W9-BXF-641

THE WRESTLER'S
CRUEL STUDY

THE
WRESTLER'S
CRUEL
STUDY

A NOVEL

STEPHEN
DOBYNS

W. W. NORTON & COMPANY

NEW YORK   LONDON

c. 1

M

The text of this book is composed in 11.5/14 Sabon,
with the display set in Cochin Bold, at 50% horizontal scale.
Composition and manufacturing by the Haddon Craftsmen, Inc.
Book design by Margaret M. Wagner.

Library of Congress Cataloging-in-Publication Data
Dobyns, Stephen, 1941–
The wrestler's cruel study / Stephen Dobyns.
p.   cm.
Includes bibliographical references.
I. Title.
PS3554.02W73 1993
813'.54—dc20   92–40861

ISBN 0-393-03511-5

W. W. Norton & Company, Inc.
500 Fifth Avenue, New York, N.Y. 10110
W. W. Norton & Company Ltd.
10 Coptic Street, London WC1A 1PU
1 2 3 4 5 6 7 8 9 0

For
Francine Prose
and
Howie Michels

Contents

The same subjects are treated by both heretics and
philosophers, and they deal with them in the same
way. Where does evil come from and in what does
it exist? Where does the human race come from,
and how did it come to exist? And the question
posed by Valentinus in particular: Where does God
come from?
—Tertullian, *On Prescription Against the Heretics*

What is portrayed by wrestling is an ideal
understanding of things; it is the euphoria of men
raised for a while above the constitutive ambiguity
of everyday situations and placed before the
panoramic view of univocal Nature, in which signs
at last correspond to causes, without obstacle,
without evasion, without contradiction.
—Roland Barthes, "The World of Wrestling"

What I am afraid of is not the frightful shape
behind my chair, but its voice; also not the words
but the terrifying unarticulated and inhuman tone
of that shape. Yes, if only it would speak as human
beings do.
—Friedrich Nietzsche, "Aus den Jahren 1868–9,"
quoted by Ronald Hayman in
Nietzsche: A Critical Life

The Devil is not to be blamed for everything: there
are times when a man is his own devil.
—Saint Augustine, quoted by Peter Brown in
Augustine of Hippo

THE WRESTLER'S
CRUEL STUDY

1
WOOL

First of all we need a place to stand. Not like Archimedes; he desired a place from which he could topple the earth with his little stick, send it tumbling like a bent hoop through the dark. We only want a place to look from: a helicopter passing over the city, a dirigible stationed high above Central Park, an East Side penthouse balcony and a man who can't sleep, for not only do we need a place to stand, we need a pair of eyes. A man who can't sleep then. In the morning he must appear in court. His wife—soon to be his ex-wife—hopes to take this penthouse from him and the man is full of fret and worry. How could the wonderful romance of his life become such a shambles? In his slippers he paces back and forth and occasionally he pours himself a little whiskey—Jim Beam green for its smoky taste. It is early autumn; it is past midnight. North toward Metropolitan Hospital sirens are sculpting elaborate curlicues of warning. Is there ever a moment when we don't hear sirens? Even at this hour all the senses are being addressed. Searchlights weave murky sentences across lowering clouds. Somewhere a building is burning; a whiff of smoke gives the air a bitter edge. The man looks down. From thirty stories the few people on the avenue become abstractions. What is that fellow wheeling? A baby carriage at this hour? No, it is a shopping cart full of his things. That's probably his word: "things." "Keep the fuck away from my things, man!" Ragged clothes, a pair of shoes, sheets of cardboard, a few returnable bottles: the detritus of a lifetime of treasures.

The man on the balcony glances off to his left and sees the sparkle of the East River. In the thoughtful mode induced by whiskey, he considers all the people being born right now, all the people dying: little folks pushing their way through the revolving door, other folks being shoved, kicked, eased toward death's blank street. He thinks of all the people full of fear right now; all the people who are having a knife stuck into them just as his wife is metaphorically sticking a knife into his own soft belly. And if these buildings lined up along the avenue were dominoes, why, he'd give them a shove. He'd watch them fall all the way down to the Bowery and then he'd laugh and somewhere his wife with her new lover, entwined in their square knot of passion, would hear his laughter and her palms would begin to sweat. She would regret turning the knife inside of him. She too would feel the terror that lay over the land.

The man on the balcony smacks a fist into his palm and turns away. It is then he sees them: across the avenue and down, a movement on the wall of an apartment house, two dark figures descending from the roof, first one, then the second directly above the first. Do they have ropes or are they clinging to the concrete and brick with gluey finger pads? From this distance it is impossible to tell. How long their arms appear and how short their legs. Window washers? Sneak thieves? What are they wearing to make them appear so brutish and fat? The man on the balcony thinks of the binoculars he keeps inside on the mantel. He hurries to fetch them. Whoops, he loses his slipper. Where did that pesky foot warmer disappear to? He finds it by the French window and puts it back on, standing on one leg and swaying a little from the whiskey.

The binoculars are not on the mantel but on the bookshelf, and by the time the man returns to the balcony, the two figures are gone. What could they have been and what were they after? The man stares at the building through the binoculars—a gray apartment building of perhaps twenty-five stories. Only a few lights are burning and nothing can be seen through the windows: sometimes a shadow, sometimes a television's blue light. After a moment the man gives it up and looks off down the avenue. A mongrel dog is burrowing into a mound of trash. Further along a car is being broken into. Two men are wrestling at the mouth of an alley. Actually, they could be dancing: twirling and jabbing and kicking up their feet.

The woman leaning over her bed folding lingerie is blond and twenty-five. She has spent several hours washing clothes, ironing blouses, and this final sorting and putting away is her last task before settling down for the night. It is twelve-thirty and she hopes to be asleep by one. Already she has brushed her teeth and wears a white cotton nightgown that reaches her ankles. She is quite beautiful and like many beautiful women she sometimes pauses with her head erect as if listening to something far away or as if preparing herself for a photo session. In these moments she resembles a piece of statuary. Around the collar of her nightgown is a border of green leaves, red cherries and interlocking green stems. On the third finger of her left hand is an engagement ring with a large diamond surrounded by rubies and emeralds. As she moves her hands, the ring flashes and glitters almost as if it were talking.

The woman's name is Rose White and occasionally she takes an article of clothing—brassiere, camisole, panties—lifts it to her nose and sniffs. How sweet it smells. How soft the white cotton feels to her fingertips. Even the reed basket is white and rests on the white bedspread of the single bed. But then, as she begins to fold a white camisole, something jarring catches her eye. Reaching deep into the basket, she gingerly extracts a pair of panties and holds them at arm's length: red silk bikini panties with a black fringe. In the dark window she is reflected holding the panties. In the mirror over the dresser she is reflected holding the panties. They aren't hers. They belong to her sister, Violet White. Perhaps Violet has come to use her shower again. Violet has always been passionate and forceful. Rose White believes that she loves her sister, but if a panel could be slid aside in the back of her head and the multiple television screens of memory could be switched on, then what complicated scenes might be observed there: Rose White age six discovering that the sugar poured onto her cereal by Violet White, also age six, is actually salt. Rose White age twelve tied up in the basement by Violet White also age twelve while a large brown rat sniffs her toes. Rose White age eighteen waiting over an hour on the steps of the Metropolitan Museum for Frankie, her first boyfriend, then sadly returning to her parents' apartment only to discover Frankie and Violet White also eighteen giggling in the bedroom.

Rose White flicks the panties onto the bed. She can't imagine wearing them. They would show through the fabric of her dress, a red smudge for all to see. She imagines wearing them to Mass. How embarrassing it would be. She imagines wearing them to work at P.S. 97. How the third-graders would laugh. Then it amuses her to think of how her fiancé, Michael Marmaduke, would react if she wore such panties. He wouldn't like them, of course. He would be confused just as she is confused. For her to wear such panties would be like wearing a costume. For a moment, she wonders how her sister can wear such things, but then she thinks she should be glad that her sister wears any underwear at all.

Rose White lifts the folded lingerie and carries it to the dresser. She takes small steps: a movement between a tiptoe and a dance. Opening a drawer, she pauses. On top of the dresser is a photograph in a silver frame showing a man in silver trunks, a silver cape and silver elf boots sitting astride a white horse. The man has ringlets of blond hair and wears a noble expression. His eyes are focused somewhere beyond the photographer as if his ears had just registered the first notes of a maiden's scream. This is Rose White's fiancé, Michael Marmaduke, although in the photograph he is not Michael but Marduk the Magnificent. The photograph gives the impression of wildness tamed, power in the service of goodness. Hercules might have looked like this, or Cuchulain, or Lancelot. But enough of the wildness remains to make Rose White feel all prickly inside. Tomorrow, after school, they will meet outside F.A.O. Schwarz and Michael will take her to an exhibit of nineteenth-century music boxes. Afterward they might have a light dinner, if there is time before Michael has to be at Madison Square Garden at eight-thirty.

Rose White stacks the underwear in the drawer, then carries the white nightgowns to the closet. A lamp burns on the night table next to the bed, its pink shade casting a rosy glow. Light too enters from the window: streetlights, lights from other apartments, the darker glow of the city entering this bedroom window at the twentieth floor. All of a sudden something slides across this darker glow, shutting it off. Rose White has her back to the window and does not notice. Instead she is staring down at the floor of her closet and counting to herself. Then she pouts and presses a finger to her lips. Two pairs of flat black shoes are missing. She knows where they have gone. Violet has taken them. Her sister uses up shoes in the way a surgeon uses up rubber gloves. It's the dancing, the constant dancing.

The room is quiet. From the clock radio in the kitchen a classical FM station plays Mozart's *Eine Kleine Nachtmusik*. Occasionally we hear the muted honk of a horn or the castrato bray of a car alarm or the accelerating rumble of a bus. Each night when Rose White sleeps a device beside her bed repeats the sound of waves washing against a beach or the sound of wind through pine trees. But now comes another noise: a bumping at the window. Startled, Rose White turns and sees nothing but darkness, as if a curtain had been hung across the outside. Before the oddness of this can suffi-ciently strike her, the window bursts inward and a rush of noise erupts from the street, all the cars, all the honking. Fragments of glass spray onto the rug. And the great blackness which had briefly obscured the city bursts through the window as well. With both hands pressed to her mouth Rose White stumbles back into the closet, falls among the shoes. The blackness is a black gorilla and behind it at the window appears a second gorilla. It hops through the open space onto the rug. On its head the second gorilla is wearing a pair of small yellow headphones. Attached to a belt around its waist is a yellow Sports Walkman. The gorilla is snap-ping its black leathery fingers, which make a dull plop-plop sound.

"Yo, fuck, man, we got ourselves a little wool!"

The first gorilla is trying to detach itself from the pieces of window frame. It heaves its long arms and shakes its head. Although its ugly face is expressionless, it appears unhappy. The gorilla has yellow teeth and red lips. Its small eyes are the color of nicotine stains and they dart back and forth. Although naked it displays no genitalia.

"We ain't here for fun," says the gorilla.

Rose White crouches in the doorway of the closet. Her forearm is pressed to her forehead while her other hand holds down the hem of her white nightgown. Equal to her shock at the appearance of the gorillas is her shock that she hasn't lost consciousness. Abruptly, she jumps up and dashes toward the bedroom door, hardly noticing the glass that cuts her feet.

"Catch the wool, man!"

The gorilla who was wrestling with the window frame hops across the floor and grabs Rose White at the doorway, snatching at the collar of her nightgown and ripping it. With its other paw it catches hold of her thigh and tosses her into the air.

"Yo, she's light!"

The gorilla tosses her again, then tosses her to its pal, who grabs Rose White, presses her to its snout and sniffs.

"This wool's got sweet flesh, man."

The gorilla by the door lopes across to the window, its knuckles trailing on the rug. "No fiddlin, man, we be here for work alone. Look, she's cut her little feets."

The gorilla with the Walkman sniffs Rose White's feet. "Sweet feets, man." The gorilla tosses her up and catches her again. Rose White has been waving her hands and making high shrieking noises. The terror in her head is like a great balloon getting fatter and fatter. All of a sudden she goes limp in the gorilla's arms.

"She done fall asleep. Poor thing's wore out."

"You scared her, man. Let's scat." The gorilla leaps to the windowsill and reaches into the dark. Catching hold of a rope, it swings out into the darkness and begins to climb.

The gorilla with the Walkman hops onto the sill. Rose White hangs limply over its shoulder. The gorilla turns its head, bumping her hip with his snout. It snaps its gorilla lips against the white fabric of Rose White's nightgown, tugging at it. "Ummm, I'd like to eats you up!" Reaching into the dark, the gorilla grabs the rope and starts hauling its thick self up toward the roof while making puff-puff noises. A few drops of blood roll from Rose White's delicate feet and tumble toward the street. Far below a homeless fellow is pushing a shopping cart toward an alley. Maybe he is struck by the drops of blood, maybe not. He shuffles forward in black boots several sizes too big for him. The boots go flap, flap on the sidewalk and the wheels of the shopping cart go squeak, squeak. These two sounds make a rhythm and to this rhythm the man is singing a little song to the tune of "Here We Go Round the Mulberry Bush."

"I got a story and nobody cares; I got a story and nobody cares; I got a story and nobody cares: I might as well bark, bark, bark."

2

Muldoon: Pforta

My name is Primus Muldoon and I am speaking to the air. Not as a man strolling through the park might mutter to himself or a man staring in the bathroom mirror or a man in a bar—you know those bars with Irish names on the outer avenues?—a man in a bar might stagger to his feet and pronounce a few incomprehensible words said in anger or confusion so that the bartender grows alert before the man slopes back down again with his elbow in a puddle of beer. No, I am speaking to the air, although it might be in any one of those other places as well. My name is Muldoon and I am a manager, but call me a director, a manipulator of men. I train them in falsehood, that honorable word which is the most distinguished of all the names we give to truth. I introduce them to their contradictory fragments so they may discover the nature of unity. And didn't Nietzsche say that our body is a social structure consisting of many souls? I teach my charges how to attach a name to that body: how to marshal their souls. And didn't Nietzsche also say that only a man who is deeply divided can perceive wholeness? So it is with Muldoon.

But what is this wholeness? Is it form or substance? And is there a difference? We strip a layer from the onion and find another onion. We strip the mask from the human being and find another mask. Perhaps without the mask, there is no face to present. Perhaps we strip off this final mask and find only wind in a dark place. We strip away the mask to disclose the drain at the bottom of the sink and the whole self trickles through it. But isn't this mask also a bandage and without it wouldn't the face fly apart? Doesn't the mask protect the wearer against breakage? The mask unifies the face, holds the face together. It may also heal. Then call me a healer: Dr. Primus Muldoon.

So form equals substance: the mask is the face, the layers of onion are the onion, the bandage becomes the wound. What name do we give to this mask? I call it Gimmick. And what do I do that makes me a manager, a manipulator of men? I train them in the perfection of the Gimmick. And who are these men? I call them grapplers with the chimaera, strugglers against desolation, contenders with the mystery. You might call them charlatans. You might call them bogus. Together it is possible to call them wrestlers. I direct a school. You would say I run a gym. I call it Pforta after the school near Naumburg which Nietzsche entered in 1858 ten days before his fourteenth birthday. You would read the name over the door and call my gym the Meat Market. I say that I teach Sparta in the morning and Athens in the afternoon. You would say that before lunch we engage in the tricks and subterfuges of fraudulent wrestling and after lunch we work on our Gimmicks, which you consider little more than stage names, cartoon titles. But didn't Nietzsche argue that one should always live in disguise? After all, if form is substance, then one exists as one's disguise: to be is to be the Gimmick. You would call this illusion. But didn't Nietzsche also say that truths are illusions whose illusoriness has been overlooked?

Be that as it may, you would probably describe me as owner and operator of the Meat Market, a gym in north Jersey. You call it north Jersey; I call it north Jersey. And you would see me as trainer, manager and agent for a half-dozen men and women whom I call grapplers with the chimaera (frauds, to you) and, out of the need to compromise, we will call wrestlers. You see how words lead to a diminishment of the truth?

But wrestling, you say, entails violence and suffering. Human beings pounding each other's heads. Isn't this brutality for the sake of brutality? The arbitrary punch in the mouth that results in a few cheap laughs? Shouldn't we be nice to each other? Once again we are struck by the reductiveness of language. Please! Spare me the cant that argues that man's true desire is for harmony while it is only nature that creates conflict. The truth is—and we all know what truth is—fighting is the food the soul loves best, while painted on the south wall of the Meat Market are the words of the Master: "A more complete human being is a human being who is more completely bestial."

And in the same way the young Nietzsche entered Pforta that gray October morning, so these young men and women come to me: confused, fragmented, out of work. Once they had a sense of who they were, but the world has snatched that from them. Once they saw the path beneath their feet, now they walk in cloud. At best they have a hankering (I would call it dream). Otherwise they are nothing; they have been stripped bare. And this is how I want them to arrive. Isn't it a precondition for becoming that one not have the least idea of what one is? Save me from the men and women who think they know themselves. When someone claims to know himself, then he is the one who will become what he is not, while the nameless, innocent and ignorant—these are the ones who will discover their true identities. Within reason of course.

They appear at my doorway, nervous, shuffling their feet. Perhaps someone gave them my business card, perhaps they noticed the sign outside the door. And I welcome them. Do I ask their names? Never. Let them give their names when they feel ready, let them give them as a gift. You would say I allow them to hang out. No such thing. I let them absorb the ambience. There are free weights, a universal gym, speed bags. There is a jogging machine, a rowing machine, the usual Nautilus paraphernalia. I offer them coffee. I point out the Coke machine. And slowly they declare themselves. Were I to name them, they would panic. Were I to ask their business, they would flee. Some never give their names. Some tiptoe back to the street, preferring their fear, than to trust being woken from their dreams. But others begin to engage themselves. A few words, a few sentences, until eventually they unreel the sorry pages of their lives. Some of these will climb into the ring, if just to visit, if just to feel the bounce of the floor. But only a few ever declare themselves grapplers with the chimaera. Some decide to study with me, others find other managers, other gyms. Whether they stay or go elsewhere, at least the healing process has begun. But let me introduce you to a few who have stayed.

Imagine a police lineup. We sit at the back of a dark room in the middle of a row of wooden theater seats. Our seats squeak when we move and we must be careful to make no noise. Before us is a brightly lit stage. On the white wall are measurement marks going up to seven feet. The wall is scuffed and there are greasy circles where people's heads have rested. The stage itself is none too clean. We see gum wrappers, a crumpled paper cup, a torn page from the comic section of last Sunday's paper. Mostly there is grit: sand, dried mud, particles from the streets, the stuff they pile on top of coffins: grave grit. A door opens. A voice cries out, "Move all the way to the end!" Four men and a woman shuffle onto the stage. They look angry, threatened but also vaguely lost as if they had misplaced a vital part of themselves. Clearly they wish to be elsewhere. Their arms hang at their sides; their hands dangle forgotten and functionless. They blink their eyes against the harsh light and squint into the dark room where we are sitting. Quite a rough-looking crowd, don't you think? Don't worry, they can't see us.

But what's this? Two men in uniform wheel a large packing case onto the stage. It is built from rough pine boards and must be heavy. See how the men are out of breath, how beads of sweat pop from their foreheads? They wrestle it off the trolley and stand it up at the end of the line, where it towers over them. This is the surprise we are saving for last.

Take a look at the first man. Certainly, you'd remember if you had seen him before. A bald black man with a gold ring in his ear. His nose is a sprawl, as if it had fallen from a great height before hitting his face. But look at his body. Can you imagine the muscles beneath that black sweatshirt? Were you to measure his biceps you would find they are twenty inches. And his size: six feet six and three hundred pounds. Of course when he wrestles the announcer claims he is seven feet tall and four hundred pounds, but that is part of his Gimmick. Maybe he's forty years old. In the ring he has had many names: the Scourge of Solomon, Mad Mustapha, the Black Hercules. When he first came to me years ago there were scabs over his body and he had no name at all, although even then he dressed in black. He sat on a stool and said nothing. His hands shook. There were days he never lifted his eyes from the floor. He barely weighed 160 pounds. After the third day I left hamburgers next to his feet, little gifts wrapped in wax paper. A week later he still hadn't touched them and the packages made a small hill. The second week the hill grew bigger as the man diminished even more. I spoke to him quietly. "To abstain from violence, injury and exploitation, isn't this a denial of life? Isn't life a matter of over-powering what can be overpowered, namely the weaker? If you want to grow, doesn't this mean imposing your power on others and isn't it no more than sentimentality to see this as wrong? Isn't life itself the will to power?"

Of course the change didn't happen right away. I had to talk to him often. Before we could work on the muscles of his body, we had to strengthen the muscles of his soul. We had to develop the muscles of his intention. But one morning I entered the gym to find that the mountain of hamburgers was gone. He still sat on his stool with his elbows on his knees and stared at the floor. He still was thin and covered with scabs, but his belly, instead of being a sad indentation, was a protuberance, a delicate drumlin of flesh, and I knew I had succeeded. Indeed, the first word he articulated within my hearing was a belch. The change came slowly. He ate. He began to work out. He spent hours jumping rope, hours with the Roman Chair. Dumbbells, barbells, cable crossovers, squat, curl, shrug, crunch—he bulked up. He took on mass. His skin grew shiny, a rich chestnut.

One day I found him standing in front of me. His body was sheathed in glistening muscle. His abs were rumble strips. His pecs resembled the twin halves of a leather medicine ball. His traps formed a small mountain behind his neck, like the hump on the shoulders of a fighting bull. "What is done out of love," I said, "always occurs outside of the confines of good and evil."

He reached out a blunt finger and poked me in the chest, making me step back. He was already well over two hundred pounds. "My

name's Thrombosis," he said in his deep voice. "I'm the blockage.
I'm the stopper. Show me who to destruct."

"The biggest danger in fighting monsters is becoming a monster
yourself."

"Man, I be mean in the service of clean. Slap me five and spare
me the jive."

Did we become friends? Let's say we reached a mutual respect.
Were he trapped in a burning building, I would risk my life to save
him. We don't complain to each other or tell each other our
troubles. Does that keep us from being friends? But Thrombosis
became my greatest aid. He is loyal. He runs the gym in my
absence. You will say, but who is Thrombosis? What did he do
before? Does it help to know that he grew up in South Carolina,
that he spent time in prison? No. Thrombosis is enough. He's the
stopper. You desire personality traits? He doesn't like people to
walk up behind him. He eats nothing but beef and dietary supplements. He keeps a canary named Larry in a black cage. He has a
girlfriend named Flash who does roller derbies. The music from
Tristan and Isolde makes him cry. He loves to discuss his 'Tude:
his good 'Tude and bad 'Tude. The point of life is to develop a
good 'Tude, because a good 'Tude means winning. You want to
know where he came from? He was born in my gym. He was born
in Pforta.

The others have similar stories. To some there is sadness: betrayal, desertion, a lover run off with another man or woman. To
others there is enigma. Take the woman next to Thrombosis. That
green leotard displays every muscle. But she wasn't always like
that. Once she was skinny and her name was Maud. She ate only
cantaloupe and weighed under a hundred pounds. See those Wonder Woman bracelets? Beneath them are scars suggesting a gloomy
history, a momentary giving up. Her dark hair didn't have that
richness when she showed up at my gym two years ago, chain
smoking and abusive. In place of words she had a repertoire of
snarls. She took a folding chair, leaned it against a wall, sat down
and watched. Sometimes I sat beside her. "Every superior person,"
I told her, "dreams of a secret castle where they might be freed
from the rest of humankind, but to live in that castle means never

to gain knowledge." And another time I said: "Independence is only a privilege of the strong."

One day she walked over to the ring. I don't know who was sparring at the time. Some poor fellows. Maud was as thin as ever. Climbing into the ring, she became entangled in the ropes. I thought just the ropes would defeat her. People paused to watch. The squeaking and clanking of the weights and pulleys subsided. The two men practicing falls looked up in surprise. She wore cowboy boots, I remember that, red cowboy boots with cups of shiny steel on their pointed toes. "Hey," said one of the men, "you gotta put your name on the sign-up sheet."

"Here's my name," she said. And before the man could react she planted the steel tip of her cowboy boot into the soft ropy mass of his genitalia. Because of the theatrical nature of our combats the male practitioner often forgets to wear a protective cup. Certainly this fellow wasn't wearing one that afternoon. He swooned. The other fellow barely had the chance to say "You better watch yourself!" before Maud raked his face with her nails, leaving on each cheek a series of parallel lines, a staff of music upon which might be jotted the glissando of his startled cry. Maud looked casually around the room, which had grown unusually attentive. She was smiling. "Dentata," she said. "My name is Dentata."

Of course in the next months she had to be taught not to cause pain. This initially grieved her but she found it easier to be gentle when wrestling with women. I became her agent and found her matches. You may have seen her work under the names Killer Kali, Medusa, Isis the Insane. Always she is after me to arrange combats with men, but the law forbids. With her current muscle mass and training in karate the results would be unfortunate. "Be careful," I told her, "a person obsessed by a wrong is an ugly sight." Even so she sometimes disappears for a few days and returns bruised but happy. No, not happy. Like a cat after a large meal, she is digesting the rewards of her retribution. And sometimes toward the back of one of the papers will appear a few short paragraphs describing mysterious assaults on isolated men where no warning was given and nothing stolen.

As for these others standing before us, the sinewy red-haired man next to Dentata chose the name Liquidity. He aspires to the power of water. Be careful of him. It is easy to forget he is watching. Black suit, black shirt, black tie—he thinks of the night as his color. In the ring he is sometimes Loki, sometimes Coyote, sometimes Cain.

Next to him is that squat rectangle of muscle with thick black hair poking out of the collar of his T-shirt—his name is Cashback. He gives better than he gets. Clearly he is the shortest of the group but he is like one of those high-calorie protein bars that swells and overwhelms. Vulcan the Vicious he is sometimes called, or Mulciber the Maniac, or Hephaestus the Hunchback. See how those dark marks on his face make him look singed? He has always lived close to the fire.

Next is the fat one, although such fat is deceptive. Prime Rib, he calls himself. Often he works with his two brothers in triple tag team specials: Prime Rib, Prime Rate and Prime Time. Prime Rib's fatness is like the softness of quicksand. By himself he is sometimes the Death Buddha, with his brothers the Maniacal Musketeers. Where did they come from? From orphanages and foster homes. Where did they get their fat bodies? I gave them to them. Their bodies are like gift boxes around secret jewels: the ruby of anger, the emerald of loss.

These five that stand before us—Thrombosis, Dentata, Liquidity, Cashback, Prime Rib—those names lie between the names they were born with and the names they assume. And as they had no choice over their baptismal names, neither have they a choice over the names they assume. This is my great affliction. Do you think I chose the name Death Buddha or Killer Kali or the Scourge of Solomon? These names come from the Wrestling Association. At best I received some choices and my charges chose between them. But if Dentata decides not to be Isis the Insane, that honor must fall to someone else. And if Dentata quits the ring to became a fireman or homicidal maniac, then another Isis must be found. Can you guess how it hurts me as an artist to have these choices denied me? Here I have devoted my life to drawing these poor souls up from the mire. It has been the shaping force of my career. When I protest, it is suggested that I am unhappy in the Association and perhaps it is time to retire. Obviously, these are threats. But when has a dragon ever died from the venom of a snake? I endure. I make plans. It is only with my last charge, my liberating angel, that some freedom was allowed. Saying this, perhaps it is time to examine the box at the end of the stage.

I clap my hands and the men in uniform hurry to remove the screws from the lid. The squeaks of metal against wood are like little shrieks of warning.

But wait, let's first speculate on the nature of chance. Think of those frisky sperm with their snapping tales. If your father had bumped his elbow at the moment of ejaculation, if he inhaled instead of exhaled, if he had thrust deeper instead of pulling back, then who is to say that the particular spermatozoon that determined your unique physical and spiritual being would have won the race. Instead of tall, you might be short. Instead of intelligent, you might be stupid; instead of male, female—all because an elbow was jiggled or not jiggled in a single instant of time. Because of our vanity, we think we were destined to be born, but truly we were destined not to be born; all probability was arrayed against us and a lucky chance prevailed. But that is just the beginning. How much happens because of the equivalent of a jiggled elbow? If you turned right instead of left when you took that deep breath, you might have inhaled a virus that could kill you. If you had taken the Triboro Bridge instead of the Midtown Tunnel, you might have crossed the path of a gigantic garbage truck whose brakes had suddenly failed. How often have such things occurred?

One late morning in early fall I was driving through a section of Teaneck I had never seen before. Taking a short cut, I had become lost. Moreover I felt sick that morning and it was only with the greatest effort that I had risen from bed. So I was driving down a street which I had reached by chance, in a town I had reached by mistake, at a time of day when I was normally elsewhere, on a particular day when I should have stayed in bed, and as I was driving along I saw a gymnasium—Bernie's Pump House—that was entirely new to me.

I decided to pay it a visit.

It was a seedy place without any showers: cracked linoleum, free weights gathering dust, the rancid smell of old liniment. Gobs of pink bubble gum decorated the edge of the water fountain. But beyond the broken stationary bicycles and teetery leg tables, a blond giant of a man was locked in combat with a rowing machine in a way that brought to mind Washington crossing the Delaware: exercise at the service of nobility. His eyes focused on mine, his rowing slowed, and some strange communication occurred between us. Across the thread of our exchanged glance our egos tottered out like tightrope walkers and a bond was established. But now we must take a look inside that box. Gentlemen, are you ready?

Soon they will have it open. Is that last screw giving the short guard some trouble? No, he has it now. Let me adjust the light. Do you see my treasure? He's only six feet four but we call him six-six. Forgive my dressing him in a tiger skin, I couldn't help myself. At least I haven't greased him, although you've probably guessed that the equipment at the Meat Market includes several tanning beds. All my wrestlers look as if they had just arrived from Acapulco. But despite that pleasant bronze color, one rarely sees such silken skin upon a man. He's twenty-five, or so he believes (I'll get to that later). Now let him step forward. Impressed? That blond hair is the real article, although when I first found him it wasn't so long. Of course he doesn't have the muscle mass of Thrombosis, but he has better definition. Do you see how the veins rest on the muscles like snakes on the surface of a pond? His waist is twenty-eight inches and his chest is sixty. He'll certainly never wear an extra extra large again. These days a tailor's clients are either stockbrokers or body builders. High forehead, long nose, full lips—see those white teeth? They've never been capped. Would you believe they came like that? And the jaw: what I like about a square jaw is that it gives a sense of determination even where none exists. Even when terrified, a man with a square jaw looks brave as long as you don't peer into his eyes. This fellow's eyes are always calm, although personally I find that light blue color somewhat spooky, like looking into water. The eyes give nothing away. Because of them, Liquidity nicknamed him the Death Angel until I asked him to stop. It created the wrong tone. Later of course Liquidity saw its inappropriateness. Do you find him flawless? Look at his ankles and you will see his only blemish. Where those nasty scars came from nobody seems to know, least of all this fellow himself, but they circle each ankle. When he wrestles he wears elf boots and so the scars are concealed but they remain one of his several mysteries.

I would call him beautiful if the word were not the vanity of our species. Nothing is beautiful, until man makes it so. We call the world beautiful in order to humanize it and make it less threatening. But that very artificiality allows us to manipulate Beauty as one of many possible Gimmicks. It suggests strength and regeneration. It suggests virtue and protection. Although with a makeup pencil we could make this fellow suggest the opposite. But why should we do that? Far easier to create the illusion of ugliness than beauty, and here, stepping out of this box, is incarnated beauty itself, at least in human eyes. But do you remember that playful bit of dialogue of Nietzsche's where the god Dionysus complains that Ariadne's ears would be more beautiful if they were long, like a donkey's?

All my other charges showed up at the Meat Market bruised and beaten. This fellow was still walking victoriously through the world (rowing, at any rate). All the others came to me nameless, then discovered their names. This fellow already had a name, or a sort of name because he was adopted as an infant and bore the name that his stepparents gave him. That morning at Bernie's Pump House my path seemed obvious. I made my way toward him, stepping across the loose plates of barbells which had been scattered irresponsibly across the floor.

"My name is Primus Muldoon," I said, "and I'm the director of a school."

The young man stopped rowing and held out his hand. "Mike Marmaduke." His grip, like his voice, was surprisingly soft.

"Michael Marmaduke?" I asked.

"Sure," he said.

"Have you ever thought of wrestling?"

"Wrestling?"

"Professionally."

"Wouldn't that mean hurting people?"

"We flirt with hurt. Pain's just part of the game."

"Game?" asked Michael, getting to his feet, and I was pleased to see that he towered above me.

"Our conflicts are more theatrical than athletic. Pain is just a notation in the script."

"Ah ha," he said. "I've wondered about that."

Right away I had hit upon an essential characteristic of Michael's nature which would seem to preclude him from violent activity. He was gentle. A lesser manager of men might have returned to his car. But can you imagine the power of gentleness as a Gimmick? Certainly this Michael Marmaduke was neither barbarian nor villain. And what made this gentleness so effective was that Michael already possessed that part of the Gimmick which is most difficult to fake. I mean sincerity. Not only was he gentle, he was sincerely gentle.

"It could mean a lot of money," I told him. "Fame, popularity. You could buy a new car."

"I don't drive."

"You could hire a chauffeur."

He scratched his forehead. "I'm not that kind of guy."

"I run a gym," I told him, keeping it simple. "Can I buy you lunch?"

"Nah, I brought my lunch. But I got some extra. You feel like some plain yogurt and pecans?"

"I love pecans," I told him.

So it began. During lunch he told me about himself and that afternoon I drove him to the Meat Market. He said he worked for Parks and Rec in Paterson but hoped to go back to school for his teaching certificate. He came from some Pennsylvania town near the Delaware Water Gap where his stepparents ran a grocery store and rented out cottages in the summer. He had an equanimity that seemed positively sleepy. At first I feared he might be stupid, but he was attentive and twice he pointed out squirrels that seemed bent on dashing in front of my car. I asked if he had read Nietzsche but he had not. However (and this must be taken as a plus), he had heard of him and knew he was a philosopher.

At the gym I introduced Michael to Thrombosis and Dentata, Cashback, Liquidity and Prime Rib, and I observed their admiring looks. Michael's gentle manner was obvious in every gesture, and I was struck by how quickly Dentata absorbed this fact and had neither desire nor necessity to knee Michael in the groin, which is her normal inclination when meeting a new man. It turned out that Michael had wrestled in high school, before being dropped from the team because of his refusal to hurt anyone. But at least he knew his way around the ring. By the end of the afternoon I had his name on paper.

Don't think it was smooth sailing. There is no such creature as the natural artist. One must study. One must learn one's craft. But Michael was diligent. I corrected his body mass. I taught him holds and falls and how to suffer. But the gentleness, which would be a virtue in the ring, was a nuisance in his training. I would put him against Thrombosis, just a test match you understand, and the moment that Thrombosis contorted his face to indicate discomfort, Michael let him go.

"What are you doing?" I would shout.

"I don't want to hurt him."

"You don't think that's real pain, do you?"

"Then why'd he cry out?"

Thrombosis would be stamping around the ring. "Because that's my fuckin job, man. It's in the script!"

It took several months before Michael could tolerate expressions of suffering without releasing his opponent. It was as if these facial contortions made his hands burn.

"Are you sure it doesn't hurt?" he would ask Liquidity after hurling him to the mat.

"Sure I'm sure," Liquidity would answer, getting to his feet. "I already said I was sure. Sure, sure, sure!"

Even in Michael's first matches he nearly abandoned the script when the suffering of his opponent seemed especially acute. Fortunately, the stratagem he devised to avoid anxiety became a key element of his Gimmick. He learned to shut his eyes and smile. "Bliss Killer," the fans dubbed him. Truly, there was something awful about how at the very moment when Michael was twisting the head from some ruffian's neck, he would close his eyes and beam like an angel. It was this smile that led me to develop the coup de grace for which he became famous. I called it "the Bosom of Abraham." Sportswriters dubbed it "the Abraham." It resembled a caress, a brotherly embrace, except that the victim was upside down while Michael had his arms around him from behind and pressed his victim's shoulder's to the mat. At the moment of victory Michael would crouch down with his knees squeezing his victim's shoulders and his arms squeezing his waist and he would smile beatifically and slowly close his eyes. The crowd would go wild and chant, "Abraham! Abraham!" The referee would slap the mat three times and the match would be over.

But I could not order Michael to do this. He had to be convinced. He had to be impressed by superior logic. About two months after his introduction to Pforta he came into my office at the back of the gym and flung himself down in a chair. The walls of my office are covered with the photographs of wrestlers with one great photograph of the Master being dominant. Although alone, it felt as if we were in a crowd.

"What's the point of this suffering?" asked Michael, pushing his hands through his blond hair. "Why is the pain necessary? I mean, this kind of wrestling doesn't do anything except make money. It's just wrestling for the sake of wrestling. It's selfish and mercenary and I'm not sure I can do it."

I chose my words carefully. "Of course, if wrestling were empty as you suggest, I would retire at once. But perhaps you are looking at it falsely. Perhaps you are searching for some moralizing tendency and not having discovered within the ring any attempt to improve your fellow human beings, you complain that wrestling is purposeless. But let's look at it another way. Doesn't wrestling praise? Doesn't it glorify? Doesn't it select? By doing these things doesn't it strengthen certain valuations and weaken others? You think this is an accident, something in which the soul of the wrestler takes no part? But, listen, is the wrestler's basic instinct directed toward wrestling or is it directed toward the meaning of wrestling, which is life? And if it is directed toward life, then isn't it directed toward the very essence of life, which is struggle and triumph? Wrestling is the great stimulus to life. How then could it be imagined as purposeless and aimless?

"Perhaps another question remains: wrestling also brings to the surface much that is ugly, hard and questionable. Perhaps it is wrong to display such ugliness to the world. But then let's ask what a great wrestler communicates of himself in the ring. Doesn't he display the condition of fearlessness in the face of what is frightening? This condition of fearlessness is of vital importance because this is what the wrestler communicates to the audience. Every wrestler is a great communicator. That is partly what makes him a wrestler. Bravery and composure in the face of a powerful enemy, in the face of great hardship and suffering—it is this victorious condition which the wrestler singles out and which he glorifies. Doesn't this give us a great example? Doesn't this instruct us and help us to survive as human beings? How then can you call wrestling purposeless?"

We talked many times but always my message was the same: "wrestling as the stimulus to life . . . the example of bravery and composure in the face of a powerful enemy." Ultimately Michael came to accept it. And when he did, he began to change. Not only did his body bulk up, but his spirit bulked up. His eyes acquired nobility and his natural quiet resembled the self-confidence of a great cat. It became time to choose his Gimmick.

You will say I had no business in this, that I have already described myself as a receiver, rather than an originator of roles. But I knew how the Association worked and I knew if I could hit upon a perfect fit between wrestler and Gimmick, then my suggestion might be accepted. Given Michael's nature, he had to be a hero. No Snake Man for him. No Judas or Brutus or Mussolini the Muscle Monster. On the other hand, because of his gentleness, the more conventional role of hero was denied him. Hercules, Roland, Lancelot—gentleness was not part of their nature. Galahad was a possibility but Galahad's virginity was a problem. Although gentle, Michael wasn't virginal. It seemed I must find a Gimmick from among the Divine, but again there were problems. The Eastern religions were too violent and the Western religions too kind, while pure monotheism limited the number of gods to choose from. I decided that the god I needed must come from someplace in between, that is, the Middle East.

I settled on Marduk, the Babylonian god of beauty and strength who becomes king of the gods and defeats Tiamat the Chaos Dragon, snatching from her the tablets of destiny. In preparing for the battle Marduk fills his body with flame, creates seven hurricanes and climbs into his storm chariot. He is the rider on the clouds armed with bow and arrow, a club, lightning bolts and a great net held at each corner by one of the four winds. Tiamat attacks with a great army which includes her oldest son, Kingu the Birdman, the Centaur and Scorpion-Man. Marduk challenges Tiamat to single combat and roots her to one spot with his net. In the words of the Babylonian tablet:

> As Tiamat opened her mouth to swallow him,
> Marduk struck her with the tempest before she could close her lips.
> The fierce winds took hold of her belly,
> Her insides blew up and she opened wide her mouth.
> Marduk then let fly an arrow which split her belly,
> He sliced through her guts and stabbed her heart,
> He squeezed her fast until her life was extinguished.

Having killed Tiamat, Marduk splits her open like the shell of an oyster. Out of the top half of her body he makes the sky and out of the bottom half he makes the earth. Then he proceeds to take care of Kingu and Scorpion-Man and out of Kingu's blood Marduk makes the first human beings.

You might ask, where is the gentleness? But by pitting Marduk against the great dragon in order to create heaven and earth and give birth to man, it could be argued that the ends were gentle even though the means were violent. Also, it was Tiamat who attacked: she had advanced upon Marduk. She wanted to eat him. Marduk was only defending himself. He was the innocent victim of circumstance, while by rescuing the tablets of destiny he made certain that the worst aspects of chaos (flood, famine and general destitution) might be alleviated.

All that remained was to convince the Association. Not, I thought, an easy task. Besides gathering a mass of material on Marduk and his combats, I made videotapes showing Michael in action. I displayed his strength, his agility, his clear hero potential, while with succinct clips I showed him at a local playground pushing toddlers on swings and manning the teeter-totter to give an indication of his gentleness.

The response from the Association was a fax which read: "Your suggestion has been accepted." No praise or thank you. But soon came a schedule of matches and the inevitable meddling, while before each match came directions on how the match must be run. My only other victory was to convince the Association that Michael should be Marduk and nobody else. No flying him out to L.A. as Maximilian the Muscle Man. All that remained was to perfect him as the great communicator I knew he could be. "Become hard," I told him. "Your greatest gentleness must become your greatest hardness. Wrestlers who think only of their own defense make themselves weak."

At last he was Marduk the Magnificent. Strip away the Gimmick of Marduk and there lay Michael Marmaduke. But wasn't this Gimmick as well? And what lay beneath it? Years ago, I believed in Gimmick in the service of truth, in the service of revolution, in the service of the advancement of mankind. Now I believe only in Gimmick. It combines obviousness and mystery, blatancy and secrecy. This is who I am: Primus Muldoon. I have mass. I have history. I believe in the Gimmick and the individual (is there a difference?). But when all is said and done: who is Primus Muldoon? Or, to quote Nietzsche, "To talk about oneself a great deal is also a way of concealing oneself."

3

FUNNY COIN

Now our attention is caught by a yellow cab rushing west on 42nd Street. Which yellow cab? one might ask. This cab is easy to spot because it is going faster than the others. See it down there zigzagging in and out of traffic? It looks like a late-model Chevrolet. Whoops, the driver veers briefly into the lane of oncoming traffic. He's taking a big chance. It is just past eight o'clock and dark. The month is October, the weather is mild. Although the street is full of cars there is a slight lull with the disappearance of the theater crowd.

Let's zoom in a little closer. The driver is middle-aged and black. Can you see his face beneath that Mets cap? No matter. But certainly you see the cigar clamped between his teeth. He never smokes them, just chews them. The name on the license over the glove box is Hurkle Simmons. How he got the name Hurkle is a long story but it needn't concern us here. Hurkle is with us only long enough to give his passenger a ride between the Plaza Hotel and Madison Square Garden.

For that matter there are two passengers seated in back, but only one is human. The other is stuffed. Let's take a look at the stuffed one first: an oversized polar bear with a bright red grin.

The bear is easily three feet from snout to rear paws and it is programmed to sing, speak or growl depending where on its belly it receives a slight poke. In fact, the man next to the bear hasn't quite worked out the intricacies of the mechanism and he is careful not to touch it. Several times he has accidentally set the thing singing and then it has been nearly impossible to shut it off: an event signaled by the phrase "Bye-bye for now!" In the store the bear had a rather noble expression but here in the cab it looks foolish. Also the occasion of its purchase as a gift has frighteningly gone by and now even the sight of its black snout is a source of anxiety.

The man himself is Michael Marmaduke, the celebrated wrestler, although he might be hard to recognize because of the dark glasses and Irish tweed hat pulled down over his blond hair. A dark raincoat is buttoned to his neck and the collar is turned up. But he is clearly a large man with broad shoulders and he occupies most of the backseat, while taking care not to bump the bear. Hurkle Simmons suspects his passenger might be Michael Marmaduke, partly because he looks like him and partly because they are going to the Garden. In ten years driving a cab Hurkle Simmons has had many famous passengers, including Stephen King and Muhammad Ali, but he has a soft spot for wrestlers.

Michael tries to ignore the driver glancing at him in the mirror. As Marduk the Magnificent he is scheduled to enter the ring at eight-thirty, less than half an hour away. It is late, but he can't help that. In fact, he barely thinks of events lying ahead. All his thoughts are directed at the past. Waves of trepidation keep sweeping over him and he has to calm himself with deep-breathing exercises. And each time he tells himself there must be a logical explanation. Perhaps she was delayed at school or perhaps there was a problem with her sister. And who is Michael thinking about? Why, he is thinking about his fiancée, Rose White, who he was supposed to meet outside of F.A.O. Schwarz on Fifth Avenue at four o'clock. If she had to be late, then why hadn't she called F.A.O. Schwarz and told a clerk that her fiancée was waiting outside? But perhaps she didn't have the chance. What if there was an accident? And again the wave of anxiety splashes over him.

As for the bear, Michael bought it for Rose White at F.A.O. Schwarz that afternoon and then had to hold it while waiting for her outside the store. Michael hates being recognized as Marduk the Magnificent and so in public he often wears a hat and dark glasses. Sometimes he even wears a black wig and mustache but he didn't wear them today because Rose White likes to tease him about them. But outside the toy store Michael felt people staring at him, until he pulled up his collar and pulled down his hat and tried to tuck his whole face behind his dark glasses, until he resembled a spy or some other desperate character: a desperate character holding a three-foot polar bear with a bright red grin. Michael waited forty-five minutes, then went inside and called, then waited outside some more, then went inside and called again, and in this manner two hours had passed. He also signed three autographs, although he swore to the people that he was not Marduk the Magnificent. They—a couple from Iowa and a teenager from the Bronx—said they didn't care. The resemblance was close enough to give the autograph validity with their friends. So in two cases Michael signed his name Ernesto Palooka and once he signed it Primus Muldoon, as a joke. He disliked being untruthful, but even more he disliked being fussed over as Marduk the Magnificent when he wasn't working.

Who Michael didn't telephone was Rose's sister, Violet, or Nurse White as she liked to be called. He told himself he didn't have her number, but he could have found it. She made him nervous. She was like a seventy-eight-RPM record among a lot of thirty-three-and-a-thirds. The last time he had seen her—which had been purely by accident—had been in Washington Square. Rose White suggested that he and her twin sister had been destined to meet. Violet White had been accompanied by half a dozen rather melancholic women, other nurses he supposed. He had stopped; it was only polite. Violet had been dressed in dark colors. Her black hair was pulled back from her face and her lipstick and eye shadow resembled gang graffiti on a white wall. Apart from that, she looked very much like her sister. Violet had said, "I bet you have the prettiest blood." He thanked her and tried to hurry on, but she had detained him with questions about wrestling and how he felt about hurting people. And she insisted on calling him Bromios, even though she knew his name was Michael. He couldn't get it out of his mind.

Apart from his anxiety about Rose White, Michael has begun to feel distracted by the cab driver, who keeps glancing at him in the rearview mirror. The driver looks at him and raises his eyebrows, then looks at him and shakes his head. Michael is still wearing dark glasses even though the sun went down two hours earlier. Even so, he knows what is coming.

As the driver waits to make the left turn onto Ninth Avenue, he peers at Michael in the mirror, then twists around and squints between the brim of his Mets cap and the upturned tip of his cigar. "Hey, aren't you Marduk the whatever?"

"I'm afraid you've got the wrong fellow," Michael answers. It occurs to him that Rose White may have been kept after school by her principal, who has been hinting that he might have her transferred to a gifted program.

"I seen you wrassle," says Hurkle Simmons.

"You must be thinking of someone else."

"Then how come you're going to the Garden?"

"Actually I'm going to Penn Station."

"Then how come you want to get out at the stage entrance?"

"Just a coincidence, I guess."

"Well," says Hurkle Simmons, "I hope you whop him. I guess you could say I'm a sucker for the good guys."

Michael decides not to answer. He does not see himself as lying. If the driver had asked, "Aren't you Michael Marmaduke?" he would have said yes. It is just that Marduk the Magnificent exists only at certain occasions, and this particular taxicab ride isn't one of them. Besides, Michael dislikes having anything intrude on his thoughts about Rose White and his concern for her.

He has known her a year. They met at a play put on by fifth- and sixth-graders at P.S. 6, the Lillie Devereaux Blake School at 81st and Madison. Michael went with the Koperskis, who live down the hall and whose daughter, Una, had the role of the dog Nana in *Peter Pan*. Rose White was in charge of the scenery. Marmaduke was introduced to her at the reception and couldn't take his eyes off her. With her white dress, blond hair and pale skin, she was luminescent, as if he could read a book by her in a dark place. He praised her for the excellence of the pirate ship, which, he said, looked just like the real thing. It was a remark that he hadn't known he was going to make until he made it. Since then they had been dating and in July they had gotten engaged.

The cab is approaching Madison Square Garden.

"Tell me," says Hurkle Simmons, "when some big bozo lifts you over his head and slam-bangs you down on your back in the ring, does that hurt or what?"

"I don't know what you're talking about," says Michael.

The cab pulls up to the curb. A crowd of gawkers hanging around the stage entrance hurries toward it, maybe thirty people, maybe forty. Most are teenagers but there are older people as well, including several old women. A few people have Instamatic cameras. When they see the cab and the large shape in the backseat their faces take on the expressions of hungry people sitting down to a large meal. They are fans and will not be fooled. An athletic-looking young man several yards in front of the others ducks down for a better look. A beatific expression softens his features. "Marduk," he says. Others hear him. "Marduk! Marduk!" they begin to shout. Half a dozen policemen and security guards hurry after the crowd.

"I thought you said you weren't Michael Marmaduke," says Hurkle Simmons, handing him a receipt with his change. His tone is slightly aggrieved.

Marmaduke gives him a dollar tip. "You never asked me that. You asked about the other one. I'm not that other one until I get inside."

"Well, what about that fall? Does it hurt?"

"I don't know. You'll have to ask the other one."

"Jesus, you're difficult. Well, I hope you bash him. You sign this city map for me?"

Michael takes the map and scrawls something across it. He is aware of excited faces pressed to the windows of the cab. Flashes are going off and making him blink. He returns the map.

"Who the fuck is Ernesto Palooka?" says Hurkle Simmons.

"My nom de guerre," says Michael, preparing to get out of the cab.

"Speaking of bears," says Hurkle Simmons, "don't forget that white one."

Marmaduke has indeed nearly forgotten the bear. He grabs it but grabs it too roughly and the bear begins to growl. "Darn," he says. He pushes open the back door and the open space is immediately filled with eager faces and hands clutching multicolored autograph books. He decides to get out the other door onto the street side and grabs the door handle.

If we were looking down from above, the cab would resemble a yellow beetle being attacked by ants. The policemen and security guards in their uniforms appear as boss ants and they know that devouring the yellow beetle will only make the other ants sick and so they are trying to drag them away. At this moment the yellow beetle dies and its soul emerges from the backseat. The soul is small and white and is being borne high in the air by a slave ant in the employ of the yellow beetle. The attacking ants make leaps at the small white soul of the yellow beetle but they can't reach it. The slave ant tries to push its way through the attackers toward the boss ants who understand that their fellows will only become nauseated if they eat the small white soul. Explosions of light occur all around the dead beetle. These may be fireflies in the pay of the ravenous ants or they may be spiritual emanations bursting from the small white soul. Look, look, the yellow beetle is crawling away!

Michael's features are contorted into a smile. What he hates about these occasions is the pushing and shoving, which means they afford opportunities for accidentally hurting someone. Michael hates to hurt anyone. Unfortunately, he is in a hurry, and while Marduk the Magnificent sometimes signs autographs, he, Michael Marmaduke, mostly doesn't.

"Marduk! Marduk! Marduk!"

Michael forces his way toward the policemen as he tries to quiet the bear, which has begin to sing: "When you go out in the woods today, you're in for a big surprise . . ." He keeps punching the bear in the stomach while maintaining his rigid smile.

"Sign my book! Sign my book!"

The autograph books are shoved in Michael's face as if their owners feel he won't notice them unless their covers touch his flesh. Now the dark glasses have become a nuisance. It is hard to see and the glasses keep getting bumped. Michael sticks the bear under his arm—it has begun to laugh—and removes the dark glasses. A sigh like an escaping whoosh of air is heard as his pale blue eyes are revealed to the crowd. As he shoves his way forward, he resembles a Cranach stag behung with dogs. People keep trying to give him things: flowers, boxes of candy, unknown objects which he gently pushes back to the giver, while trying to maintain his smile. But then people try to put things into his pockets or tuck them into his jacket. As he pushes forward an elderly woman tries to insinuate a bunch of white chrysanthemums into the front of his raincoat. He looks down at her gray face with its expression of religious devotion. The woman is replaced by more autograph books. A box of candy falls to his feet and is crushed. Something else is pressed into his hand, something cold and round. Michael slips it into his pocket.

All of a sudden a clear area blossoms before him and the teenagers clinging to his raincoat fall away. Into this space hops a lummoxy fellow with sandy hair and pimples. He wears a red sweatshirt depicting an ugly crocodile face under the words "Rahab the Ragged Rascal." The fellow is in his early twenties and appears wild with rage. He is hunched over and his twitching fingers are outstretched toward Michael.

"All right, you fuck, you think you're so fuckin tough, I can take you, you fuck!"

Michael is uncertain whether he has seen this lummoxy-looking fellow before or if he is just a familiar type. In any case Michael doesn't like him.

"I'm goin to kill you, you fuck, I'm goin to rip your head right off your fuckin neck!"

The man with the Rahab sweatshirt lunges forward and at that moment he is grabbed around the neck by two policemen. In the ensuing excitement, Michael slips past and is joined by two security guards. The three men—joined as closely as Siamese triplets—burst across the sidewalk and through the open stage door of the Garden, which slams shut behind them.

"Thanks, fellas," says Michael.

"Anytime, Mr. Marmaduke," says one of the guards, whose name is Solomon. "Nice bear."

The bear has begun to sing again: "You're in for a big surprise . . ."

"You think so?" says Michael. "I can't shut it off."

The other guard, who goes by the name of Spoiler, steps forward. "My kid's got one of those. I can do it." Spoiler pokes the bear directly above the heart, or what would be the heart if the bear were a mortal creature.

"Bye-bye for now!" says the bear.

"Thanks, Spoiler," says Michael. But both guards are looking over Michael's shoulder at a huge black man dressed in a leopard skin who is rushing toward them with his fists raised above his head. It is Thrombosis.

"Michael, where you been? You gotta be on in ten minutes!"

Michael is immediately grabbed by Thrombosis, who begins hurrying him toward the dressing rooms. He tries to keep the bear away from Thrombosis's big hands, because if the bear starts laughing or singing, Thrombosis will simply whop it. So as they hurry down the hall Michael continues to hold the bear high above his head, as if the bear were the important person of their group and not Michael Marmaduke himself.

"Rose White was supposed to meet me," says Michael. "She didn't show up."

Thrombosis opens the door of a dressing room and pushes Michael through it. "Tell me later, man." Already Thrombosis is stripping away the raincoat. The bear soars across the room and lands on a couch. The Irish tweed hat follows it.

"Dentata's waiting with the horse, man. You coulda called. Your 'Tude must be fucked up real bad." Thrombosis's voice is very deep and thick with vibrato like Paul Robeson singing the first few bars of "Old Man River."

Michael is unbuttoning his shirt, trying to get his fingers between Thrombosis's hands, which are as big as boxing gloves. "Rose White's never been late before," he says. "What if she's had an accident?"

"You want an accident, man? You got twenty thousand people

waiting out there. You don't show and there'll be one hell of an accident. You haven't even seen the script."

"I win, right?"

"That's not the point. This is three falls. There's a lot of rhetoric." Thrombosis shoves a paper at him. His round black face is as shiny as a greased bowling ball, and his teeth flash. "I'll get you dressed and do the makeup. Will you get your fuckin little hands out of the way or do I have to slap them?"

Michael sits in front of the mirror wearing only his jockey shorts. Instead of looking at the paper, he looks at a coin that he has found in his pocket. He has no idea where it came from. What a funny coin, he thinks. It appears to be brass and is the size of a silver dollar. On one side is the face of an angel with a halo and on the other is the face of a devil with horns. Both faces are smiling, but the heavenly smile is kindly and the other is unkindly. Michael flips the coin, then catches it angel face up. He flips it again and it lands devil face up. Somebody must have given it to him after he got out of the cab.

"What the fuck you doin, man?" demands Thrombosis.

"Someone gave me a funny coin."

Thrombosis makes a noise like a unhappy sewer. "The script, man, you got to look at the script."

Michael decides to work the coin into his routine and sets it on the table. Then he turns to the script. He is perfectly still, concentrating on the paper, as Thrombosis hurries around him fussing with his hair and applying makeup. Sometimes during a wrestling event Primus Muldoon appears in Michael's corner, but mostly it is Thrombosis, in the role of Nasamon the Nubian Giant, who coaches Michael, keeps track of the script and often takes enraged swipes at Marduk's opponent, especially if the opponent has been cheating. For big events in Madison Square Garden, Dentata works as well. She is Nemesis, Goddess of Retribution, and has been known to injure male fans who make the mistake of sitting too close to her holy wrath.

Thrombosis raises Michael's left foot and smears cream of aloe on the scars surrounding his ankle. Then he raises the right foot. Sometimes the scars become chafed and swollen. He draws on the white silk socks and then the silver elf boots.

If we pulled back to the farthest corner of the room, we would be struck by contrasts: the blackness of Thrombosis, the whiteness of Michael Marmaduke; the muscular bulk of Thrombosis, the muscular definition of Michael; the rushing movements of Thrombosis, the absolute stillness of Michael as he studies the sheet of paper. The room is dark except for a circle of lights around the mirror. It is just eight-thirty and from somewhere we hear a rhythmic thumping: bam-bam, bam-bam! These are the impatient feet of thousands of fans. Now, added to the feet, is a huge voice which is the blending of thousands of voices. At first the voice is a rhythmic mumble but as it increases in volume a single name becomes audible: Marduk! Marduk!

Thrombosis abruptly steps back. "Done!" he says.

Michael sets the paper on the table, picks up the coin, and rubs his thumb against it. He looks in the mirror. Everything exists within the reflection except Marduk himself. Michael is like a theater waiting for an event. The mask of Michael Marmaduke is replaced by the mask of Marduk the Magnificent, but Marduk hasn't arrived. He must be summoned. Michael looks into his eyes in the mirror. The gold and silver mascara makes his blue irises resemble the distant suns of uncharted solar systems. Michael focuses on the black pupils. He thinks about power. He thinks about Ea, father of Marduk; Ea, the god of wisdom and the source of all magic. He thinks of how Absu, the sweet water abyss, wants to slay Marduk even before he is born but how Ea the All-Wise throws the cloak of enchantment over Absu, putting him to sleep. And then Ea kills Absu and he constructs a wonderful chamber out of his body and he calls the chamber "Absu" and within this chamber the birth of Marduk takes place and he is born fully grown and never was there a creature so beautiful and never was a creature so powerful and from Ea's cloak of enchantment there comes the cloak of power and it is like a cloak of cobwebs, a cloak of fog that seems to drift from the mirror and come to rest on the shoulders of Michael Marmaduke with the cool touch of mist, and the shoulders of Michael Marmaduke become the shoulders of Marduk the Magnificent.

Marduk stares into the mirror. He roars.

"Fuckin A!" says Thrombosis.

4

FAITHFUL AND TRUE

We are focused on a brown, gelatinous substance and we see strange movements within its depths. It contains in fact various shades of brown with a blackness at the center. The movements seem caused by powerful currents pushing the blackness from side to side. Let us move back a little. The substance assumes an orblike shape surrounded by a ring of pink, then a textured whiteness. Could it be one of those globes with which Gypsies tell the future? What is happening? Not only are we looking into this brown orb but it seems to be looking at us. We move back a little further and find we are staring into the eye of a horse. The eyelid closes, then opens. The great pupil shifts from right to left as if the beast were nervous. It tosses its head and we lose sight of the eye altogether. Here is a nostril. Here is a bridle of silver. We are still too close.

We pull back twenty feet and there, seated upon a white horse, is Marduk the Magnificent poised on the gangway seconds before his entrance into the Garden. Marduk is clothed in white linen over which is a white robe that appears to have been dipped in blood. The bottom half is splotched with red and looks wet. Across the robe are the words "King of Kings." Marduk's face is white with white powder and around his eyes are many shades of red, silver and gold, making his eyes seem to burn with an intense flame. Caught up in his blond hair is a crown with many diamonds which traces words in some unknown alphabet. Between Marduk's teeth he holds a sword; ruby rings flash from his fingers and gold bracelets from his wrists. His legs are bare and upon his right leg are tattooed the words "King of Kings" in red letters, and upon the left are the words "Faithful and True" in black letters. In his left hand he holds the key to the abyss and a gold chain, and in his right hand, along with the reins, he holds a small microphone. He is seated upon a golden cowboy saddle. The horse's bridle and bit are of the whitest silver. Every now and then Marduk makes a soothing noise and pulls back on the reins because the horse is nervous and dislikes this waiting. The horse is rented and is named Joey.

A few feet in front of the horse stands Dentata in her role of Nemesis, Goddess of Retribution. Over her shoulders she wears a golden robe and upon her head is a crown with twelve stars. She stands on a small cart that is silver and resembles the moon, as if she had the moon beneath her feet. The cart is electrically powered but Dentata also holds a leopard on a leash and the leopard seems to be pulling the cart. Don't look at the leopard too closely. It is old and has no teeth.

Behind Marduk's white horse stands Nasamon the Nubian Giant. He too is dressed in golden robes and wears a golden turban with a single star in the center of his forehead. The blackness of his face is like the bottom of a well. Within his arms he carries Marduk's weapons: a silver bow and a quiver of silver arrows, a silver club, several silver lightning bolts, a silver net which is the net that will be held by the four winds.

From the Garden itself comes the stamping of thousands of feet which accompany the chant: "Marduk! Marduk!"

A row of a dozen policemen stands on either side of Marduk, and six more block the end of the gangway. These men appear intensely bored. Their only solace is that they are not out on the street busting dope dealers. They tend to be older men and nearly all have trouble with their arches. Adolescents with flash cameras keep springing in front of the policemen blocking the gangway. The adolescents hastily point their cameras toward Marduk the

Magnificent and snap off quick shots. The flashes of light disturb Joey the rented horse. The policemen wave away the adolescents as one might wave away gnats on a lazy afternoon.

Nasamon the Nubian Giant gives Marduk a slight poke with a silver bolt of lightning. "Let's get the show on the road."

Marduk rises up in the silver stirrups. His blood-dipped cloak swirls around him. His blond locks quiver. Back in the gangway someone has turned on a wind machine. A policeman loses his cap and it rolls forward among the kids with cameras. Marduk stands in his stirrups and concentrates on his own magnificence. Once more he becomes mighty and terrible. Once more he becomes thunderer and howler. He removes the sword from his mouth and gives it to Nasamon. Marduk raises the microphone and, as he speaks, his words erupt heavy with reverberation from a hundred speakers throughout the Garden.

"Come, let us gather for a great banquet! Let us feast on the flesh of kings, of commanders, of mighty men, of horses and their riders, on the flesh of everyone, free and slave, great and small!"

His words are followed by the trumpet blast of Aaron Copland's "Fanfare for the Common Man." Almost instantly the fanfare is overwhelmed by the roar of the crowd. The air throbs like wind whipping through willow trees. The goddess Nemesis moves forward in her moon cart drawn by the leopard, Vengeance. The colored spotlights make the twelve stars in her crown dance and flash. Next comes the white horse, and Marduk enters the Garden. The bloody sword is again between his teeth. He lifts the golden chain and key to the abyss. The wind tousles his golden hair and ripples his cloak dipped in blood. His smile is terrible and joyful. His power is gentle and ruinous. The white horse rears up and tosses its head. Lastly comes Nasamon the Nubian Giant. One might think he would be borne down by his load of weapons, by the lightning bolts and bow and arrows and great silver net. Instead they seem to bear him up and his strides are light and massive.

On either side of Marduk hurry the two rows of policemen. No longer do they look bored. Instead they appear anxious, even frightened. At times like these the older ones begin to think of retirement. They stare into the crowd that threatens to push against them. A teenage boy rushes toward the white horse and is pushed back. A girl in a denim jacket flings herself down on the concrete before the moon cart and the leopard Vengeance and is immediately dragged away. The hugeness of the noise is like a silence. It is like a great ache in the ears.

Then, above the roar, comes the voice of the announcer, an ancient fig-shaped sack of a man dressed in black and standing in the center of the ring. Long ago he wrestled under the name of the Slam-King. Now days he works up the crowd and is called Mr. Lightning. His words are doleful and the contortions of his face express severe dejection.

> "The cities sighed, the people
> Were plagued by the serpent-dragon.
> The people died and decreased in number
> Their corpses were flung on the dung-heap.
> For their lamentation there was nobody
> To listen, nobody to answer to their cries.
> 'Who brought forth the serpent-dragon?'
> 'The sea brought forth the serpent-dragon.'
> Enlil drew a picture of the dragon in the sky.
> Ten yards across spread his giant mouth.
> At fifty yards the dragon could snatch birds
> From the air and grind their bones.
> He raises his tail and sweeps away
> A third of the stars of heaven
> And hurls them to the ground.
> All the gods of heaven flee the monster.
> Who will rescue the people of the cities?"

Mr. Lightning puts one hand to his forehead, shielding his eyes from the lights, and stares out into the Garden. Soon he notices Marduk the Magnificent approaching on his white horse. Mr. Lightning hurries to the edge of the ring.

"Who comes forward?" cries Mr. Lightning.

The white horse rears up and Marduk shakes the key to the abyss above his head. "It is I that comes forward! Marduk the Magnificent! I will rescue the people of the cities! I will restore the tablets of destiny!"

Mr. Lightning stretches his arms toward Marduk. The crowd of twenty thousand are on their feet, shouting and whistling. Mr. Lightning permits himself a hopeful expression.

> "Can you draw out Leviathan with a hook,
> Press down his tongue with a cord?
> Can you put a cord through his nose,
> Can you pierce his jaw with a hook?"

Marduk simply nods. By now he has reached the ring and dismounts. The two rows of policemen shield him from the crowd. Every few seconds a fan runs forward and has to be pushed back. Marduk climbs into the ring and strides to each of the four corners, holding up the bloody sword in one hand and the golden chain and key in the other. He calls out to the crowd, and his voice bursts from a hundred speakers: "Cast off the works of darkness and put on the armor of light!"

The twenty thousand voices speak as one voice: "Marduk!"

Again he lifts up the sword: "Sit at my right hand until I make of your enemies your footstool!"

"Marduk! Marduk!"

The policemen encircle the ring. They shift from foot to foot and look nervously at each other. This is the time they like least, the time they feel these twenty thousand excitable fans will attempt to join Marduk in the ring. Don't think it hasn't been tried. Each one of these men has an unpleasant story. Nasamon the Nubian Giant is holding the horse, which keeps trying to rear up. Even the leopard, Vengeance, looks unhappy.

Marduk raises the key to the abyss. "Rahab will be your footstool!"

"Marduk! Marduk!"

During these moments Mr. Lightning has been glancing up the gangway. Abruptly his face collapses in terror. He scurries to the opposite side of the ring. From the speakers erupts the wild beating of kettledrums. The twenty thousand fans fall silent.

Mr. Lightning points with a trembling hand. His words rise fearfully above the beating drums: "His roaring is the floodstorm, his mouth is fire, his breath is death!"

Suddenly a giant crocodile rushes into the Garden flanked by twenty policemen. Although the crocodile appears ferocious and the policemen seem full of fear, their fear is directed out toward the crowd, rather than in toward the crocodile, which is making great bellowing noises and raking the air with its claws. An Indian warrior with war paint and feathers hurries on either side of the crocodile. Between them they hold up a banner on which is printed a picture of a gigantic, fiery-red dragon with seven heads and ten horns, and on each head are seven diadems. Each warrior grips a tomahawk between his teeth.

Mr. Lightning screams out to the crowd, "It is Rahab the Reckless, Rahab the Ragged Rascal, the Arrogant One, the Grand Dragon of Badness!"

The crocodile rushes toward the ring, and the policemen rush with it, as do the two Indians holding the banner. There are screams from the audience and people throw things like beer cans and cushions. The policemen wear determined but aggrieved expressions. As the crocodile approaches it becomes clear that Rahab is in fact a very large man wearing a crocodile skin over his head and shoulders. The head of the crocodile has red eyes and two rows of huge white teeth. Mr. Lightning has fallen to the mat paralyzed with terror. His arms cover his head and he is quaking. Marduk has given his sword, chain and key to the abyss to Nasamon the Nubian Giant. He leans against a padded turnbuckle and appears very relaxed. He flips a coin into the air, catches it and flips it again.

The rushing crocodile stretches out its arms as it nears the ring. The two Indians, called Gog and Magog, begin howling and running toward Nasamon the Nubian Giant and Nemesis. The four are abruptly engaged in a fierce struggle, or perhaps it is a primitive form of greeting, because they fall apart as suddenly as they came together, although the Indian who attacked Nemesis seems to be limping. Vengeance the leopard has fallen asleep. Joey the rental horse is eating something. The kettledrums still echo from the speakers. Rahab's policemen join with Marduk's policemen, and both groups appear substantially relieved.

Rahab the Arrogant One climbs into the ring. He leaps up and down screaming and bellowing at Marduk. Mr. Lightning remains prostrate on the mat. Although Rahab is full of rage, he doesn't approach Marduk. The kettledrums begin to fade. Marduk yawns and takes a few steps toward Rahab. He reaches up for the microphone hanging above him and shouts into it.

"Behold, Rahab, I am against you! You are the fat crocodile lying in the midst of the stream that says, 'The water is my own; I made it for myself.' But I will put hooks in your jaws and make the fish stick to your scales. I will drag you out of your rivers with all the fish still sticking to you. And I will cast you forth into the wilderness and I will leave you there where you shall be neither picked up nor buried but left as food for the beasts of the earth and birds of the air!"

Rahab appears to go crazy. He climbs up the turnbuckles and balances on the post. Then he leaps into the ring, bellowing and beating his chest. His feet pounding the mat make a terrible racket. Marduk is indifferent. Mr. Lightning remains prostrate. Rahab screams and screams. Marduk again takes the microphone.

"You, Rahab, are a crocodile, making the water bubble, fouling the waters with your feet and dirtying the streams. I will haul you up with my net and hurl you into the open field. I will strew your flesh upon the mountains and fill the valleys with your bones. I will drench the whole earth to the tops of the mountains with your gushing blood. And when I have blotted you out, I will veil the heavens and darken the stars, covering the sun with a cloud and the moon shall cease giving her light!"

The crowd roars its approval. People—mostly the young and nimble—jump up and down on their seats. Mr. Lightning returns to life and gets to his feet. He appears perfectly calm and pulls down the microphone. "In this corner," he shouts, "stands Rahab the Reckless, six feet eight inches tall and weighing four hundred and fifty pounds." There is a storm of protest and boos.

"And in this corner at six feet six and weighing three hundred pounds is Marduk the Magnificent."

Hysterical appreciation.

"This is a championship match of three falls!"

More hysterical appreciation with threats shouted at Rahab, who keeps sneering and making faces at the crowd.

Rahab and Marduk remove their paraphernalia. Rahab gives

his crocodile skin to Gog and Magog. Marduk gives his cloak and white linen shirt to Nasamon. He removes his championship belt, holds it up so that people may cheer, then gives the belt to Nasamon as well. He removes his crown. He removes his rings and golden bracelets until he wears nothing but his golden trunks and elf boots. He flexes his muscles. His body resembles an overinflated machine.

Rahab finishes disburdening himself, and the referee, a gray, tubercular-looking man known as Slick, checks Rahab for hidden weapons. Marduk, as faithful and true, has no use for hidden weapons. He continues to lean against the turnbuckle flipping a coin. Slick raises both hands and lets them fall. There is a sudden hush. The match has begun. Marduk slowly pushes himself away from the turnbuckle, flips the coin one more time, glances at it, then flips the coin into the crowd. Let's take a close look at it spinning through the air. There is the face of the angel with the halo. How joyful he looks. There is the face of the devil with his horns. Now there's a mean-looking puss. First one, then the other. Closer, it is just a brassy blur. Closer still and it is nothing. The crowd roars approval.

5

How May I Serve You

At the peak of its trajectory the coin moves back into view and begins its descent toward Section H on the northwest side of the ring. Among the colored spotlights, the coin is just one more bit of glitter, and most of the people following its course have lost sight of it. Besides, in the ring terrible events are taking place. Rahab the Arrogant One has rushed at Marduk and his great scaly breast has smashed against Marduk's smooth white skin. But one stubborn fellow in Section H still has the coin in sight. Like most everyone around him, he is standing up and craning his neck in order to see better. He is about thirty-five, of average height, dressed in jeans and a green sweatshirt that says "New York Giants." He is squinting into the lights as if he were at the very brink of a religious experience. His name is Wally Wallski and he is an out-of-work fisherman. Beside him is a dark shadow, but we will get to that later.

Wally Wallski is here by chance. A sick buddy gave him the ticket, and if his wife Claudine knew that instead of pounding the sidewalks in search of employment he is planted in the Garden watching a theatrical event which amusingly describes itself as professional wrestling, she would shy a frying pan at him, the

relationship between Wally Wallski and his spouse being somewhat like the relationship between a walnut and a hammer.

But now the coin is completing its arc. With his eyes fixed on its
shining promise, Wally Wallski climbs onto his seat. He is crouching and alert. Like many professional fishermen, he is a thin man:
wiry with leathery skin. Suddenly he leaps into the air, high above
the heads of the men and women around him, makes a mighty
swipe with his right hand and shouts, "Hah!" Then he tumbles
back to the floor pressing both hands to his chest.

"You okay?" asks the dark shadow by his side.

But Wally Wallski doesn't even hear him over the cheers and
groans of the twenty thousand fans. Wally Wallski sits on the cold
concrete and he holds up the shiny coin as if he meant to eat it.
"I'm lucky now!" he keeps saying. "I'm lucky now!" He turns the
coin over. He looks at the angel's face; he looks at the devil's face.
Standing up, he doesn't notice that he has torn his shirt or has dirt
all over his pants: crimes which will bring his wife's wrath down
upon him. All he can think about is his good fortune in snatching
the coin out of the air: a coin flipped by Marduk the Magnificent.
"Whatta day," Wally Wallski keeps saying.

Let us leave him for a moment and turn our attention to the
dark shadow by his side. The shadow has focused on the coin in
Wally Wallski's hand and committed its two faces to the tidy file
cabinets of memory. Now he is looking back at the ring. He is a
smallish man, perhaps five feet eight and quite thin. His meager
black hair is slicked back flat over his head so that his widow's
peak bisects his shiny forehead in a distinct black V: V as in
Vicious. He has a long nose and receding chin. He has dark eyes
and small teeth which incline inward. He wears a double-breasted
dark suit with padded shoulders and under those shoulders one
can easily imagine that he has no body at all, or no human body,
at any rate. Standing, he bends forward as if unaccustomed to
being on two legs. Long ago he acquired the name Deep Rat, and
that has subsequently replaced any name he originally possessed.
As far as he knows he has always been Deep Rat. And just as a ton
of coal can be compressed to a single diamond, so the past for him
has been compressed to small zones of comfort and discomfort.
For the discomfort, he still expects retribution. And for the com-

fort, there was never enough. Comfort and retribution form the sole motivations of his life, with retribution having the edge, because he has been known to endure cold and wet just for the pleasure of sticking someone who deserves to get stuck. And the memories of retribution rest like sweet things in his mouth.

Deep Rat is not a wrestling fan. He is here on business. For him Marduk the Magnificent is just a meal ticket. Marduk is not even a curiosity, because Deep Rat has no interest in anything untouched by his twin areas of interest. But because Deep Rat is being paid, his attention is focused on the events in the ring. All the rest—the noise, the hysterical crowd—are as far away as China. Even the fishy-smelling man at his side has been forgotten. When Deep Rat takes an interest in something, he leans forward and lifts his head as if he were sniffing.

In the ring Rahab the Ragged Rascal has lifted Marduk high over his head, holding him up to whatever spirit of darkness Rahab worships. We hear a lot of anxious mewling from the crowd. Rahab's elbows are locked and Marduk must be ten feet above the mat. Rahab begins to turn, slowly at first, then faster. Those who have seen Rahab wrestle all realize this is a dire moment. Rahab has begun a move called the Twister. In fact, if one listens, one can hear the word being spoken by worried fans—"The Twister," they say, "he's doin the Twister"—but Deep Rat pays no attention to this. He simply watches Rahab turning faster, and he wonders, mildly, how Marduk will free himself from this predicament.

Now the kettledrums begin again. Nasamon and the Goddess Nemesis pace nervously back and forth at the edge of the ring, and Nemesis makes catlike hisses at the Indian chieftains: Gog and Magog, who look particularly peppy and smug. The one point of peace and tranquillity in the entire Garden appears to be Marduk himself as he reclines in the gigantic paws of the Grand Dragon of Badness. Marduk's arms are at his sides and he seems asleep. If one could calculate the sinking hearts within this arena one would have a downward motion comparable to the grand cataract at Niagara Falls. The only happy spirits are a few Rahab fans: misfits and malcontents caught up in a perverse Romantic spirit which will someday land them in jail. Every other heart but one is awash with dread. That single exception is Deep Rat, whose heart—it resembles a block of oak chiseled into the shape of a question mark—is indifferent.

The kettledrums reach their crescendo, and at that very moment Rahab the Ruthless plants his two great feet and attempts to bring Marduk crashing down to the mat, where his spine will be crushed and his skull turned to jelly. But as Rahab is beginning the great sweep downward, Marduk twists in his hands and kicks at Rahab's shoulders, which deflects his descent, sending him not to the mat but over toward the ropes, which are not ropes at all but thick elastic cords like the cords on a gigantic slingshot. Marduk hits the ropes with such force that his body is propelled back over the curtain and nearly to the first seats before the counterforce of the elastic takes effect, hurling Marduk back into the ring. And do you see how he has positioned himself with his elf boots pressed together like the warhead of a gigantic torpedo? It is a pity this happens so quickly, because one would like the chance to savor Rahab's sudden awareness of the reversal of his fortune as Marduk rockets toward him. But there is no chance. Marduk's boots connect with Rahab's chin and the Grand Dragon of Badness is bludgeoned to the mat. Marduk walks over and puts a foot on Rahab's chest. Imagine great black X's drawn across Rahab's eyes. Slick the referee drops to his knees, peering at Rahab's flattened shoulders. Then he strikes the mat three times as the crowd goes wild.

Slick gets to his feet and hauls down the microphone. "The first woe is past; and, behold, the second woe cometh quickly!"

Rahab, who had seemed dead, pops to his feet fully refreshed, because, after all, this is the first of a three-fall event and the night is young. As for Marduk, the slingshot maneuver clearly exhausted him. He staggers to a turnbuckle unprepared for the awful embrace that Rahab wants to inflict upon his person. Rahab pursues Marduk as Marduk attempts to catch his breath. Rahab tries to grapple and is thrown off. Rahab grins and makes happy crocodile noises. He kicks out and appears to make contact with Marduk's stomach—at least there is a loud noise—even though Deep Rat can still see the colored spotlights twinkling between the sole of Rahab's boot and Marduk's vulnerable flesh. Marduk nearly falls and his handsome face, in its expression of suffering, resembles the erosion patterns on a drought-stricken landscape: deep cuts and ravines, the terrible inroads of pain. Before Marduk can recover, Rahab the revengeful has leapt on Marduk's back and is hammering the champion's head against the turnbuckle as the crowd shouts out the number of times that Marduk's brow makes contact with the seemingly concrete-block texture of the padded cushion. ". . . eight, nine, ten . . ." Rahab releases his victim and Marduk stumbles across the ring with his hands pressed to his eyes and forehead. Even though the champion is suffering intense pain, he struggles not to show it. Even in adversity his valiant nature is in the forefront.

Deep Rat glances around at the audience. If Marduk's suffering expression were a loud noise, then the face of each wrestling fan would be its little echo. Next to Deep Rat, Wally Wallski's countenance is a study in distress as he clutches the coin to his chest. He appears to be wishing on it and mutters a few desperate words over and over. Deep Rat doesn't understand all this fooling around. What this Marduk fellow should do is haul out a pistol and shoot that big fucker. Why waste time? This is what Deep Rat would do. This is what any sensible person would do. And the fact that Marduk doesn't do it is plainly a sign of weakness. That big black guy in the fancy turban could easily be packing a .38 beneath his orange robes and instead of running back and forth like a terrified toddler, he could give Marduk the gun and let Marduk stop this nonsense once and for all. Deep Rat hadn't quite understood this wrestling business when he first arrived, but now he's got it figured out. It is spinelessness parading as valor: rabbits dressed as pit bulls. And the crowd, they're just the same. Deep Rat's been around. He knows mice when he sees them. Marduk's just a big mouse. Marduk the Squeak-Squeak, Marduk the Trembler with Pink Eyes.

In the ring Rahab the Ruthless once again has Marduk raised above his head. Once again he is turning round and round and again one hears the whispers of the crowd: "The Twister, oh my God, the Twister." Again the kettledrums erupt from a hundred speakers. But this time Marduk doesn't seem relaxed but limp. He doesn't appear to be waiting, but unconscious. And when Rahab begins his great sweep to hurl Marduk to the mat, the champion makes no clever acrobatic move with his elf boots. A telephoto lens would indicate the grenade-popping sweat drops that burst from Rahab's scaly forehead as his powerful arms surge into the equivalent of turbodrive, and, like twin sequoias toppling at the identical moment, they begin their descent with Marduk lolling in their grasp. This is how night descends. This is how plague strikes. Rahab lets loose his hold on Marduk's delicate flesh and the champion plummets like a comet toward the mat.

Let us consider the noise his body makes when it strikes. Even miles away people must hear it: families gathered to discuss the confused state of the world, nuns at their prayers, the mayor going over his budget. Suddenly comes an explosion which seems not so much outside them as within them. It erupts in the deep cave where fear hides. It touches them like a knife point at the back of the neck. Children whimper. Adults imagine early graves. They feel chilled and glance around for sweaters. They feel despairing and once more they think they should move from the city. But where could they run? Where hide when every hiding place would betray them?

In the Garden, Marduk's contact with the mat is accompanied by the crash of kettledrums. The champion bounces up several feet and hits again. "Boom!" go the drums. Rahab falls upon him like a fat man falling on a meringue. How can Marduk breathe with that scaly chest pressed to his mouth? Slick the referee seems reluctant to begin the count. He is gazing at the ceiling, where a white pigeon flutters between the rafters. The Indian chieftains Gog and Magog are throwing bananas at him to get his attention. The goddess Nemesis has her head bowed. Nasamon the Nubian Giant beats his chest. At last a banana bounces off the back of Slick's head and he notices Rahab sprawled on Marduk's lifeless body. Slowly, he turns. He lowers himself to the mat and peers at Marduk's shoulders. Slowly, he strikes the mat as if his hand were difficult to lift: one, two, three. Rahab the Outrageous leaps to his feet and declares himself champion. He springs toward Nasamon to grab Marduk's championship belt. Slick pursues him to explain this is a three-fall event and only two falls have occurred. Rahab looks at his closed fist and raises three fingers pensively. He looks back at Marduk still lying on the mat. Rahab again throws himself across Marduk's shoulders and shouts at Slick to begin the count. Slick refuses. The Indian chieftains Gog and Magog climb into the ring. Nemesis and Nasamon the Nubian Giant climb in as well. Magog grabs Slick the referee and receives a kick in the belly from Nemesis.

Deep Rat turns away from the action to buy a cherry pop from a kid hurrying by with a loaded tray. Then Deep Rat accuses him of short-changing him a quarter, which is the sort of thing Deep Rat does by habit. Sometimes it works, sometimes it doesn't. This time it doesn't. By the time Deep Rat looks back at the ring, Gog and Magog, Nemesis and Nasamon are back on the floor and Slick is hauling down the microphone. "The second woe is past; and, behold, the third woe cometh quickly."

But what's this? Marduk is still lying on the mat. People begin shouting, "Wake up! Wake up!" Rahab rubs his great paws together and runs his tongue around the outside of his mouth. His tongue is dark blue like a chow dog's. Rahab sidles toward the unconscious Marduk. Slick tries to push him away. "Wake up! Wake up!" Slowly Marduk begins to stir. Rahab grapples with the referee and roughly elbows him aside. Rahab runs across the ring and leaps up, twisting his body into a mighty swan dive. He means to come crashing down on Marduk's helpless form. "Wake up! Wake up!" Rahab the Rotten falls toward Marduk like the sharp tines of a fork toward the yolk of a poached egg. Then, at the last possible moment, Marduk rolls aside and Rahab crashes to the mat and bounces. Oh, that hurt! Oh, how much does Rahab regret his impetuous nature. Marduk gets to his feet. The crowd chants his name over and over. Deep Rat looks around with scorn. "Marduk the Mouse," he says to himself. Rahab the Remorseful also crawls to his feet. He is unhappy and much of the spirit has gone out of him. When Marduk slowly approaches, Rahab backs away. It is as if Rahab had never understood the nature of pain until this moment and now he wants no part of it. He would change his life if he could. He would become a postman. But Rahab should have thought of this before. He must take responsibility for his actions. Why should Rahab be different from anyone else?

The short nap seems to have done Marduk good. He smiles at

Nemesis, Goddess of Retribution. Let's get on with it, he seems to say. Let's get the job done. Rahab is distressed to witness Marduk's renewed vigor. It seems like cheating, and he mumbles crocodile protest noises to Slick the referee. But Slick hasn't forgotten how Rahab pushed him around, and he shrugs. There is a lot of philosophy in that shrug. A lot of Plato, a lot of Hegel. Rahab had better face the facts, it seems to say. Rahab had better get with it. Rahab takes a deep breath, charges Marduk and is easily thrown aside. He has hurt himself—perhaps he has twisted his ankle. He grimaces and hobbles around the edge of the ring as Marduk waits, flexing his pecs and smiling at the crowd.

Deep Rat is disgusted. If he were not here on business, he would walk out. He glances at Wally Wallski, who is sniggering happily, as if Wally Wallski had caused this turn of events with his *sotto voce* supplications. Deep Rat gives Wally Wallski an elbow jab in the ribs and then pretends it was an accident. Sorry, sorry, I just got excited. Wally Wallski hardly notices.

Deep Rat wonders about his employer. What could be the purpose of this? He has deep respect for his employer as someone who doesn't fool around. Is it Marduk's destruction that his employer has in mind? Blackmail, treachery, some form of catastrophe? Deep Rat hasn't received his final instructions.

In the ring Marduk has hurled Rahab against the ropes, and when Rahab comes bouncing back, Marduk downs him with a flying leg kick. The fans are on their feet. They know the end is very close. Marduk is full of vigor and Rahab appears exhausted. He crawls away from the champion. All he wants is to return to his swamp and suck in the little fish, to lie in the primordial ooze and gossip with his belly. Marduk grabs his leg and pulls him to the center of the ring. Rahab struggles to his feet. Marduk grabs the Rascal's wrists and begins swinging him around, going faster and faster until he is just a blur. Marduk lets go and Rahab hurtles into the ropes and bounces back again, tumbling over and over. Marduk smiles. Instead of dropping Rahab with a final kick, he catches him as one might catch a rolled-up mattress. But look, he has caught him upside down! Marduk lifts Rahab up and smashes his head down to the canvas. Boom! go the kettledrums. Then he begins to squeeze.

"It's the Bosom of Abraham!" says Wally Wallski.

"Fuck you," says Deep Rat.

Marduk squeezes harder. Rahab's chow-dog tongue protrudes from his mouth. His eyeballs inflate like little balloons. "Abraham! Abraham!" chants the crowd. Marduk forces the Arrogant One's shoulders down to the mat. His smile broadens and he closes his eyes. His smile is like the kiss of an angel. One imagines that Florence Nightingale wore that smile in the Crimea when she visited the beds of the dying. "Abraham! Abraham!"

Slick the referee ducks down to check Rahab's shoulders. Rahab's tongue extends half a foot. Slick strikes the mat three times and Marduk releases the Grand Dragon of Badness, letting him topple into a defeated heap. The match is over.

Slick hauls down the microphone. "And the great dragon was cast out! The old serpent, he who deceives the whole world, was cast out onto the earth!"

Slick lifts Marduk's hand into the air. "You rule over the proud swelling of the sea; when its waves rise up, you quiet them! You crushed Rahab like a carcass, you scattered your enemy with your mighty arm!"

The Indian chieftains Gog and Magog apprehensively crawl into the ring to scrape their comatose potentate off the mat. Rahab needs to be carried away. Gog and Magog struggle under his weight. The twin lines of policemen close around them to prevent members of the crowd from getting in a few licks, a few quick karate chops.

Marduk the Magnificent straps on his golden championship belt and raises his hands over his head. From the loudspeakers comes a deep paternal voice.

> "By his power he stilled the Sea!
> By his cunning he smote Rahab!
> By his winds the heavens are cleared,
> His hand pierced the twisting serpent!
> Lo, these are the outskirts of his power;
> What a faint whisper we hear of him!
> Who could understand his mighty thunder?"

Most of the twenty thousand fans are on their feet and begin to chant the words they find printed in their programs. "Was it not you that cut Rahab into pieces, that pierced the dragon? Was it not you that dried up the sea, the water of the great deep?"

Nasamon the Nubian Giant puts the great cloak dipped in blood upon Marduk's shoulders, sets the crown upon his head. Waving and smiling, Marduk climbs from the ring. Again the warm paternal voice erupts from the loudspeakers.

> "O Marduk, thou art indeed our avenger!
> We have granted thee kingship over the universe entire!
> When in assembly thou sittest, thy word shall be supreme!
> Thy weapons shall not fail; they shall smash thy foes!
> O lord, spare the life of him who trusts thee,
> But pour out the life of the god who seizes evil!"

Deep Rat pushes past Wally Wallski. It's time to get busy. Although the aisles are full of people, Deep Rat easily gets through them. He is a master of the scuttle. Around elbows and over shoulders, he sees that the white horse has been led back to the ring and that Marduk is climbing into the saddle. Marduk waves to his fans. His smile is like a warm breeze occasionally felt in early spring. Deep Rat squeezes through the crowd in order to cut him off near the gangway. Two rows of policemen shield Marduk from the embraces of his fans. People throw flowers. Copland's "Fanfare for the Common Man" blares from the speakers. Even Nemesis, Goddess of Retribution, looks content.

Right at the spot where the gangway disappears under the seats, Deep Rat insinuates himself into position like a splinter into a thumb. Two policemen stand before him but they are big, with space between them. Marduk the Magnificent approaches on his prancing white horse. When Marduk is only five feet away, Deep Rat slides between the policemen. He spreads out his arms and bares his chest. "How may I serve you?" he cries out. "How may I help you find what is lost?"

Deep Rat only has the chance to see Marduk's startled expression before the two policemen seize him and drag him away. But that expression is enough. It is like honey on his tongue.

6

No Hero

It feels like we are looking down the single powder-specked barrel of a shotgun but actually it is a long corridor with dark gray walls. At the end is an open door. Two men stand in the doorway. We are hastening toward them and there is the sound of footsteps clattering on the tile floor. Around us are Marduk the Magnificent, now simply Michael Marmaduke in fancy wrestling dress, and his friends Dentata and Thrombosis in their sun and moon outfits. All three are in a hurry and their minds dwell on future events: friends to meet, problems to solve. Thrombosis and Dentata are extremely pleased with the conduct of the match and keep slapping Michael on the back and congratulating each other. Michael smiles, but his mind is on Rose White and his anxiety is like a pain in his side. The corridor is dim. Hallways in burning buildings are bleary like this one.

While we have a moment, let us look at the two men waiting in the doorway. They are quite short and wear dark overcoats and dark fedoras. If the fedoras were removed one would see the men are going bald. Both are about fifty and the accumulated problems of their lives have left significant autographs scrawled across their features. They are thin-lipped and their teeth are stained with nicotine. Although laughter as a concept must not be new to them and they have most likely experienced the smile, the chuckle and guffaw, their present expressions indicate that it hasn't happened recently. Their faces are neither handsome nor ugly, simply well trafficked. Because of their clothes and their age and their height, the men look like twins, but in fact they are unrelated. Indeed, they don't even like one another and each suspects the other of trying to copy him, not out of respect but just to get his goat. Even their names are similar, Brodsky and Gapski, and this too irritates them, and each sees the other as one of the heavier crosses he must bear in this life. Look how they stand, crowded in the doorway. Do you see how they elbow and jostle each other? This sort of proximity is hateful to them. Each detests how the other smells and looks and sounds, although these characteristics are identical for both. Even their farts smell the same, because they tend to eat in the same cheap restaurants, although mostly at separate tables. Then why are they together? you might ask. They are together through the whim of their superior, a man named Sapperstein. There is little enough amusement in Sapperstein's life but it amuses him to see Brodsky and Gapski working as partners as if the two short men were Sapperstein's entry in a three-legged race. We will never meet Sapperstein, but already we know a great deal about him. And whenever we encounter Brodsky and Gapski, then we must also imagine Sapperstein, who has united them and who has few pleasures except for this one, and who is sniggering as he considers Brodsky and Gapski bumping together through the world as if the left leg of one and the right leg of the other were strapped together and tied up in a burlap sack. And what do these men do? Brodsky and Gapski are police detectives and they are unaccustomed to bringing cheer into people's lives.

As the wrestlers approach the door, Brodsky, who stands on the left, lifts one hand as a signal to Stop. Although he might be impressed by their bulk and regalia, he gives no sign of it. "Which one of you people is Michael Marmaduck?" he asks.

"Duke," says Michael.

"Whatever," says Brodsky, glancing at a pad in his hand.

"You know a Rose White?" asks Gapski. The police detectives

talk as if they had missed a lot of sleep, as if they were more interested in naps than conversation.

"She's my fiancée," says Michael. He glances at Dentata and Thrombosis in surprise. "Has anything happened?"

"When did you see her last?" asks Brodsky.

"Wednesday evening. Is she all right? Who are you guys?"

Perfectly synchronized, Brodsky and Gapski reach into left-hand breast pockets, withdraw identical eelskin wallets and flip them open to show their police ID. "You talked to her since then?" asks Gapski. They return their ID to their pockets.

"Last night. What's going on? I was supposed to meet her this afternoon but she didn't show up. Is she all right?"

Brodsky looks at Gapski and raises his eyebrows. "He wants to put us out of work," he says.

"He wants to ask all the questions," Gapski replies.

"I bet he's the kind of guy who gives cops a hard time," says Brodsky.

"I hope we don't have to teach him a lesson," says Gapski ruefully. "I hate having to teach lessons."

Both Brodsky and Gapski are a foot shorter than Michael and each is half the weight of Thrombosis, who towers above them. Even Dentata could lift either police detective with one finely chiseled hand and lob him into a nearby wastebasket. Even so, the three wrestlers are subdued. They aren't fools. They know the difference between the real world and the play world.

"I'm just asking because I'm worried," says Michael quickly.

"You got a right to be worried," says Brodsky.

"In fact you shouldn't be worried," says Gapski, "you should be terrified."

At that moment Rahab the Arrogant One appears behind the two policemen. He is so big that if one squinted, it might seem that Brodsky and Gapski were Rahab's grade-school children. It could be a tense moment if it really were Rahab, but it is only Ronnie Reuther, who portrays Rahab in the ring. He has already shed his costume and is on his way home. He wears a London Fog raincoat and a blue beret. With him is his wife, Myrtle.

"Good match," says Ronnie. "You coming over for oxtails on Saturday? You know how Myrtle cooks them."

"I'm not sure," says Michael.

Ronnie looks at the two policemen and begins to realize that something is amiss. "You okay?"

"Yeah, I'm fine. I'll give you a call tomorrow."

"If there's anything I can do . . ."

"Don't worry."

Ronnie and his wife move past them into the long hall. His Gimmick put away, he leaves the Garden, impassive, anonymous, carrying a small suitcase and arm in arm with Myrtle, who has been his wife and helpmate for twenty-five years.

"You know Rose White's apartment up on Madison?" asks Brodsky as if posing a trick question.

"Sure," says Michael. "I mean I'm her fiancée, like I said."

"You better come with us," says Gapski. Not only must both men tilt back their heads when they look up at Michael, but they also have to hold on to their hats to keep them from falling off.

"Can't I change first?" Michael lifts the edge of the white cape dipped in blood.

"Make it snappy and don't pull any tricks," says Brodsky.

Michael puts a hand on Dentata's shoulder. "Will you do me a favor and call Primus Muldoon?"

Detectives Brodsky and Gapski plan to take Michael up to Rose White's apartment and confront him with the evidence. Since the drive from the West Thirties to the East Eighties will take a while, let's turn our attention to Wally Wallski, who has pulled a blue jacket over his New York Giants sweatshirt and is exiting the Garden along with twenty thousand contented fans. Deep Rat has already disappeared. No telling where he's gone. He's a slippery customer.

Wally Wallski emerges onto Eighth Avenue. It is ten-thirty and the night is cool. He knows he should go home to Brooklyn, but there he will encounter the recriminations of his wife Claudine and just the thought leaves a sour taste in his mouth. Perhaps he will stop for a beer, but then she would smell it on his breath. Perhaps he'll get a hot dog, but then she'll accuse him of wasting money.

He feels the lucky coin in his pocket and turns it over. It's been such a lucky night that it would be a shame to go home too early.

Wally Wallski wanders around the corner to the stage entrance in hopes of seeing somebody famous leaving the Garden. Perhaps he will even see Marduk himself. About thirty people are standing near the door. They are happy and eager and many hold small cameras. Half a dozen policemen stand impassively under a red exit sign. Wally Wallski takes his place next to a ragged-looking customer wheeling a shopping cart full of his things. The two men look at each other and their eyes meet.

The man with the shopping cart assumes a hopeful expression. His name is Beetle and everything he owns is in this cart. He might be forty; he might be seventy. He might be Norwegian; he might be Tunisian. At the moment he is ageless and gray. "You want to hear a sad story?" asks Beetle.

Wally Wallski moves back a step. "I don't know," he says.

"It's about something I did when I was a lot younger," says Beetle, pushing his shopping cart toward Wally Wallski. "You want to hear it?"

Wally Wallski looks apologetic. "I'm just here to have fun," he says. Then he digs in his pocket. "Here's a buck. Buy yourself a hot dog."

Beetle sighs and takes the money. "I could make it short," he says. But Wally Wallski is already moving up 31st Street.

As he walks, Wally Wallski asks himself how he will be able to explain the missing dollar to Claudine. He is half tempted to jump the gate at the subway, even though he has never done such a reckless thing. And what if he gets caught? On the other hand, what if his wife learns that he gave a dollar to a bum? Wally Wallski is a terrible liar. He will get flushed and stutter and finally admit what happened. "You gave a dollar to a bum?" Claudine will ask in the same voice that she might ask, "You slaughtered an entire kindergarten class with a machete?"

Wally Wallski takes the lucky coin from his pocket and flips it. Angel face up and he will jump the gate. It lands on his palm devil face up. He decides to try for two out of three. He flips the coin again, but as he reaches for it, he stumbles and the coin falls to the sidewalk and rolls. "Oh no," cries Wally Wallski. He runs after

the coin. He is on the dark side of the Garden and there are few
people about. The coin hops and turns and disappears into an
alleyway. Wally Wallski puts on a burst of speed and turns the
corner after the coin.

The alleyway is shadowy and Wally Wallski is hunched over
with his eyes focused on the pavement. He sees the glitter of the
coin and dives for it. Just as his hand closes around it, he realizes
he is not alone. He is aware of at least half a dozen vertical legs.
Worse, he's about to crash into them. "Watch out!" he shouts.
"Comin through!" He crashes into the legs.

Instead of protest or complaint, the air erupts with gunshots:
Bam! Bam! Bambambam! Wally Wallski lies on his belly with his
hands pressed to his ears and the lucky coin clutched in his fist.
There are groans and shouts. Bambambam! Then silence. Wally
Wallski peeks between his fingers. A man is standing in front of
him. Two others are lying in clumsy heaps.

"You okay?" asks the man. He has a deep voice like a country-
western singer.

Wally Wallski does a quick inventory of his body parts. "I guess
so."

The man reaches out to help Wally Wallski to his feet. The smell
of cordite tickles Wally Wallski's nose. He checks to see that he
still has the coin. He does.

"My name's Lenguado," says the man, giving Wally Wallski his
card. "You saved my life. I owe you one."

"What's going on?" asks Wally Wallski nervously. He tucks the
card into his pocket. The man is no more than a dark shape.

"These guys wanted to kill me. If I were you, I'd take a powder.
It wouldn't help to have your name in the papers."

"I'm already travelin," says Wally Wallski, backing out of the
alley.

All the way to Brooklyn, Wally Wallski tries to figure out what
happened. He remembers chasing the coin. He remembers the legs.
Then everything was gunshots and shouting. As far as he can tell,
the lucky coin saved his life.

When he arrives home, Wally Wallski discovers that Claudine
is waiting up for him. It used to be in scenes like this that the wife

has steam coming out of her ears and she is clutching a rolling pin with which she is gently tapping her palm. But times have changed. These days wives like Claudine already have the rolling pin built inside them.

"And where have you been?" asks Claudine. She wears a peach-colored robe and her hair is in rollers. These rollers don't improve the quality of her hair; rather, they appear to have a defensive purpose, as if with them she might batter down locked doors and barrel through crowds of shoppers at Macy's sales. She is a big woman and has the figure of a linebacker.

"Uh, just over, you know, in the city, dear."

"Did you find a job?"

Let us not embarrass Wally Wallski. Suffice it to say that in five minutes he has told his wife all about the wrestling and he is hoping that he won't have to reveal the fact that he gave a dollar to a bum. He also hopes not to mention the coin which he is turning over and over, frantically, in his pocket.

"And what else, you flimsy excuse for masculine enterprise?" Claudine is perched on the kitchen table as on a throne and Wally Wallski sits before her on a wobbly kitchen chair, trying not to glance at his wife who looks, he thinks, too bright and shiny.

"Ah, ah . . ." And then Wally Wallski remembers the shooting. "I would have gotten here earlier," he says, "but I was busy saving a man's life in a gang fight."

Of course Claudine doesn't believe him. He insists. She scoffs. Then Wally Wallski remembers that he has the man's card. "Look, he gave me his card."

Claudine plucks the card from her husband's outstretched hand like picking a canapé from a tray.

"Harvey Lenguado?" she asks.

"I guess so. I mean he said his name was Lenguado."

"You know who he is?"

"Sure, he's the guy whose life I saved."

"No, you idiot. He's one of the biggest realtors and developers in the city. What'd he give you for saving his life?"

"He gave me his card."

Claudine reaches forward and gives Wally Wallski's face a pat.

It is not affectionate. It is with pats of equal force that she kills the cockroaches that stream over the counters of their small kitchen. "No, stupid, he gave you nothing. You saved his life and he gave you nothing! First thing in the morning, you go to Harvey Lenguado and tell him he owes you one. Tell him he has to get us a new apartment. You understand?"

Wally Wallski looks around. He and his wife have two small bug-infested rooms on a noisy boulevard and dope dealers live on either side of them. "But haven't we been happy here?" he asks.

Most people's eyes are round; Claudine's appear pointed. Instead of answering, she stares at her husband in such a way that the image of a rolling pin springs into his brain: a disembodied rolling pin zapping through the air like a torpedo. And Wally Wallski winces as he imagines how it would feel to have this rolling pin come crashing down on his fingers.

We now move back an hour to Rose White's apartment. It is nearly eleven-thirty. Michael arrived with the police detectives Brodsky and Gapski ten minutes ago, and Primus Muldoon showed up five minutes later. Muldoon is a small man, not much bigger than the detectives, but he has a huge brown mustache. It is such a big mustache that it seems like a mustache with a man attached, rather than the other way around. He wears a sport coat with brown- and mustard-colored squares and a mustard-colored golfing cap. Muldoon is indignant and he keeps removing the golfing cap and slapping it against his leg. Each time he slaps it, a little cloud of dust explodes into the air.

"You mean you bust in here," he is saying, "find the broken window, find the blood, find my client's photograph, and so you arrest him? Just what police academy do you call your alma mater? Dumbo Tech?"

All four men are in Rose White's bedroom. Brodsky and Gapski stand side by side by the window. They keep elbowing and bumping one another, but neither moves away. Michael sits in a chair by the closet with his face in his hands. The sight of blood has not only frightened him, but turned his stomach. Even though there is not a lot of it, the stains are readily visible on the white rug. Michael keeps imagining possible scenarios as to what might have happened and each has an unhappy ending.

"We had to start somewhere," says Brodsky. His tone is more stubborn than apologetic.

"You gotta open the book before you begin the story," says Gapski. Both Brodsky's and Gapski's voices are high-pitched and they speak quickly, clipping off the words.

Muldoon paces with his hands clasped behind him. Each strand of his graying, sandy-colored hair pursues its destiny without regard for its fellows. "You police types," he says, "behave impudently toward your experiences: you exploit them."

"A clue's a clue," says Brodsky.

"Even the redwood," says Gapski, "grows from a tiny seed."

That morning somebody noticed the broken window and the building superintendent was notified. He knocked on Rose White's door and got no answer. Assuming she was at work, he tried to enter but found the door was locked from the inside. He sought help and the door was removed. The apartment was empty. There were traces of blood on the bedroom rug. The window, of course, was smashed. The super called the police. The big question was what had happened to Rose White. She had not gone to work. Presumably if she had jumped out the window, her body would have been found on the street below. Even if somebody had stolen her body, there would have been blood, some kind of mess, but the laboratory experts found nothing. Consequently, Brodsky and Gapski turned their attention to the roof. Here they discovered scuff marks but nothing more. Indeed, there was nothing to say that the scuff marks were significant. Another possibility was that Rose White had been lowered or raised to another apartment. Detectives questioned the occupants of the building, but everybody claimed ignorance and surprise. Personally, Brodsky and Gapski favored the roof theory, which is what led them to think of Marduk the Magnificent.

"Marmaduck's athletic," says Brodsky. "This would require somebody athletic."

"He hates heights," says Muldoon. "He's a gentle guy. In the ring, let's face it, he's a terror, but that's just business. Outside of the ring he's just like you or me, only nicer. What about her twin? Does she know anything?"

"The nurse?" asks Gapski. "She was at the hospital. Nice woman, you should have seen how upset she was."

Michael raises his head. Something colorful by the bed has caught his attention. Bending over, he finds the same panties that Rose White discovered the previous night: red silk bikini panties with a black fringe. He holds them up uncertainly.

Brodsky and Gapski have immediately noticed. Whatever their shortcomings, they are professionals and their eyes are quick.

"Hey," says Brodsky, with an ersatz grin, "it looks like our girl's a party girl."

"Anybody who wears stuff like that," says Gapski, "must have lots of athletic friends."

Jostling and bumping each other the police detectives hurry to examine the panties. "I thought you said Rose White was a quiet girl," says Brodsky, plucking the panties from Michael's fingers.

Michael feels no particular surprise about the panties. His response is identical to Rose White's. He assumes that some of her sister's clothes got mixed up in the wash. "I don't think they're hers," he says.

"Listen to the guy," says Brodsky. "Isn't that a story we've heard before? Nobody likes their sweetie to have a secret life."

"She not my sweetie," says Michael. "She's my fiancée."

"Whatever," says Gapski.

Michael glances toward Muldoon and shrugs. He wants to help but he is stunned by Rose White's disappearance. He is also unhappy that Brodsky and Gapski seem to find her disappearance a nuisance rather than a challenge. Frustrated, Michael returns to his chair. He remembers encountering Violet White one Sunday afternoon in this very apartment. She was dressed entirely in red. Rose White intended to drive her sister out to Flushing to visit a friend. Violet didn't drive because she was epileptic and, despite her medication, she occasionally had fits, mostly petit mals, but sometimes a grand mal that might occur on the street and cause a commotion. Violet would come out of these episodes strangely invigorated, and her sister accused her that day of not taking her pills in order to bring about an attack. Michael was standing next to Violet White at the time. She reached out and stroked Michael's cheek while scratching him with one red nail and leaving a mark: a single red line. Speaking to him rather than to her sister, she said, "Remember, my dear, creation and destruction are inseparable." To tell the truth, she gave Michael the shivers, but she was enough like her sister that whatever chemistry in Rose White worked on Michael's romantic feelings, a certain amount existed in Violet White as well. He would look at her with dislike and then have a mental image of caressing her that would be so vivid that Michael would have to yank down the shades on his own imagination.

Brodsky and Gapski have finished playing with the red silk panties and Brodsky has folded them and put them in the pocket of his coat. One might wonder whether they will ever reach the evidence drawer. "What we want from you, young fellow," says Brodsky, pointing at Michael, "is a list of your girlfriend's pals, people she worked with, everybody who knew her."

Primus Muldoon stands near Michael puffing on his pipe. "And then can he go? He needs his sleep."

"We might have to arrest him," says Gapski.

Brodsky rubs his palms together so they make a whispering noise. "A night in jail might have a salutary effect."

Muldoon exhales a cloud of smoke. "My client will give you ten minutes. Then, if you don't let him go, I'll make a few calls which will guarantee you guys finish your tours guarding the heavies and growlies at the Garden. Believe me, busting crack houses in your bare feet would be a safer proposition."

Thirty minutes later Michael Marmaduke sits on a bench on Fifth Avenue waiting for a bus to take him down to Number One University Place, where he has a condo. The two policemen are off pursuing leads and Primus Muldoon is driving back to New Jersey. Michael is not alone on the bench, but we have yet to meet his companion, so let's take a closer look. First of all, he is quite old. He is old and his clothes are old and his overcoat is old and his shoes are old, but he is not shabby. His name is Jack Molay and he is a mysterious figure. At first glance he appears harmless, although it might be asked why he is sitting on a bench at the edge of Central Park around midnight on a cool October night. Michael assumes he is waiting for a bus, although he never asks. Jack Molay's white hair is longer than is fashionable but it is not unkempt and it appears to have been recently cut. He has a long horsey face and were he to stand up one would see that he is a lanky sort of fellow and limber for his age. His eyes are so dark that they appear black, but most likely they are deep brown. Jack Molay leans forward and his hands are supported by a cane topped with an ivory handle carved in the shape of a head with a face on each side, like Janus the double-faced Roman god of doors and beginnings, although it is not Janus. One face is smiling and the other is leering: a subtle but distinct difference. The head with two faces reminds Michael of something but he can't recall what it is.

"And what do you think has happened to your fiancée?" Jack Molay is saying. He has a slight French accent, which Michael thinks makes him sound distinguished.

"Well, she can't have flown out that window and she didn't jump, so somehow somebody must have kidnapped her."

"Quite an ambitious undertaking," observes Molay.

As can be seen by their conversation, Michael has already described something of his predicament. Michael felt drawn to the old fellow simply because Molay apparently had no sense of who Michael was, didn't ask for an autograph and, while friendly, appeared unimpressed when he discovered Michael's occupation.

"So you're a wrestler?" Molay had asked.

"It's like wrestling. I mean, it resembles wrestling."

"Perhaps it is like French boxing," said Jack Molay. "I've done some of that in my time. They use their feet."

"No," said Michael, "it's more like play-acting."

"And you make it up yourself?"

"I get directions. I could be in the movies, but it's in the wrestling ring instead."

From these subjects they had gone on to discuss the vanishing of Rose White. Jack Molay seemed curious but wasn't pushy, which was a relief, because Michael found most of the world pushy, even his manager, Primus Muldoon, whom he truly respected. It seemed everybody was always trying to get him to do something, everybody except Rose White, and now she was gone.

"So what do you plan to do next?" asks Jack Molay.

Michael is about to say that he hopes something will turn up, that maybe Rose White herself will wander back home and say the whole thing was an incredible mistake, when all of a sudden there is a screech of brakes and a rusty Chevy slides to a halt a few feet away. The driver's door opens and a man tumbles out, then gets to his feet and staggers around the front of the car.

"Hey, I know you!" shouts the man, who is large, ragged and drunk. "You're Marduk the Dumbfuck. Let's go, man! Let's have it out! I can take you with one fuckin hand cut off at the wrist!" The man whips off a Yankees cap and hurls it to the street. He has tousled black hair and wears an army camouflage jacket with the name McCurdy stenciled on the front.

Michael glances around for a policemen, but the streets are empty. Way up Fifth Avenue he sees his bus. "I don't know what you're talking about," he says as politely as possible.

"Talking about my ass, man," says the raggedy fellow. "I'm going to beat you into a splop of jelly. Let's go, big guy!" The man hunches over with his hands outstretched and his fingers quivering in a parody of wrestling ring decorum.

Embarrassed, Michael gets to his feet. "I'm afraid you're making a mistake."

Let's take a moment to inquire into the possible courage or cowardice of Michael Marmaduke. Is it possible to dislike combat and not be a coward? First, let's state once and for all that Michael is a man of great personal bravery. Just last summer when visiting his stepparents in Pennsylvania, he happened to be at the lake when a canoe with two elderly fishermen overturned and sank. Michael never hesitated but swam out into deep water and helped the men to shore. Both said later they'd been sure they were goners. If people were trapped in a burning building, Michael would rescue them. If someone were lost in a blizzard on a mountain top, Michael would be the first to strap on his snowshoes. But grappling with blizzards and burning buildings is a different order of business from bopping somebody on the nose. It isn't courage that Michael lacks but testosterone. He is sorely deficient in the competitive instinct. He did well in high school football not out of any interest in winning and losing, but in order not to make his coach angry. In college he avoided sports altogether. Instead, he enjoyed those field trips where people try to see how many different kinds of birds they can spot or how many wildflowers they can locate.

"Look," says Michael to the man who may or may not be named McCurdy, "I just want you to get in your car and drive away. I'm asking you politely."

"Let's have it out!" shouts the man. "Let's get this settled once and for all!"

Michael stands back from the curb. The man who may or may not be McCurdy approaches cautiously. He has clearly seen a lot of wrestling, because he has got all the maneuvers down pat. He is big but soft-looking. He is the sort of man that Thrombosis would stuff into a trash can blindfolded, but Michael has always believed it is better to use reason, even with a madman. Jack Molay has moved into the street and looks north toward the approaching bus, which has stopped for a light a block away. He is holding up his cane in order to catch the driver's attention.

"I hope you got your health insurance paid up!" shouts the man. "You gonna be broke in places you didn't know could break!"

"Let's talk this over," suggests Michael. "Maybe you've been unhappy."

"Maybe I'll kill you all at once," says the man. "Or maybe I'll make you beg for mercy."

The bus pulls away from the light. How slowly it moves. It is an older model and its engine must be clogged. Still, the driver sees Jack Molay and, like a log in a slow-moving stream, the bus begins to drift toward the curb.

Michael feels a certain anxiety. He imagines the old man hopping on the bus and deserting him. He thinks of a time that he had to restrain a friend who was drunk and how hard it is to restrain a person without doing him an injury. Then he sees a strange thing. The old man has gotten down on all fours and is kneeling behind the man in the army jacket. Michael can't figure what he is doing. The bus has almost reached them and is opening the door. Jack Molay is making encouraging expressions at Michael, who remains mystified.

"I'll rip you like wings off a fly!" shouts the man.

Jack Molay kneels about a foot behind him. He keeps beckoning to Michael, who wears a puzzled look. The bus has drawn to a complete stop and the driver has a hey-let's-get-the-show-on-the-road sort of expression. Unfortunately, the bus is on the other side of the man with the army jacket. Then, as if Michael Marmaduke's mind were a darkened room and someone snaps on a 250-watt bulb letting illumination flood all corners, he catches on.

"Hey!" he shouts, jumping toward the man in the army jacket.

The man steps backward, bumps against Jack Molay and falls to the pavement. Both Michael and Jack Molay scramble for the bus. They jump on the step, the door closes and the bus pulls away, leaving the man with the army jacket sitting at the edge of Fifth Avenue.

"Whew," said Jack Molay.

Michael fumbles in his pocket for exact change.

The bus driver is staring at him and his face moves from doubt to uncertainty to wonder. It is like watching the sun come out from behind a cloud. "On my bus," he says, "Marduk the Magnificent rides free."

Michael drops five quarters into the box. Then he glances at Jack Molay, who looks embarrassed.

"I'm afraid I only have a check," he says.

Michael digs in his pockets, then glances at the driver, who still looks as if he's won the lottery. "The money's for him. Thanks for the free ride."

"Will you sign my paperback?" asks the driver. He might be Puerto Rican or Cuban. Maybe he is forty.

"Sure," says Michael, wishing he didn't have to. He takes the copy of *Gone with the Wind* which the driver is holding out to him and signs his name on the flyleaf.

"My kids aren't goin to believe this," says the driver.

Michael and Jack Molay move toward the back of the bus, which has about half a dozen sleeping passengers. They take a seat across from the rear exit.

"I've been thinking about your problem," says Jack Molay. He sets his cane between his feet and rests his chin on the knob.

"Oh, yeah?" asks Michael. Rose White's absence is like a constant loud hum in his ears.

"Maybe you could find her yourself."

"Me?"

"Why not?"

"I'm no hero," says Michael. "Heroism is only my Gimmick."

"You do seem rather nonaggressive." Jack Molay suggests this as if he were afraid of offending Michael.

"Gentle's what they usually call me. Often it only gets in the way."

"You shouldn't dismiss it so lightly," says Jack Molay. "Someone's bound to find it useful. But maybe I could help with this Rose White business. I've got contacts."

Michael starts to say, "You're joking," but says nothing. He is thinking about heroism, and as the bus reaches the Plaza, he glances out at F.A.O. Schwarz. He imagines the stuffed animals waiting quietly in the dark. It seems to Michael that they could sooner become flesh and blood than he could become a hero.

7

Dance—One

A round hand mirror is being turned a foot or so away from a candle in a brass candlestick. The mirror has an ivory frame and long pointed handle. The hand holding the mirror is obviously a woman's: delicate ringless fingers, long tapered nails with a colorless polish. The woman wears a white gown and the mirror reflects the part below the neck, which the woman pulls aside to reveal one of her breasts. On the left breast above the nipple is the tattoo of a green leaf, perhaps an ivy leaf. The woman turns the mirror to get a better look at the leaf, admiring it. A red spot marks the leaf like a single drop of blood. The light from the candle throws shadows on the breast and white gown.

The woman leans toward the candle and turns the mirror, staring into her face: a thin face with a long straight nose and full lips formed into a half kiss, half pout. The high cheekbones create indentations in her cheeks, small valleys of shadow. The woman turns the mirror back and forth and her reflection moves across the glass. Her dark eyebrows are slivers of two dark moons, her forehead is high and narrow. It is a beautiful face and its features are delicate and fine. Between the parted lips can be seen twin rows of small perfect teeth.

This is Violet White, and she is unhappy with her face. She focuses on her eyes. They are dark brown but the white has a yellow cast. Where did that yellow come from? Her forehead seems too narrow, her face too long. She understands, of course, that it is a beautiful face, but she feels it is not as beautiful as her sister's. What does Rose White have that she doesn't? No yellow shadow mars her eyes and her face lacks that thinness, that hunger. Rose White's face has color and warmth. It lacks her sister's suggestion of anger. It lacks darkness.

And what has Rose White's beauty won for her? As Violet considers this, she begins to think of Marduk the Magnificent. How handsome he is, how wild, and Violet White's breath quickens as Marduk's image strides across the fields of her imagination. Then she thinks of Michael Marmaduke, her sister's fiancé. Although handsome, he has been domesticated. It is not merely the difference between a wild animal and a tame animal. Michael Marmaduke has all the passivity of a lump of clay. He is like a car without a motor. He and Marduk may be equally handsome but that is their only similarity. They are twins in the same way that she and her sister are twins, but they are twins within one body. They are like twin villages on a single mountain with no roads running between them. And again Violet White considers how such roads might be constructed.

Violet turns the mirror so that it again reflects her breast and the tattoo of the ivy leaf. She touches the leaf with the fingernail of her right index finger as she thinks of Marduk and Michael Marmaduke. She imagines how Marduk might touch her and the rough sensuality of that touch. Then she imagines the timid caresses of his twin, like being licked by a kitten. Gradually in the background we begin to hear a rhythmic noise like the drip, drip of a leaking tap but it is too loud for that. It's a single drum being tapped very slowly: tum, tum, tum. Now there is another, a higher one beating faster: tintintin. Now a third drum somewhere in between: tem, tem, tem. Now comes the rattle of a tambourine. Violet White puts down the mirror.

Turning with her, we see a large room—more like a loft than a room. It is difficult to guess its size because the space is lit only by candles and we see just darkness fading away on all sides. From somewhere comes a draft and the flames of the candles—all in brass candlesticks—twist and shiver. Maybe there are fifty candles, maybe more. A dozen young women are scattered across the room, moving slightly from foot to foot. All wear white gowns that reach their ankles. At first they seem like nightgowns with long sleeves, but these gowns are tied at the waist and have too much fabric. They are not for sleeping but dancing. The faces of the women have been powdered and are very pale. As Violet White moves toward them, we see she is dressed like the rest, although she is taller and her face is not powdered. She touches one of the women, lets her hand trail across the woman's shoulder. Where are the drums? Are they a recording? No, off to the left we notice a floor tom-tom with a silver shell. The person playing has his back to us. We guess he's a man but it's hard to be sure. He wears some kind of fur jacket and his black hair covers the collar. The other drums—we hear two or three more—must be back in the shadow.

One of the women holds a tambourine, and she beats it slowly against her thigh. The top of her gown is unbuttoned, and we catch a glimpse of her breast. Look more closely. Do you see that she also has the tattoo of the ivy leaf? Again she hits the tambourine against her leg. More women join them, perhaps eight or ten. To the left, tethered to a white column, stands a white goat with a golden collar. A mask of a man's bearded face is attached to the column; the eye holes are great black circles. On the floor by the column are several large bowls full of a dark red liquid. Next to one of the bowls is a basket of figs.

The drums beat faster. The women wear black slippers and their soles whisper against the floor. Perhaps there are twenty-five women but the space is so large that there is no suggestion of crowding. As the movement increases, the candles flicker as if keeping pace with the drums. Violet White moves between the women, twisting and spinning, letting her hands trail across them, as if she were tying them together. The women turn, dipping and spinning, their arms drifting out at their sides. Now we hear the sound of a flute, ascending and descending the notes of its register.

A second flute joins the first and the two streams of notes intertwine and pull at each other. More women appear from the shadows. Perhaps there are thirty-five or forty. The drums, now too many to count, beat even faster.

Blending together, the women move rapidly across the floor. All wear white gowns, and despite differences in their hair, it seems that the many women are really part of a single woman, rushing and spinning across the candlelit space. If we look closely we can still see Violet White as she moves between them, but here too the distinctions are blurred, as if she also were an aspect of the whole, while the drums beat faster and the flutes—surely more than two —rise to a scream and the sound of many feet resembles an angry muttering, a harangue, as the women swirl within the shadows, spin around the column with the mask, twirl around the white goat, which is hunkered down and terrified.

Now another figure runs onto the floor. It wears a golden mask with a snout and two horns, the mask of a bull, and it seems not dancing but staggering, and the women circle around it and bear it up. Is the figure a man or a woman? It is impossible to tell. It wears a red gown and its head is entirely covered by the mask. But look, its hands are tied behind its back. And it seems not dancing but attempting to flee as the women twist around it and caress its face with their hands. And still the drums beat faster and the flutes become a single shrieking. The figure with the bull's mask runs from one side to the other as the women turn it back and bear it up when it starts to fall.

Amidst all the other drums we now hear a bass drum louder than the others and beating more slowly—THUMthum . . . THUMthum—like the beating of a heart. Another masked figure appears on the floor. At first it seems familiar, then we realize it is someone wearing the mask that hung from the pillar with the black beard and black eye holes, and looking over at the pillar we see the mask is gone. Is the person wearing the mask a man or woman? We can't tell, although it seems taller than the others. It too is dressed in white and on its feet are black slippers. The women fall away from the dancer with the mask of a bearded man, as it makes its way toward the figure with the mask of the bull, and we realize that the deep drum belongs to the bearded man, that the women dance to Pandemonium, but the figure with the mask of the bearded man dances to the sound of his own heart.

The bearded man spins toward the bull but instead of caressing it like the women, he runs into the bull, knocking it aside. Suddenly the drums grow louder and faster and the women, still in their dance, rush toward the bull, knocking it to the floor. The figure with the mask of a bull scrambles to its feet but then again it is knocked to the floor. It gets up and tries to run but the bearded man flings himself upon it, then the women fling themselves upon it as well so there is a struggling heap of white bodies. But again the bull gets loose and there is blood on its white gown. The women form a circle around it, and whenever the bull tries to break from the circle, it is pushed back to the center. The bearded man is also in the circle and he moves around the bull and every few moments he rushes at it; and his own drum, the deep one, the slow one, begins to beat faster.

Now one of the women joins the bearded man in the circle and she too runs at the bull and appears to bite at it. A second woman joins them, and a third. The music is just a roar except for the deep pounding of the bass drum. The figure with the mask of the bull is being crowded into a smaller space and cannot break free of the circle. The women have their mouths open as if shouting or singing but the noise is so great that they can't be heard. Now the bull appears to fall and the women fling themselves upon it and the center of the floor is a mass of bodies heaving and pulling as the noise grows louder and even the deep drum is beating so quickly that it is like a single sound.

Then it is over. The drums stop. A shrieking is heard, then it is gone. The women roll off the pile and crawl away. The figure with the mask of the bearded man appears out of the pile of bodies and drags itself toward the pillar. It lifts the mask from its head. Look, it is Violet White. She places the mask on the pillar and sits down. She leans against the base of the pillar and closes her eyes. The whole room is quiet except for the nervous bleating of the goat.

More women crawl from the pile and collapse on the floor. After another moment we see the figure with the mask of the bull lying by itself. Its red gown is torn and we see scratches on its white skin. The women move away. Even the goat has grown silent. The women appear to be sleeping. Some have streaks of blood on their faces making it seem that they too wear masks. Candles have been knocked over and the room is darker.

After another moment a cat appears out of the darkness. Is it really a cat? It seems too big. Perhaps it is an ocelot, perhaps a wildcat. Its coat is a yellow color and its tail swishes back and forth. The creature makes its way across the floor. The white goat sees the cat and begins to bleat, but the cat has no interest in the goat. It makes its way around the women, treading delicately on its large paws. It reaches the column and sniffs at Violet White's feet, then it moves toward one of the large bowls. It lowers its heads and sniffs at the dark red liquid, then it touches its tongue to the surface. It raises its head and a few red drops fall from its whiskers. The creature looks at the sleeping women. It looks at the figure with the bull's mask lying motionless on the floor. Then once more it lowers its head to the bowl and begins to drink and the room is silent except for the lap-lap of its tongue.

8

MULDOON: THE GIMMICK ONION

Do you like my mustache? It is to my upper lip what a fur coat is
to a bear, what the Statue of Liberty is to Manhattan when one
approaches after days of bobbing across the Atlantic. Give me
your tired and your poor and I'll set them to collecting returnable
bottles. Nietzsche once wrote that a large mustache gives a man
the appearance "of being military, irascible and sometimes violent." That's why he loved his own. It is true that I had my
mustache before reading that sentence but when I discovered it in
Morgenröte I let my mustache grow even bigger. I fertilized it. I
removed its shackles. My mustache became the controller of its
own destiny. Nietzsche's mustache of course was thick and luxuriant. All his words passed through it and it filtered his every breath.
One can legitimately ask if he breathed the world or if he breathed
his mustache. In the same way that all history is contemporary
history, so all the world for him was mustache-flavored. My mustache, I believe, is larger and even more luxuriant. Is chestnut your
favorite color? I know it's mine. People see my mustache before
they see me. They respond to it, talk to it, develop entire relationships with it even before they make my acquaintance. It is the
gauge through which I am measured. As we observe a panther

through the bars of its cage, so I am observed through my mustache. It creates certain expectations. It suggests definitions. It is an intrinsic part of my Gimmick, the apparatus of Primus Muldoon.

Consider the cowboy belt, plaid shirt and baseball cap of the truck driver. Consider the beard and pipe and tweed jacket of the academic. There is also the leather jacket and cap, the tattoos of the motorcycle rider, the scraggly beard and beer belly. What is the effect of such apparatus? It encourages the viewer to make definitions about these people before any hard evidence is presented. And of course one observes oneself through one's own apparatus. The motorcycle gang member whose single ambition it is to be a motorcycle gang member looks at himself in the mirror and says, "I look like a motorcycle gang member." This makes him happy. Ditto the truck driver and the academic. Consider the apparatus of the artist, the apparatus of the doctor. All styles of clothing, haircuts, makeup, all aspects of one's appearance are potentially apparatus, are aspects of Gimmick. Anything added: facial expressions, methods of laughter (the guffaw, the tinkling giggle), all sighs, peculiar walks, all aspects of activity and inactivity which project information about the actor may be incorporated into Gimmick. Clearly this behavior is tied to memory. We associate stethoscopes with doctors because of our experience, and the doctor wears the stethoscope around his neck—even if he never, never uses it—to remind us of that memory. Consequently, to adopt aspects of any stereotype is to adopt aspects of Gimmick, and that very familiarity is a source of comfort to both the perceived and the perceiver. It contains within it the idea of correctness, of being at one with one's own view of the world. Have you ever watched a university professor stroke the leather elbow patches on his tweed jacket? His expression is the same as a baby sucking on a pacifier in those moments before it drifts off into its afternoon nap.

But wait. All definitions are reductive, and having linked Gimmick to stereotype I stray into oversimplification. Consider how God is brought into existence by the act of faith. We need to believe and so God appears. Faith invents God. And in the same way that faith invents God, so does male desire create woman. Without male desire a woman is only a female *Homo sapiens*. It is male desire that changes this biological baby factory into a woman. It also allows woman to put on the Gimmick of "desira-bleness." Equally, it is female desire that changes man and allows him to put on one of his many Gimmicks, which makes him appear desirable or strong or protective, although male and female desire are very different.

But let us concentrate on the Gimmick of Desirableness as it appears in women. It is the customary passive role of woman that makes her Gimmick necessary to her: she waits and therefore she has to arouse the man to action, which she does through her Gimmick. Male desire creates the illusion of desirableness which the woman, putting on the Gimmick of Desirableness, perpetuates by strengthening male desire. Desirableness, among other things, is the promise of future satisfaction, and by skillfully controlling the Gimmick of Desirableness the otherwise passive woman is able to exert control over that future. All elements of fashion are the knives and brass knuckles of a woman's Gimmick—lipstick, eye makeup, lingerie, jewelry, push-up bras.

Nietzsche said that when we believe we perceive greatness in a human being what we actually see is the actor of that person's own ideal. A man wants to impress others as a great philosopher so he acts out his fantasy of how a great philosopher behaves. Why else would he wear those peculiar whiskers and seem never to be listening? By enacting his own ideal, the man appears great. Isn't this also true of a beautiful woman? Isn't she also the actress of her own ideal? And what is ugliness? Perhaps it is just the afterecho of what was once seen to be beautiful—the atavism of an older ideal, which is also what Nietzsche calls evil: the atavism of an older ideal.

First the child is born. That is the beginning. First there is the individual, which of course is not an individual. It is simply a blob. Then comes the assumption of the Gimmick. Cuteness is a Gim-mick. The parents desire to see cuteness and so the child dons the Gimmick of Cuteness. It becomes cute in response to the adults' wish for cuteness. We put on aspects of Gimmick in order to affect how others see us, secondly we put on aspects of Gimmick to affect how we see ourselves. What is the individual? The individual is the Gimmick. How cynical, you say: surely, beneath the Gim-mick lies the true individual. Perhaps there exists a trace of individual, perhaps a soupçon. But by the time we reach adulthood we are so covered with Gimmick that whatever we once had that was individual, that was peculiar only to us, is hardly a shadow. Remember that Gimmick is form pretending to be substance. Does substance truly exist? Remove the mask and we find another mask. Peel the onion and there is always more until at last there is nothing—just a smell on the fingers and a tear in the eye.

So you see why I honor my mustache? It is more Primus Muldoon than I am. Or rather, I am mystery; my mustache is actuality. It gives information about me. The fact that such information may be false is unimportant. We are a nation of newspaper readers. Doesn't that prove that we value apparent information—that is, illusion—over truth? If Thrombosis were to approach you in a dark alley your heart would probably stop beating. Huge and black, he wears the Gimmick of Violence in the same way I wear my mustache. But I know him as a kind man who is the sole protector of a pet canary and who discusses the novels of Toni Morrison with his girlfriend. You would be safer with Thrombosis in a dark alley than with your own mother.

But listen, there must be something in him that yearns for violence even if it is inaccessible. Why else would he choose that Gimmick over another? All his life Nietzsche was proud of the small slanting scar across the bridge of his nose which he received at the age of twenty in a duel. Yet he was a gentle man. All his life he was proud of his time in the army, that he was the best horsemen among thirty recruits. The fact that he had been a lance corporal in the artillery and bore a dueling scar—these became aspects of his Gimmick. These were aspects of what he wasn't but yearned to be. Perhaps the woman who appears desirable is herself yearning for desirableness while believing herself to be intrinsically undesirable. Michael Marmaduke is a gentle man but perhaps he yearns for the violence and power of Marduk the Magnificent. Were you to confront him with this, he would deny it. He despises violence. The sight of blood makes him ill. When he is Michael Marmaduke, he is not only gentle but he surrounds himself with proof of his gentleness.

Consider, for instance, Rose White. To tell the truth, I have never liked her. She is as exciting as Welsh rabbit. I am sure she is an excellent third-grade teacher. She is sweet and gentle and feels that dogs shouldn't go poo-poo on the sidewalk. The fact that he is engaged to her affirms for Michael his own gentleness. But this doesn't mean he is gentle, rather it means that he wants to see himself as gentle. Perhaps his gentleness is as much a Gimmick as his violence. And who is he really? Perhaps it is too soon to say. First comes the individual (the blob), second comes the Gimmick. And what does Michael Marmaduke receive from the Wrestling Association? He receives permission to be violent and gentle at the same time. All wrestlers have the appearance of power, wildness, and intoxication. In reality they are quiet, organized, and rather boring. One of the dullest evenings imaginable is a dinner of oxtails in the house of Rahab the Arrogant One. And for a special treat he will show you his collection of 1940s baseball cards.

The whole Wrestling Association is dream posing as intoxication. They are logicians dressed as whirling dervishes, bank clerks made up as tarts. The Association chooses the Gimmick of every wrestler. It places the cloak of frenzy on the shoulders of the accountant. It sells apparent intoxication to the immutable unwashed many. But the sellers, the planners, the dreamers have never touched a drop. They're peddling Kool-Aid with a Jack Daniel's label. That is what I hate about it. Where is our liberty? Michael Marmaduke is trapped by the twin illusions of gentleness and violence, unable to become either. Like a woman's desirability, his Gimmick is as much his prison as his freedom. Who would he be without it? He is gooey protoplasm around a granite question mark.

Let us liberate the intoxication from the prison of the dream. Let us not pretend to be violent, let us become violent. Let us liberate our Gimmicks. I want to unleash my mustache and send it into the world. I want the Association to stop pushing me around. I want the day off. I want a weekend. I want the chance to be bad. Let us open the doors of our prison to see what sort of person emerges —free of Gimmick, free of lie. The child that totters through the prison doors, is it angel or demon, Samaritan or thug? Our philosophy must begin not with astonishment but terror!

9

STRIFE

It has taken Wally Wallski much of Saturday morning to locate the home of Mr. Lenguado: a renovated brick warehouse down on Fulton Street within sight of the East River. It is a sunny morning and Brooklyn twinkles across the water. Wally Wallski tries to let the warm weather and pleasant atmosphere cheer his heart—as an unemployed fisherman he has a certain nostalgia for the water— but, in truth, he has had a bad night and his ribs ache. His wife Claudine did not exactly beat him but she elbowed him fiercely in her sleep, at least she claimed to be sleeping, and at last Wally Wallski decided to sleep on the floor. But it was not quite the last because when Claudine got up to pee around five a.m., she stepped on his stomach, hard. After that, Wally Wallski was unable to drift back to dreamland. Around seven-thirty, he roused himself and prepared Claudine's coffee and bacon and eggs, and after arranging the tray and delivering it to her in bed, he set off to find Mr. Lenguado.

"It's got to be a nice place," Claudine called after him. "I'm not moving from one dump to another."

Now, fingering the lucky two-headed coin in his pocket, Wally Wallski looks up to the open second-story window of Mr. Lenguado's home and he can hear strange singing, more like chanting with horns and drums. Actually someone is listening to the first act of *Turandot* and the strangeness consists of the crowd of Puccini's Chinese women singing "Gli enigmi sono tre, la morte è una!" or "The riddles are three, death is one!" while the executioner's men sing about grinding and sharpening the ax.

Wally Wallski cups his hands into a trumpet and stretches his neck toward the window. "Mr. Lenguado!" he calls. "Are you in there? I got a favor I gotta ask. My wife Claudine is unhappy in our place and wants a nice apartment. Mr. Lenguado! Do you hear me? It's Wally Wallski! I saved your life!"

"Ungi, arrota, che la lama guizzi, sprizzi fuoco e sangue!" sing the executioner's men. "Oil it, grind it, let the blade flash, let spurt the fire and blood!"

"Mr. Lenguado, do you hear me? My wife Claudine thinks you should help us out. . . ."

It seems to Wally Wallski that a chill wind has begun to blow and several dark clouds are drifting across the sky.

"Mr. Lenguado . . ."

"Enough!" cries a powerful voice over the sound of the executioner's men singing, "Morte! Morte! Morte! Morte!"

"Do you think I am deaf?"

"Mr. Lenguado, my wife thinks you should help us find . . ."

"O testa mozza! O esangue!" sing the women of Peking. "Oh, severed head! Oh, bloodless one!"

A piece of paper floats down from the second-story window, making zigzag curves in the air. "Go to this address!" cries the voice. "A truck's already on its way to your old place to pick up your stuff. Be careful about bothering me again!"

Wally Wallski leaps up and catches the piece of paper. The address is an apartment building in Brooklyn Heights. "Oh, thank you, Mr. Lenguado, and my wife Claudine thanks you too."

"Vieni, o amante smunta dei morti!" sing the men of Peking. "Come, oh gaunt lover of the dead!" Then the window slams shut and all is quiet except for the wind blowing dark clouds across the sky and a single crow perched on a No Parking sign and making menacing squawks. But Wally Wallski is too happy to notice. Clutching his lucky coin, he walks quickly toward South Street.

There is a bounce in his step and hope in his heart. He'll take the bridge. He'll walk all the way to his new apartment. And when he arrives, Claudine will be there and they'll celebrate. They will drink sparkling apple juice out of champagne glasses. To heck with dark clouds. No sprinkles and a little thunder can trouble his life.

But thirty minutes later, as Wally Wallski is walking across the Brooklyn Bridge, a terrible thing happens. He has stopped to admire the view and is looking upriver to where a few sailboats are scudding along in the breeze. Preparing to pass beneath him is a large gold-colored motor launch, with several decks and brightly dressed people standing around with drinks in their hands, at least Wally Wallski assumes they are drinks because they are really too far away to tell. The word "yacht" never enters Wally Wallski's mind because actually the boat resembles a large floating apartment house with awnings and terraces and all that seems to be missing is the doorman.

But as he is thinking about the floating apartment house, he is also looking upriver toward a building on the Manhattan side which is gray and stunted and one of the ugliest buildings that Wally Wallski has ever seen and he wonders what the building could be used for. Perhaps it is one of those places where children are stunted or old folks are shouted at. And as he is thinking about the floating apartment house and wondering about the ugly gray building, he is also flipping the lucky two-headed coin over and over.

Well, anybody can do too many things at once. Wally Wallski flips the coin and catches it. He flips the coin and catches it. He flips the coin and bump, it hits his knuckle and bounces away, bounces to the sidewalk, bounces up between the bars of the protective fence and into the air above the East River, where the sun seems to leap upon it, making the coin twinkle as it tumbles down through the vast vaults of air.

"Oh no!" cries Wally Wallski. "My lucky coin!"

The coin tumbles toward the yacht where the brightly dressed people are drinking, chatting and enjoying the warm October morning. And the only person on the yacht—called the *Boeski* after the money man—to notice the coin is a girl of about thirteen with blond braids who is deathly bored. Her name is Beacon Luz and she wears a blue sailor suit. The *Boeski* is her daddy's yacht.

Beacon Luz sees the man on the bridge and sees something fall from his hands. At first she thinks it is a cigarette butt, then she sees it twinkle. She is sitting on a chaise lounge covered with green canvas cushions on one of the after-afterdecks and she is drinking a cherry Coke with a tiny amount of rum, which makes her feel considerably grown-up and vastly superior to all these boring people who are drinking large amounts of rum with a tiny bit of cherry Coke in a drink called a Washington Libre (because Washington cut down a cherry tree, remember?).

Beacon Luz watches the shining golden object tumble nearer and nearer and she springs to her feet because she is afraid it will hit her and, Plop!, the coin lands on the chaise longue and sinks several inches into the green cushion. Picking it up, Beacon Luz observes the angel face on one side and the demon face on the other; and she feels the warmth of the coin in her hand and no longer does she feel bored and contemptuous of the people around her. Instead she feels extremely lucky. Squeezing the coin, she looks up at the Brooklyn Bridge and waves and waves, catching one last glimpse of the man high above her before the *Boeski* glides under the center span and he disappears from view.

Leaning over the railing, Wally Wallski sees the small figure in a blue sailor suit waving at him. He considers running to the other side of the bridge and throwing himself after the coin but there are too many cars and he thinks he would miss the gold-colored yacht and even if he hit the yacht it would probably be the end of him because he no longer feels lucky. In fact, he feels very unlucky; he feels he will never be lucky again. He stares over toward the ugly gray building in the distance and he wonders if he should blame its ugliness for his ill fortune, but although Wally Wallski is sometimes foolish, this does not make him a fool, and he knows that he has nobody to blame for the loss of the coin but himself. Slowly he turns and continues across the bridge toward Brooklyn Heights, but he carries no pleasant feeling in his heart about what he will find there.

But let us go back and follow Wally Wallski's gaze toward the ugly gray building, as if his gaze made a tight rope and we were gliding along it. We move very quickly and have no fear of falling and in another moment we slide through an open window to discover a nurse and a figure swathed in bandages in a wheelchair because the ugly gray building is a hospital and we are now inside one of the upper rooms. The room has two beds but both are empty. Attached to the wall is a television with the sound turned off, but we can see the great yellow body of Big Bird from Sesame Street rushing in circles and waving his trifling wings as if his life were in danger. Moving to the left we realize that the nurse is Violet White. She is dressed all in white and her beautiful face is a dark shadow. Pinned to her black hair is a white cap. Violet stands behind the figure in the wheelchair and she is unwinding the bandages surrounding the person's head. Is it a man or woman? The person is small for a man and wears a blue hospital robe, but looking at the feet we can see they are a man's feet: big and bony and with black hairs on the toes.

Violet White's long fingers unwind the bandage and the white cotton gauze piles up on the floor next to her shoes. Her face is calm but bears perhaps the slightest trace of expectation as if she were looking forward to receiving a gift. The man sits perfectly still. His narrow hands rest on the arms of the wheelchair and his fingers curl over the ends. Now the top of his head appears out of the bandage. He has straight black hair brushed back over his skull. The hair is thinning and shines as if greased. Shortly we see that the hair forms a widow's peak, a distinct V bisecting his forehead. Perhaps there is something familiar about it. The forehead is narrow and the sharpness of the widow's peak has a violent quality. Next are revealed the small black eyes and long narrow nose and, yes, we recognize the face at last. This is Deep Rat, who sat next to Wally Wallski during Marduk the Magnificent's combat with Rahab the Arrogant One. Do you remember the receding chin and the small teeth that incline inward? Here they are before us.

Violet White removes the last of the white gauze and steps back.

She appears unsurprised to find Deep Rat beneath the bandages. Maybe she is breathing just a tiny bit faster.

"And what have you been doing?" asks Violet White as she puts her hands to her hair to adjust her small white cap.

Deep Rat turns the wheelchair to face her. When he smiles, his teeth look as if he hoped to nibble something. "I've been roaming around," he says. "I've been roaming around the earth and walking up and down upon it."

"And what have you done with Michael Marmaduke?"

"I have planted my face in his memory."

"And what of our plans?"

"Everything has been prepared according to your wishes, Nurse White."

"Make it difficult, otherwise he won't believe you."

Deep Rat begins to assume a condescending expression, then thinks better of it. "Spreading strife is my greatest joy," he says.

"Don't let him get killed."

"Killed?"

"Make it difficult but don't get him killed."

Deep Rat again makes one of his nibbling little smiles. "Nothing is certain in this life."

Violet White moves to him slowly, takes one of his hands and begins to stroke it. "You have sweet little paws," she says. "It would be a pity to see them smashed."

Deep Rat maintains his smile but the pleasure has gone out of it. He tries to remove his hand. Violet White squeezes it, then releases it. The wheelchair slides back a foot.

"I have no happiness but your happiness," says Deep Rat.

Violet White nods, then leaves the room, seeming to forget Deep Rat the moment he disappears from sight. She walks as if her feet never touch the floor. She walks without looking back. Proceeding down the hall, she passes room after room and through open doorways we can see bandaged men and women sitting up in bed and watching TV sets attached to the walls. Most have their faces covered with white gauze. Are these lepers? From what do they suffer? As a matter of fact, these men and women have paid a lot of money for the privilege of wearing these bandages and beneath them they have new noses, new lips, new cheeks, the fat has been scraped from their facial bones, their ears have been trimmed, small tucks have been taken in their wrinkles, and someday, when the white cotton gauze is removed, all their flaws will have disappeared. Their only danger will be that other people—the blemish-ridden majority—will try to kiss them to death, and never again will their wishes be refused.

Violet White enters an office and locks the door behind her. Then she goes to a file cabinet and takes a videocassette from the top drawer. She moves quickly and her starched white skirt whispers around her. One can detect a trace of nervousness, almost clumsiness, in her gestures. A Mitsubishi television and VCR stand on a table by the wall. Violet inserts the cassette and adjusts the controls. Rummaging among the papers on the table, she finds the remote control wand, steps to the desk and perches on the edge so that her white shoes barely touch the floor. Violet waves the control wand and fast-forwards the tape. Suddenly Marduk the Magnificent appears on the screen. Violet pauses the tape. The image flutters slightly and it seems that Marduk's muscles are pulsating as he stands in the ring with his arms raised above his head. Violet waves the wand and right away a dark winged monster appears behind Marduk the Magnificent. It is Pazuzu, king of the evil spirits of the air, the demon of violence and fever. Pazuzu springs at Marduk's back, but, as if he had eyes behind his head, Marduk leaps aside and trips Pazuzu as he rushes past so that the monster crashes to the canvas.

The referee pulls down the microphone and shouts into it, "Put on the armor of goodness, so that ye may be able to stand against the wiles of the Devil. For we wrestle not against flesh and blood, but against principalities, against powers, against the rulers of the darkness of this world, against spiritual wickedness in high places!"

In all his blond glory Marduk puts his elf boot onto the center of Pazuzu's chest. Then he throws back his head and roars and his golden locks tremble. A caged lion half a mile away might sound like this. Violet White waves the wand, backing up the tape, and increases the volume. Marduk roars again and the caged lion

comes closer. Violet waves the wand again and Marduk roars a
third time, this time it is still louder and the leaves of an aloe plant
on the windowsill shiver and quake. Violet waves the wand a
fourth time and in rooms up and down the hall the bandaged men
and women anxiously raise their hands to their faces, touching the
white protective gauze as once more the strange roaring violates
their fantasies and dreams.

Some lives move easily on greased ball bearings. Others move like
one sandpaper block against another. Wally Wallski stands next
to his new fireplace with his head bowed and his hands folded
behind his back as his wife Claudine discusses the shortcomings of
their new apartment.

"Nice, certainly it's nice," says Claudine. "But nice means cute
and cute means small."

"But we've never lived in such a nice place in our lives," says
Wally Wallski, who is without hope. The apartment has four
furnished rooms and an eat-in kitchen. The cream-colored walls
have been recently painted. The bright red side-by-side refrigerator
includes an icemaker and a cold-drink dispenser.

"Maybe you have never lived in such a nice place," says Claudine, whose hair is in rollers, "but I've lived in all sorts of places
before I met you and many were a lot grander than this. I once
even lived in a place with a grand piano."

"No roaches, no rats, no drug addicts, can't we be happy here?"
asks Wally Wallski. In his mind's eye he sees the golden coin
tumbling toward the boat as big as an apartment house. And
didn't everything good in this world fall with it?

"It's a matter of what a person's used to," says Claudine reason-
ably. "And I've been used to bigger places. This guy Lenguado has
his thumb pressed to the real estate pulse of the entire city. He can
make five thousand doormen leap through hoops. You mean this
is the best he could come up with? It doesn't even have a king-sized
bed."

"I think it's a great place," says Wally Wallski gloomily.

"You don't know squat," says his wife Claudine. "You go back to this Lenguado character and tell him you want a condo with a king-sized bed and you want it in Manhattan, Upper West Side. No more Brooklyn for me. After all, you saved his life."

Wally Wallski wonders what Marduk the Magnificent would do with a wife such as Claudine. He lets the question hang in his mind like a drop of water on a faucet.

"Hey," says Claudine, "we're on a roll."

Let's take a moment to check in with Beacon Luz, whose father's yacht, the *Boeski,* has just docked in the North Cove Yacht Harbor under the shadow of the World Trade Center. Deck hands in matching blue caps are securing cumbersome lines to the bollards and the gangplank is about to be let down. A whistle blows. Guests prepare to disembark. But first in line is Beacon Luz, her daddy's favorite, who intends to buy several pocketfuls of Godiva chocolates from the chocolatier in Winter Garden. Afterward she will watch Marduk the Magnificent on the TV and nibble the chocolate so that it lasts through the entire show. Impatiently, she turns back and forth and her two blond braids swing across the shoulders of her blue sailor suit. She will be glad to get away from these boring guests once and for all. As she waits she squeezes the golden coin that has fallen to her from out of the sky and she knows that she is a lucky girl, the luckiest girl in New York.

Standing on the dock directly in front of Beacon Luz's eyes, but not seen by them, is a ragged-looking fellow with a shopping cart full of his things. He has a hopeful expression and stares toward the *Boeski* as if his life might be looking up. Truly, he thinks, it seems like a boat full of generous people. He does not notice the two private security men in blue blazers who are hurrying toward him with indignant expressions. Instead he is staring at Beacon Luz and thinking how pretty she is and how kind she must be. He thinks she is someone who might possibly want to hear his story. It is a sad story and he can hardly wait to tell it. The ragged man's name is Beetle and we have met him before.

Now the moment has arrived. The gangplank touches the dock. Beacon Luz jumps forward. Beetle takes a step and is grabbed by the two security men. There is a brief struggle which results in the following tableaux: one security man pulls Beetle's feet and the other pulls his hands. By exerting opposite pressure the two security men lift Beetle into the air, making a sort of bridge stretched out horizontally several feet above the sidewalk. Beacon Luz scurries under this bridge as she clutches the coin. Although her blond braids brush Beetle's buttocks, she is aware of no other human being. Written across her brain the word *chocolate* flickers its neoned message into each of Beacon Luz's taste buds. She can hardly run fast enough.

10

RUBBER

Once more we hurry through the air. It is night, early morning in fact although the sun won't rise for another four hours. A light drizzle is falling and the gray liquid seems to ooze from the darkness. We rush quickly above the street and beneath us rushes a dilapidated Econoline van with a broken muffler. Once it had a color, perhaps green. Now it is no more than a mood, a depressed one. And where is this van? It is speeding north on Greenwich somewhere below Canal Street. See the old brick warehouses? Not much warehousing goes on these days, although there's the Bazzini Company—specialists in dried fruits and nuts—and as we pass it we can just catch the smell of peanuts being dry-roasted. Let's duck down and look through the windows in the van's rear doors. Here's our chance as it slows for a light. Of course it won't stop and the van coughs and roars as the driver guns the motor. Already we have a sense of this van as an outlaw van as it rocks back and forth across Greenwich and its muffler bellows its displeasure into the cool night air. Peering through the rear windows we see Michael Marmaduke sitting on an overturned five-gallon white plastic bucket. Michael has his arms outstretched and pressed against the sides of the van. There is nothing Christlike about this gesture; he simply has a dread of being catapulted through the front window. Where're the seat belts? he keeps thinking. He is also depressed by all that has happened, and like a bass clef strumming along beneath the alto, the deep notes of his grief for the missing Rose White harmonize with the high notes of his trepidation.

Before him on the floor a young man in a red leather jacket flips something over and over. At first we suppose he is flipping a coin but looking closer we see it is a condom in a sheath of red plastic. The man is talking, yelling actually, over the noise of the muffler. "Everything we see, man, is fundamentally dogshit. I mean, you gotta ask yourself about the Nazi who made it. Was he ignorant, or just fuckin dumb." He holds out the condom to Michael. "Did I give you one of these?"

"Thanks," says Michael, taking the condom. "You've already given me a couple."

"You can't have too many," says the man, whose name Michael has understood to be Clancy. "That fuckin Nazi Ialdabaoth, man, what a loser."

Including Michael and Clancy, there are six men in the van, plus a pile of bricks, which explains why the van rides so close to the pavement and scrapes its muffler at the intersections. Three men ride in front: the driver and a fellow in the passenger seat, or "shotgun" as it keeps being called, as well as a man crouched between them. All three are in their early twenties and wear similar red leather jackets. Across the back of each jacket is written V-A-L-S in silver studs. One might guess this is the French word for "waltz" and sometimes these gang members are called the Dancers by the unenlightened who choose to heckle and aggravate, which irritates the Vals no end because they have no stomach for frivolity. Vals have nothing to do with dancing. As Clancy has explained: "Valentinian Gnostics, man, and we're goin to stomp ass!" It should be pointed out that the man riding shotgun cradles a real shotgun in his lap.

Next to the pile of bricks is crouched a fourth man in a red leather jacket. He holds a brick in his right hand and keeps slapping it into his left. What is his function? Let us watch him in action. The van skids to a halt before a fashionable men's clothing store. No iron grate protects the front window, and behind the glass stand several mannikins wearing raincoats and holding umbrellas which they are in the process of opening as they glance anxiously toward a fictional sky. As the van comes to a stop, the side door bursts open and the man—the others seem to call him Correction—leaps from the van, hurls the brick at the plate-glass window and shouts, "Fuck you, Sophia!" The window disintegrates and one of the mannikins topples over. Then Correction jumps back into the van and the driver roars away.

If we focus on Michael's face, we can see his expression move from the province of long-suffering to the province of I've-had-about-enough. On his mind's big screen appears a likeness of Jack Molay, the elderly gentleman we met last night with Michael at the bus stop. Jack Molay is wearing an oversized overcoat and holds a cane, the ivory handle of which displays two faces looking in opposite directions. For a moment the likeness is superimposed on an imagined plate-glass window and suddenly a brick comes crashing through it. These are hard feelings indeed for such a gentle man as Michael Marmaduke.

As for what are Valentinian Gnostics, Michael has no idea, but this doesn't bother him. He assumes, wrongly, that they are connected to Valentine's Day. His lack of concern is based on tact. He knows Evangelists, he knows Spiritualists. He knows Tarot readers and astrologers. He knows practicers of voodoo and a rather scary Brazilian cult. This is New York: people believe all sorts of stuff. When your neighbor comes home with a black rooster in a wooden crate, it is best not to ask questions. Were Michael to learn that Valentinus was a Christian teacher who founded the last great Gnostic school in second-century Rome, he would be interested, mildly, even though the Vals are Valentinian Gnostics in the same way a Brooks Brothers shirt is a Brooks Brothers shirt after ten thousand washings: that is, a rag. What Michael doesn't ask himself is why these young men should have become Valentinian Gnostics. That question comes later.

Clancy is still talking. "Think of it this way, the whole mass of people have been enslaved by their scummy bodies. They fucked and had kids and their kids fucked and had kids according to the likeness of their spirit. And they closed their hearts and hardened themselves according to the meanness of their spirit. But we're goin to see that the hardship gets turned around. Have another rubber."

"That's okay," says Michael, not wanting to let go of the sides of the van. "Why d'you think you're right about this?"

"We know, man."

"How do you know?"

"Because we been revealed to ourselves. I been redeemed. I got the Knowledge."

"And what does this knowledge get you?" asks Michael.

"Hold on a sec."

The van skids to a halt and its wheels scrape the curb. Michael slides forward and must hang on to the side panels, which hurts his fingers. Correction leaps out. Michael has a glimpse of a women's clothing store, a window of dresses and shoes, before a brick shatters the glass.

"Fuck you, Sophia!" shouts Correction as he climbs back into the van.

"Knowledge," says Clancy proudly, "this Knowledge tells me who I was and what I've become. It tells me where I was and why I was made to fall. It tells me where I am hastening and when I will be redeemed. You can't beat it, man. It puts all the cards on the fuckin table."

"That's a mouthful, Clancy," says Michael Marmaduke.

Clancy leans forward and hisses at Michael. "Not Clancy! Clemency! My name's Clemency!"

But let's pause before getting too far ahead of ourselves. How did Michael Marmaduke meet these fellows in the first place? We need to go back to early that Saturday morning when Michael was woken by a hammering at his front door. It was the super with an Express Mail package.

"Something for Marduk the Magnificent," said the super.

"Don't call me that," said Michael sleepily.

The package contained a videocassette. Still half asleep, Michael slipped the cassette into the VCR and turned on the television. What he saw on the screen instantly roused him to wakefulness. It was Rose White. She was in a kind of basement chained to a wall. Chains encircled each of her slim wrists and were attached to hooks high above her. Rose White leaned desperately toward the camera. "Michael," she cried, "you must save me! I'm being . . ." Then the screen went dark.

With uncertain fingers Michael rewound the tape and watched it again. Rose White wore a white nightgown. She looked so fragile that her very fragility seemed lodged like a bone in Michael's throat. Then he called Brodsky and Gapski, who worked out of a precinct house on the East Side. They told him to bring the cassette to the precinct right away. It's Saturday morning. Don't these guys ever get a day off? The answer is no.

One has so often seen these precinct houses on TV shows that little needs to be said. Let us simply remark that the genetic makeup of the criminal is often claimed to be identical to the genetic makeup of the policeman with perhaps only one chromosome being different. When one observes these criminals in captivity, one sees how ten of them are kept in a jail cell designed for four. In the same way, in the precinct house, one finds ten desks in an office designed for four. And just as the jail cell is ugly, so is the precinct office ugly, with chipped furniture, dirty green walls and the only decoration a framed photograph of the mayor, and look, some joker has stuck a gob of chewing gum onto the mayor's nose. There's not even a flag, for Pete's sake. This is the office which Brodsky and Gapski occasionally occupy. They occupy it now. Their gray suits are rumpled; their fedoras are crushed. Around the collar of each of their white shirts is a similar gray ring. Do you know the expression "a murdered necktie"? It is not so much a style as a result of years of necktie abuse. Upon each of their murdered neckties is a similar egg stain. It should be remarked that both have a criminal air about them. They appear sullen and unhappy with their lot. It used to be the case that policemen were sometimes asked to take part in police lineups, just to flesh out the number of people onstage, but they were so often identified by the victim as the attacker or robber or assaulter—as, in fact, the criminal—that the practice was stopped. This is the main difference between the physical appearance of a criminal and the physical appearance of a policeman. The criminal appears less guilty.

When Michael entered the office there was a certain rustling of paper from the other half-dozen men and women, who realized this blond giant, as he was often described on TV, was Marduk the Magnificent. And if he had not been part of their job, Brodsky and Gapski might also have responded with interest. However, since Michael made up part of their current caseload, they pretended not to see him and only glanced up from their desks after Michael had cleared his throat several times.

"Oh, yeah," said Gapski. "Marmaduck."

"Duke," said Michael.

"Whatever," said Gapski.

"And you got some kind of tape recording?" asked Brodsky.

"A videocassette."

"Well, I guess we gotta see it," said Gapski.

Both men shuffled some papers, pushed back their chairs and got to their feet. They felt keenly aware that they were a foot shorter than Michael Marmaduke and they stretched their necks and stretched their backs and stood on tiptoe in a way to suggest they were suffering a violent pain in the rectum, and by such contortions they reduced the height difference by a single inch.

"We can go into the chief's office," said Brodsky. "He's not in today." It should be noted that Sapperstein, their boss, never works weekends.

Sapperstein's office was small and also crowded with file cabinets but at least it had only one desk. On a table was a TV and VCR. Above it hung a dartboard with the face of Yasir Arafat which had never been removed from its dusty gift-wrap cellophane. The green venetian blinds were half closed, giving the room an underwater tint. Brodsky turned on the TV, inserted the tape and fiddled with the controls, and after a moment the enchained Rose White appeared on the screen. "Michael," she cried, "you must save me! I'm being . . ." And again the screen went dark.

Brodsky and Gapski exchanged a look, something rare in itself given their dislike for each other. Then Brodsky rewound the tape and played it again. Then he played it a third time.

When the tape finished Brodsky and Gapski sat back in a pair of metal folding chairs and knitted their fingers into little contemplative tents before their faces.

"Where'd you get the tape?" asked Brodsky.

Michael explained how it had come by Express Mail. He had even brought the package. Gapski inspected it, then tossed it onto Sapperstein's desk. "I may be way outta line," said Gapski, "but I got a feeling you really hate this Rose White lady."

"What?" said Michael, astonished.

"In fact we were talking to her sister," said Brodsky, "and she said you and Rose White have been doing a lot of arguing."

"Are you serious?" said Michael. He couldn't imagine why Violet should tell such falsehoods.

"You're a strong kinda guy," said Gapski. "You coulda climbed down that wall with no trouble."

"But she's my fiancée! Why would I have done that?"

"You're tired of her, see," said Brodsky. "You want to get outta the relationship but she threatens to go public on your kinky habits and this will hurt you in the magazines. The fans won't like it. Consequently, you fake a kill."

Michael sat in a chair and the policemen stood on either side of him so that with Michael sitting and them standing, Brodsky and Gapski were just his height. If Michael hadn't been so amazed, he would have grown angry. "But I love her!"

"It's a known fact that love is next-door neighbor to hate," said Gapski.

"Hey, we all got feelings we don't understand," said Brodsky. "You're just a victim of your inner needs."

"If you come clean with us," said Gapski, "we'll see to it that even in Attica, you get to wrestle."

"You guys are nuts," said Michael. "If you're going to make stupid charges, then I get to call a lawyer. But none of this will help us find Rose White."

An hour later Michael Marmaduke was walking out of the precinct house with Primus Muldoon's lawyer, who liked pin-striped suits and had all the polish of the interior of a Rolls-Royce. His name was Truman Butterfield and he only left his East Side old-lady practice to pursue an interest in female body builders, which had originally led to his connection with Muldoon.

"Those guys," said Truman Butterfield, referring to Brodsky and Gapski, "are strictly crack-house fodder."

"They're in charge of finding Rose White," said Michael, holding the door for Butterfield, whom he always called Mr. Butter-field.

The lawyer paused on the sidewalk. "Are you close to this Rose White?"

"She's my fiancée."

"Too bad," said Mr. Butterfield philosophically. "But I can't understand the reason for the videocassette unless the kidnappers intend to ask for money. Maybe you should stay close to the phone."

"Good idea," said Michael. "I've got to be on TV tonight but my answering service can take the calls."

Until it was time to get ready to leave at eight o'clock, Michael sat no farther than a yard away from the phone. His stepmother called. Thrombosis called. Dentata called. Prime Rib called. Liquidity called. Cashback called. Every time the phone rang, Michael's adrenaline rose to the tips of his ears. When he realized the call had nothing to do with Rose White, his hopes tumbled to his arches. At last he turned his calls over to the answering service and crawled into the shower, feeling he had spent the whole day running up and down stairs. As the water beat against his power-ful trapezius and latissimus dorsi, Michael thought for the hundredth time about Jack Molay, the old fellow he had met the night before. Molay had said that perhaps he could help Michael find Rose White, but Michael had hardly paid attention. Now he regretted not asking for his card.

Primus Muldoon picked him up a few minutes after eight in his black Volvo 740. In preparation for his TV appearance, Muldoon had brushed out his mustache until it protruded several inches from his upper lip and resembled a fur bumper for his nose. "Butterfield told me about this morning," said Muldoon. "You heard anything?"

"Not from the kidnappers. For Pete's sake, I don't even know if they really *were* kidnappers." Michael strapped on his seat belt. A Wagner opera was playing quietly. Michael knew it was Wagner because Wagner was the only composer Muldoon ever played. "I just wish I had more faith in those policemen."

"They are systematizers and I mistrust them," said Muldoon. "The need for a system suggests a lack of integrity."

The TV show was a teaser for upcoming wrestling matches. Frankie Fallon was the host and he called his half-hour program *Barbarians in the Garden*. The lapels on Frankie's double-breasted gold sportcoat were so wide that had he attached a battery pack, then, like Icarus, he could have flown. The jacket had a thick rectangular shape, like a box, and Frankie appeared trapped inside. It was the jacket who was boss of this show. People spoke to it, they flattered it. Did we say it had rhinestones? It had rhinestones.

Looking past the jacket, although few people got that far, one was aware of crowds of perfectly capped teeth and a crow's wing of thick jet-black hair that cut diagonally across Frankie's forehead. Beyond the teeth and hair, one met a wide face, a nose like a big toe and a breakneck voice that addressed everybody as "guy" and used phrases like "more bang for the buck." Beyond that was like going beyond the breakers and roaring surf: there was only mystery and the gray expanse of the sea. Was there a Mrs. Frankie? Were there little Frankies? What made Frankie sad and what did he regret? Or was he, like the set of a western movie, all facade? Did one burst through Frankie's front door to meet nothing more than dusty back lots and alleyways?

Marduk's opponent was the serpent Apophis, who, like Rahab the Reckless, had never mastered the power of speech. Away from the ring he was Leon Molta, a nervous man who dealt with his nervousness by knitting mittens, and there wasn't a wrestler in the Association who hadn't at one time received a pair of Molta mittens. These were black wool mittens and during the colder months many a wrestling fan outside Madison Square Garden would squeeze his poor brain trying to guess why so many fierce-looking wrestlers were wearing black mittens, as if they were the badges of a secret club and not the physical tokens of Leon Molta's existential angst, the fuzzy black tears of his terrified soul.

The serpent Apophis was positioned on one side of the stage with a chain around his neck which secured him to a post, and if it weren't for this chain there might have been trouble, because Apophis kept flinging himself against it and making vicious squealing noises, maddened equally by the proximity of Marduk and his inability to speak. Apophis had an Egyptian trainer called

Nassim who wore a turban and carried a little tasseled stick with which to beat Apophis when he grew obstreperous. Nassim was actually Leon Molta's cousin, Ivan, and in his off hours he was studying to be a pastry chef. When he arrived at the studio he had brought several raspberry walnut cream pies, which everyone, including Michael, had hurriedly eaten.

Marduk the Magnificent stood on the other side of the stage dressed in golden robes, smiling and looking benign. In truth he was worrying about Rose White and he kept flashing on the video showing her chained to the wall somewhat as the serpent Apophis was chained to the post. Was she in pain? Did the kidnappers intend to call him? And he kept thinking about Jack Molay and how he might find him.

Frankie Fallon was shouting into the microphone: "From the torrid slime pits of Africa the bitter hatred for all that is pure and noble had for many years galled the poisoned heart of the serpent Apophis until he crawled up from his sewer and made his slow way to Manhattan to wreak destruction on the forces of decency!" Here Frankie Fallon turned to Apophis, who was pressed against the very end of his chain and raking the air with his claws. He was a gigantic creature and his height was exaggerated by elevator elf boots which raised him a foot above Frankie Fallon and his golden sport coat.

"Mr. Apophis," asked Frankie, "just what is it that you dislike about Marduk the Magnificent?"

"Arghh, arghh!" said Apophis.

Nassim struck at his charge with his tasseled stick, then took the microphone. "The beast is driven crazy by virtue. It is the question that constantly torments the purely evil: why was good ever permitted into the world?"

Frankie Fallon crossed the stage to where Marduk stood with Primus Muldoon. "And you, Marduk, what do you think of your chances against this man-eating beast?"

Marduk had two responses. First he tilted back his head and roared a great full body roar so that Frankie Fallon held on to his hair and the serpent Apophis scurried back behind Nassim the Egyptian and peered nervously over his shoulder. Then Marduk said, "I can only hope to do my best, and if I am successful, then

I must give the credit to all those fans who have faith in me and who have given me such encouragement."

"And is there anything you want to tell your fans?" asked Frankie Fallon.

Marduk's scripted answer ran, "Just to have hope and trust and love for one another." Instead, he broke the Association's cardinal rule: he stepped out of his Gimmick. "Is Jack Molay out there? I need to talk to you."

Frankie Fallon took a few steps back and the serpent Apophis stopped tugging his chain. There was an awkward silence.

Primus Muldoon hurriedly took the microphone. "Jack 'Meatbucket' Molay is the cruelest combatant on the western circuit and Marduk wants him to stop beating up on his friends."

Relieved, the serpent Apophis returned to screaming and raking the air with his claws.

But once they were back in the dressing room, Primus Muldoon asked, "Just what was that Molay stuff? We could get fined."

Michael sat at the light table rubbing cold cream into his golden makeup. "I would have asked about Rose White, but she's probably not watching TV. This Jack Molay said he could help me find her."

"Who is he?"

"Some old guy I met at a bus stop."

Did Michael really believe that Jack Molay might be able to help? He both did and didn't. Jack Molay appeared wise and mysterious and these qualities indicated that he would hear and respond. Jack Molay was also old and seemed financially troubled, not to say broke. These qualities suggested that he wouldn't respond. It depended on where one put one's faith, the reality described by newspapers or the reality described by poets. And although Michael didn't read much poetry, it seemed that wrestling formed part of the same artistic genre and so he put his money on mystery.

And when Michael left the TV studio around ten p.m., there was Jack Molay leaning against a parking meter and scratching his nose with the ivory handle of his cane.

"I received an awful videotape of Rose White," said Michael, shaking his hand. "She needs help."

"Why don't you tell me about it," said Jack Molay.

They went into a Greek coffee shop and Michael Marmaduke described the frustrations of his day. Plink-plink *Zorba the Greek* music came from a radio in the back. "If she's really been kidnapped," said Michael, "then why don't the kidnappers call?"

"Maybe it's not money they're after." Jack Molay had ordered hot cocoa and he cupped his hands over the steam.

"What else could they want?"

"Maybe they want you."

"They still have to call, don't they?"

"Perhaps they will contact you in some other way."

"But you'll help me?" Michael leaned across the table. About ten other men were in the coffee shop and by their stares he knew that most recognized him. A small wizened man in a dirty apron was picking up dirty plates and throwing them into a plastic bucket. Michael felt that the crashing noise exactly duplicated the jangling of his own overstimulated nerves.

"I know some clever people," said Jack Molay. "Maybe they can help. But it might be difficult to find them."

"What business are they in?"

Jack Molay held the ivory handle of his cane toward Michael, showing him the smiling face, then the leering face. Michael noticed that the leering face had little horns. "They're in the business of trying to discover how evil came into the world."

"And you can take me to them?"

"No, but I can lead you to people who know where they're to be found. But you'll have doubts."

"I can deal with doubts."

"These will be big doubts."

Michael wished he could see the other man's eyes but they were hidden by the brim of his hat.

"I can deal with big doubts."

"A hero," said Jack Molay, "is not only someone who acts. A hero is also someone who endures. As force is the expression of strength, so is endurance the expression of gentleness. Marduk's strength is matched by his endurance and wisdom."

"I can endure a lot," said Michael, hoping it was true.

So it was that Michael had found himself standing alone near the exit ramp of the Holland Tunnel where it circled around to Hudson Street. It was after midnight and he was waiting for a green van that was supposed to come along at any time. But he had already waited half an hour and he was cold. Still, he asked himself: Is my endurance only good for thirty minutes? He wore a stocking cap so he wouldn't be recognized and must have looked like a beggar because a few passing cars had flung him quarters.

Jack Molay had left him there, dropping him off from a cab.

"You're not coming with me?" Michael had asked.

"Just don't lose faith and you'll be all right."

"And who's the guy I'm looking for?"

"He's called the Master of Ceremonies."

"And he'll be in the van?"

"No, but they might be able to take you to him."

Michael heard the van long before he saw it because of the broken muffler. Then, observing the three red-jacketed men sitting in front, Michael felt a whisper of doubt. If rowdiness were a city, then here were its citizens. Michael stepped off the curb and waved at the driver.

The van swerved and braked. The driver—Michael later learned that his name was Retribution—leaned out and gave him an appraising stare. Then he said, "Ain't you Marduk the Magnificent? Why you wearing a funny hat?"

"I'm looking for the Master of Ceremonies," said Michael.

"Sure, hop in," said Retribution. Then he held out his hand, offering something. "Want a rubber?"

11

SNAKES

For the fifth time in the space of two hours the Econoline van screeches to a halt, the side door slides open, Correction leaps out and flings a brick through a plate-glass window. We must envy him this. Flinging a brick through a plate-glass window is one of the most satisfying pleasures life has to offer. This is a men's clothing store on Park Avenue on the northwest corner of Union Square: nice jackets and raincoats. Half a dozen men are hanging around despite the drizzle. When Correction hurls the brick, they are stalled as motionless as the pleasant-looking mannikins in the window. Each is thinking, Should I run or should I pretend to be invisible? All opt for invisibility. One of them is a homeless fellow with a shopping cart.

"Fuck you, Sophia!" shouts Correction. He jumps back through the side door and the van roars away.

Inside, Michael relaxes his hold on the sides of the van. "Just who is this Sophia anyway?" he asks.

Clancy, or Clemency as he seems to prefer, turns and spits into the corner. "The bitch! She's an Aeon, man. She's the very last of the thirty emanations of the unknowable Forefather of All. It was her fuckin curiosity that got the rest of us in trouble. That's why she's called Wisdom the Whore. Wisdom, hah! She didn't know squat."

The van slides around a corner and once more Michael has to brace himself. He wonders if an Aeon is like an Albanian or an Ethiopian. "Did she try to smuggle something through customs?"

"No, man, she tried to overreach herself. She tried to go beyond the limits of her ontological status. I mean, if the unknowable Forefather had wanted Sophia to know about him, then he would have tapped her on the shoulder and told her. But she didn't want only knowledge. She yearned for him, she burned for him. She wanted to possess him with her mind. The idea of him made her hot all over."

"Were they or weren't they related?" asks Michael, who, as an orphan, has conflicted feelings about kinship.

"He made her," says Clemency, "and she figured that made him responsible. But what can you know about the Unknowable, right? I mean the one fuckin thing you know about the Unknowable is that it's unknowable, which is basically zip."

Correction leans over Clemency's shoulder. "You gotta understand that old Sophia burned and burned until the Aeon Horos— whose name means Limit—came along and slapped some sense in her, making her stop. Of course by then it was too late."

"You better believe it," says Clemency. "Her burning passion just floated away from her. Even though it had been aborted, it still had life: a living fetus drifting through the void. This hypostatized passion had been flung from the Fullness by Horos, but it continued to live."

"And this happened recently?" asks Michael. It occurs to him that they are describing a video game.

"No, man, this is older'n Adam," says Clemency.

"Can you imagine this monster?" asks the Vals crouched in front whose name is Tribulation. "Born out of Sophia's wish for her own father, the little bastard floated through the void. And you know what, it grew. It got bigger!" Tribulation moves back to sit next to Clemency. The van takes another corner and they all slide to the left.

"Not only that," says Clemency, "it's got a name. Ialdabaoth, it was called: Child of Chaos."

"Or Sakla," says Correction, "Prince of Darkness."

"Or Sammael," says Tribulation, "the Blind God."

"This monster didn't know a fuckin thing," says Retribution. "He's got three names and he doesn't know nothing. He doesn't know his mother. He doesn't know his father. All he knows is that he's lonely."

Only the young man riding shotgun hasn't spoken. His name is Retaliation. He turns around to face Michael and the barrel of his sawed-off shotgun bumps the window. "Actually, he's got a fourth name. They also called him Error."

Let's pause a moment. In the heresiological literature we find half a dozen accounts of the Valentinian system. Irenaeus, Hippolytus, Clement of Alexandria, Epiphanius and Origen—all purport to know the truth of Valentinianism and all differ from each other. From Valentinus, who was expelled from the Roman church in 143 A.D., we have only a little hymn called "Harvest" and a fragment that states that man was made by inferior angels. The school of Valentinus was split into two sections: the Italian (based in Rome) and the Anatolian or Oriental, which was active in the Mideast. One imagines the Roman world as packed with crotchety old guys wearing old sheets who loved to argue. There is much disagreement in Valentinianism, and Irenaeus scolded the followers of Valentinus for "inconsistent teaching" and trying to "improve upon the master."

How Valentinianism moved from the Roman Empire to the streets of New York may be attributed to the pessimism of our times. Dualism is a gloomy system arguing that good and evil are of equal strength and seeing creation as a mistake. On these two points the Vals are passionate. "Life," they say, "what a fuckup!" From which it can be supposed that their own dualism (Valentinianism) arose in response to what they saw as the ugliness of the world and by being Vals they feel they have found a way to reduce the ugliness. Michael knows little of this. He is getting only a fuzzy snippet of Valentinianism. Still, he understands they are a religious group neither better nor worse than Evangelicals, Spiritualists, Episcopalians or the practicers of Voodoo, all of whom are in the business of figuring out how current events got the way they are, meaning confused.

The van again swerves to a halt and the side door is thrown open. Correction leaps out with a brick and hurls it at the window of a shoe store on Eighth Street. The glass shatters.

"Fuck you, Sophia!"

Correction jumps back in the van. "There're some Snakes back there," he says. "You better get moving."

"And you know what this asshole Ialdabaoth did because he was lonely?" asks Retribution, turning onto Fifth Avenue.

"He fuckin made something," says Retaliation. "He got lonely so he thought he'd make hisself a little friend."

"He made a monster," says Correction.

"He made us!" says Tribulation.

"But it wasn't really us," says Retaliation. "It was a Frankenstein's monster kind of us."

"That's right," says Clemency, "because Sophia saw what was going on and she said, 'Oh, fuck, that's one ugly sucker.' "

"So she flew down," says Tribulation, "and she gave this creature part of herself, part of her own essence."

"She fuckin blew on him," says Correction.

"The big Pneuma," says Tribulation.

Correction leans past Michael to look through the rear window. "Those snakes are still back there," he tells the driver. "We don't want them to catch us."

"Snakes?" thinks Michael. He braces his hands against the sides of the van as Retribution takes another corner. He feels the grim resignation that he feels in the dentist's chair when his teeth are being worked on.

"This Pneuma or Spirit connects us to the Unknowable," says Retaliation. "And it sits in us like a blank sheet of paper ready to take down the Logos, the Big Word itself."

"The Pneuma," says Clemency, "gets the Logos through Gnosis, which is Knowing. We know, man. We're the Vals!"

"We got the knowledge!" says Correction.

"We got the power!" says Retaliation.

Michael wishes he could see outside. He is aware of the van going increasingly faster and it is hard to keep his seat on the bucket. He can see Retribution checking his mirrors and turning around to look out the back. More important, Retaliation has broken open his shotgun and inserted two shells. The sound of the shotgun snapping shut is a tiny noise amidst all the others but to Michael Marmaduke it is strangely deafening.

"But Ialdabaoth," says Retribution, turning in his seat, "is out to gobble up more light. He gets fat on it. And Christos is trying to get it back again. We all got some of this light inside us, and each time we make babies, we keep spreading it around. We dilute it."

"But we don't want that," says Correction.

"That's right, no more babies," says Tribulation.

"That explains the condoms," says Michael. The van is rocking back and forth and above the sound of the muffler comes the sound of motorcycles. Certainly more than a couple.

"Fuckin A," says Clemency. "No more babies!"

"Ialdabaoth didn't know what he was at," says Tribulation, crouched by the rear window and looking out. "He made every fuckin thing but he did a bad job. He made it ugly."

"And the only reason that the world sometimes seems pretty," says Retribution, "is that we're not lookin at the thing itself, we're looking at the Pneuma inside it and the Pneuma's pretty."

"The fuckin Pneuma's beautiful," says Clemency. "That's why we gotta save it. That's the point of Salvation. I mean, we don't need Salvation because of Adam and Eve. We need Salvation because of what happened before creation. Before we got here!"

"Salvation," says Retaliation, "means returning the Pneuma or Spirit to the Unknowable Father of All!"

"After all," says Clemency, "it's basically his biscuit."

Michael Marmaduke falls off the bucket as the van rounds another corner. Leaning against one wall, he props his feet against the other. Once again he is overswept by feelings of doubt. But weren't these the very doubts that Jack Molay had warned him against? How can he feel confident in his ability to trust when already he is feeling distrustful?

"Snakes coming up on the left!" shouts Tribulation, still staring out the rear window. There is the roar of a motorcycle.

Retribution swerves to the left and the van crashes against something right below Michael's feet. The thin metal wall is bent inward, possibly in the shape of a handlebar. Michael moves his feet. Retaliation scrambles back to the rear window. "I'll take care of them!" he shouts.

"How will you know when Salvation happens?" asks Michael.

"Darkness, man," says Correction, "that's where Ialdabaoth lives. When the Unknowable Father gets back the Pneuma, we're goin to have nothin but light."

"Snakes on the right!" shouts Retaliation. He lifts the shotgun and begins hammering at the rear window with the stock. The glass shatters and the roar of motorcycles is louder.

Retribution swerves to the right and again there is a crash. Michael thinks they are on West Street somewhere near Washington Market Park. The van is swerving and Michael's stomach feels queasy. He wonders if this is the kind of endurance it takes to be a hero.

"So why throw bricks through windows if you're already saved?" Michael asks.

"It the fuckin Matter, man," says Retribution. "Matter is bad. Matter is made by Ialdabaoth. Didn't you get it? He got lonely so he made himself some Matter to keep himself company."

"And because the Matter was so fuckin ugly," says Retaliation, "Sophia added a dash of Spirit, a little breath of the Aeon, a little Pneuma."

"So that's what we are," says Clemency, "ninety-nine percent Matter and one percent Pneuma."

"There's a fuckin dozen Snakes, man!" shouts Retaliation. He raises the shotgun and fires. Within the van the noise is so loud that it is like getting one's ears boxed. The van turns west on Vesey and the rear end fishtails back and forth.

"But why smash store windows?" persists Michael. He presses his feet more firmly against the opposite wall.

"It's the advertising, man!" says Correction, shouting toward Michael's ear. "The fuckin business world is in the business of glorifying Matter."

Again Retaliation fires the shotgun and again Michael feels he has been punched in the head.

"The whole fuckin point of advertising," says Retribution, turning around in his seat, "is to make it seem that Matter has Spiritual qualities when in fact it has absolutely none."

"Fuckin zip," says Clemency.

"Can you imagine it?" says Correction. "Spirit hates matter and Matter hates spirit and these fuckin advertising people try to pretend that Matter and Spirit love each other."

"A fuckin lie," says Tribulation. "Matter's evil, man. It's evil and it's ugly."

"So you look at these shop windows, right?" says Clemency, shouting into Michael's ear. "And each one is trying to tell you that your Spiritual qualities are going to be beefed up by buying these shoes . . ."

"Or raincoats . . ." says Correction.

"Or lingerie . . ." says Tribulation.

"Or sport coats . . ." says Retaliation.

"Or dresses . . ." says Retribution.

"And what happens when you think this shit?" says Clemency.

And the others reply in unison: "You make more babies!"

Retaliation fires a third time. "Snakes on the right!" There is a roar of motorcycles. The van swerves right. "You missed them, goddammit! Don't let them near the front window!"

"I mean the purpose of evil," says Correction, leaning toward Michael's other ear, "is to spread the Spirit over a bigger and bigger area, to make everything darker."

"That's what evil is," says Clemency, "the Big Darkness!"

"They're coming up on the left," shouts Correction. The van swerves. "You missed them again!"

"Watch the front window!" screams Tribulation.

"Who's the Master of Ceremonies?" asks Michael.

"He's the main man," says Correction.

"He keep us talking," says Clemency.

"He keeps us from killing each other," says Tribulation.

"He makes art from our crud," says Retaliation. "We give him raw material and he makes something fantastic out of it."

"Snakes on both sides," shouts Retribution. Retaliation crawls forward with the shotgun.

"Who're the Snakes?" asks Michael with increasing anxiety.

"Snakes, man, they're not even Christians!" shouts Clemency.

"They think they got the knowledge, but we got the knowledge!" shouts Correction.

"We're the Vals!" shouts Tribulation.

"Watch the window! Watch the window!"

At that moment something hits the front window and it disintegrates. A brick bounces across the floor of the van, followed by hundreds of little pieces of glass. The shotgun explodes again. From all around comes the roar of motorcycles. Michael sees something like a bag flung through the front window. The van is swerving dangerously back and forth and the tires are squealing. Clemency and Correction are shouting. The bag hits the floor and breaks apart. A tangle of snakes seems to burst from it, dozens of small black-and-green snakes, which begin to separate, wriggling away as the tangle slides across the floor.

"Jesus," says Michael Marmaduke, who hates snakes.

12

DISILLUSIONMENT

The snake in Michael Marmaduke's lap is an eight-foot rattlesnake with bright red eyes and fangs several inches long. Coiled up, it resembles one of those undersized spare tires which are only safe at slow speeds. It also appears angry, although Michael feels that all snakes have a moody look. At least, he has never seen what he'd call a happy snake, unless it was a sleeping snake. Luckily, this snake is in a cage covered with thick wire mesh. A white mouse is also in the cage but at the moment the snake appears indifferent to the mouse. The mouse sits very still as if pretending to be a small snowbank. Michael knows if he thought hard he could discover some symbolic meaning in the mouse, but looking again at the snake's fangs he decides it is not a meaning to which he cares to be privy.

If we move back, we see that Michael is wedged into the cigar-shaped sidecar of a black motorcycle roaring north along FDR Drive just north of the Williamsburg Bridge. The cyclist is dressed in black leather and painted on his black helmet are two red eyes so that the helmet resembles the head of a snake. Behind this motorcycle are ten others driven by similarly dressed young men but this is the only motorcycle with a sidecar.

"It's a good thing you're a friend of the Master of Ceremonies," shouts the cyclist, whose name is Rattler. The roaring of the motorcycle—an old Triumph Bonneville—reminds Michael of the roar of Niagara Falls heard from the deck of the *Maid of the Mist*.

"I need to talk to him," shouts Michael. "My fiancée's been kidnapped and I'm told he can help." He is sitting several feet beneath Rattler and has to twist his neck in order to see him.

"The M.C. can do anything," shouts Rattler. "He takes our gang fights and turns them into truth." Then: "Be careful about shaking my snake. He don't like it."

Michael holds the snake very carefully. Really, it is the motorcycle that is doing the shaking, leaping from pothole to pothole; Michael is only riding. But it is not the discomfort of the sidecar which bothers him so much as the presence of the snake. He can't remember when he first decided he disliked them. Probably he was born with it: a twist in his genetic makeup, a skewed chromosome with snake-hatred written across it. So when the bag of snakes came hurtling into the van, Michael felt he had reached his limit. Grabbing the side door, he yanked it open so hard that the handle broke off in his hand. By then the van was out of control and executing pirouettes down Lower Broadway. In the midst of a pirouette Michael hopped to the curb. He was quickly surrounded by men in black leather with the word "Snakes" written across their backs. Ophites, he later discovered they were called. Although feeling rather fed up, he asked if they knew the Master of Ceremonies, and once the young men decided that he was not a Val, they offered to take him. Of course they also recognized him as Marduk the Magnificent. In the meantime the van had straightened itself out and disappeared in a puff of exhaust smoke and a cry of "Fuck you, Snakes!"

Now they are rushing north on FDR Drive and Michael has noticed that tied to the back of every motorcycle, even Rattler's, is a cage full of snakes, not one or two snakes in a milk crate but a whole packed box.

"So you like snakes, do you?" shouts Michael, trying to be conversational.

Rattler glances at him. He is a large black man but only the tip of his nose and the bottom part of his face are visible; all the rest is covered in black leather and over his eyes are World War II aviator goggles. Michael is aware that he is seeing less than one percent of Rattler's skin so the rest might be any color at all.

"Snakes is boss, man," shouts Rattler.

"What about the Big Pneuma?" shouts Michael, trying to give the impression of being someone in the know.

The motorcycle swerves. "Fuck the Big Pneuma, man, there ain't no fuckin Big Pneuma. Thass jes raggedy bullshit. What's a smart wrassler like you hanging out with Dancers anyway?"

"They were going to take me to the Master of Ceremonies."

"They couldn't take you outta a paper bag! All that Christos shit, all that Ialdababble! That's jes fantasy, man. They is only one sucker you gotta pay attention to and thass the snake. I mean, the *Big Snake*!"

"Where do you find this snake?" asks Michael, hoping to learn its location and elude it.

"Every little snake, man, is a part of the Big Snake, so to see the Big Snake, you jes look a little snake in the eyes, jes like a little bird, and you start to feel dizzy jes like a little bird, and in that dizziness, in that big swoon, well, that's where you meet the Big Snake. Face to face: like a kiss."

Michael considers what it would be like to kiss a snake. Cold lips, sharp teeth. The thought disagrees with him. On his left is the United Nations, on his right the river. Traffic is light and the motorcycles roar past whatever cars—cabs mostly—are out at this hour. The sidecar is about a foot off the pavement and resembles a motorized skateboard. Michael feels if he flexed his muscles, the sidecar would explode. He is aware of the Vals' condoms in his pocket—he is sitting on a lump of them—and thinks that the sidecar is like a condom, a giant full-body condom. He also thinks about Ialdabaoth and Sophia with regret. He is like someone who has spent a long time learning a foreign language and has just reached the realization that he will never use it.

"So who is this snake?" shouts Michael.

"You ever thought about why the world doesn't fly apart?" answers Rattler. "Big fuckin round thing spinning through space—why doesn't it just bust into millions of pieces? I'll tell you why. The Big Snake's got hisself wrapped right around it with his tail in his mouth. He keeps us tight together. He keeps us a fambly. How you goin to explain it otherwise?"

"I never thought of it like that," answers Michael.

"Those Dancers talk about the Big Pneuma and the Unknowable Father of All. You don't need that shit. You only need your own sense of right and wrong. And you know where you got dat?"

"From my parents, I guess, or my stepparents. I was adopted."

"Yeah, but where did they get it and where did their parents get it? See what I mean? Who got it first?"

There is a thrashing in the cage. Looking down, Michael sees that the white mouse has disappeared, while the rattlesnake has a lump in his throat that Michael realizes is not sadness. He thinks about right and wrong and who might have made the original distinctions. No wonder that Ialdabaoth is also named Error.

"You tell me," shouts Michael.

Rattler slows to take the 96th Street exit. The ten other motorcycles tighten ranks behind him.

"The fuckin Garden, man. The snake shows up in the Garden and teaches Adam and Eve the difference between right and wrong. This stupid god, he makes 'em, but don't finish 'em. He leaves them dumb. You ain't finished till you know right from wrong!"

"Didn't the snake get them in trouble?" says Michael. His stocking cap has blown off and his blond hair blows in the wind.

"That's what the Christians say. How can you believe folks who says the meek will inherit the earth? That's loser talk. All I know is that Adam and Eve was strollin through the Garden singing doo daa doo daa and the snake comes along and sets them straight. It was the main teacher, man. If it weren't for Mr. Snake, you'd still be digging under rocks for your protein. The Garden, man, that was Disneyland. You can't spend your life in a place like that. You gotta grow up. The Tree of Knowledge gave them the big distinction. Thass what's important, man, the Big Distinction!"

"So how'd the snake get in the Garden?" asks Michael.

"Sophia put him there, of course, but it was the big snake that told her to do it, the big Leviathan hisself."

"So you believe in Sophia after all?"

"Sure, man, but our Sophia and the Dancers' Sophia is not

necessarily the same Sophia. Even the Cainites believe in Sophia, and they don't believe in much else."

"Who're the Cainites?" asks Michael.

"We plan to be meeting them shortly," says Rattler. "I hope you're ready to wrassle."

"I only want to find the Master of Ceremonies."

Rattler turns up First Avenue. "That comes after."

The fact that Michael hasn't heard of the Snakes doesn't worry him. Every day he sees signs on storefronts advertising some religious group and he guesses the Snakes are just one that he missed. But given the practices of the second-century Ophites (Greek *ophis*: serpent) and Naassenes (Hebrew *nahas*: serpent), which included eating bread that snakes had fooled with and kissing snakes on the mouth, one may wonder if the cult had much staying power. You can only kiss so many snakes before wanting to call it quits. Yet something existed in Ophism that spoke to Rattler and his pals. Who made us smart? The Big Snake made us smart.

There are few cars on the street. In several doorways Michael sees sleeping figures, and he thinks of his own soft bed with regret. The rain has stopped but the streets are still wet and lights reflect off the pavement.

"Why were you chasing those guys in the van?" asks Michael.

Rattler downshifts and the motorcycle backfires. "The Big Eradication, man. I mean, Ialdabaoth made Adam and Eve. He made the Garden of Eden, which means Delight. But it didn't happen like the Vals say it did. Like it says in their Bible, 'For the Archons' Delight is bitter and their beauty is lawless. Their Delight is deceit and their tree was hostility.' Now that tree weren't hostility. That tree saved us. It was by eating of the tree we discovered that Ialdabaoth was full of shit and we turned away from him. The Big Snake was the start of *gnosis* on earth. The Vals don't believe that stuff, so it's our job to stomp them."

"That seems a little extreme," says Michael.

"Can't be helped. You got a plague, you stomp it out."

"And the Cainites?"

"Shit, they don't believe it either. I mean, Cain snuffed his brother because his brother was no good. I'll accept that. But it was the snake told him to do it. The snake knowed that Abel was no more'n an Ialdabaoth stooge. You know what the mark of Cain was? It was a little snake tattooed on the forehead. But these Cainites don't believe in no snake. They don't believe the Leviathan keeps the world from flying apart. They think it was Cain that taught us the difference between right and wrong all by hisself. They think the mark of Cain was a little pissed-off fist so they gots themselves little dumbfuck fists tattooed on their foreheads. Don't that beat all? How can you let dumbfucks like that go around breathing the same air you breath?"

Michael shifts himself in the sidecar, which is chafing his knees. "Wouldn't it be better to live and let live?"

"Thass what the Master of Ceremonies says, but I can't see it. When a cockroach is squatting on your ham sammich, do you say live and let live? When a rat strolls across your kitchen table, you blows him a little kiss? No, sir, you stomp 'im. Thass why you're Marduk the Magnificent and thass why we brought you along tonight. We respect you. You don't take shit and we don't take shit. But right now you're about to do a little work. The time for talk is past."

It is on the tip of Michael's tongue to say that contractual obligations to the Wrestling Association deny him the pleasure of free-lance matches, but then life suddenly speeds up. Rattler swerves around the corner of a dark street and up ahead Michael sees another Snake off his motorcycle and crouching by a garage door. Just as Michael is wondering what the fellow is doing, the Snake jumps away and there is a flash of light and an explosion as the door disappears in a yellow cloud of smoke.

Rattler guns his motorcycle. "You in charge of the boss snake," he tells Michael. "Don't let anything get it mad." Then he shouts to the riders behind him: "Grab yourself a serpent!"

The motorcycle surges toward the smoldering garage door and Michael hears a popping noise reminiscent of gunfire. He ponders the nature of fear. Although he knows he is in danger, what worries him most is that he might do something to make Primus Muldoon angry. As the motorcycle roars through the doorway, Michael notices that Rattler is steering with his knees. In each of his upraised hands, he clutches a fat black snake. Michael takes a firm grip on the cage in his lap. Although he dislikes snakes, he is a kind man and he doesn't want the rattlesnake to feel anxious, especially on a full stomach. Ahead of him he sees people running. The noise in the building—a kind of warehouse—is much louder. The popping noises are also louder and Michael decides they must be gunfire after all. A bullet ricochets off the front of the sidecar.

Now let us look down from the ceiling. We watch the action from a spot near one of the forced-hot-air heaters. The room is smoky and we think there must be a fire but then we see that one of the Snakes is throwing smoke bombs from the door. Within the smoke are brightly colored lights—red, yellow, green—and we see that the room is hung with traffic lights. Given the fondness for symbol on the part of the Valentinian Gnostics, Ophites and Cainites, we assume the presence of a dozen flashing traffic lights has some import beyond the purely decorative. Perhaps they signal the entry of evil into the world. Perhaps they caution us as we wind our way through the traps and pitfalls of right and wrong. At the moment there is no one to ask, because the thirty or so visible Cainites—all wearing dark green leather jackets and sporting small fist tattoos on their foreheads—are scrambling like ants when one gives the ant hill a good kick. A few have pistols and take aim at the motorcycles roaring through the remnants of the front door. One might think it an easy task to pop a rider off his bike with a .38, but then one would be reckoning without the snakes. As the riders burst through the door each hurls the two snakes he grips in his upraised hands toward the startled Cainites, then digs into the box attached to his rear fender for a couple more. From our place near the ceiling the snakes resemble flying black streamers and the air is full of them. It is tricky to take aim with a .38 and deflect snakes at the same time. As a result, although many weapons are being fired, the question of accuracy is problematic, and several bullets have struck the forced-air heater to our left even though we chose this position because of its ostensible safety.

The warehouse is very noisy what with the roaring of the motorcycles over which rise a variety of human screams much in the way the tips of icebergs rise out of the sea. The riders are executing a series of figure eights as they pursue the Cainites in the smoky gloom punctuated by the red and yellow and green flashing traffic lights. The motorcycles smack the fleeing Cainites and ride over them, leaving black tread marks on the backs of their green leather jackets. They zoom up stairways and leap over tables. They hop barrels. They roar over the top of a stationary Chevy Impala. And everywhere there are snakes: flying through the air, wriggling across the floor, wrapped around young men's extremities. Rattler, on the lead motorcycle, and Michael Marmaduke, in the sidecar, function as a battering ram sweeping the Cainites before them. Michael clasps the rattlesnake's cage, and the tense expression knotting his features might be mistaken for fear but actually it is nausea. He hates bumpy rides and is growing carsick. He is also approaching the moment when he will articulate the brief sentence: I have had enough!

There. Do you see it? We can observe the sentence cross his forehead like a news flash crossing the Times Building in Times Square. Michael begins to relax. He knows what he must do. Reaching toward the headlight of the Triumph Bonneville, he turns the ignition key, pulls it out and sticks it in his pocket. The motorcycle glides to a stop as Rattler stares at him. We assume that Rattler is astonished but because of his helmet and World War II aviator goggles, no facial expression is visible. His mouth, however, is slightly open.

Once the motorcycle is motionless, Michael hands Rattler the cage with the snake and climbs from the sidecar. It is a tight fit and he tears his raincoat. Then he gives the key to Rattler and makes his way toward the smashed door of the warehouse, cleaving the chaos like a sharp knife through a flank steak. Two green-jacketed Cainites hiding behind the Chevy Impala leap at him with paleolithic clubs: the weapon of choice among the Cainites, supplemented by the occasional .38. Michael yanks the clubs from their grasp, grabs the young men and sets them gently on top of the Chevy Impala. Michael doesn't want to hurt anyone. He only wants to go home. A motorcycle roars at him. He pushes it aside. A man leaps at him from a balcony. Michael catches him and sets him down on his feet. A snake comes flying through the air. Michael grabs it and releases it on the floor unhurt. Then he reaches the door. Is he done for the night? Not quite.

Out on the sidewalk Michael stops to catch his breath. His coat is torn and his knees feel bruised. He decides not to look for a bus but splurge on a cab even though it must be 120 blocks to his apartment at One University Place. He pushes his way, gently, through the crowd gathered by the front of the warehouse and hears people say, "Marduk the Magnificent, Marduk the Magnificent!" Michael shakes his head at their error but has no energy for argument. Up the block he sees a yellow cab and he moves toward it. His legs ache; his back aches. He begins to imagine the comfort of his bed, the luxury of his pillow. But these hopes are premature. As he reaches the curb, he feels some hard object being shoved into his back. His first impulse is to swat it away, then he decides to see what it is.

Turning, he looks down on two skinny young men dressed in mustard-colored leather jackets. The men readjust their pistols so they are pointing at Michael's belly.

"What the fuck you doin in there, buster?" says one young man. "You a Cainite or a Snake?"

"Hey, it's Marduk the Magnificent," says the other. Both have many angry-looking pimples and there is something wrong with their hair, which seems unusually thin and dandruff-clogged.

"I've been trying all evening," says Michael, attempting to keep the frustration out of his voice, "to find the Master of Ceremonies. I'm told he can help me with a problem."

At that moment there is a low rumbling noise and a purple Ford Galaxy with purple-tinted windows glides up to the curb.

"Maybe we can help you find him," says the first young man.

"'Course you gotta help us first," says the other.

"Maybe I'll just go home," says Michael.

The first young man shoves the pistol into Michael's belly. "You got no choice," he says.

Michael wants to refuse but knows that Primus Muldoon will be unhappy if he gets shot. One of the young men opens the back door. Across the back of his leather jacket are the words "Mars Boys" in gold studs. Another young man is in the backseat. He is pimply and attempting to grow a beard, but the scant blond whiskers seem in need of fertilizer. His cheeks resemble photographs of crop failures in Ethiopia. "Hey," says the young man, preparing to slap Michael five, "I recognize you!"

Half an hour later all Michael knows for certain is that he is somewhere in Queens and that the Mars Boys are Marcionite Christians. There are five of them: three in front and two with Michael in back. The car is crowded, moving fast, and there is rap music on the radio. The car also has the sour smell of dirty bodies, as if the Mars Boys hate to use soap. They are on their way to settle a score with the Toots—Tertullian Christians. Later they swear to take Michael to the Master of Ceremonies.

"The Toots fucked up the Book of Luke, man," says the man with the sickly whiskers on Michael's right, who introduced himself as Billy Pontus. "Like Luke didn't even fuckin write the Book of Luke, it was written by Paul himself, but the Toots fucked with it. Like the man says, 'Great is the blindness of those who read.' It gets so you don't know who to believe. It's all there to tempt you. It's there to make you fuck up!"

Michael twists in his seat to give himself some more room. "But what do you mean there are two gods?"

"Easy," says Billy Pontus. He holds a dismantled pistol and he is oiling each part, even the bullets. "There's the Just God and there's the Good God. The Just God's the god of the Old Testament and he's a fuckup. An eye for an eye and a tooth for a tooth. What kinda god is that? But that's not to say he's the Devil. The Toots say he's the Devil and they're wrong. The Just God is just a fuckup. But he made us. He made the big messola. And if it weren't for Jesus, we wouldn't have the Good God at all, because basically he can't be bothered with us. We're just small fry to him. We depress him. But Jesus bought us with his own precious blood and gave us to the Good God. And he wants us to help him free the spirit. And you know what that means?"

There is a pause while Michael thinks what this might mean and then all five Mars Boys shout in unison: "No more fucking!"

"Not even with condoms?" asks Michael.

"Not ever. Only the fuckin Vals believe in condoms. We hate the Vals. We kill them!"

"But isn't killing wrong?" asks Michael.

"There you go again," says Billy Pontus. "Right, wrong, good, bad, justice, injustice—these are the tricks that the Just God uses to keep you tied in knots. You gotta say no to the whole bundle. Perpetual abstinence is where it's at!"

"It seems like a peculiar system," says Michael.

"It was the Just God that invented it," says Billy Pontus, re-assembling his pistol, which has black electrician's tape wrapped around the butt. "Can you imagine how stupid he must've been to invent something like sticking your weenie into a bacteria-ridden hole? Then to be born outta that hole, just like coming outta a sewer? We gotta put a stop to that. It's not clean and it fucks up the light. It dilutes the power of the soul!"

"Wasn't Jesus born like that?" asks Michael.

"That's what the Toots say, but it's a lie," answers Billy Pontus. "Jesus sprang outta the brain of the Good God. The Good God had a lively good thought and that was Jesus. He popped into the air like a dancer outta a birthday cake. Doesn't that make more sense than weenies in a hole?"

"The smart thing," says the man on Michael's left, who has introduced himself as Frankie Pontus, "would be to have them surgically removed. That's what Origen did. That's what a lotta them did, all those Essenes and followers of Attis. Lord knows, we got those folks too. New York's a big place. They just lopped it off. But to me castration's just a crutch. You gotta say no with your heart. Say No to Pussy. That's where it's at."

"You see," says Billy Pontus, sliding a clip of bullets into the butt of the pistol, "it's lust that keeps the world going and imprisons the spirit. Lust keeps the world in the hands of the Just God. Like we're his vibrator toy. We're his big dildo!"

"Don't you think it might be better to cut it off?" asks the driver, Louie Pontus. "I keep having these dreams."

"We already been through that!" says the man next to him.

"I don't know," says Charlie Pontus, who is riding shotgun, "if it were just removed altogether, then maybe it wouldn't be such a distraction. Like it nags, man. It whines at me."

"You gotta say no!" says Billy Pontus. "Unless the decision comes outta your heart, it's not the real thing."

"Sometimes I just wanta slice it off," says Charlie Pontus.

"Me too," says the driver. "I wanna give it the old heave ho! I'm tired of being strong. Sometimes I think I'm too weak to be strong!"

Billy Pontus leans forward and taps the driver on the back of the head with his pistol. The car swerves. "Man, you know what happens to heretics? The same fuckin thing that's about to happen to the Toots."

Michael flexes his latissimus dorsi to give himself more room. He suspects the Mars Boys are pimply and smelly because they don't take care of themselves. They need vitamins. They need a good gym. "What do you know about the Master of Ceremonies?"

"He's the big organizer," says Charlie Pontus.

"He's like a union boss," says Louie Pontus.

"He smooths out all the rough places," says Frankie Pontus.

"He's at the center of the center," says Billy Pontus.

"He makes beauty from our violence," says Freddy Pontus.

"And you'll help me find him?" asks Michael. He recalls the doubts Jack Molay had warned him about and how he had protested. Yet at the moment—and by the illuminated dial on his watch he sees that it is four in the morning—he wishes he were home in bed. But even as that sensation sweeps over him, he thinks of Rose White and his eyes begin to water.

"Sure we'll help you," says Billy Pontus, "but you gotta help us kill these Toots first. We need someone to break down the door, and you're just the one to do it, big guy."

"We're comin up on their clubhouse," says Louie Pontus.

"Cut the lights," says Billy Pontus.

"You know, once you've said no to right and wrong," Frankie Pontus tells Michael conversationally, "it makes a lotta things easier. I mean, you just say, fuck it. You come to a red light: fuck it! It's time to pay your taxes: fuck it! Your landlord wants the rent: fuck it! Even food I can cut down on. Eat only supplements. Washing? Who cares? Cutting my toenails? What's it matter? It's just pussy that poses the big problem. It keeps singing to you. It keeps trying to whisper in your ear."

"Don't talk about it!" shouts Louie Pontus, slowing the car.

"I can't stand it!" shouts Charlie Pontus. "I just gotta cut it off! Novocain, I'll get some Novocain!"

"Be quiet now," says Billy Pontus. "You'll feel better after you kill some Toots. You'll be freeing their immortal souls. Believe me, they'll thank you later. Let's go!"

The Ford Galaxy has come to a stop off Rockaway Boulevard in Ozone Park. There are trees and in the distance is Kennedy Airport. Michael decides he is not going to knock down any door or help anybody kill anybody. He gets out of the car. The street is dark with some houses, a garage, several small shops. A dog barks. The five Mars Boys begin moving toward the garage.

"Come on!" urges Billy Pontus.

Michael takes one step, then another. He is determined to turn around and run in the other direction. He just has to make up his mind to do it. But he hates running and he worries about Rose White. The Mars Boys are about ten feet ahead of him. It is at this point that a cab turns down the street. The Mars Boys duck into the shadow. A second dog begins to bark. From the airport, Michael hears the roar of a jet engine. The cab slows and comes to a stop next to Michael Marmaduke. The back door opens and a two-headed cane protrudes from the darkness. One face is smiling, the other is grim.

"Would you like a ride?" asks Jack Molay.

Quickly, Michael Marmaduke enters the cab. "Maybe I don't have what it takes to be a hero," he says. "I feel deeply disappointed." The cab accelerates down the street.

"Disappointment," says Jack Molay, patting his arm, "is an effective form of instruction."

13

RICE PUDDING

In his more meditative moments Wally Wallski tries to rack up metaphysical mileage out of the fact that some days are bright and cheery and others are cloudy and glum. This Sunday morning, for instance, the weather is decidedly gloomy, and its gloominess seems to match Wally Wallski's own gloominess as he walks up Fulton Street toward the renovated brick warehouse which is the home of Mr. Lenguado. Of course Wally Wallski knows that his gloominess and the sky's gloominess are coincidental. His gloominess is caused by his wife Claudine, who isn't happy in their new apartment in Brooklyn Heights but demands a condo on West End Avenue. As for the sky, no telling why the sky is gloomy. Maybe a meteor poked it in a painful manner. Maybe some practical joker has sown the fleecy white clouds with dry ice and gotten them mad. Maybe the birds are acting up again. And surely it is cloudy all over, not just around Fulton Street. In New Jersey it is cloudy. In Connecticut it is cloudy. No one is lying on the beach today. No one is packing a picnic basket. But was it cloudy when Wally Wallski left Brooklyn Heights less than an hour ago? He doesn't think so.

The street is empty, not even any passing cars. Across the sidewalk one Styrofoam cup chases another in a way that seems contentious, as if the second bore malice for the first. From somewhere nearby comes the conversational slither of stringed instruments and operatic singing; then, incorporated into the music, comes a woman's scream. This is followed by a question shouted in a foreign language which Wally Wallski knows to be Italian because many of his fellow fishermen are Italian.

"Che grido è questo mai?" Why did she scream?

Wally Wallski hesitates, then continues putting one foot in front of the other. The music rings no bells with him. He's not much for opera anyway. We, however, floating above the street, find something familiar about the music—perhaps it is Mozart, perhaps Gluck—and we wait for another clue. Wally Wallski can see the windows of Mr. Lenguado's flat with their green window boxes and red geraniums. The music surges toward a dramatic moment. Wally Wallski decides that Mr. Lenguado has the radio on again. There is another scream.

"Che grido indiavolato! Leporello, che cos'è?" What a scream! Leporello, what's going on?

The name Leporello tips us off and we realize the music is *Don Giovanni*. This is the moment when the statue of the Commandant comes to Don Giovanni's house for dinner and his servant, Leporello, opens the door and screams. Wally Wallski hardly hears the music. Its combined notes form a faint tinkling at the doorway of his consciousness. Instead he feels crushed down by the dark sky, which he imagines divided into the half belonging to his wife Claudine and the half belonging to Mr. Lenguado. They are twin Himalayas crushing his heart. To Wally Wallski the tidy apartment in Brooklyn Heights is the nicest place he has ever lived. To Claudine it is an affront to the dignity of the person she would like to become.

Wally Wallski cups his hands into a trumpet and raises up on his tiptoes toward the window. "Mr. Lenguado," he calls. "Are you in there? I got a favor I gotta ask. My wife Claudine is unhappy in our place and wants a nice condo. Mr. Lenguado! Do you hear me? It's Wally Wallski! I saved your life!"

From the window comes the sound of knocking, followed by more Italian.

"Qualcun batte! Apri!"

"Io tremo!"

It is the statue knocking. "Open the door!" shouts Don Giovanni. "I'm afraid," cries Leporello.

Wally Wallski waits on the sidewalk. The air grows colder.

"Mr. Lenguado, are you in there? I got a favor I gotta ask. It's me, Wally Wallski, the guy who saved your life."

Suddenly, there are two long blasts from the orchestra, followed by a pause and then a third blast. "Don Giovanni!" cries the bass voice of statue. "A cenar teco m'invitasti, e son venuto." You invited me to dinner and I have arrived.

"Mr. Lenguado, are you up there?" shouts Wally Wallski over the music. He is surprised by how dark the sky has become.

A shadow passes across the window. "What do you want?" comes the voice of Mr. Lenguado. It is not a friendly voice.

"My wife Claudine . . ."

"Didn't I warn you about bothering me again?"

"A torto di viltate tacciato mai sarò," sings Don Giovanni. No one will ever accuse me of being afraid.

Wally Wallski puts his hand on his head to keep his hat from blowing away. "We just have a little problem. My wife Claudine felt sure you could fix it."

"What kind of problem?" shouts Mr. Lenguado. When Mr. Lenguado shouts, the red geraniums quiver in the window boxes.

Why is the air so cold? Wally Wallski asks himself.

"Pentiti, cangia via, è l'ultimo momento," sings the statue. Repent, change your life. This is your last moment!

"No, no," responds Don Giovanni, "ch'io non mi pento!" I will not repent!

"I think it's a great apartment," shouts Wally Wallski. He wonders if he can ask Mr. Lenguado to lower the music. Better not, he thinks. "But my wife says it doesn't quite suit her."

"Why not?" shouts Mr. Lenguado. His voice is so full of static that Wally Wallski expects flashes of lightning to burst from the dark window.

"Pentiti!" roars the statue. Repent!

"No!" cries Don Giovanni.

"The coloring is off," says Wally Wallski.

"It can be painted!" shouts Mr. Lenguado.

"The neighbors are noisy," says Wally Wallski.

"They can be moved!" shouts Mr. Lenguado.

"The school district is not the best," says Wally Wallski.

"You don't have children!" shouts Mr. Lenguado.

"Ah," shouts the statue, "tempo più non v'è!" Your time is up!

"It's too small," cries Wally Wallski. "My wife Claudine thinks it's too small! She wants a condo on West End Avenue with a king-sized bed!"

"You're pushing your luck," shouts Mr. Lenguado.

Now a chorus of demons is singing. "Tutto a tue colpe è poco!" No horror is too terrible for you!

"Mr. Lenguado, I saved your life. You gotta help me!"

"Chi l'anima mi lacera? Chi m'agita le viscere?" sings Don Giovanni in pain. Who torments my soul? Who agitates my body?

A piece of paper floats down from the open second-story window. "Go to this address!" cries Mr. Lenguado. "A truck's already on the way to Brooklyn Heights to pick up your stuff. Think wisely before bothering me again!"

Wally Wallski catches the piece of paper. The address is a building on the corner of West End and 89th Street. "Oh, thank you, Mr. Lenguado, and my wife Claudine thanks you too."

"Che inferno, che terror!" shouts Don Giovanni, then he screams. Don Giovanni is dragged down to hell. The scream tumbles from the window like a net toward the sidewalk, but Wally Wallski is already hurrying away and the music passes from his mind. Its little notes bounce on the pavement behind him. Wally Wallski decides it will rain at any moment and he wants to get to the subway. A pit bull tied to a parking meter barks and lunges at him. Wally Wallski shakes his finger at the dog. His happiness is almost complete. He pauses: what is missing? Ah, if only he hadn't dropped Marduk the Magnificent's two-headed coin, then he would be truly happy. But hasn't he been lucky without it? Now he and his wife Claudine can have the life she has always wanted. Perhaps he is only being superstitious.

At the corner is a man pushing a shopping cart. It is Beetle, the homeless fellow we have met before. He wears an oddly colored raincoat—plaid and stripes all at once—and seems very thin and lumpy at the same time. The shopping cart appears full but it is covered with black plastic so we can't say what it contains. It too is lumpy. Beetle's face is as gray as the clouds: a long face, and his eyes and nose look like features drawn on the trunk of a sycamore tree. When we first met him outside Madison Square Garden, we couldn't guess his age. Now we'd say he is about sixty. But he could be fifty and he could be seventy. His hair is thick and coarse and sticks straight up from his head. If one squints, he looks like a bottle brush.

When Beetle notices Wally Wallski striding toward him full of purpose, his face becomes more focused; and we observe what, in a religious person, would be a sense of mission. His whole body, every bit of tissue, becomes pointed at Wally Wallski.

Beetle moves his shopping cart so that it blocks the sidewalk. "You want to hear a sad story?" he asks.

Too much has happened to Wally Wallski for him to remember seeing Beetle before. Still, something strikes him as familiar.

"I'm in a real rush," he says.

"I could make it short."

Wally Wallski digs in his pocket. "Here's a buck. Buy yourself some grapefruit." He doesn't know if Beetle likes grapefruit but he hates giving money if he feels someone has a drinking problem.

"It's about something I did when I was a lot younger," says Beetle, taking the dollar.

"If I don't hurry, I'll get really yelled at," says Wally Wallski, dodging around the cart.

"You need to change your life."

Wally Wallski stops to consider this. "If I changed my life, Claudine would kill me." Better to be half dead as Wally Wallski than completely dead as somebody else. He hurries up Fulton Street toward the subway.

Beetle looks after him and sighs. The sense of mission drains from his face. He turns toward Wall Street. Even on a quiet Saturday he enjoys leaning back against the walls where the money lives. Although it chills his body, it warms his heart.

If one were to peek into Beetle's head, one would not find words. Rather it would be like looking down a tunnel much like a subway tunnel with the tracks all rusted and the roof caving in.

If one had a flashlight, one could pick out strange drawings and rudimentary frescoes on the walls. This old head has had lots of abuse: too much drinking, too much dope, plus all the guilt. To tell the truth, the guilt has been the worst. All those mornings when Beetle pounded his forehead shouting, Regret! Regret!—these have taken their toll. The drawings in the tunnel of Beetle's consciousness are a little smudgy and dampness has eaten into the corners. Some are impossible to decipher. Take this one, for instance: a woman's face, but who she is or what she is doing is obscured by the wreckage. Here is a scene of a man being beaten. Here is another of a tombstone. Then vagueness, vagueness. But here is one clearer than the rest. It shows a young man leaning over a trash can in which there is some kind of creature. Is it a hairless monkey? No, it is a baby. And look, its feet are handcuffed together. How old is this baby? Certainly no more than a few days. It doesn't even have a diaper, just a towel under its bottom, and this at least allows us to determine its sex: a little boy baby. Glancing again at the man's face, we see that it is long, just like Beetle's, and has his same startled expression. Is the man putting the baby into the trash can or taking him out of the trash can? That's the trouble with wall paintings. There's no movement. And now the whole tunnel is shaking. Beetle must be pounding his head again. We better get out before the roof falls in.

Back on the sidewalk we see Beetle smacking his brow with his palm. He has a story to tell, but no one wants to hear it. If he could only transfer the pictures in his head to the walls of these buildings, then people might pay attention. There would be a real ruckus. He might even get on TV. Ahead of him, Beetle sees a girl with two long blond braids standing at the corner of Maiden Lane. She is flipping a coin and watching it glitter in the sunlight. Yes, the sun is just beginning to come out again. It might be a nice day after all.

Once more the glow of possibility suffuses Beetle's cheeks. He pushes the cart a little faster and it bounces over the cracks in the sidewalk. Objects rattle within it: clinking and clanking noises. Beetle imagines the girl's sympathetic ear turned toward him. He sees himself as easing the burden of his story off his shoulders and onto hers. But if his mind were not so damaged from abuse, he would realize he has seen this girl before. Yes, it is the same girl that he saw running down the gangplank of the *Boeski* when it tied up at the North Cove Yacht Harbor the previous morning. Her name is Beacon Luz and she has Wally Wallski's coin. There it is, flipping through the air, on one side a happy smile, on the other side a smirk.

Beetle brings the cart to a stop beside her. "Do you want to hear a sad story?" he asks.

Beacon Luz does not even turn in his direction. "Beat it, grease-ball." Even though she is only thirteen, she feels much more grown-up, and the world feels too crowded for her, too tight, as if it were a shoe that she was growing out of. She feels if she only had the power of Marduk the Magnificent, she could make herself some elbow room. Such is her ambition.

"This story will make you cry," says Beetle hopefully.

Beacon Luz digs into the blue blouse of her sailor suit and withdraws a small whistle. "See this whistle? If I blow this whistle, four big men will appear out of nowhere and pound you."

Beetle gives his cart a push. He knows about whistles like that one. But he wishes there were some way to begin his story with words powerful enough to grasp his listener by the lapels, words which would be undeniable, words not even invented yet. But all he has in his head are pictures. And between the crumbling cave paintings of his interior and the first words of their verbal enact-ment lies something like the dark space extending between the earth and the moon. All he can say is: "You're positive?"

"Don't say I didn't warn you," says Beacon Luz, lifting the whistle to her lips.

But by now Beetle is already ten feet away and moving down Pearl: rattle, rattle, rattle. Wall Street is only two blocks south. He will hang a right and go rest his shoulders against the New York Stock Exchange and let the building's sleeping financial power energize him.

Beacon Luz returns to flipping her coin. When it travels out on its little arc, a smidgen of anxiety swells within her; and when it returns to her palm, her happiness is like the rising sun. She flips it higher and higher as she moves slowly up Maiden Lane toward the Chase Manhattan Plaza, where her daddy is in a meeting. Up into the sunlight flies the golden coin, glittering and twinkling as it flips over and over. Down into the shadow it falls again, landing smack in the center of Beacon Luz's outstretched hand: sometimes with the smiling face looking up at her, sometimes with the leering demon. Behind Beacon Luz trails a gray Mercedes with tinted windows. It has a sinister aspect, but one needn't worry. The four big men inside, if not the friends of Beacon Luz, are at least paid to watch over her. They live, as it were, at the other end of her whistle.

But look, Beacon Luz is not paying attention! The sidewalk is cracked. She is not watching where she is placing her feet in their black patent-leather slippers. All her thoughts rest upon the golden coin, flipping up into the light and tumbling down into shadow. It is as if Beacon Luz were riding on the coin, as if her face were up there with the two others. But her face is not on the coin and it is a mistake to think otherwise, because suddenly her foot slips on a loose bit of concrete. As she stumbles, she turns her attention from the glittering arc of the coin and it doesn't fall back to her hand but slides between her open fingers and falls to the sidewalk, where it bounces and rolls into the street.

"My coin!" she cries. The coin rolls along the gutter and Beacon Luz runs after it. The coin jumps across cracks in the pavement and is deflected by pebbles and pieces of glass. How quickly it rolls. Beacon Luz leaps for it, lands on her belly and the coin darts between her outstretched fingers, rubbing between them with a kind of goodbye caress.

From her horizontal position she stares out across the gravel, and so close is the roadway to her chin that it resembles the surface of the moon. The coin bounces, clinks against a grating and disappears. A few seconds later she hears a faraway splash. With a practiced motion Beacon Luz draws the whistle from her sailor suit, inserts it in her mouth and blows. What a scream it makes! Every pigeon within a four-block radius experiences a pang of anxiety. And four big men come exploding out of the gray Mercedes. They wear gray double-breasted suits with padded shoulders and all their buttons are ready to pop.

"Where is he?" shouts one.

"Who hit you?" shouts another.

They pull Beacon Luz to her feet. "My coin!" she cries.

The four big men look around for someone to beat up, but the only person in sight is a crippled kid on a stumpboard about half a block away. Still, if the crippled kid were any closer, these guys would pound him.

"My lucky coin fell down the sewer," cries Beacon Luz. "You have to save it!"

It takes a few minutes for the four big men to understand what has happened. If these guys were geniuses, they would be in another line of work. They pull off the grating and stare down into the smelly blackness. Each wears a fedora and each has a hand clapped down on the crown to keep the fedora from tumbling down into the dark and each thinks how much he gets paid and how much it would be worth to climb into that foul hole and perhaps there just aren't that many bucks in Manhattan.

"I'd be happy to go down, miss," says one, "but my shoulders won't fit through the opening."

"And I can't swim," says another.

"My asthma's been acting up," says the third.

The fourth just stutters, "My, my, my . . ."

"If you don't get that coin," says Beacon Luz, "you'll go back to flippin burgers at Pizza Land."

"We'd need a rope," says the first.

"We'd need a light," says the second.

"There're rats down there," says the third.

"And even worse," says the last.

There is a small commotion at knee level. "Is something wrong?" asks a voice. It is the kid on the stumpboard. His name is Zapo and he is fifteen. He looks like a beggar but actually he sells syringes and has tips on horses running at Belmont. The four men see a greasy-looking kid in an oversized tweed jacket and with no legs: just two stumps about five inches long. Each wonders briefly how the kid lost his legs (a bus ran over them), then turns away.

"Beat it," says one.

"Get lost," says another.

"My coin fell down the sewer," cries Beacon Luz. Big tears roll down her cheeks. "And these bozos won't get it for me."

"I can get it," says Zapo.

"Oh, please, please . . ."

"But what will you give me for it?" asks Zapo.

"I'll give you anything in the world!"

Zapo considers. His face is gray with dirt and scabs spot his forehead. There are rags wrapped around his knuckles so he can push himself along on the sidewalk. "Will you let me live with you and be your pal?" he asks.

"Anything, anything!" says Beacon Luz.

"You're sure you'll let me live with you and be your pal and sleep in your little bed?"

"Of course," cries Beacon Luz. "I've always wanted a pal."

"Shake on it," says Zapo, stretching out a hand.

The four big men take a step forward, but Beacon Luz gives them a stern look and they move back. Beacon Luz takes Zapo's hand. "My pal," she says.

Zapo wheels himself to the open hole and looks down. One can hear the bubbling of water. If the smell emerging from the hole had a shape, it would resemble a *Tyrannosaurus rex*. "Don't let any-one swipe my stumpboard," says Zapo. He crawls off the board and disappears down the hole headfirst.

The four big guys scratch their heads. Beacon Luz waits and taps her foot. A helicopter passes overhead in the direction of the Downtown Heliport. Several minutes creep by.

Suddenly a hand emerges from the hole and grasps the edge of the grating. Then a second hand appears as well. Between its knuckles is the golden coin. On one side a kindly face, on the other a sneer. "Help me up," cries Zapo.

Beacon Luz stares down at the coin. Then she quickly bends over, plucks the coin from between Zapo's fingers and jumps back.

"Hey!" cries Zapo.

As if that cry were a signal, two of the big men step forward and each puts a fat black brogan on one of Zapo's small hands. They do this for about three seconds and when they step back the hands are gone. Moments later there is a splash. Beacon Luz is already walking toward the gray Mercedes. One of the big guys picks up the stumpboard and drops it down the hole. There is a second splash. The four big guys follow Beacon Luz to the Mercedes. She is not flipping the coin. It is buried in her left fist and she is squeezing it tightly, as if she wanted to squeeze it into her body or as if she wanted to hurt it.

The four big guys are happy. They feel they have done a good morning's work and they are ready for lunch. Pig knuckles is what they feel like today. Pig knuckles with applesauce and boiled potatoes and maybe a small green salad, because it is Sunday and they've got to be nice to their stomachs.

Of course many people are in the mood for lunch at this hour, but let us look at just two of them. The police detectives Brodsky and Gapski are finishing lunch in a First Avenue deli on the East Side. All through the meal they have been smoldering at each other. Ostensibly they are discussing the Rose White disappearance. A witness has come forward claiming that she saw two gorillas climbing down the side of Rose White's building on the night she disappeared. Nobody is happy with this information, but it has to be investigated. Sapperstein tells Brodsky and Gapski to get busy. Now they have talked to the woman and have made other discoveries as well. They have discussed what they have learned over their sandwiches, but in the past few minutes something has occurred to create an emotional impasse.

You see, both have ordered rice pudding for dessert and each thinks the other has ordered the pudding as a mockery of his own personal dignity. It would occur to neither that they have an equal fondness for rice pudding and each thinks the other has a sort of rice-pudding agenda. They face each other across the yellow Formica and each wears a gray fedora. Their fedoras are not like the fedoras worn by the four big men accompanying Beacon Luz. Those were fat healthy fedoras, glowing and well brushed. The fedoras of Gapski and Brodsky have been around the track. If in the precinct house an impromptu Mexican hat dance might erupt, these fedoras would be at their center. In fact, Brodsky and Gapski each hate the other's fedora and sometimes one will accidentally sit on the other's fedora, or step on it, or knock it downstairs, or throw it out the window, or drive over it in a patrol car. So each fedora bears the marks of Brodsky's and Gapski's detestation, and if, just out of the shop, each fedora once looked exactly like the other, now—crushed, beaten and approaching their end—they remain identical. Leaning forward over the table the men resemble mirror images of each other. Their chins are set similarly. Their eyes have a similar glare. Their right fists are clenched similarly around their spoons.

From the female insomniac, they have heard the story about the gorillas. And from the super of a nearby building they heard a story about a white van with two big furry guys inside and a lot of commotion. And from the driver of a garbage truck they heard a story of a white van with New Jersey plates and how a woman seemed to be screaming. But all of this has been forgotten during this tense moment over the rice pudding.

"You prick," says Brodsky, *sotto voce.*

"You penis," whispers Gapski.

"You turd," murmurs Brodsky.

"You shit," mutters Gapski.

Even in their curses they are destined to duplicate each other. Both lean forward until only a few inches separate them. They resemble book ends waiting for a book. What could be the title? *Trouble in Mind* or *Bad Times Ahead.* Then Brodsky takes his spoon, sticks it into his rice pudding, removes a good-sized dollop and catapults it viciously into Gapski's left eye. Let's hold this scene a moment. Do you see how the entire eye socket is coated with the shiny white rice pudding dotted with specks of cinnamon? The combined constabulatory expertise of Brodsky and Gapski— sixty years of police work—has been reduced to this dollop of rice pudding in the eye. The search for Rose White, the grieving heart of Michael Marmaduke, the tribulations of Primus Muldoon, the strange ambitions of Violet White—all have been condensed, abbreviated, diminished and downgraded to a dollop of rice pudding. And of course where there is one dollop there is bound to be another, just as soon as the action resumes and Gapski can shove his own spoon into his own pudding. But let us tiptoe away before that can be allowed to happen.

14

SPARROW

This is how Violet White tells the story to her companions.

"And the tall woman bent over Semele and asked, 'Why does he hide himself from you? If he really loves you, why won't he let you see him?' And Semele answered, 'It is night. He comes in darkness. How can I see him?' And the woman bent closer and asked, 'But haven't you wondered what he looks like? You let him take your body, yet his face is unknown to you? What if he is a monster?' And Semele answered, 'If he wanted me to see his face, he would show it to me.' And the woman's breath touched Semele's skin and the breath was cold. 'Are you such a slave to his desires?' she asked. 'Are you his slut that he can stick you to the mattress whenever he chooses? Don't you bear his child within you? Until you know him, you are only a thing he uses and discards. You are no better than the cloth he takes to clean himself.' And Semele answered, 'But how can I see his face when he hides it from me?' The woman touched Semele's cheek and where her finger rested the flesh turned cold. 'Ask him to grant you a wish. If he truly loves you, then he will grant it. Ask him to reveal himself. Ask to see his face.' "

Violet White pauses to take a drink of water. She wears her

nurse's uniform and a white cap is pinned to her black hair. Around her, reclining on cushions, are a dozen other young women dressed in white. They sprawl across each other, legs over legs, arms draped across each other. Several appear pregnant. The room has white walls and a white floor. It is a corner room with four windows: two facing east, two facing north. From down on the floor all we can see is blue sky. Several pigeons strut back and forth on a window ledge, and for a moment we hear their cooing. Violet White sets the glass on the floor and leans back against one of the women, resting her head between her breasts.

"But Semele was frightened and when her lover arrived that night in the darkness, she said nothing and her lover had his way with her and then departed. The next day the woman came again and asked, 'What if he is a monster? What if you bear a child with a monster's face? Think how people will treat you.' When the woman went away, Semele thought about her words. The woman seemed her friend but really she was her lover's wife and her words were the beginnings of her revenge. That night when her lover returned he could tell something was disturbing Semele and he asked, 'What is the matter?' and she said, 'Nothing, nothing is the matter.' But still he knew she was troubled and he asked again what bothered her. Then Semele said, 'If I asked a favor, would you grant it?' And her lover said, 'What sort of favor?' But his desire was satisfied and this made him generous. And Semele said, 'How could it be a true favor if you knew what it was beforehand? To give me what you can easily dispose of is to give me your charity.' And her lover laughed and said, 'All right, I will give you whatever you ask.' And Semele was quick and she entwined her fingers in the hair on his chest and she asked, 'Let me see your face, because I want to know what our child will look like.' And then her lover grieved because he knew he had been tricked and within Semele's request he saw the movements of his wife, the marks of her jealousy. 'You cannot see my face,' he answered. 'Then what are your favors worth if you withdraw them so easily?' asked Semele. 'You don't know what you ask for,' said her lover. And Semele tugged at his chest hairs and taunted him. 'I only ask for what is mine. I ask for what you promised. If your word is worth nothing, then the secret we share is also nothing and why should

I honor it?' Her lover grew angry and realized he had no choice
and must take a path that would destroy Semele and that the path
had been devised by his wife. 'I will show myself tomorrow night,'
he told her."

Violet White pauses again. She is aware of the eyes of the other
women upon her. Despite their apparent languor, she can feel their
attentiveness. She sips her water and glances toward the window.
She tries to picture Michael Marmaduke, to give palpability to the
thought of him walking across a room or sitting in a chair. She
imagines him being transformed into Marduk the Magnificent, as
if he took all the light that lay outside of himself and thrust it deep
inside himself. A yellow cat enters from another room and walks
around the outside of the group of women. Several women reach
toward it but the cat avoids their touch. It moves to a triangle of
sunlight on the floor and lies down within it. Then it begins washing itself.

"The next night Semele's lover came after everyone was asleep.
And he seemed hungrier and more passionate than before and he
took her without letting her speak. Her hands could feel the muscles of his body and their great strength and she wondered how she
could have thought he might be ugly and she almost regretted
asking to see his face. But she was also curious and she told herself
that she needed to see him for the sake of the child she carried
within her. And when her lover was finished and rolled away, she
said, 'Remember your promise.' For a moment he made no response, then he moved back and she heard his feet upon the floor
and in the darkness she could see the shape of his body, a greater
darkness. He's getting a light, she thought. Then, all at once, the
light began and briefly she thought it was the candle, but it grew
brighter and was too bright for a candle, too bright for the largest
fire, and briefly she had a glimpse of face, the goldenness of his
skin and great golden beard, but it too brightened and a great heat
pushed out of it and the heat burned her and she covered her face
with her arm and then her arm began to burn and her skin began
to blister and she could smell the burning of her hair.

"Her lover watched her burn. Her skin blackened and the bed-
clothes caught fire. He watched her twist within the flames trying
to cry out. At last he reached into the fire and he drew out her

baby, Bromios, a fetus of six months. Then he took a knife and slit open his thigh and he placed the baby within the wound and with fishing line he sewed it up again. And all that was left of Semele was a pile of white ash on the floor. Her lover reached down and took a few flecks of ash and put them on his tongue. Then he departed. And this is why Bromios was called the twice-born, the god of the double door."

Violet White glances around her. One of the pregnant women is rubbing her belly. Another rolls away. Violet can feel their attention drift back to their own lives. She walks to the window, and as she approaches the glass, two pigeons, one white and one black, fly up into the air. She follows their path until they disappear around the side of the building, then she looks north toward the Williamsburg Bridge. Ahead of her are the four smokestacks of the power station on 14th Street. She considers the goldenness of Marduk the Magnificent and how his muscles would feel beneath her fingers. She thinks of the size of him and how he would feel on top of her and how her breath would be pushed from her body. It amazes her that her stupid sister has never slept with him, that she has been saving herself for her wedding. And where is her sister now? Is she alive? And what does Violet White hope about her sister? Better not even ask.

An autumn haze covers the blue sky. Violet thinks of the trees turning color outside of the city. She knows that the gym where Marduk trains is called the Meat Market and that it is in New Jersey. She imagines it surrounded by maples and oaks now turning bright yellows and reds. She imagines Marduk continuing to sculpt his body and how the light from the autumn colors casts a glow across the room and how the sweat on his body must shine. But it is not Marduk but the kitten Michael Marmaduke. Then she thinks of Deep Rat. This is the day he will begin his teaching.

There are no windows in the Meat Market, only two television monitors: one shows whoever appears at the front door and the other shows the parking lot (there have been break-ins). Both screens are black-and-white. Although part of a tree can be seen at the edge of the parking lot, its leaves are various shades of gray.

In any case, Michael Marmaduke's eyes are shut. Dressed in shorts and a Gold's Gym T-shirt, he lies on an exercise bench holding two forty-pound dumbbells high above his chest. Slowly he lowers them to the side to below the level of the bench and it feels that his arms are being ripped from their sockets. Then he raises the dumbbells high above his chest so they touch, a little click like a kiss. Then he lowers them again. From across the room it appears as if Michael is attempting to fly, or perhaps he is already flying: the slow wingstrokes of an albatross high above the lonely waters of Antarctic seas.

Michael's thoughts are elsewhere. Although part of his mind concentrates on the dumbbell flyes, the remembering part is focused on two weeks he spent on Cape Cod with Rose White in July. They rented bikes and each day Rose White would pack a lunch and they would bicycle off to the National Seashore to find a new beach. Rose White's skin is very delicate and she wore white muslin from her neck to her ankles, as well as a broad-brimmed straw hat with a pink ribbon. Michael wore dark glasses and a baseball cap so he wouldn't be recognized. Several times he wore a false mustache that Dentata had given him. Each day he strapped a pair of forty-pound dumbbells to the back of his bike and used only the highest gear in order to toughen his thighs. Then, after they found a beach, he would work on his pecs and abs as Rose White read out loud from Jane Austen. They had finished all of *Pride and Prejudice* and half of *Sense and Sensibility*. Michael simply couldn't get over how polite people used to be.

He and Rose White rented adjoining motel rooms in North Truro and pushed their beds against the wall so they were separated by only an inch of particle board. Michael was certain he could feel Rose White's warmth through the wall. After going to bed they tapped out messages early into the morning. They even bought a book on Morse code and when Michael proposed marriage on the last day of their vacation, he did it in dots and dashes at two a.m. Four times Rose White asked him to repeat himself to make sure she hadn't misunderstood. The next morning, when he brought her breakfast, he placed a diamond engagement ring between the two halves of her English muffin.

As the dumbbells click above Michael's head, he wonders where the engagement ring is now. In his mind he replays the videotape that he gave to Brodsky and Gapski. Again he sees Rose White's delicate hands chained above her. Was she wearing the engagement ring? Michael doesn't think so. Again he hears her voice, "Michael, you must save me! I'm being . . ." and then nothing.

Michael swings himself off the bench and puts the dumbbells on the floor. Then he presses his hands to his head. If Rose White was kidnapped on Thursday, she has now been gone three days. And what has been done? Michael thinks of his quest the previous evening for the Master of Ceremonies. He feels certain that if Jack Molay had not rescued him from the Mars Boys, he would have gone on from one peculiar group to another.

"And what have you learned from your evening?" Jack Molay asked him.

"Not to take rides from strangers."

"No, you learned many people are engaged in defining the nature of evil and there's great disagreement as to its source."

"Why don't the police arrest those guys, those Snakes and Cainites and Dancers?"

"They do, but they find it difficult to understand their preoccupations. When the police discover the corpses of five Cainites, they blame it on drugs and not pre-Augustine heresy. Language is reductive and explanations are the most reductive of all. Think of the definitions of life and how little they describe life. The Vals and the others are theological pessimists who are engaged, to the best of their abilities, in defining the nature of evil in order to eradicate it."

"They seem more interested in eradicating each other."

"That is their confusion. Before they combat evil, they have to combat all that disagrees with them. Evil begins with anything which is other."

"Just like the Yugoslavians."

"Or any mixture of groups. But do you remember what St. Paul wrote to the Corinthians? He said, 'There must be heretics among you so that those who are genuine may be recognized.'"

"And this will help me find Rose White?"

"Your question is also reductive," said Jack Molay. "You ask how to find Rose White, but that might be the wrong question.

Knowledge is a matter of knowing what questions to ask."

"So what should I ask?"

But Jack Molay refused to answer directly. "There must be crooks so that the honest can be recognized. There must be heroes so that the cowardly can be recognized."

"That's all determined by the Wrestling Association. Who's a crook, who's a hero—they figure it out beforehand."

"And does the word 'darkness' define the dark?"

"It describes it. Anyway, you just flick a switch and there it is. Dark is the absence of light."

"Is evil just the absence of good?"

Michael felt exasperated. "Why do you have to be so philosophical all the time?"

"Why indeed?" Jack Molay answered. "But listen, if your gentleness is a virtue, your passivity is a fault. You must pursue your ignorance and destroy it. You must activate yourself."

"Meaning what?"

"Meaning you should have stayed with the Mars Boys."

Twelve hours later the conversation still sits badly with Michael. He doesn't see how the evening brought him closer to Rose White, yet he also feels that he never got his words fixed on what the evening was about, as if his words were a torn paper bag and the subject—whatever it was—kept tumbling out again.

It should be understood that despite Michael's perfect physique, he is, in a way, disabled. Had he worked on his mind as he has worked on his body, he could be a modern-day Aristotle. But he hasn't, and consequently his character has been inexactly formed. Truly, it can be said that he has never felt fear. He never thinks of the future and rarely considers the past. He has never been faced with an insurmountable problem. He has never learned to think. Even though he graduated from college, that required little cogitation, while the changes in his life were mostly caused by outside stimuli. He took the job with Paterson Parks and Rec because it fell open at the right moment. He began wrestling because Primus Muldoon discovered him. Michael is kind, moderately intelligent, unambitious, and has floated through his twenty-five years like a small white cloud through blue sky.

Consider now his dilemma when faced with the disappearance

of Rose White. Without anger, aggression or ambition, Michael is at a disadvantage. There is nothing crafty about him, nothing sly, nothing that weighs the odds and seeks an opening. And although in the ring he may give the impression of aggression and craftiness, that is only the script. Also, it is Marduk the Magnificent, while he is Michael Marmaduke.

Michael walks to the parallel bars. He must work on the lower parts of his pectorals and complete a set of parallel-bar dips before starting his cable crossovers. He jumps onto the bars and supports himself with his arms straight beneath him. A dozen other men and women are working out, and the gym smells of sweat and liniment. Dentata is doing leg curls. Liquidity is at the lat pulldown machine and the weights clink over and over. Each time he pulls the bar behind his neck, a lock of red hair falls across his brow. Liquidity is often cast as a villain. He has played Cain and Genghis Khan. But apart from his training, he spends much of his free time as a volunteer at a soup kitchen. It was just the chance of being born with high cheekbones and red hair that has made him suitable for villainous roles.

Across the room Muldoon is arguing loudly with an ex–midget wrestler who is high up in the Wrestling Association. Earlier, Muldoon told Michael, "Anything I can do to find Rose White, believe me, I'm in your corner." And Michael knows this is true. But what Michael wants is for Muldoon to take charge of the search because—one—he trusts him and—two—he doesn't know how to do it himself. But Muldoon has his own life. That's the trouble with people, thinks Michael as he lowers himself on the parallel bars, the center of your life is not the center of their life. Your only rescuer can be yourself. And the articulation of this commonplace fills him with regret.

Muldoon is puffing out his mustache and shouting, "D'you think Van Gogh painted by numbers? D'you think Beethoven had one of those little drum machines and let strangers fiddle with the dials? How can I create if you tell me what to create?"

The ex–midget wrestler stands in front of Muldoon like a bollard pin to which the yacht of Muldoon's frustration is moored. In the ring he had been called Crow; now days he is Johnny Korzeniewski. He is completely bald and his scalp shines as if waxed.

"You're not supposed to create," he says, "you're supposed to direct. Maybe you can direct creatively, but mostly you're supposed to follow instructions."

"Do you think Mozart followed instructions?" shouts Muldoon.

"You're not Mozart."

"But this is a stupid idea! Satan versus Santa Claus? Who made up such lunacy?"

"They both wear red suits and have tails. It will be a visual thing."

"Santa doesn't have a tail!" Muldoon's face grows purple.

"He has a white piece of fluff on the back of his suit. It could be a tail, a sort of bunny tail. Look at their names—Satan, Santa —it's only dyslexia that makes them different. We're billing them as brothers and one of them went bad. Brother of darkness, brother of light. It will be a grudge match. Satan has his pitchfork and Santa has his bag of tricks."

"Get out!" says Muldoon, making a threatening gesture.

"You refuse to do it?"

Muldoon deflates a little. "I just have to think about it."

Johnny Korzeniewski is not a bad guy and besides he is only carrying a message. He puts his hand on Muldoon's arm. "Haven't you ever wondered who was stronger, Satan or Santa Claus?"

Primus Muldoon pounds his fists against his forehead. "Absolutely never!"

"Well, millions have," says Johnny Korzeniewski, "and now the Wrestling Association, through your creative genius, will show the world who is toughest."

"I am hardly able to wait," says Primus Muldoon.

Michael is just finishing his last set of parallel-bar dips when he sees a man walking toward him across the gym, someone he feels he has never seen but who has a familiar unfamiliarity. The man wears a double-breasted dark suit with padded shoulders and beneath his coat there appears to be no body, or at least the fabric is so loose that there appears to be nothing but cloth in the way that a cartoon ghost appears to be nothing but white sheet. The man has a distinctive widow's peak that divides his narrow forehead and his eyes resemble black marbles. Michael may not recognize this fellow, but we do. This is Deep Rat, and he looks so hungry that we begin to worry, because we know that the hungers of such a creature as Deep Rat are not appeased by food.

"I have come to help you," says Deep Rat, and his sentence is one hundred percent toneless.

"How so?" Michael wonders if this fellow is going to try to sell him insurance. From across the room he sees Dentata looking at Deep Rat suspiciously.

"I was in a bar and I overheard a man say he had seen a videotape of a woman chained to a wall and he laughed and said the woman was your girlfriend."

We must imagine Michael Marmaduke staggering back, although he really didn't. He is too stunned to move. But even he, deep inside, feels that he has staggered and nearly fallen.

"A woman?" he asks.

"A young woman, I forget her name."

"Rose White?"

"Perhaps that was it."

"You didn't go to the police?"

Deep Rat stares into Michael Marmaduke's face, and Michael realizes that the man never blinks, as if his eyes were the kind one buys in a taxidermist's shop. "I didn't go to the police because I didn't know if it was serious. I felt I should talk to you about it and then you could decide what to do. After all, she's your girlfriend."

"What's the bar?" Michael's brain is working very fast but the movement is like wheels in deep mud: lots of action but no forward motion. He continues to feel stunned.

"The Blood Factory."

This is a bar in Lower Manhattan not far from the mouth of the Holland Tunnel which attracted participants in the pseudo-violent sports: wrestling, roller derbies, gladiatorial combats, ninja scrimmages. Although Michael doesn't drink, he had once gone to meet a friend. The bar, for all its bloody demeanor, was one of the few places a wrestler could socialize without being gawked at. No cameras were allowed and the bouncers discouraged patrons beneath a certain professional body mass.

Michael takes a step toward Deep Rat, who is perhaps eight inches shorter and half as wide. "Who was talking about her?"

"I don't know his name but I've seen him there before."

"What were you doing there?"

"I'm studying to be a referee. I go there to make contacts. If you want, we can go later. Even if this man isn't there, we can find out who he is. Don't worry about the trouble, I'm one of your biggest fans. Why do you think your girlfriend is chained to a wall?"

"She was kidnapped Thursday night. I've been waiting to hear from her kidnappers. You think I should call the police?"

"Sure. I mean, if you can't handle it yourself. I'm just trying to help."

"What time should we go?" Michael realizes that the small man speaks without the slightest emotional inflection.

"Around ten."

"Okay if I bring a friend?"

"Whatever you feel comfortable with," says Deep Rat.

Just two short scenes and we can end the chapter. Oddly enough, both concern explosions of anger. The first deals with Wally Wallski's wife Claudine. Let's look at her for a moment. She is not an attractive woman, and while this remark may seem to be the death gargle of the stymied voice of male hegemony, it is also the view of everyone—male and female—who has made her acquaintance. Power is what she likes, and if she had a modicum of patience, she might have become governor. But she is like a fisherman who keeps yanking her hook at every imagined tug. Now days we understand that her unpleasantness is probably caused by an excess of peptic acid or a mild chemical imbalance in her cerebral cortex. To call her greedy or mean-spirited or bullying is to privilege those adjectives that rose to popularity in the Romantic era and have been put to sleep in this age of Nuevo Reason, or almost. These are not matters of right and wrong. Claudine is our sister and we must see that to foreground the differences between her and ourselves does not mean that she is at fault but that we are confused. At most we can say she is a trifle pushy, but even that aggressiveness is the result of her being the plaything of male hegemony. She is the victim of her chemistry and environment.

And when we say that she is physically unattractive, aren't we privileging definitions of beauty which are not only bound to outmoded Romanticism but also to a capitalist system of spend-spend-spend that prejudices those of us that cannot appear on the cover of *Cosmopolitan*? So what if Claudine is somewhat heavy? Who devaluates heaviness? So what if she constantly keeps her hair in rollers? Who are we to define what hair should be? So what if her round face is as red as a beet and her clenched fists are raised above her husband, who kneels before her with his eyes squinched shut?

Claudine stands in front of the mantel of her new twenty-by-twenty-five-foot living room of her seven-room condo on West End Avenue. She wears an ankle-length black sable coat which she found in the closet. You can tell the sables were wild and not raised in little cages because of the white tips within their fur. The living room is furnished with a Bokhara carpet and a leather sofa and chairs. A Bonnard watercolor of a garden scene hangs above the mantel. And what is Claudine saying with force enough to propel little drops of spit into the air around her husband's head?

"You little fuck, when I say this shit heap is too small, I mean it's too small! You go back to that crook and tell him you want a red-brick townhouse on Gramercy Park! You saved his life, didn't you? Well, he owes you one, the asshole! You tell him that the fucking tap in the fucking bathroom drips and there's no champagne in the fridge!"

Our second scene foregrounds the father of Beacon Luz, who is a real creep. He is nicknamed the Snowman, not just because of the temperature of his heart, nor because of his connection to drugs, nor because his eyes resemble two black coals, but also because in his physical shape he truly resembles a snowman. He is a great white blob. With him it may be doubted that his behavior is due to chemistry or environment. He was simply born bad. Bad blood, bad genes, bad chromosomes—the whole porridge should have been thrown out. And what has his badness brought him? Immense wealth. Leisure time. Beautiful women. Where many people faced with a possible illegal action hesitate and say, "Better not take the chance," the Snowman has surged forward and filled his pockets with gold.

At the moment he is standing at the head of the dinner table with his wife (a crushed and abject slave), his mistress (soon to be replaced), half a dozen cronies whose conversation consists entirely of phrases like "Wow, that was a smart thing to do, boss" and "Wow, I guess you told him, boss" and "Wow, boss, you're really the baddest guy around!" and his only child, Beacon Luz, who is staring down at her plate.

In the doorway on the far side of the room we glimpse a legless kid on a stumpboard wearing an oversized tweed jacket. His hair is matted with filth and his narrow face is smudged and gray. Even though we see him for only three seconds before the door slams shut, we recognize him as Zapo, the fifteen-year-old syringe salesman who rescued Beacon Luz's lucky coin from the sewer. It is because of Zapo that the Snowman is shouting.

"You told him he could fuckin sleep in your fuckin little bed? Are you outta your fuckin mind?"

It is hard on the page to indicate the force of the Snowman's words. Perhaps they should have been printed in another color: something bright and forceful. To say the Snowman is angry is insufficient. If the Wolf in the story of the Three Little Pigs had had such lungs, he could have blown down the brick house as easily as those made of sticks and straw. When the Snowman yells all the napkins flutter and the cowlicks on his cronies' heads hop about.

"You fuckin told him you'd be his fuckin little pal?"

"He saved my lucky coin," says Beacon Luz into her plate. "And besides, I didn't really mean it."

"Where is this fuckin coin?" shouts the Snowman. "You know what that slimeball would do in your little bed?"

The Snowman reaches out an oversized hand and snatches the coin from Beacon Luz's fingers. Without glancing at it, he hurls it toward the open window. Now, watch carefully. The golden coin spins over the heads of the sycophantic cronies, over the head of the soon-to-be-replaced mistress and over the head of the abject wife, it spins toward the window and we can see both the angel's smile and the demon's sneer, it spins through the bronze aluminum frame and out into the Manhattan sky. We are on the thirty-fourth floor of a building at the southern tip of Manhattan. The coin we assume will fall to the street. But at that moment, outside the window, a hand appears and catches the coin in the way a fan sitting along the third base line might snatch a foul ball. The hand snatches the coin and disappears. Let us say at once that the hand belongs to Sparrow and that he is a window cleaner. We shall meet him again.

15

MULDOON: LIVE DANGEROUSLY

What does it mean to be Primus Muldoon? It means being a complete solitary, an outsider without the comfort of a single friend. Between me and the vast social void which passes for contemporary American culture, there gapes an infinity. No one who possesses friends can grasp the meaning of solitude. Not even if he is surrounded by people who hate him is a man truly alone. And do you know what it means to be genuinely solitary? I doubt it. Because he who is alienated is also unparalleled. He who is desolate is also unique. Wherever there have been powerful dictatorships, totalitarian governments, tyrannical religions, wherever there has been intolerance it has hated the solitary thinker, for such thought can create a hiding place that no tyranny can reach: the cavern of inwardness, the labyrinth of the heart. This cavern is where the lonely hide and where they encounter their greatest danger, for the smell of this cavern aggravates all tyrants. They can't stand the freedom of the solitary thinker, the philosopher who has thrown off the shackles of convention and cultural expectation.

"Belief in truth," wrote Nietzsche, "begins with skepticism about everything held to be true." Can you see how such thought is the province of the true solitary? Consider wrestling and how the so-called sports critics see it as false. Wrestling for them is not sport but spectacle. They argue that true sport, such as baseball, football, etc., imitates life, which presupposes certain definitions—certain conventional ideas—as to the nature of life. In fact the so-called sports critics view wrestling in the way that deconstructionist critics view literature. Namely, bogus. They see it as full of lies, which presupposes certain definitions—certain conventional ideas—as to not only an approach to truth but also the very existence of truth. They point to their Ph.D.s and claim to know better than anyone in history. And as the deconstructionists privilege the essay, so do the sports critics privilege conventional sport. Both groups lay claim to some faddish definition of truth without realizing that truths are merely the irrefutable errors of mankind.

Wrestling, like literature, is not an imitation of reality. It is metaphor. You say the best man or woman doesn't win in wrestling? Well, what of it? You say that the actions are not spontaneous but follow a script. Doesn't a script exist in life as well? In wrestling everything has been stripped away except black and white, good and evil. Only the absolute exists. In wrestling, everything is presented completely. Nothing remains in the shade. Each action throws off its parasitic meanings and offers to the public a pure and full signification, rounded like Nature. What is given is a perfectly lucid metaphor of reality, an ideal understanding of things. One experiences the euphoria of man raised above the daily morass of ambiguity, uncertainty and equivocation. Here at last signs correspond to causes, without obstacle, without evasion, without contradiction.

What wrestling gives us is the substance of literature without the diluting presence of language. True, it is violent and often cruel, but isn't it time to admit that violence and cruelty have their virtues? I welcome all signs that a more manly and warlike age is about to begin, an age in which valor will again become honorable. This age will carry heroism into the pursuit of knowledge and wage wars for the sake of thoughts and their consequences. To this end we need warriors who cannot leap into being out of nothing; men and women characterized by cheerfulness, patience and contempt for all great vanities, as well as by magnanimity in victory and tolerance regarding the small vanities of the vanquished; men and women possessed of keen and free judgment; men and women who are accustomed to command with assurance and are no less ready to obey when circumstances require; men and women who are in greater danger, more fruitful and happier! Michael Marmaduke is such a man. Dentata is such a woman. And Thrombosis, Liquidity, Cashback and Prime Rib.

Consider how my heroes are seen by the audience. They are the metaphysical "others" of the spectators. They become their representatives, the tools to lift them from the trivial and enable them to strike a blow against all that is frustrating and penning them in. Conversely, the villains represent all the trouble in one's life: the cop, the bureaucrat, the bad doctor, the sleazy dentist. And through their heroic "others," the spectators at last defeat all that has defeated them until they feel vindicated and triumphant.

But why should the spectators need a metaphysical other? you ask. The answer is they have become corrupted. The majority of men and women are frightened and lazy. They conceal themselves behind their opinions and customs. Even though each knows that he or she has only one chance on earth, they hide this fact out of fear of their fellow creatures who insist that everyone must behave the same way. But why should a person fear his fellow creatures and act as they do? Simply out of sloth, because to behave honestly would make trouble. It would make each person a nuisance. It's hard work to be honest. Only those who possess an artistic temperament hate this indolent life of borrowed ideas and conventional opinions. They are the only ones who dare to speak out. They become everyone's bad conscience. They are the only ones who believe in the uniqueness of every human being. Only these solitaries show this uniqueness as beautiful and worth study. Only these managers and trainers of great wrestlers. And when an artistic temperament like this appears to hate his fellow creatures, it is only their laziness that he hates: a laziness that makes them look like products off an assembly line, that makes them seem indifferent and unworthy of instruction or companionship. A member of society, a spectator, a wrestling fan who wants to discover his true uniqueness must overthrow his complacency and cease being comfortable with himself. He must listen to his conscience, which tells him: "Be yourself! What you are doing is not really you." By teaching valor and cruelty in the name of virtue, my wrestlers teach the audience not to be frightened and lazy. They teach them how to live.

We know of course that each wrestler's Gimmick is not the truth, but an amalgam of conventional definitions pretending to be true. In this conventionality lies the tragedy of wrestling. What occurs in the ring is not Right versus Wrong but False Right versus False Wrong with a third character, the audience, fiercely believing in the battle. And even if False Right seems to win, he or she wins against types (the bureaucrat, the tax collector, the policeman), and the types will ultimately triumph. False Right is fighting against the sea. Marduk the Magnificent seems to win but his enemies are legion. There will always be another. To fight against the supposed villains of society is to accept the clichés of society, to accept society's definitions of right and wrong.

And where do these ideas of False Right and False Wrong come from? They come from the Wrestling Association, and they are an example of decadence, which is the result of feeling guilty for being powerful. The power is turned inward. The power exists to protect the status quo, not to change it. Instead of freeing the managers like myself, like Primus Muldoon, to create their own stories, they force a story upon us. But that is not a story, that is a cartoon. And that too is a Gimmick, the Gimmick of how the society sees itself. It is designed to keep the society free from change. And what if that Gimmick were destroyed?

Behind the glorification of wrestling by the Wrestling Association I find the same thought as behind the praise of any nonpersonal activity for the public benefit: the fear of everything individual. At the bottom of the Association's belief that wrestling must present societal stereotypes of right and wrong is the idea that wrestling is the best policy, the best way to let off steam, that wrestling keeps everybody in harness. This idea of wrestling obstructs the development of reason and the wish for independence. For such a cheapening of wrestling—the stereotypes that the Association foists upon us—uses up much of the audience's nervous energy and takes it away from reflection, brooding, dreaming, worry, love and hatred. The Wrestling Association always sets a small goal before one's eyes and permits easy satisfactions. It argues that a society in which the members continually work hard will have more security: and security is now adored as the supreme goodness. Security, my friends, is death. It is rot and corruption! The secret of the greatest fruitfulness and the greatest enjoyment of existence is to live dangerously! Live at war with your peers and yourselves!

16

LAVA LAMP

Let us rest a moment atop this streetlight on the corner of Vestry and Greenwich. It is nighttime, ten o'clock, and few people are about. Do you see that brick warehouse with its black double door? Do you see how it has an illuminated great splatter of scarlet above the lintel? It looks like blood pulsing from a wound nearly three yards across, and the fat drops seem to slide down the wall to form a pool on the sidewalk. If you stood next to it, you would see it is truly in motion. Red stuff in plastic tubing circulating from the great wound above the door, trickling down the wall in several plastic-covered streams, then gathering in a plastic receptacle on the sidewalk, where, presumably, it is pumped to the top again. This is the Blood Factory.

Now let's observe who goes inside. See those two dark shapes gliding along the sidewalk? It requires only a moment to realize they are wearing roller blades. How long before every mugger owns a pair? Purse snatchers at thirty miles per hour. If we look closely, we realize these shapes are male and female despite their almost complete physical resemblance: black leather pants, black leather jackets cut off at the shoulders to expose tattooed arms, silver spikes attached to their elbows, bright red Mohawk haircuts and about thirty-five (each) little rings through their noses, ears and lips. One can also infer several tongue studs, nipple rings, perhaps a penis ring, a clitoris ring. Can you imagine the pain if one of his rings links with one of hers in a moment of passion? Better not think about it. Personally, we often wonder, What if their mothers saw them?—those dear little baby ears now pierced with so many holes, those dear little baby noses. It is not that this heavy metal couple on roller blades is in any way reproachable, just that they have journeyed such a distance from the womb.

As we watch them enter the Blood Factory, we draw certain conclusions about what lies inside. But let's look at this next couple coming up from Hudson Street. Not only are they dressed as cowboys, but both are bowlegged and totter on the tall heels of their Tony Lama boots. It is hard to see their faces because of their ten-gallon hats. The man twirls a lasso and the woman wears fifty petticoats, each a different color. As they enter the Blood Factory, we begin to modify our earlier assumptions.

Now look closely. Here comes a cab. It draws to a stop before the shimmering pool of blood and the back door opens. At first we are aware of darkness, then of hair. It appears to be two great monkeys, no, they are gorillas, and as they hurry inside the Blood Factory, we realize we have met them before. Is it possible there are more than two gorillas even in as big a place as New York? Quite unlikely.

Several minutes go by and then we see three figures walking up from Hudson. The one in the middle we recognize as Michael Marmaduke. The combination of size with that golden hair makes him instantly recognizable. He wears a brown leather jacket and jeans. No costumes for him, thank you very much. On his left is a smaller figure who doesn't seem to be walking within the shadow so much as drawing it around him. He appears to wear the shadow as a garment. See how he slides along? Even without seeing his face we know it is Deep Rat.

On Michael's right is the wrestler Liquidity, who we first recognize by his red hair as he passes under a streetlight. Like Deep Rat's his gestures have a certain fluidity, but while Deep Rat's fluidity is a movement away, an avoidance, Liquidity's is always toward. After all, he is a wrestler and he is prepared, at least visually, to do battle. He has been here before and is appropriately dressed: black pants, black shirt, black cape, a silver chain around his neck. He is Loki, the trickster, the one it is easy to underestimate.

Just what *is* appropriate at the Blood Factory? you ask. Perhaps it is helpful to learn that the owner of the Blood Factory, an ex-wrestler called Scab, had originally considered naming his bar the Gimmick Redux. The Blood Factory is where the Gimmick is freed from its chains and that boundary between reality and fantasy is at last eradicated. Yet if Primus Muldoon were with us, he might ask, "But isn't that a Gimmick as well?"

Inside, the room seems filled with smoke, but whether it is real smoke or fake smoke is hard to tell. Within this murk are rotating colored spotlights which illuminate different areas of smoke, changing them from red to green to yellow. Maybe it is not smoke but fog. The bar is in the center of this space like a hub inside a wheel. There is music of a sort: several atonal guitars and a percussion section of kitchen utensils. Some people are dancing, but most are standing around, sipping drinks and looking at everyone except at their ostensible companions.

The two bouncers are big, bald-headed men in leopard skins and their job is to turn away the straight and narrow. Liquidity slaps them five. Michael nods. Deep Rat looks past them to more important matters. In truth, Michael is not altogether happy. He dislikes what he calls license, the chance of events going haywire. There must be three hundred people in the Blood Factory, and Michael is perhaps farthest from the concept of Gimmick. His Gimmick—Marduk the Magnificent—is also his burden. It means that people keep bothering him, wanting his autograph, wanting to wrestle. They think he is Marduk the Magnificent every day of the week, whereas actually he is Michael Marmaduke, ex–Parks and Rec employee and orphan boy from the Delaware Water Gap who considers East Stroudsburg, Pa, his home. He has a certain innocence, a certain naiveté. Others might find him shallow or dull. He looks at the gladiators, wrestlers and cowboys and he feels they are playing dress-up.

But Primus Muldoon would argue that a healthy life requires conflict. It is necessary to identify your opposite and struggle with it, not to become your opposite—that would be impossible—but to become something in between. See this oversized fellow at the bar drinking a martini and dressed as Attila the Hun? He is a milkman from Bridgewater who believes that it makes him a better milkman to masquerade on weekends as a mass murderer. Holding a knife between his teeth on Sunday makes the cream taste sweeter on Monday. All these people are caught up in a struggle with who they are not in order to change who they are. Perhaps across town there is a bar of real murderers, rapists and lovers of carnage who are sitting around in little pink dresses drinking tea. These cucumber sandwiches are just divine, they say. Pass me another onion cake, they say.

Even a naked corpse displays Gimmick. Breasts have been added to or decreased, bodies have been tanned or left white. Biceps have been monkeyed with, hair dyed or coiffed, bottoms trimmed, faces lifted. Plastic surgeons have grown rich. Even a skeleton has elements of Gimmick: gold teeth, legs shortened, nose straightened, bones smoothed down. Only as a handful of ash is a human being free of Gimmick, although coffin, burial plot and noble tombstone contain Gimmick as well. And what is Gimmick again? How you want to see yourself and how you want to be seen. Truly, one's Gimmick is one's Significant Other.

And is Michael Marmaduke really free of Gimmick? Let's say the pleasures he receives as Marduk the Magnificent confuse him. Let's say he has ambivalent feelings. The gentle part of his nature looks with apprehension at his strength, seeing it as violence; the strong part of his nature looks with scorn at his gentleness, seeing it as mush. Consequently, he is torn.

Michael stands near the bar sipping a nonalcoholic beer (Kaliber) and feeling ill at ease. Several complete strangers have greeted him affectionately, slapping him on the back and making him cough. Some fellow dressed as a panzer commander has asked if he wanted to wrestle and Liquidity gave him a shove. Deep Rat is off looking for the person who has seen a video of a girl chained to a wall. Every now and then Michael notices him resurface among the crowd like a prairie dog on a cartoon show.

Within these first minutes not much has happened worthy of attention except for one event. When Michael entered the Blood Factory and the name *Marduk, Marduk* buzzed around the room like a ball around a roulette wheel, there was a slight commotion toward the back as two big hairy fellows headed for the rear exit. Have you ever seen gorillas walk on tiptoe? They hoped to make their getaway without fuss. But perhaps Deep Rat noticed, because there is little that escapes his quick dark eyes. A door slammed and Michael felt an unexplainable chill. "A goose walked across my grave," he said to himself.

"So how come you don't hang out here?" Liquidity is saying. He has to raise his voice over the general noise.

Michael glances at the crowd. Although the room is jammed, there is an open space around him which exists so he can be seen. Michael neither likes nor dislikes this. It only strikes him as curious. "I don't tend to go out much at night," he says, "unless it's to get a sandwich or see Rose White."

Liquidity has met Rose White and likes her, mildly, but she is not, he feels, his kind of girl. She's a girl you'd be afraid of hurting if you hugged her too hard. Even holding her hand, you might accidentally crack a few bones. Kissing her, you might chip her tooth.

"I don't suppose Rose White's ever been to the Blood Factory," he says.

Michael can't imagine it.

A moment later, Deep Rat shows up dragging a large man in the camouflage fatigues of a Desert Storm commando. Michael is impressed that although Deep Rat is half the soldier's size, he is the one showing the power.

"This is Blackhead," says Deep Rat in his toneless voice. "He's the one who told me about seeing a videotape of a girl being tortured."

"I didn't see it, I only heard about it," says Blackhead, nervously. "I was just bragging. It's wrong to brag."

Michael is struck by the man's fear, which makes him look hunched, makes his eyes seem loose in their sockets.

"Where'd you hear about it?" he asks.

"I forget," says Blackhead.

Deep Rat is wearing boots to make him appear taller. He plants a heel on Blackhead's instep and Blackhead groans.

"Don't hurt him," says Michael. He puts a hand under Blackhead's chin so that the Desert Storm commando is forced to look at him. Blackhead has short-cropped gray hair and there are black charcoal marks under his eyes. "Please, that woman is my fiancée. If you know something, I wish you'd say."

"You promise not to tell?" Blackhead's fear is almost a smell.

"I promise."

"It was Troll. He's got the tape. But don't tell him about me. He'll hurt me. He likes to hurt things."

"Troll?" asks Michael, who has never heard of him.

"He used to be a wrestler," says Liquidity. "He went crazy. One of those guys who decides never to take off his makeup ever again. Like these days he's a troll."

"Don't say I said anything," asks Blackhead. "You promise?"

"Sure," says Michael. He wonders what it would be like to never take off his makeup, to be always Marduk the Magnificent roaring and stamping his feet. "We won't say anything."

"He lives below the subways, way down deep." Blackhead tells them about a disused lavatory in the subway station in Union Square. A service closet at the back conceals a trapdoor and a ladder leading down.

"But be careful," says Blackhead. "He's got no inhibitions left. I'd go in after he's asleep. Maybe you can surprise him."

"That doesn't sound fair," says Michael.

"You don't try to be fair with creatures like Troll. He's left fairness way behind. He's got that tape. He's got lots of tapes. Torture tapes, snuff tapes. He calls them his cartoons."

They take a cab to the Union Square subway station. The whole way Michael and Deep Rat discuss fairness. Liquidity stares from the window and wonders what it would be like to become Loki the Trickster, to become the Trickster for life.

"I'm not sneaking up on anyone who's asleep," says Michael. "We'll go in, say what we want, and this Troll person will have to respect our honesty."

Deep Rat disagrees. "We'll sneak down there and smack him with a brick. Then we'll tie him up and question him. We'll even put matches to his toes if we have to."

Michael insists on buying tokens. Even with the token in his hand, Deep Rat appears to slide under the gate. He pockets the token for a rainy day. There has been a breakdown and the station is crowded. Along the walls about a dozen homeless men are curled up covered with newspaper and sheets of plastic.

Deep Rat and Liquidity move in front of Michael as a flying wedge to conceal his identity. Even so, he is noticed.

"I know you!" shouts a man. "I can take you! I can take you any day of the week! Marduk the fuckin Magnificent, ha!"

A heavyset black man in a sweatshirt comes running at Michael. Perhaps he is drunk, perhaps crazy. In any case, his grasp on reality has slipped. The man begins to rush past Deep Rat but somehow his darkness becomes entangled with Deep Rat's darkness. Deep Rat makes a sudden movement and the man slips to the concrete with a startled look in his eyes. Deep Rat hurries on. Michael and Liquidity follow him. When Michael glances back, the black man is sitting up and rubbing his head.

The door to the disused lavatory is locked.

"You're strong," says Deep Rat. "You push and the door will open. If necessary, we'll fix it later."

Michael leans against the door. The wood makes a slight groan, then the door opens. Deep Rat realizes that Michael has great skills which are wasted on him. Still, Deep Rat smiles warmly, because he is supposed to be Michael Marmaduke's friend.

It is dark in the ex-lavatory. Deep Rat takes a little flashlight from his pocket. They enter slowly and Deep Rat closes the door behind them. The door to the service closet is unlocked. Liquidity is aware of a lot of insect life on the floor but he doesn't want to investigate. Inside the closet is a trapdoor. Deep Rat lifts it up. In the darkness of the closet is the even greater darkness of the hole.

"I am scared shitless," says Liquidity, "and I don't care who knows it."

Michael has curiosity, a desire not to act badly, a desire not to get dirt on his clothes, but no fear. "Shall I go first?"

But Deep Rat goes first. After all, he has the light.

The ladder going down from the trapdoor is a rusted metal ladder bolted to the wall. Liquidity feels a clammy draft coming up from below. There is also a stench. It smells to Liquidity like decomposing meat. Even in the ring, Troll was an unpleasant character. One of those guys who didn't follow the script and did little things to hurt you. There had been complaints. Liquidity remembers him as a big blobby hairless guy with red eyes. Maybe he was six foot eight, certainly over six-six. A big guy who liked to hurt people and now he has refused to take off his makeup.

Troll.

Liquidity counts the rungs and by the time he reaches a hundred he's at the bottom. Even this scares him. One hundred rungs is a long way to fall. As a trickster he is not accustomed to approaching problems head-on. Obliqueness is what he's all about. If he was doing this on his own, he'd lure Troll out of his cellar and smack him from behind. Further along he can see Deep Rat with the light, then the huge shadow of Michael Marmaduke. Liquidity imagines something sneaking up on him and he hurries forward so he is practically tripping over Michael's feet. The smell is stronger down here. Thicker somehow, a mixture of locker room, slaughterhouse, and sleazy restaurant.

From somewhere ahead comes a noise like a burbling toilet: guttural and wet. Liquidity keeps bumping into Michael and whispering, Excuse me, excuse me. The floor is slippery and Liquidity doesn't like that, nor does he like the spiderwebs that float across his face. The burbling noise has a nasal quality. Suddenly Deep Rat flicks off the light. Liquidity considers the nature of fear and what it is that makes him want to scream uncontrollably.

When Deep Rat turns off the light, Michael stops. Then Liquidity bumps into him and says, "Ooomph." All three stand very still. After a moment, Michael grows aware of a dim light somewhere ahead of them.

"Be very quiet," says Deep Rat. He moves forward again.

It occurs to Liquidity that he is moving forward only because he is afraid of Michael's disapproval. He is perhaps risking his life for fear of this disapproval. Perhaps all action, he thinks, lies between the pull of two or more fears, or if not fears, then what in the realm of fear would correspond to a precancerous condition. As the whole world is precancerous, so is it prefearful. Liquidity wishes he could go someplace to think about this. He is aware of the light getting a little brighter, the burbling noise a little louder.

After another minute, the three trespassers reach the source of light. In fact, there are two sources of light. One is a lava lamp about four feet tall. Within it red, blue and green fluids enact the drama of an upset stomach. The other source of light is a large television screen which shows nothing but flickering gray dots.

Between these two lights is a king-sized bed and on the bed is a huge white creature. He is so big and nasty-looking that if we had mentioned him before mentioning the lights, nobody would have paid attention to the lights, and they too—in a much smaller way —are important. Liquidity, for instance, never looked once at the lava lamp and sees only the monster on the bed, although he is also aware of bones on the floor, big bones. The thing on the bed is naked except for a dark jockstrap. It is hairless and parchment-colored. It lies on its back with its mouth open and it is snoring. It looks like a sumo wrestler gone bad but it is bigger than a sumo wrestler. This is Troll, and he is presently at his nicest, i.e., coma-tose.

Liquidity realizes this is his last chance to run. The big bones on the floor have unnerved him. He hopes he won't inadvertently wet himself. He takes a step backward as Michael steps forward and clears his throat.

"Mr. Troll, I have a question. I need some information. My name's Marmaduke. Michael Marmaduke."

Suddenly Troll is sitting straight up in bed. "What the fuck!" he says. Even sitting he appears to be over six feet.

"I need to ask you about a videotape," says Michael.

Although he is about to wet himself, Liquidity is impressed by the coolness of Michael's voice.

Now Troll is off the bed and standing before them. He has moved very fast, and Liquidity thinks it is wrong for people this big to move so fast. It makes it unfair for everyone else: those others who think only of running and hiding. Troll appears about six inches taller than Michael Marmaduke and twice as broad. He is the sort of creature that one measures in acreage.

"How the fuck you get in here?" he roars.

"I need to find out about this videotape," says Michael. "You see, my fiancée's been kidnapped . . ."

"My fuckin cartoons, man!" shouts Troll. "You want to steal my cartoons!" And before Michael can answer, Troll grabs him by the lapels, lifts him as if he were a puppy (Michael must weigh about 250 pounds) and throws him at Liquidity. All of this is an enactment of Liquidity's worst fears.

"I'm goin to eat you, man," says Troll.

Michael collides with Liquidity, then gets to his feet and dusts himself off. "Perhaps I haven't made myself clear. I'm told you have a video showing my fiancée. She's been kidnapped."

Michael and Troll stand between the two light sources: the flickering TV and the lava lamp. The shadows from the lava lamp move up their bodies like little elevators. The TV makes it seems as if they are covered with snow. Michael looks attentive but relaxed. He is thinking that he probably doesn't have to worry about hurting this big guy. He is thinking he is probably unhurtable. "Perhaps you could tell me where you got that video," he says. "It's very important that I find out."

Troll doesn't appear to be listening. He hunches over and reaches out toward Michael, who backs up.

Will the Bliss Killer have the chance to put Troll to sleep in the Bosom of Abraham? Let us not draw out the suspense. In the battle that follows, Michael is badly beaten. Although he is strong and knows many wrestling holds, these holds are based on the assumption that the other person—his antagonist—will permit him to take hold, permit himself to be grabbed. After all, it's in the script. Troll doesn't do this. When Michael reaches out, Troll simply leaps forward and tackles him. There follows about five minutes of extreme violence in which the TV is smashed, the lava lamp is overturned and Michael is bruised. Liquidity hits out several times, but in the complete darkness, he doesn't know who or what he is hitting.

Then, unexpectedly, there is a crunch and a groan and a moment of silence. A small light flicks on which illuminates a brick on the floor and Troll's feet with the toes pointing toward the ceiling. "Run," says Deep Rat.

Liquidity needs no second invitation. Michael limps after him. He hurts in ten places, and this interests him because he has never really hurt before, except once when he fell out of a tree. Still, he doesn't dawdle. Deep Rat runs ahead with the light. After a minute or so there is a roar from behind them.

"I'll grind your bones!" roars Troll.

They hear him running after them: a stamping dragging noise. Liquidity is amazed at his own speed. With Troll behind him, he feels he could win a marathon. Deep Rat reaches the ladder and begins to climb. Liquidity is second, Michael third. Michael is depressed that he has been unable to make himself understood but is unwilling to try again. Is he afraid? Let's say he realizes language has its limitations. He hears Troll reach the ladder and the whole ladder shakes as he begins to climb. Michael sees the light above him. Deep Rat is at the top. Then Liquidity climbs through the trapdoor. When Michael climbs through, he sees Liquidity with the light and Deep Rat standing with a cinder block. There is a puffing and panting as Troll continues to climb the ladder. Deep Rat steps to the trapdoor and drops the cinder block down the hole. Michael hears a brief whistling noise, then a crash and a scream and another crash, then silence.

Brodsky and Gapski are working late, but still they don't like being disturbed. In the world of upset they see themselves as disturb*ers* rather than disturb*ees*. They have been discussing Russian roulette. Each sees this is a potential way out of their problem—the chance that one of them might die—but neither cares to be the first to take the plunge. They are deadlocked.

All of a sudden there is a knock at the door. Startled, the two detectives look up to see Michael Marmaduke.

"Look what the cat dragged in," says Gapski.

Both policemen are wearing brand-new lime-green suits. Each went out the previous evening to buy a suit which he would have sworn his partner would never buy and, by chance, each hit on the color lime green, which both, in fact, detest. Believe us when we say there was a tense moment when Brodsky and Gapski laid eyes on each other this morning. Now, in order to individualize their green suits, each has worked all day to make his suit dirty in his own personal manner. Brodsky's has egg stains, coffee stains and ink stains. Gapski's has oil stains, ketchup stains and smears of white paint. They can barely wait for the moment when they can go home and change into pajamas and slippers. And now comes this oddball to bother them.

Michael holds up half a dozen videotapes that Deep Rat snatched up from Troll's lair. "I think you better look at these." He has already glimpsed bits of them back at his apartment and what he saw sent him downstairs in search of a cab.

Brodsky and Gapski don't feel like seeing any videotapes, especially videotapes turned up by amateurs. Still, deep within their idiosyncrasies lies a whisper of professionalism. They are also aware that they will get yelled at if they make a mistake.

Brodsky takes the tapes and holds them as if they were hot. "Where'd you get them?" He reaches up and pokes Michael in the chest with a little finger. "Did you steal the tapes?"

"Breaking and entering, burglary and assault could keep you out of the ring for quite a while, big guy," says Gapski.

Michael feels that Jack Molay may be correct about the reductiveness of language. First he tries to talk to Troll, then he tries to talk to Brodsky and Gapski. Michael knows that behind his words exists logic, reason and good intention. Yet his sentences fall flat. Each explanation is just another confusion. Describe a banana and people think you are talking about oranges.

"Just look at the tapes," suggests Michael.

They go into Sapperstein's office with its VCR and cellophane-covered dartboard showing the face of Yasir Arafat.

"This better be good," says Gapski. He puts the tape into the machine and sits on the edge of the desk to watch. Brodsky sits beside him.

On the screen a man in a wolf costume lies on a table and another man raises a knife and plunges it into his belly. Out of the belly pop an old woman and a little girl. They appear very happy. They quickly gather up rocks and put them into the wolf's belly. Then the man sews up the hole. The man in the wolf costume climbs off the table. He finds it very hard to walk with rocks in his belly. The other three laugh and laugh. The man in the wolf costume staggers till he comes to a pond. He falls in the water and doesn't come up again. Just bubbles. The old woman and little girl and the man with the knife all begin kissing each other. The screen goes dark.

Brodsky and Gapski have witnessed many unpleasant things but this video is very competitive. They both search for adjectives to describe the video—nasty, disgusting, appalling—but each thinks the other will choose exactly the same adjective and so he remains silent. Brodsky inserts another tape into the machine.

On the screen we see seven sleeping girls. Each wears a cap and has a round ugly face. On the sheet in front of them are chicken wings, a chicken's head and some bones. One of the girls has a bone in her mouth, a second holds a chicken claw as a child might hold a rattle. An ugly-looking man sneaks up behind the girls. He reaches out and touches their caps and smiles. Then he takes a butcher knife and proceeds to cut the little girls' throats. It makes quite a mess. A tiny boy sticks his head out from under a table and laughs and laughs. The screen goes dark.

"I don't know," says Brodsky.

"Me neither," says Gapski. "I just don't know what to say."

"Troll called these his cartoons," says Michael.

"Sick," say Brodsky and Gapski in unison. Gapski puts a third tape into the machine.

A woman hurries down the cellar stairs. She keeps pausing to look back over her shoulder. Her hair is messed and she is distraught. She wears an old-fashioned dress that reaches her ankles. Coming to a big door, she takes a key and unlocks it. Ten women hang from hooks on the wall. Their throats have been cut. Their bodies have been mutilated. The camera carefully investigates the wounds on each body. The living woman turns back toward the door and screams. The screen goes dark.

The next two films contain similar material: a boy being cooked in a pot, people being sliced or stabbed. Brodsky and Gapski are tempted to call Sapperstein himself but it is after one a.m. and they are afraid of his disapproval.

The sixth video shows Rose White. She is in a cage hanging from a crane on the roof of a tall building under construction. The crane turns, swinging the cage toward the camera. The sky is blue and spotted with fleecy white clouds. Rose White looks all scrunched. She wears a white nightgown. "Michael, save me," she calls. "I'm being . . ." Then the screen goes dark.

"That looked like Brooklyn," says Gapski.

"My idea precisely," says Brodsky.

Ten minutes later Michael is in a squad car heading toward

Union Square. Actually, he is in a procession of ten squad cars. He keeps thinking of Rose White crammed into the cage. He wishes he were unconscious and he understands how some people can be overtaken by attacks of amnesia. It has begun to rain and the streets are all shiny.

The police cars double-park at the subway station and the policemen run down the steps with Michael leading the way. He takes them to the disused lavatory, then to the service closet in the back. A policeman pulls up the trapdoor. The police have big lights. They have pistols, shotguns and a deep seriousness. They descend the ladder. The ones in front wear bulletproof vests. At the bottom they find a small pool of blood and a cinder block. They are in a cavernous space beneath the subway. The policemen fan out looking for Troll. Michael leads Brodsky and Gapski over to the TV, the lava lamp and king-sized bed.

Let's look down from a high place. There's plenty of light and plenty of action as the police run back and forth, darting from post to post. They find bones on the floor and don't like these. Nor do they like the unpleasant smell. Off to the left we see the broken TV, the broken lava lamp and the bed all messed up. The oil from the lava lamp has made a puddle on the floor, which is already filthy and stained with reddish fluids. Now and then a rat scampers from one hiding place to another. And there is Michael with Brodsky and Gapski. Michael towers above the two detectives, who wear fedoras and smoke cigarettes. Brodsky and Gapski each hold a bone. The bones are long and look like leg bones. If one could glance into the detectives' heads, one would see the pictures of various animals—cows, horses, oxen, mules, elk, buffalo, moose, antelope: animals which have great big legs. What Brodsky and Gapski are doing is trying to imagine a suitable animal which is not a human being because these bones look a lot like human leg bones and if they are human bones then Sapperstein is going to be very angry that he wasn't called earlier.

As for Troll, he is nowhere to be found.

17

ERNEST HEMINGWAY

When Sparrow cleans windows, the cleaning is only part of the job. The other part is the climbing and the enduring of high places. That is the part he likes best and the part he is best at. If truth be known, he is a mediocre cleaner but an A-plus climber, and these two valuations cancel each other out to keep him steadily employed.

Sparrow has always been Sparrow. In fact he was baptized Sparrow: Sparrow Gonzalez. And he sometimes wonders if it wasn't being called Sparrow that kept him small. If he had been called Eagle or Condor, then perhaps he would have grown up to be a big fellow, because although his name is Sparrow, he is also called Pipsqueak, Half-pint and Smidgin. But he does not like these names and does not answer to them. He is five feet tall and if he had had the right breaks he would have been a jockey like his cousin Jaime, but his life did not take that particular turning and so he is a window cleaner instead. In order to be a jockey or groom or stable boy, one must be very calm. One can't do anything to upset the horses, and, if truth be known, Sparrow has a temper. Do you know those people who are just waiting for the world to insult them? Sparrow is like that, and it has affected his life.

Although in his mid-thirties, he is still single and has no friends. It is hard to be Sparrow's friend, because he is always saying, "What'd you mean by that crack?" or "I don't like that kinda talk," if, in his company, you ask for a small beer, small Coke or small pizza. In fact, if you use the words "small," "little," "minute," "minor," "picayune," "puny," "skimpy," "tiny," "petite," "microscopic," "miniature" or "midget," then you will arouse his wrath. "I take exception to that," he'll say. Consequently, people avoid him. Consequently, he is lonely.

But today, Monday, he feels lucky. Just yesterday he was working overtime cleaning the windows of a penthouse condo in Gateway Plaza when a wonderful golden coin came flipping out the window. And he caught it. Lightning reflexes, that's how his manager billed him in those Golden Gloves flyweight competitions, where each match, for Sparrow, became a grudge match. He grabbed the coin and proceeded to lower his platform, because he knew that what he had caught was valuable and its loss was a mistake. And only moments later he heard a scream: "Come back! I want my coin!" But Sparrow lowered his platform to an empty condo, then he ducked through the window and ran for the elevator. Once down on the street he hailed a cab and only when seated in the backseat did he take the time to see what he had captured.

First of all, he was sure it was gold, because it felt heavy like gold. Secondly, it had two wonderful faces. On one side was an angel, on the other a devil. We of course already know this, but for Sparrow the coin was a surprise and he kept turning it over. What a nice smile the angel had. And the devil: how sinister! He wanted to tell the driver about how lucky he'd been to catch the coin but he didn't trust him. The driver was from Russia or Iraq or Istanbul —some bad place where people normally stole other people's lucky coins. Obviously the driver would try to keep the coin for himself. But Sparrow also felt a pang of loneliness. Here he was in the midst of an extraordinary event and he had no one to share it with.

"Take me to Cooper Square," he told the driver. This was three blocks from his apartment on Avenue A, but he had something valuable and he didn't want the driver to know where he lived.

Sparrow hurried home. It occurred to him that the rich people who dropped the coin might be able to trace him through the window washing company, so he wanted to pack a suitcase and disappear for a while. He didn't need much and he didn't own much. Property just drags you down, was how he saw it.

He spent the night in a cheap hotel near Seward Park. Half the guests stayed up drinking late, the other half got up early to give their drinking a head start. Sparrow slept with the coin clenched in his fist and the fist under his pillow. It gave him sweet dreams in which he caught trains on time and was surrounded by people who liked him. When he left the hotel Monday morning, he felt that life was looking up.

We now have Sparrow at his best. It is nine o'clock Monday morning and he is walking east on Canal Street. He plans to turn north on Chrystie because he wants to see some trees and maybe these trees—it being late October—have some color. By this we can see how Sparrow has allowed optimism to distort his reason. Trees don't turn color in Manhattan in October; they become jaundiced and brown. But right now Sparrow loves the world and loves his fellow creatures, even though what passes for love in Sparrow would be mild dislike in Mother Teresa. He clutches his coin in his right hand and although he doesn't flip it—he is too suspicious for that—he keeps raising and lowering his hand as if he were flipping it, flipping a coin encaged by his own tight grip. Everything in Sparrow's life is turning up roses and his only complaint is his lack of companionship. And at this moment Sparrow sees Bernard.

It is rush hour and the sidewalk is crowded but there is an island of open space around Bernard, who stands looking up at the clouds. You know the old chestnut "Hearts turned to one purpose alone trouble the living stream"? That's Bernard. People are veering around him like a current around a boulder. He wears blue institutional coveralls and a zippered green sweatshirt and his hair has been shaved close to his head and there are little nicks in his scalp and from this we can determine that whoever cut Bernard's hair was not paid by Bernard to do it. He was paid by someone else and he didn't care if Bernard liked the haircut or not. The barber just didn't give a damn, and at five o'clock he probably went home and complained to his wife about what a lousy day he had had.

Normally Bernard lives in a semiprivate mental institution in Brooklyn but two days ago he stopped taking his pills and last night he felt clear-headed enough to walk away from the grounds. He walked and maybe he slept a little because the night was mild apart from a brief shower and then he walked some more and now he finds himself on Canal Street and he has never seen Canal Street before, but more than Canal Street, he likes the clouds: clouds from the west, clouds carrying the beginnings of winter, clouds flecked with the shadows of southern-flying birds.

So Bernard stands in the middle of the sidewalk and people give him a wide berth because to live in New York City for more than twelve hours is to develop a wacko-sensitivity level and Bernard doesn't measure up well on the scale. On other occasions Sparrow also would follow the example of the crowd, because his wacko-sensitivity level is very high and such a sensitivity means avoiding those oddballs whose next actions cannot be anticipated and this could easily be true of Bernard, but just then Sparrow catches a glimpse of Bernard's eyes.

They are light blue and the size of saucers. But it is not their physical characteristics that are important but what they suggest. These eyes suggest extreme gentleness and sensitivity. They suggest a fondness for all living creatures and a complete absence of anger, violence and a sense of competition. It might be hypothesized that lobotomy patients have eyes like these or that the eyes are the results of Bernard's medications, which for twenty-five of his forty years have kept him as happy as a houseplant. The eyes also suggest a mild sadness, a melancholic discontent that so deeply touches Sparrow's tepid heart that he immediately adjusts his steps to bring himself to Bernard's side.

"Tell me," says Sparrow, tugging at Bernard's sleeve because Bernard is about a foot taller, "why do you look so sad?"

Bernard looks down at Sparrow and gives a little smile that shoots like an arrow to the center of Sparrow's soul. "I am sad because I am hungry and I have had nothing to eat."

"Come with me," says Sparrow. "I'll get you plenty to eat."

Sparrow feels no surprise to see Bernard following him. He squeezes the lucky coin and decides that Bernard is just another good thing that has happened and now he has had a couple of good things after a long period of drought.

He turns down Bowery to the Silver Palace, which opens early and has a minuscule waiting period between the *I want* stage and *I eat* stage. Soon Sparrow and Bernard are settled at a table. Waiters walk by with carts laden with food. The idea is to take whatever you wish and the plates are added up at the end.

"They say the dim sum is good here," says Sparrow.

Bernard tries the dim sum. He tries the steamed pork dumplings, beef and oyster sauce, sweet and sour pork and the Peking duck. He tries the vegetarian rainbow miracle, flounder stuffed with chestnuts and baked conch stuffed in its own shell. He tries the bean curd stuffed with chopped shrimp and the roast squab and the chow fun. He finishes up with melon and tapioca and then gets a fortune cookie. The fortune tells him: "Beware of anyone driving a white van."

"That's funny," says Sparrow, "I've never seen them get that specific. I wonder what model?"

"A Ford Econoline," says Bernard. "The wacko-catchers at the hospital use them: white Ford Econoline vans."

"Wacko-catchers?"

"The men who come after the people who escape. I hate them and they scare me." Bernard carries such a residue of a lifetime of being medicated that he uses words like "hate" and "scare" in the same tone of voice that he might say "rabbit" or "ice cream."

"I'll protect you," says Sparrow. The absence of emotional nuance in Bernard's voice makes Sparrow very happy. "Let's take a walk and watch the trees change." The waiter tallies up the plates. It's quite a pile.

They walk back up Bowery toward Chrystie Street. Sparrow has told Bernard about many of the difficulties in his life. The difficulty of being five feet tall. The difficulty of never making it into racing. The difficulty of failing as a fighter. To all this Bernard responds with intense sympathy of a certain kind, meaning that the words are sympathetic—what a shame, what a pity, how terrible—but the tone is perfectly flat and devoid of emotion. That is how Sparrow likes it, and soon he plans to tell Bernard about the good things in his life: how he is great at buzzing around at high altitudes and about the lucky coin with its two faces. But before Sparrow can tell him about the coin, Bernard says, "I'm tired. I think I'll take a little nap."

"Yes, do," says Sparrow. "Just lie down on this bench and I'll sit at the other end." By this time they have reached Chrystie Street with its row of trees.

Bernard lies down on the bench. "I'm very happy," he says in the same tone of voice that he might say "My shoelace is untied." Within two minutes he is asleep.

Sparrow sits at the other end of the bench inspecting his lucky coin and every now and then giving it a cautious flip. He is paying so much attention to the coin that when he hears the truck door slam, he looks up with surprise. There is the white Ford van parked at the curb and coming toward Bernard across the sidewalk is a very tall and very fat man who must have a regular name but at the mental hospital he is only called the Grabber.

"There's the sleazebag," says the Grabber. "He's had me up all night." And he takes out a syringe and prepares to give Bernard a shot that will return him to the vegetable state that the Grabber likes best.

Sparrow jumps up and stands between the fat man and his new friend. "Don't do it," says Sparrow, "or I'll make you poor!"

"A little fuck like you?" says the Grabber. "How could you make me poor?" And he pushes Sparrow aside and jabs the needle into Bernard's leg. Bernard briefly opens his eyes, sees the Grabber, registers a soupçon of terror, and then his beautiful blue eyes go blank. The Grabber throws Bernard over his shoulder and heads back to the van.

Sparrow gets there first and stands between the Grabber and the sliding door. "That's going to cost you," says Sparrow.

"Get outta my way, half-pint," says the Grabber. "I gotta get this bag of trash back to St. Elmo's." He again pushes Sparrow aside, throws Bernard into the van, climbs into the driver's seat and drives away.

On the back of the van is written the address of the hospital. Sparrow takes a pencil and jots it down on a scrap of paper.

Actually he doesn't feel so bad. After not minding heights, being unforgiving is what Sparrow is best at.

"I once did something awful," Beetle says to his new friend, who isn't listening as closely as Beetle would like.

"If I ever get legs," says Zapo, "I'll do everything I can to help you."

They sit leaning against the wall of Gateway Plaza, and thirty-four floors above them Beacon Luz and her father the Snowman are doing whatever rich people do on a Monday morning. A bank manager passing in a helicopter would see the Snowman sitting on the veranda, talking on the telephone and getting a manicure from a beautiful woman. He might also see Beacon Luz sitting on the floor of the vast living room with a Monopoly set and two mirrors positioned like other players. Beacon Luz is playing Monopoly with the reflections of her left and right profiles and she is winning. But she is also sad. Her lucky coin is gone and her father is angry at her.

"I found a baby in a trash can," Beetle is saying. "Can you imagine that? Its ankles were handcuffed together. I had the darnedest time getting them off."

Zapo has a piece of charcoal and draws broken hearts on the sidewalk, although they look more like broken eggs than broken hearts. "Why do you think Beacon Luz doesn't like me? Is it me she doesn't like or is it that I don't have any legs? But if she doesn't like a thing that doesn't exist, then don't her dislike and my nonexistent legs cancel each other out? It would seem then, logically, that she must like me. I mean, if she doesn't like what's not there, then she should like what exists, right?"

Beetle sits in the shade of his overladen shopping cart. "This baby had the prettiest blond hair," he says. "Of course I couldn't leave it in a trash can. I almost did, though. I walked away, then went back. The moral pressure was huge. You can rob a bank or shoot a guy, but you can't leave a baby in a trash can."

"Actually I'm faster on my stumpboard than anyone on two legs," says Zapo. "I can really rip. And even though I have no legs,

I'm still quite tall. I've got a long torso, long neck and a long head. If I had legs proportionate to the rest of my body, I'd be well over six feet. I'm really a very tall person, it's just the fact that I don't have any legs that makes me short."

"So I take the baby outta the trash can," says Beetle, "and I ask myself, What am I going to do with it? Here I am an ex-con with a record of nervous disorders and they find I'm carrying a baby with its legs handcuffed together. You know what the cops would've done to me? No way could I stay in the city."

"I even work for the Snowman," says Zapo, correcting the jagged edge of the broken heart so it looks less like a broken egg. "I work for the Snowman like a janitor in Trump Towers works for Donald Trump. These syringes I peddle. One nickel from every sale goes straight to the Snowman. That's a lotta nickels. And this is just for starters. I plan to work my way up in the organization. Basically I'm an idea man."

"So I started to walk," says Beetle. "I walked right over the George Washington Bridge. I'd never even been in New Jersey before. People are always talking about New Jersey. To tell you the truth I didn't think it was so hot."

At this moment a black BMW pulls up and two rough-looking men in double-breasted suits hurry out of a doorway where they have been concealing themselves. They catch Zapo's eye because they are the sort of men who sometimes hit him up for syringes. A rectangular-looking bald man gets out of the BMW and the three proceed to have a private conversation five feet away from where Beetle and Zapo are sitting, from which it may be understood that they see Beetle and Zapo as hardly human and certainly no threat.

"He sends his bodyguards down first," says one of the rough-looking men. "They check the area and check his car, then the chief bodyguard calls back upstairs."

" 'Clean as a whistle' is what he always says," says the second rough-looking man.

"From that point," says the first man, "it takes the Snowman between five and seven minutes to get downstairs."

"But on the average," says the second man, "he walks outta that elevator at ten a.m. sharp."

"How many bodyguards?" asks the rectangular-looking bald man, who also wears expensive Italian sunglasses.

"Two in the elevator and a third in the car with the driver."

"And how many guys will you need to take care of them?"

"Four plus us," says the second man. "That's three in the garage and three to wait for the elevator. Then I call up, 'Clean as a whistle,' and the Snowman'll come down. Won't he be surprised when he pops outta the elevator and finds six guys waving a lotta machinery in his face."

"Seven," says the rectangular-looking bald man, who proceeds to pat a bulge over his heart. "I'll teach him to fuck with me. After Tuesday, no more Snowman. He's going to get melted!"

As a rule Wally Wallski doesn't drink—his wife Claudine objects to the financial waste—but sometimes he pops into a bar for a quick beer just because he needs something sustaining. Late Monday morning he is in O'Leary's Pub on First Avenue in the low Sixties, sipping his fifth beer of the day. What he should be doing is asking Mr. Lenguado for a new place to live, but he's afraid. All night Claudine complained about cramped quarters, although their West End condo has seven large rooms. It wasn't her body that was cramped but her spirit. Her spirit felt as if it were sleeping in a birdhouse and it kept waking her up. And every time her eyes rested on Wally Wallski sleeping like a baby she elbowed him in the ribs. Although Claudine's upper and lower arms are puffy and soft, each elbow is as sharp as a tack. It was this sharpness that kept driving itself between Wally Wallski's deepest sleep and a state of panicky wakefulness, and it happened a dozen times between midnight and six o'clock, when Claudine felt that her husband had slept long enough.

"All right, asshole, rise and shine. It's time to tell old man Lenguado we've lived in this slime pit long enough."

She didn't even give Wally Wallski time to shave or drink a cup of coffee, and under his shirt he still wore his pajama top with its picture of Marduk the Magnificent. Wally Wallski staggered from his building and headed east toward Central Park to think: a process which entailed striking his forehead and asking, "Why me?" In fact he was engaged in an act of careful measurement, comparing his terror of Claudine with his terror of Mr. Lenguado. It was what some psychologists used to call an Avoidance-Avoidance situation and others referred to as a Double-Bind. In any case, he didn't know what to do. He was stalled, perplexed, dead-ended in a moral cul-de-sac.

If we invited a panel of experts to analyze Wally Wallski's predicament, their advice might be as follows. The psychiatrist from Harvard might urge Wally Wallski to convince his wife that she is privileging certain stereotypes of financial success and that Wally Wallski's duty is to bring them both into therapy.

The psychiatrist from Yale might ask Wally Wallski why he chooses to infantilize himself not only in his interpersonal relationships but in his interests, i.e., wrestling. Doesn't he comprehend that by refusing admission to his adult self, he is falling victim to those economic forces that foreground Fun-fun-fun instead of allowing him to develop a foundational sense of social responsibility which will enable him to cultivate a more constructive self-image?

The psychotherapist from Columbia might argue that Wally Wallski has been degendered and emasculated by being dissevered from his self-selected profession (being a fisherman) and that his inner profundity will only access cornucopian fruition with full employment. Possibly Wally Wallski needs to be retooled as a traffic policeman.

Wally Wallski, on the other hand, sees the problem in terms of getting yelled at. Either he will be yelled at by his wife or yelled at by Mr. Lenguado. It is his failure to think his way through this predicament that leads him to O'Leary's Pub at ten in the morning. What beer does for him is to let him subdue the Claudine/Lenguado controversy and let the rest of the world reassert itself. It may not reassert itself in any meaningful fasion—after all, Wally Wallski is getting drunk—but at least it lives and breathes. And as the rest of the world reasserts itself, Wally Wallski becomes aware of an important discussion at one of the tables.

Three English professors from Hunter College are having a colloquy, although the words "English" and "professor" are no longer part of their vocabulary. They are theorists in textual studies and it is only to their dean that they are still English professors.

As theorists they are engaged in the production of significant texts in the same way that Chaucer and Shakespeare and Milton once produced significant texts, but while the texts of Chaucer and Shakespeare and Milton have been deconstructed—that is, they are going down—the texts of these three gentlemen from Hunter College have been superstructed—that is, they are going up. And in the same way that two elevators in a skyscraper can pass each other—one ascending and the other descending—so these three gentlemen from Hunter College believe their texts have passed the texts of Chaucer and Shakespeare and Milton, and that what the theorists' texts lack in imagination—although, in their way, they are very imaginative—they make up for in theoretical expertise, an expertise which has led them to the conclusion that a rose by any other name is not a rose and may be a hot dog or, in fact, a can of tuna fish.

" 'Of man's first disobedience, and the fruit of that forbidden tree, whose mortal taste brought death into the world'—just what kind of bullshit is that, anyway?" says one of the three men, whose name is DeMaus.

"By pointing to the man," says the second of the three, whose name is Vogel, "the whole problem becomes a gender issue."

"Even the word 'first,' " says the third, whose name is Sosage, "privileges defunct mathematical systems."

"And what is it to be disobedient?" asks DeMaus. "Doesn't this valorize a methodology of behavior which it is our duty to question?"

It might be assumed that DeMaus, Vogel and Sosage are up drinking rather early. In fact, they are up drinking rather late, having begun the previous evening. As theorists they no longer have the tweed and facial hair of traditional academics; instead they wear black leather jackets and black pointed boots, and Vogel has an earring. All three are in their thirties and clean-shaven.

"Consider the phrase 'fruit of that forbidden tree,' " says Sosage. "Just what is 'fruit'? To point to one part of the tree and argue it is better than another part and to call that valorized part of the tree 'fruit' is to abrogate other arboreal components which certainly have individual validity, and even to say that these other components lack the taste of the supposed 'fruit' is indubitably an attempt to objectify an experience which at best is subjective and ephemeral."

"Even 'forbidden' is problematic," says DeMaus.

"Even 'tree' is suspect," says Vogel.

"To tell you the truth," says Sosage, "I'm astonished he ever got the fucking thing published."

For Wally Wallski, Milton is a town in Massachusetts, but he is impressed with the strength of conviction exhibited by these three leather-jacketed men—are they bikers?—drinking beer and shots of gin in a nearby booth.

"Defunct," says DeMaus.

"Dismantled," says Vogel.

"Demolished," says Sosage.

"Devastated," says DeMaus.

"Despoiled," says Vogel.

"Destroyed," says Sosage.

"It seems to me," says DeMaus, with the air of one struck by a new idea, "that since Chaucer and Shakespeare and Milton have been deleted, we owe it to humanity to take their place in order to avoid the creation of an unfortunate vacuum, which, we understand, nature abhors."

"Shouldn't one of us be a woman?" asks Vogel.

"Or gay?" asks Sosage.

"Perhaps," says DeMaus, "they were. Who's to say that Shakespeare wasn't a woman or gay or a writer of color? And isn't the same also true of Chaucer and Milton? Certainly the historical sources lack credibility. All we know for certain is that they were precisely not what people have claimed they were. Consequently if you choose to portray Chaucer as an African-American lesbian, I feel your portrayal will have as much credibility as those portrayals formerly in fashion."

Vogel and Sosage are struck by the truth of these remarks and they drink to DeMaus's health.

"In fact," continues DeMaus, "we could easily establish that our fellow drinkers are the entire male hegemonical canon. If we think it so, then doesn't that give it an indisputable validity?" Here he looks around and spots Wally Wallski staring at him with interest. "You there," calls DeMaus. "Come here a moment."

Wally Wallski slowly walks over carrying his fifth beer. It must be understood that five beers are perhaps what Wally Wallski has drunk in an entire year so to have five at once is to put his head in a spin. Wally Wallski stands at the theorists' table swaying back and forth.

"What dead writers have you ever heard of?" asks DeMaus.

Wally Wallski isn't much of a reader but as a fisherman he has a soft spot for Ernest Hemingway and has listened to the cassette version of *The Old Man and the Sea* several times.

"Ernest Hemingway," says Wally Wallski.

"By the power invested in me by the Modern Language Association," says DeMaus, "I make you Ernest Hemingway. I warn you of your duties and remind you of your privileges."

Vogel shakes Wally Wallski's hand. "Congratulations. I've always admired your stuff."

Sosage gives Wally Wallski a glass of gin and pats his back. "I'm really looking forward to your next book," he says.

Wally Wallski feels overwhelmed by responsibility. "What does it mean to be Ernest Hemingway?" he asks. He's not even a very good speller.

"It means you're a fisherman par excellence," says DeMaus.

"It means you're Papa Macho, the first twentieth-century tough guy," says Vogel.

"It means you are boss of the simple sentence," says Sosage. "See Spot jump. See Spot rise. Sun also rises."

"Tough guy?" asks Wally Wallski.

"No one can push you around," says DeMaus. "Can you imagine someone pushing around Papa Hemingway? *Absolutement pas!*"

"Of course," says Vogel, "you gotta quit this sexist shit."

"You gotta stop privileging the male hegemony," says Sosage.

"Racial stereotypes are a thing of the past," says DeMaus.

"Toughness in the service of theory," says Vogel. "Macho correctness in the service of macha prerogatives."

"It'll mean writing books," says Sosage, "in which no one will find a single word offensive or disturbing."

"Books where the author," says DeMaus, "will always defer to the point of view of the reader."

"But I can't write!" says Wally Wallski.

"That's just the point," says Sosage. "The books of the new Papa Hemingway are wordless and silent."

"The moment you set down a word," says DeMaus, "you compromise your uniqueness."

"What makes you great," says Vogel, "is your refusal to commit yourself to meaning."

"By being nothing," says Sosage, "you become all things to all men and women."

"And this makes you tough," says DeMaus.

"Powerful," says Vogel.

"Magnificent," says Sosage.

"Does this mean I don't have to be afraid of Mr. Lenguado?"

"Of course not," says DeMaus.

"And Claudine, will she still scare the pants off me?"

"No one will ever frighten you again," says Vogel. "Believe me, or my name's not Will Shakespeare."

"I'll do it," says Wally Wallski. "I'll be Ernest Hemingway. No one will ever push me around again."

"Let me be the first to congratulate you," says DeMaus, raising his glass of gin. "Watch out, world, here you come!"

18

GUTS AND FAST RUNNING

We sit astride a broken castle wall, or at least it resembles a castle, although it has only two stories. There are granite crenellations and five-sided windows (all broken) which bear the outline of little houses. Although we see no roof, there is a piece of blue plastic of the sort that yachtsmen use to cover their boats in winter and it has been rolled back to admit the sun because it is a bright warm day, something unusual for late October and so something to be valued. Off to our right is midtown Manhattan and we can just hear the growl of traffic from FDR Drive. To our left is Brooklyn and behind us is the dark span of the Queensboro Bridge packed with slow-moving vehicles. From this it can be determined that we are on the tip of an island in the East River. The water laps against the shore and here comes the Delta Airlines water ferry, which will shortly make its first stop at the pier at 36th Street. Once this island was called Welfare Island, but then the developers—with their eyes fixed on the marketability of a name—had it rechristened Roosevelt Island. Our crumbling perch belongs not to a dilapidated castle; rather, we are in the ruins of the old Smallpox Hospital.

Below us is a room with a broken stone floor with weeds and grass growing from the cracks. This foliage, however, has been recently trimmed, so the room appears to have a green carpet. Two men are in the room. The first, sitting in a canvas lawn chair, is Michael Marmaduke, who is trying to balance a cup and saucer on one knee and a plate of buttered toast on the other. He bears the look of someone attempting to be polite while afraid of committing the social blunder of dumping his tea on the carpet, actually grass. But beneath this anxiety exists a more complicated expression: one which rises to the surface when someone one feels one should respect says something doubtful: a combination of deference and suspicion which streaks Michael's handsome puss like stripes on a zebra.

His interlocutor is standing. He is a tall thin man wearing a green robe much like a monk's and his head is shaved. In one hand he holds a silver cream pitcher and in the other a bowl of sugar. Michael has declined both, preferring his tea straight. The man's name is Brother Thomas, and he is speaking: "It is not widely accepted that Judas Iscariot was the twin brother of Jesus of Nazareth but it is a true fact nonetheless."

"I don't think I ever heard that," says Michael politely.

"Of course that is not to say he was divine. He was more of a half-twin. When God the Father impregnated the Virgin Mary, it was through her right ear. After all, Jesus was Logos, the Word, and it is through the ear that the Word is received. Judas, the son of Joseph, was conceived more conventionally. Some say that Jesus was also born out of that same ear, but I don't know."

"It would be tricky," says Michael.

Brother Thomas nods, then offers Michael a wedge of lemon, which he declines. Both men contemplate the difficulties of giving birth to a child through the ear. Presumably it would require a very big ear or a very small baby. Then Michael takes a bite of toast. He has missed breakfast and is hungry.

"For years," continues Brother Thomas, "it was assumed that Judas Thomas, who wrote *The Book of Thomas the Contender,* and Judas Iscariot were two different men, but that is not the case. After the Resurrection, Judas Iscariot was transformed into Judas Thomas through the sacrifice, or near sacrifice, of his own life.

Later he became a famous teacher in India, where people were not prejudiced against him. And of course there was also prejudice because he was gay."

"I don't think I knew that either," says Michael.

"In *The Dialogue of the Savior*, it says how the disciples Judas and Matthew rejected 'the works of femaleness,' meaning they were gay. It doesn't say whether they were lovers, but we may assume as much. This is why Matthew tells the false story of Judas's suicide. Out of guilt for his illicit affair, Matthew spreads the slander that his lover is dead when actually he is visiting India. It was Judas's gayness that made him unpopular with the other disciples and not his apparent betrayal of his twin brother. If it hadn't been for this prejudice, Judas would have assumed his rightful place as the head of the church, instead of Peter. It must have given him some white nights during his Indian travels: there but for the grace of God, etc."

"But wasn't there a betrayal?" asks Michael uncertainly. He tries to remember if it was twenty or thirty pieces of silver. Perhaps those long Sunday mornings when Michael daydreamed through Sunday school could have been put to better use.

Brother Thomas pensively nibbles a wedge of lemon. "There was indeed an event which has been interpreted by most people as a betrayal, but the word privileges an interpretation which I and my brothers believe to be false: an interpretation that derives from the homophobia of Peter and the resultant church. But surely you can see that without this event, Christianity would be merely another minor cult."

From where Michael sits he can see two levels of stalled traffic on the Queensboro Bridge. It strikes him that wherever he looks he finds metaphors for his own dilemma: the traffic jam, the crumbling walls, the island surrounded by water, even the chain-link fence that he had to negotiate to get to the Smallpox Hospital —all remind him of his own stalled position and the impediments existing between him and the missing Rose White. He finishes his toast and sets the plate on a little wicker table.

"You remember that Jesus offered the disciples a sop of bread," continues Brother Thomas, "and that Judas was the one who took it. Many claim that the devil was perched on that sop of bread and by eating it, Judas took the devil into his mouth. But without the betrayal, there would have been no arrest; without the arrest, no Crucifixion; without the Crucifixion, no Resurrection; without the Resurrection, no religion. And Jesus knew this. He could see both past and future. Didn't he say to Judas, 'What you are doing, do quickly'? They all knew someone had to go to the authorities, but only Judas had the courage to volunteer. He went because his love was greatest, because he was Jesus's brother. Peter of course was the one who should have gone, but Peter was a coward. Look at his behavior with the soldiers. It is Peter who raises the alarm about Judas, and he is the first to speak of betrayal. He needed a scapegoat, needed to turn attention away from his cowardice. And you may very well ask yourself, who gave Judas the assignment of going to India? Once again we see Peter's hand. And why did Judas go? Because it was the most difficult task, and worthy only of the disciple with the most love. And he would have been successful if Peter hadn't stayed behind to spread slander. When he returned, all doors were shut against him. He was the traitor who had hung himself and not the one who had sacrificed himself so that Jesus could give evidence of his Godhood. Of course a few believed him, a chosen few, and they kept his story alive."

If we look closely at Michael's face, we can see different levels of activity. On the surface exists a sort of patient interest as Michael sips his tea, now cold, and glances at Brother Thomas, who paces back and forth in front of him. After all, Michael is polite, and even though Brother Thomas is just a stepping-stone on his path, he must not take that stepping-stone too lightly. No stepping-stone wants to be just a stepping-stone and each must dream of someday being a destination. But beneath Michael's courtesy burns a huge impatience, as well as the seeds of anger, which is perhaps the most surprising because Michael never feels anger and one realizes the seriousness of the events surrounding him if they have pushed him to such an extreme.

But this morning—Monday—the news media learned that Marduk the Magnificent's fiancée had been mysteriously abducted, and a few dozen of their representatives woke Michael at eight o'clock (remember that he had been with Brodsky and Gapski until four a.m.) to plague him with questions. Michael refused to see them and took his phone off the hook, but soon they were pounding on his door, having gained access through the super, who had proved himself willing to take a few bribes.

Michael fled, and fled in such a hurry that he left behind the mustache, wig and floppy hat that he often used to disguise himself. He fled out the back door and he fled on foot, and as he ran down the street, he was aware of heads turning and recognition flaring in the eyes of strangers; and he could see his name, or the name of his Gimmick, being silently articulated on the lips of the unknown many.

He came to rest at the back of a dark bar on Avenue A to consider his options. One, he could call Muldoon, who would commiserate but tell him that life was enriched by conflict. Two, he could call Brodsky and Gapski, who appeared to have lost interest in Rose White now they had discovered all those bones in possession of Troll (who was being eagerly sought). Three, he could call Deep Rat and ask what to do next. But he didn't quite like Deep Rat and he didn't quite trust him and he felt that seeing Deep Rat would only lead to more bruises. The ones he had received from Troll were still painful, and maybe it was more bruises that Michael wanted to avoid (and wasn't he alarmed to find within himself a snippet of trepidation?). Consequently, he had chosen the fourth option of calling Jack Molay (he now had his number), and Jack Molay told him just what Michael had been afraid he would tell him: to find the Master of Ceremonies.

"But how can he help me?" Michael asked.

"He may not help you at all," Jack Molay said, "but even that might help you to help yourself."

It was here that Michael felt the first glimmerings of anger. "But Rose White is in danger!"

"I realize that, but if you choose to find her yourself, you must do it with a combination of action and wisdom, and the latter means knowing what questions to ask."

"And where is the Master of Ceremonies?"

"Go to the old Smallpox Hospital and ask about betrayal. When you have learned about betrayal, you may ask about the Master of Ceremonies."

Michael had sighed, and when he recovered from his sigh to ask another question, he found that the line was dead.

If you ask a New York cab driver about the old Smallpox Hospital, he will look at you blankly. This is information best learned from your local library, and by the time Michael had discovered this and transported himself to Roosevelt Island it was late morning.

"As for betrayal," begins Brother Thomas, at last answering Michael's original question, "it depends where you are standing. Judas appears to be the betrayer, but in fact he is the savior. Peter appears to be the hero, but in fact is the betrayer. What appears false turns out to be true; what appears true turns out to be false. Why do you need to know this?"

"My fiancée has been kidnapped."

"And how will this be of assistance?"

"I don't know. Maybe it means that someone who seems trustworthy is not trustworthy and I am looking in the wrong places. But it's also supposed to lead me to the Master of Ceremonies. I'm told he can help."

"Ahhh." Brother Thomas nibbled another piece of lemon.

"Do you think he could help?"

"Perhaps, although I should think it would be an indirect sort of help. He is not a man of action."

"Do you know where I can find him?"

"The question is not simply where the Master of Ceremonies is to be found. It is also what is the ceremony."

"I don't follow you," says Michael.

"One can't be a master of ceremonies in a vacuum, just as one can't be a host in a vacuum. To be a host, one needs guests. To be a master of ceremonies, one needs a ceremony and other people. Do you know the story of your fiancée's kidnapping?"

Michael is struck by the oddness of the question. "I know she disappeared from her locked apartment and her bedroom window was smashed open. I've also seen videotapes showing her chained to a wall and showing her in a small cage dangling from a crane. What do you mean by the story?"

"One's question is what has caused a series of events and so one formulates the story of how those events were caused in order to repair them. For instance, the followers of the disciple Peter put forth a narrative to explain why life is the way it is, yet their story has little effect on current events. The world goes on as badly as before. Consequently, they must be mistaken. We Judists feel that if our own narrative were adopted, then events would change. The world would get better. Unfortunately, there are many groups and each has a narrative. The Master of Ceremonies is the one who helps to find a way through them."

" 'There must be heresies among you so that those who are genuine may be recognized,' " quoted Michael.

"Yes, that was Paul. Not much better than Peter, but at least he wasn't a coward. But my point is that you are not simply looking for the Master of Ceremonies, you are looking for the Master and all those for whom he is the Master."

"And can you tell me where he is to be found?"

"I can only tell you what is true to the Judists, which is that he can be found within the number thirty-three, which is the age of Judas at the time of the supposed betrayal."

"Thirty-three?"

"Exactly."

"And that's supposed to tell me something?"

"Only if you are ready to receive it," says Brother Thomas. "I admit it is the smallest snippet of information, but it is a beginning. Go to the Cathars. Perhaps they will tell you more, or at least they'll tell you what is true for them. But be careful. They are dualists and full of error."

"And where can these Cathars be found?"

"You might find one in the vicinity of what they call Montsegur, the Mountain of Safety, which they also call Mount Thabor, and which everyone else calls the Cloisters."

"How will I recognize him?"

"It might be a woman. In any case they wear black, robes much like my own, but with an ornate woven belt from which hangs a leather bag. Within it they keep their version of the New Testament. Many of the Cathars are also weavers and some carry small looms. They particularly like the Saint-Guilhem Cloister. They say it reminds them of Albi. Twelfth-century, you know."

Let us skip past the difficulties which Michael experiences in getting from Roosevelt Island to the Cloisters at the same time the *New York Post* hits the streets with his picture on the front page under the headline *Marduk the Murderer?* This is a dark day for Michael and it means engaging in confessional-type conversations with strangers, mainly taxi drivers, who want to know whether he butchered his fiancée.

"I don't know why all this is happening," Michael says at one point to a taxi driver named Ahmed.

"Bad karma," says the driver. "The same thing happened to my Uncle Akhbar."

"And did it get better?"

"No, he went crazy and died. But it got so bad that death was an improvement. No more pain. Hey, he was that lucky."

But having given the flavor of these events, let's advance to where Michael is sitting with Sister Esclarmonde by the fountain of the Saint-Guilhem Cloister. Around them are columns topped with strange plants and animals: more geometric than beastly. Sister Esclarmonde is seated at a table on which stands a small loom. She is an attractive woman in her mid-forties and bears the inner smile of someone who knows herself to be saved. "Yes, we still keep an office in Albi," she is saying, "but purely for sentimental reasons. After Montsegur was destroyed our time in France was basically over. Count Raymond of Toulouse burned two hundred of the Perfect—those are our priests—in a single day. Shortly before that last battle, four of the Perfect escaped with our treasure and holy books. Even though it was winter they made their way to Cathar communities high in the Pyrenees. Later they fled east and were welcomed by the Bogomil communities in Bosnia. As hundreds of Cathars kept being burned by the Inquisition, others fled to Bosnia as well. France became quite dead to us, although —foolishly perhaps—we still see ourselves as French."

"They burned people?" asks Michael incredulously. "When was this?" He thinks it must have happened during World War II.

"The citadel of Montsegur fell in March of 1244, but the last Perfect was burned in France in 1330."

Michael feels relieved. "But that's quite a while ago."

"You say that because the span of your life is approximately seventy-five years and so you think, Oh, that's nearly nine lifetimes ago. But for a big tree, it isn't much, and in the span of the world, it's nothing. In fact, your short memory makes the repetition of such atrocities possible. Oh, you say, Genghis Khan was long ago. Oh, Hitler was long ago. But your memory isn't your fault. It's a flaw built into the matter of which you are made and it's one more proof of the deviousness of your maker. You see, it was because he envied God's rule over Heaven that the Devil created this world on earth. He attacked God and was beaten, but he escaped with a third of the celestial spirits. Then when the Devil made men and women, he put one of these captured spirits into each of his clumsy creations in order to give it life. You have such a celestial spirit caged within you, and it's your duty to live a life which denies the world of matter—a life of great purity—so that at your death the spirit may be returned to God. That's why it is wrong for you to have children or eat meat, because such activities dilute your spirit."

But let's pause a moment. Sister Esclarmonde has a long story but we don't need to hear it. Pope Innocent III's crusade against the Albigensians, their slaughter and persecution by the Inquisition: these matters burn fiercely within her heart. As for her beliefs, we have heard enough to know that they resemble those of the Vals and the Mars Boys, although Sister Esclarmonde would be deeply insulted to hear this. They differ as Catholics and Protestants differ: those small controversies that led to the deaths of millions. As for Michael, he sits on a bench near the fountain and stares at a tangle of stone grape vines carved above the Romanesque columns, and within their confusion he finds another metaphor for his own predicament.

We must sympathize with him. Just as he was at a loss at how to behave when confronted with Troll, so he is at a loss now. Just as he didn't know how to fight, neither does he know how to think. He doesn't know what it means to ask the right questions. He doesn't understand the argument that falsehood is necessary so that truth may be recognized. He doesn't get this stuff about betrayal and its connection with Rose White's kidnapping. He doesn't understand what it means to formulate the story of those events in order to decipher them. If an action is seen by fifty people, Michael thinks they will agree about what happened. He doesn't realize that fifty people may have fifty different stories. And what is the story of the kidnapping? Michael feels he already knows it (meaning the events themselves) and consequently all he must do is to discover the kidnappers.

But let us again rejoin him. Michael is saying, "That business about matter and not having babies sounds like the Vals and the Mars Boys. They both talk about the evil of matter."

Sister Esclarmonde's forehead wrinkles. "They too are dualists, but there are many differences between us. That is why we find the Master of Ceremonies so necessary."

"Who is 'we'?"

Sister Esclarmonde works a red piece of yarn through her loom. A group of Japanese tourists enter the cloister and Michael keeps his back to them so he won't be recognized. Even in Japan he is famous.

"The 'we' are the Disputants," says Sister Esclarmonde. "All the different groups. Each has a representative and they meet together and argue. But they don't really argue: they dispute. And the Master of Ceremonies keeps the peace between them. It's quite a crowd."

"And where do they meet?"

"In the Lair of Christ."

"Where's that?" asks Michael.

"I'm afraid that's all I can tell you."

"So you believe in Christ?" The hope of knowledge that had brightened in Michael's brain begins to fade, but he still thinks he may learn something to give him further assistance.

"Of course. He's the chief of God's Aeons. When sent to earth, he put on the shape of Jesus of Nazareth, but that was only a disguise, because he wasn't human at all and so he didn't have to be born from a human being. All that business about the Virgin

Mary is just dirty talk. He came to earth to fight the Devil and rescue the captive sparks of divinity. It's been quite a battle, don't you think? And it's going on even as we speak."

It occurs to Michael that Christ putting on the disguise of Jesus of Nazareth would be like Marduk the Magnificent assuming the Gimmick of Michael Marmaduke. He is surprised by this thought. "Does the number thirty-three mean anything to you?"

"Only that it was the number of years that Christ bore the Figment, the impersonation of Jesus, before it became not worth his trouble."

"Do you know anyone who might tell me more clearly where the Master of Ceremonies might be found?"

"Possibly a Promethean. They like high open places. You might find one in the bell tower at Riverside Church."

"What do they look like?" asks Michael.

"They favor Greek-looking costumes. But be careful. They're hardly Christian at all. Although personally, I find pagans less abrasive than heretics."

Michael's trip from the Cloisters to Riverside Church entailed recognition by several different groups, and none of this was pleasant. Leaving the Cloisters, he was assailed by a squad of Japanese tourists with little books they wanted him to sign as well as wanting to videotape him in wrestling poses with five of their number. Michael ran for a cab and the Japanese gave chase. From high above, the scene resembled hounds harrying a stag.

The cab driver was named Vladimir and he said, "Did you or did you not kill your girlfriend?"

"I don't know what you're talking about," lied Michael. He was shocked that someone would think not only that he might commit murder, but that he would kill anybody he loved as much as he loved Rose White.

Then, once inside the church, the man who sold Michael a ticket to the bell tower said, "I know you!" To which Michael responded, "You only think you do." And of course there were more tourists, more gawkers. You see how difficult it is to get from Point A to Point B? Also, at the first opportunity, the cab driver

Vladimir phoned the *New York Post* and told someone at the city desk that he could reveal the location of Michael Marmaduke for a price. But Rose White is in danger. We can only touch upon these peripheral scenes with the lightest of fingers.

The Promethean is a tall thick man with a great white beard. He doesn't quite wear a toga, but his blousy white shirt is togalike and he wears Greek sandals. His Levi's, however, are pure American. His name is Timaeus and he treats Michael and his endeavors with the mild scorn of someone who has always seen himself as a benevolent outsider.

"You say your girlfriend has been kidnapped? Maybe you should think yourself lucky. Maybe you should just wrestle and forget these other distractions."

"I need to find the Master of Ceremonies," says Michael. He has made his way up through the carillon, three or four stories of catwalks, which he has not enjoyed, and now he is on a sort of balcony poked out over the New York skyline. They are on the south side of the tower and it is windy. Stretched out before them under a hazy sky lies all of New York with Central Park to their left and the World Trade Center way off in the distance. Michael just hopes the seventy-four bells don't begin to ring while he is up here. He has never liked heights, and although this may be a weakness, he has no wish to change, since it would most likely mean putting himself in danger by climbing to high places like this one. Life, he thinks, is short enough.

"You've been wasting your time talking to Christians," says Timaeus. "They get the story wrong. Jesus's brother isn't Judas, but Diabolos. Perhaps one can say that as Chrystos dons the illusory body of Jesus, so Diabolos dons the illusory body of Judas, but that's as far as I'll go. According to Lactantius, Diabolos is the jealous brother of Chrystos. In fact, Chrystos is the right hand of God and Diabolos the left. And they are always fighting. Lactantius believed we needed evil. He wrote, 'If no evil existed, there would be no danger, and thus no basis for wisdom.' By that argument, if there were no evil, we'd all be a bunch of dopes. Evil makes us smart. But we don't want too much. The Master of Ceremonies helps us steer a course around it. Without him, the Disputants would kill each other."

"Where can I find the Master of Ceremonies."

"Why, in the Aerie, of course."

"Do you mean something frightening, like an eerie movie?" asks Michael, not happy with what he is hearing.

"Don't be silly. 'Aerie' derives from the Latin word *agrum*, meaning 'lair.' How much do you know about Prometheus, anyway?"

"Didn't he steal something and get caught?"

Timaeus looks scornful. "When Zeus, the Demiurge, made men, he made them cretinous. They were Neanderthals and existed to do Zeus's bidding and be his servants. Prometheus was one of the lesser Aeons, but he had great sympathy for these creatures while feeling their ugliness was an insult to the Unknowable Father of All. Consequently, he stole the holy fire, meaning Spirit or Pneuma, and he blew a tiny amount into the Neanderthals. In fact, Prometheus gave them a soul. Well, when Zeus realized some of the Pneuma was missing, he summoned his Aeons. All came except Prometheus, and because of his absence, Zeus realized he was guilty. He seized Prometheus, nailed him to a cliff in the Caucasus Mountains and summoned an eagle to devour Prometheus's liver. Every day the eagle eats the liver and every night it grows back. But the Unknowable Father of All realized that Prometheus had stolen the Pneuma only out of love for him, and so he sent down his right hand, Chrystos, to do battle with Zeus, and that battle is continuing even as we speak."

"And who will win?" asks Michael.

"We hope that Chrystos will win and free Prometheus, but who knows? Zeus is very wily. But by bending our thoughts toward this battle we hope to influence it. Even though the Disputants disagree about many things, they agree about the final battle, that the forces of evil and good are locked in combat."

"But what is the Aerie?"

"The Aerie is the lair of the eagle—the place where Prometheus is bound and tortured—but it is also the meeting place of the Disputants."

"That doesn't help me," says Michael.

"It's the best I can do. For me to know the location by another name would be heresy."

"Do you know the meaning of its other names? Thirty-three or the Lair of Christ."

"Yes, that is what it is called by others, but those terms are meaningless to me."

"But is the Aerie a place?"

"Yes, it's a very high place, one of the highest in New York City, much higher than the place where we now stand."

"Thirty-three," Michael says to himself, "the lair of Christ, the Aerie." Surely some sense can be made from this.

As Michael faces the low stone wall that divides him from four hundred feet of nothingness, he hears a shouting from inside the bell tower. Glancing around the corner, he sees a TV crew trying to work its way up the catwalk. He also sees several other men and women he recognizes as press types.

"Is there any other way down from here?" asks Michael.

"Not unless you want to jump."

The very idea brings an unpleasant sensation to Michael's knees. "Then I guess I'll have to go down the regular way. It's just that I was hoping to avoid those people."

The Promethean gives a friendly shrug. "Possibly I can distract them so you can get first crack at the stairs."

"I'd be in your debt."

"Who knows," says Timaeus, "perhaps even you, somehow, will help free Prometheus from the eagle tearing at his liver. You move toward the stairs, then I'll make a terrible scream."

Ten minutes later the following scene may be observed in Riverside Park. On one of the paths runs Michael Marmaduke. How graceful he is. He runs as if he has been running all his life, which, because of his body-building routine, is almost the case. He bounces from leg to leg as if from trampoline to trampoline. Strung out behind him are about two dozen representatives of the press, while far back (one can barely see them among the trees) are several TV crews. The cameras unfortunately slow them down. Given Michael's speed, we are impressed that some of these reporters run so quick. It would be interesting to know which news organization has the fastest reporter. The *Times*? The *Post*? The *News*? The *Village Voice*? *Newsday*? *Time*? *Newsweek*? How are the wire services doing? What about the foreign press? But such a quiz would distract us from our main purpose. Descending to a point where we can peer inside Michael's head, we see a lot of activity. Thirty-three, he keeps thinking, the Lair of Christ, the Aerie. And he is also thinking about betrayal. Who can he trust if he can't trust himself? To what degree is evil more than an assigned Gimmick deriving from the Wrestling Association? Thirty-three, the Aerie, Christ's Lair, he thinks. Christ's Lair? And with this simple inversion Michael almost comes to a halt. It seems he has been struck by a sudden thought.

19

IMAGINED SQUEEZE

Wally Wallski is careening through Grand Central Station to the Oyster Bar to chow down on two dozen Chincoteague oysters when he spots the headline of the *New York Post: Marduk the Murderer?* If Wally Wallski had a friend, he might later tell this friend: "It was as if someone gave me a kick in the butt!" Wally Wallski comes to such an abrupt stop that several people bump into him. "For crying out loud," he says, still staring at the headline. Then he buys the paper to see what it has to say. Around him is the echoing cavern of the station with people rushing in every direction. It is twelve-thirty and many are thinking about lunch. If one could transform thoughts into pictures, the air would be filled with images of food: chickens here, crepes suzette there.

Wally Wallski sits on a bench like a depressed commuter who has just lost his job. Actually, he is half crocked and has a hard time focusing on the print. Only a half hour before, he left the three Hunter College professors DeMaus, Sosage and Vogel at O'Leary's Pub in his new role as Ernest Hemingway. And what does Wally Wallski plan to do as Ernest Hemingway? He plans to buy himself some oysters at the Oyster Bar because he loves oysters and his wife Claudine will never let him have any. But now everything is changed.

"He killed his fiancée? That's going too far!"

Within the paper is a photograph of the police detectives Brodsky and Gapski, and Wally Wallski decides they must be twins, they look so much alike. Wally Wallski reads that while Brodsky and Gapski do not exactly accuse Marduk of killing Rose White, neither do they rule him out. Consequently, he is a suspect. There is also a photograph of Rose White's building with a white arrow pointing to her broken window and a line of broken white dots showing the ostensible path to the roof. Wally Wallski whistles. He can't imagine climbing down a rope to the twentieth floor, then climbing back up with a girl on your shoulder, even a girl who is as light as a feather. Not even Ernest Hemingway could have pulled off such a trick, no matter what DeMaus might say. Wally Wallski feels humbled and the oysters are forgotten.

Reading the news story in his drunken state, Wally Wallski decides there is no real evidence against Marduk (at least none is mentioned), but neither has Marduk issued a denial. In fact, he has refused to comment. In the language codes manipulated by the media, refusal to comment is tantamount to an admission of guilt. But Wally Wallski can't believe it. He staggers to his feet. In his new role of Ernest Hemingway, he wishes he could help. Perhaps there is an arm he can twist or a head to bop, because he knows that Ernest Hemingway wouldn't just sit around.

But let us not carry this Hemingway business too far. It is only because he is tanked up and torn between the twin terrors of Claudine and Mr. Lenguado that Wally Wallski has let himself be influenced by strangers. It is transformation he is after: to be somebody other than himself. And if someone offered to change him into a white rabbit, he might jump at the chance. The mantle of Ernest Hemingway offers Wally Wallski a little sapling to hide behind while he decides what to do about Mr. Lenguado. And if Wally Wallski were sober, the sapling would shrink to the size of a fig leaf.

But now comes the news about Marduk the Magnificent, and for a moment Wally Wallski forgets Mr. Lenguado as he imagines Marduk's heartache for his missing sweetheart. Once Wally Wallski was also in love, and even though falling in love with Claudine was like falling in love with Alcatraz, he still recalls those tender feelings and he knows how Marduk must suffer. Wally Wallski smacks his forehead. How petty to be crushed by his own problems when Marduk's are so much greater! This is an important moment for Wally Wallski. By his own choice he is moving away from the protective sapling of Ernest Hemingway and into the open terrain ruled by those eagles of the air his wife Claudine and Mr. Lenguado, and for the time being neither seems quite so awful. Wally Wallski gets to his feet. He will sober up, then go down to Fulton Street and convey to Mr. Lenguado his wife Claudine's request: a red brick townhouse on Gramercy Park. If Marduk can face adversity, then so can Wally Wallski. After all, Mr. Lenguado can only say no. So what if he says it in a voice so loud that the leaves fall from the trees?

Wally Wallski weaves his way to a 42nd Street exit. He is still half in the bag, and reaching the sidewalk he promptly collides with a shopping cart—not one full of groceries but one full of mysterious bundles wrapped in black plastic. Once again this is Beetle, and seeing Wally Wallski, his face brightens.

Disentangling himself, Wally Wallski focuses on Beetle and finds him vaguely familiar, as if Beetle were a friend from his youth. "Isn't it awful about Marduk the Magnificent?" he asks.

Beetle pats his plastic bags to make certain nothing has been disturbed. "As ye reap," he says, "so shall ye sow. I know a story worse than that. It concerns a baby and the terrible things that were done to it. Would you like to hear it?"

"I'm too mixed up to think straight," says Wally Wallski and thrusts money at him. "Here's a buck. Buy yourself an oyster."

When Zapo, the fifteen-year-old legless syringe salesman, sees the front page of the *Post* he feels as if someone were shaking his stumpboard—so great is his admiration for Marduk the Magnificent and so deep flows his sympathy for Marduk's troubles. As he reads the article at the edge of the Bowling Green, where he likes to take the sun when he is not working, he hears the passing business types above him (he is at knee level) arguing the pros and cons of the Marduk case. "Sure he killed her. Big guys like that can't control their dicks." "Nah, he's too dumb to kill anybody. His brain's like rice from all that bashing."

Even before finishing the article, Zapo is convinced of Marduk's innocence. Although Zapo is in the throes of a personal dilemma, which we will get to in a minute, he ducks into an alley, yanks his red Marduk the Magnificent sweatshirt out of his backpack and pulls it on. He may be small but he wants to show the world where his allegiance lies. Parked at the corner of Broadway and White-hall, Zapo waits for someone to make a nasty crack and then he will run back and forth over the guy's foot with his stumpboard until the guy cries uncle.

Zapo considers Marduk's problems. Here he is wrestling champion of the world and he is still capable of being dragged down by his enemies. And what is Marduk doing? Cringing in a cellar? No way! Zapo is sure that Marduk is on the attack. Certainly if Rose White is ever rescued, then Marduk will be the one to do it. "I'm with you, pal!" he calls up Broadway to wherever Marduk must be.

But this brings us to Zapo's own dilemma. Only a few hours earlier he has heard a bunch of thugs discussing how they intend to melt the Snowman the very next morning, and since then Zapo has been brooding about his own ineffectuality. Not only is he fifteen, but he has no legs. And while he can run over the toes of one bozo and make him cry ouch, he can't do it to seven—especially seven guys with guns. Even if the Snowman were not the father of Beacon Luz, whose image is lodged in Zapo's heart just as the picture of the Quaker is lodged on a box of Quaker Oats, he would still want to stop these guys, simply because the Snow-man—in the vaguest of terms—is Zapo's boss. This certainly would be news to the Snowman, but just as water trickles down from a mountaintop, so does a bit of the Snowman's money trickle down to Zapo, and so he has a sense of obligation. Look at it this way. Zapo has no father, no mother, no relatives of any kind, no friends and hardly any acquaintances. If it weren't for the Snow-man and his crooked empire, God knows where Zapo would be. Probably selling pencils in Penn Station or in a home for dreary adolescents with kinky habits. So what if Zapo doesn't have any legs; he's got lots of heart. He's got more heart than a football team. But what he doesn't have is muscle, and the big question is how can he stop these bozos from melting the Snowman? In fact, wouldn't he be crazy to try? He'd only get stomped on. Maybe he'd get shot or have his stumpboard turned into splinters. So this is Zapo's dilemma: what, if anything, can he do to help?

But now, wearing his red Marduk sweatshirt and behaving aggressively to the passersby, Zapo takes courage. He pushes off on his rag-wrapped knuckles. He will warn the Snowman. He will burst into his penthouse condo at Gateway Plaza and say, "Snowman, seven thugs are planning to shoot you!" And as Zapo rips along at knee level, he imagines how Beacon Luz will look at him with a new light in her eye, how she will put her hand on his head and want to be his pal.

It is wonderful to have a plan. A plan can make the whole future rosy. No longer is one being sloshed about by the white waters of fate, thrown from one jagged rock to the next. To have a plan is like having a little canoe and even the fiercest rapids can be negotiated.

But an hour later, Zapo's plan is in shambles. He has tried entering through the front door of Gateway Plaza and making his way to the elevator, only to be caught by the security guards and ejected, roughly. The same thing happens when he tries the back door. Then he finds a side door and climbs six of the building's thirty-four floors (this is very difficult with a stumpboard), before being caught and thrown out again. This time he collects some serious bruises. Then Zapo tries calling, but first he finds that the Snowman has an unlisted number, and then, after he convinces the operator that it's a matter of life and death, he is blocked by the Snowman's appointment secretary, who says that for the Snowman nothing is a matter of life and death, unless the Snowman is the one doing the labeling.

So Zapo is left leaning against a wall of the Gateway Plaza exactly where he was sitting earlier with his friend Beetle when he heard the thugs planning to melt the Snowman with a lot of machinery. He feels frustrated and beaten. But because Zapo wears his red Marduk sweatshirt and because he knows that his troubles are nothing compared to Marduk's, his brain keeps ticking. Glancing around, he sees some kids in the parking lot working with their skateboards. They have made a ramp out of plywood in the shape of a bowl which enables them to zoom down one side and zoom up the other, then make a delicate turn at the lip and zoom back down again. Zapo watches for a few minutes. Then like a crocus pushing through the soil in early spring, an idea begins to blossom in Zapo's brain.

Let's take a look at Beacon Luz before we move on to other business. She is planted in front of the TV thirty-four stories above Zapo and she is depressed, but she is not depressed about anything directly connected to her own life. This in itself is noteworthy because usually it would take an earthquake measuring over eight points on the Richter scale to get Beacon Luz's mind off herself and her appetites. You think she is spoiled? Sure she is spoiled, but how could she not be spoiled with a father who ignores her except to shout, and an abject slave of a mother who only opens her mouth to complain, and a penthouse full of sycophantic toadies who only speak in order to lie? And even though their lies are pleasant (oh, Beacon Luz, Einstein was a dummy compared to you), they are still ersatz.

Ninety-nine percent of the time Beacon Luz has her brain focused on the bull's-eye of herself, because for all her problems she is the most unchangeable thing in a constantly changing environment. Paradoxically, she is both the drowning man and the straw to which the drowning man clings. Despite all the presents and new clothes and rich food, life with the Snowman is not easy.

But one percent of the time, Beacon Luz turns her eyes outward and focuses them on her hero, Marduk the Magnificent. And she is depressed because according to the TV, Marduk is in deep trouble, and Beacon Luz wishes she could help. Maybe she can get her father to shoot someone or hire a squad of pit bulls. And to show her support for the famous wrestler, Beacon Luz is wearing her Marduk the Magnificent sweatshirt. But unlike Zapo's sweatshirt, hers is forest green.

Over in Brooklyn, in a back ward of St. Elmo's Hospital, Sparrow Gonzalez is visiting his friend Bernard. It is a gloomy time for Sparrow, and the one bright spot in the dismal landscape of his present life is the lucky coin, which Sparrow clutches tightly in his left fist, which is buried in his jacket pocket.

Sparrow is seated on one side of a table and Bernard is seated on the other. They are in the middle of a large room furnished, for the most part, with green vinyl furniture and a TV turned up too loud. All the windows are covered with wire mesh. Twenty other people are scattered about the room, but, to tell the truth, they look unconnected, as if someone had come along and ripped their plugs from the wall. Some stare at the ceiling, some stare at the floor, some stare at the TV in a vague way, and if you took one of these people by the shoulders and pointed him or her at anything else, then he or she would look at that new object without an iota of added interest. Their interest level being at this moment absolutely zip. They have been medicated and their mental machinery is moving about as fast as a snail moves up a wall.

On the TV an anchorman is saying there is still no idea as to the whereabouts of Marduk the Magnificent or his fiancée, Rose White. Marduk was last seen in Riverside Park running away from reporters. The man is able to articulate this in such a manner that if Marduk were on trial, a jury would sentence him to one hundred years of solitary.

"Isn't it terrible about Marduk the Magnificent?" says Sparrow. "Isn't it a cryin shame?"

Bernard is sitting with his hands in his lap. His beautiful blue eyes have filmed over exactly like a fish's eyes when you cook it. "Ahhh," says Bernard.

"Have you always been a wrestling fan?" asks Sparrow, holding his lucky coin a little tighter.

"Ahhh," says Bernard.

"Personally," says Sparrow, "I have no doubt that this whole thing is a setup. When a guy gets to be as powerful as Marduk the Magnificent, he's bound to have enemies. Look at me, I'm absolutely nobody and I've got tons of enemies. So it stands to reason that Marduk must have millions."

"Ahhh," says Bernard.

Sparrow moves his hand back and forth in front of Bernard's dead fish eyes. There is no response. It occurs to Sparrow that Bernard is dead. Of course, he knows he is not dead, but his brain is moving so slowly that he might as well be dead. Even a goldfish has a more active mental life. And Sparrow thinks about who killed him: the Grabber. What would Marduk the Magnificent do with a guy like the Grabber? He would turn him into fudge.

"Well," says Sparrow, "I guess I'll be shoving off. But I'll drop by tomorrow. Okay, Bernard?"

"Ahhh," says Bernard.

Sparrow makes his way out of the dayroom. He wonders what he would need to rescue these people. Maybe a tank. Isn't he nervous about being stuck with a lot of nutcases? But Sparrow has spent enough time on the streets of New York to know that a cross section of the general public could be no worse. Given a choice between the occupants of a picked-at-random subway car and St. Elmo's nuthatch, he, Sparrow, would take the nuthatch.

As Sparrow leaves the building—it is one of those gloomy red-brick buildings put up at the end of the last century—he thinks again of the Grabber and how he would like to hurt him. So what if the Grabber is four times his size and as mean as a cobra. Look at all the stuff Marduk the Magnificent has to put up with. If Marduk can do it, Sparrow can do it!

Then, reaching the parking lot, Sparrow sees the Grabber's white Econoline van. Casually, he walks toward it as if admiring its simple rectangular lines. Nobody is about. Sparrow strips off his blue window washer's shirt, then removes his undershirt, which he rips nearly in half, making one long piece of cloth. Unscrewing the gas cap, he pokes the cloth down the hole, then pulls it out. The bottom is wet with gasoline. Sparrow wets the rest of the cloth with drops of gasoline, then feeds the cloth into the tank again, leaving six inches on the outside. He steps back, puts on his shirt and digs in his pockets for a match.

At that moment, the Grabber comes out of the back door of the hospital. He is six feet six and weighs three hundred pounds, and his black hair is shaped into a duck's-ass haircut in imitation of Elvis, his idol. "Hey," shouts the Grabber, "what are you doin?"

"I'm going to make you poor," says Sparrow and he lights the gasoline-soaked strip of cloth and sprints for the street. Five seconds later the Ford van disappears in a ball of orange flame and a loud roar. Up and down Flatbush Avenue people rush to their windows to see a cloud of black smoke. Even the medicated inmates of St. Elmo's blink their eyes, slowly. We hear an odd tinkling noise on the pavement which is hard to identify until we realize that the van has been turned into metallic confetti.

The Grabber crawls up off his stomach and sees Sparrow on the sidewalk. "Jesus," he cries, "look what you've done!"

"You're poor," says Sparrow, "but you're not poor enough." And he jogs off down Flatbush Avenue toward Kings Highway, where he intends to catch a bus.

The Grabber jumps up and runs after him. "Hey, stop!"

Sparrow grins. He knows the Grabber can't catch him, while if he runs fast enough, maybe the Grabber will pop his heart.

If we lift ourselves up high over the street, the following panorama is spread before us. There is St. Elmo's surrounded by trees and there are the remnants of the burning van. There is Sparrow running down Flatbush Avenue pursued by the Grabber, who is getting farther and farther behind. We hear the sirens of approaching fire trucks. But if we look up toward Flatlands Avenue we see another runner. His name is Seth and he is running southwest on Flatlands as Sparrow is running northwest on Flatbush. Seth is a handsome young man, eighteen years old, and he is in a hurry because his father Marcello is sick and the only thing that will make him better (according to his father) is a bottle of aquavit, which is some kind of brandy he used to drink in the old country. In fact, his father Marcello is so desperate that he has sent his two older sons searching for aquavit as well, but that was yesterday and the day before and they still haven't returned. The father hadn't wanted Seth to leave home because Seth is underage to buy alcohol, but Seth insisted that he could find the aquavit and at last Marcello let him go.

And now Seth is running his heart out southwest on Flatland as Sparrow is running his heart out northwest on Flatbush. From high above we see them approaching the corner, and first we think Sparrow will arrive first, then we think Seth will arrive first, and then we see they will arrive at exactly the same moment. We would warn them if we could, but it's too late for that. Sparrow and Seth collide and their left arms link and they spin around four times before they break free. But such is their fierce desire to keep running that they hesitate only a moment with their knees still pumping up and down before taking off again.

A few seconds later Sparrow slides to a halt in the middle of the sidewalk and begins frantically patting his pockets. The coin, he has lost his lucky coin! He looks back toward the corner where that young fellow smacked into him and he even runs halfway back across the street. He sees nothing flicker, nothing shiny on the sidewalk. Down Flatland Avenue he sees the young fellow's back getting smaller. Sparrow would run after him, but here comes the Grabber and the Grabber is smiling because he thinks (foolishly) that he almost has Sparrow in his clutches. Sparrow turns and begins to run, but there is no gladness in his step. Even the pleasure of blowing up the Grabber's white Ford Econoline van has faded.

And the lucky coin? It is buried deep in the left pocket of Seth's denim jacket and he doesn't even know it's there.

Now we turn our attention to the hospital where Violet White works. But perhaps to call it a hospital is a misnomer. Despite its size, it is more of a clinic and it goes by the name of El Instituto Estético. Truly, it resembles an automotive body shop where they make hot rods, because no one checks into El Instituto sick or damaged. Have you ever looked at yourself in the mirror and said, "My earlobes are too fat"? Here's where you can get them fixed. In El Instituto men have become women and women have become men, short people have become tall, tall people short, the old have become young again, at least temporarily. Genitalia have been improved with a variety of implants. Breasts, noses, ears, chins—all can be ordered from a color catalog the size of the New York phone book. You know those idle thoughts regarding how you would like to look on a summer beach, how you would like to make heads spin so fast that you can create ten thousand cricks in ten thousand necks? El Instituto makes beautiful people in the way Porsche makes fast cars, although it could just as easily produce monsters. Monsters, however, are not much in demand these days. Even so, some of El Instituto's best customers have been wrestlers who have come to have their fierceness heightened. To one fellow they gave the nose of a pig and a pair of tusks, to another they gave a set of horns and a tail.

As for Violet White, she is the head nurse on the two floors specializing in cranial improvements. Anything you want done to your head gets done here, although sad to say they only work on the exterior. If it's intelligence you want, or psychological well-being, or even happiness, you have to go someplace else. Luckily most people feel that a pretty face makes up for the rest, so even if there were a clinic where people could be made smarter or happier or more secure, the vast majority would still pick El Instituto Estético first.

On this Monday afternoon Violet White is making her rounds, urging perseverance and optimism, directing her nurses, and as she walks down the hall, she notices a man mopping the floor a few yards ahead of her. He is short and thin and wears a green uniform with a green cap pulled down over his brow. But what attracts Violet's attention is that the man seems uncomfortable on two feet and keeps bending forward as if to catch his balance.

Increasing her pace, Violet White reaches out her hand and grabs the man behind the neck. "You're sly," she says.

The man tries to turn and his cap falls off. Are we surprised to see Deep Rat? Not particularly.

"My slyness is at your service, Nurse White," he says, attempting a smile which shows off his pointy teeth.

"Only because I pay you and frighten you," says Violet. "How are your little paws today?"

"They are at your service as well."

"And what have you been doing?"

"I've been roaming around," says Deep Rat. "I've been roaming around the earth and walking up and down upon it."

"And what of your mission?"

"The evening went as well as we could hope."

"And did he believe you?"

"Of course."

"You remember what I told you?"

" 'Make it difficult but don't get him killed.' "

"Exactly," says Violet White, releasing him. "Be careful you don't make a mistake." Then she continues down the hall.

"My only joy," says Deep Rat, putting the green cap back on his head, "is to give you joy."

Violet doesn't respond. Instead of continuing her rounds, she goes to her office at the end of the hall. We observe a certain impatience to her step, a certain unsteadiness. Going to a file cabinet, she takes a videocassette and inserts it into a VCR, which rests on top of a Mitsubishi television on a table by the wall. A wrestling ring appears on the screen, and suddenly the great serpent Ur, the father of the Seven, leaps into its center. "I am the offspring of the serpent-nature and the corrupter's son!" he shouts. "I am the son of him who sits on the throne and has dominion over creation, who encircles the sphere, who encircles the ocean, whose tail lies in his mouth!"

Ur rushes back and forth across the ring striking his chest.

Next we hear a great roar and Ur falls back. Marduk the Magnificent climbs into the ring. "Hell beheld me and became weak!" he shouts. "Death spat me out and many with me, gall and poison I was to him. I descended with Death to the uttermost depths of Hell. His feet and head became strengthless!"

Violet waves the remote-control wand and there is a flurry of movement. When it stops we see that Marduk has the serpent Ur in an embrace, although Ur is upside down and facing away from Marduk. It is the Bosom of Abraham. Marduk squeezes and a blissful smile oversweeps his face. He closes his eyes. The serpent's tongue oozes from his mouth. Marduk squeezes harder. His blond hair trembles and a blond lock falls over his eyebrow. He squeezes until his lips turn white. Slick the referee ducks down, then slaps the mat three times. Marduk releases the body of Ur and the serpent collapses unconscious. Marduk places a silver elf boot on Ur's scaly chest, throws back his blond head and roars. Then he steps to the edge of the ring and speaks:

"I ascended up to the light as if on the chariot of truth, the
    Truth guided and led me.

She brought me over the gulfs and abysses and bore me upward
out of gorges and valleys.
She became to me a harbor of salvation and laid me in the arms
of life everlasting."

Through the television's speakers erupts the roar of the crowd.
Violet waves the control wand and the scene backs up. Again we
see the serpent Ur in the upside-down embrace of the Bosom of
Abraham. Violet White slows the action and the muscles of Marduk's arms pulsate. His smile ripens slowly like peach on a branch.
Violet stops the action altogether and focuses on Marduk's great
arms. She tries to imagine what it would be like to be squeezed so
hard that the air was forced from her lungs.

20

MULDOON: SOUL SURVIVOR

Can one, like Faust, have two souls in a single breast? I, Muldoon, sometimes feel that I have a hundred souls within me, a hundred different warriors wrestling for my heart. And of course Nietzsche claimed that "our body is a social structure composed of many souls." But he meant appetites and he made Pleasure their commander.

Muldoon does not mean appetites, but souls: self-movers, those which have a share of the divine. At best the appetites are the foot soldiers of the soul. But is there not within each breast the wish for darkness and the wish for light? May this not be evidence of more than a single soul? Nietzsche said, "I would rather be a satyr than a saint." Unfortunately, there was nothing of the satyr about him. He had no sexual drive. His mass of constructive thought was made possible only because he lacked a libido. No playgirls danced across Nietzsche's brain, and, ultimately, it drove him mad. Has this never been argued, that Nietzsche's madness was due entirely to sperm backup? In his madness he kept repeating: "I am dead because I am stupid; I am stupid because I am dead." Over and over. That stupidity was his lack of libido. I am dead because I lack a libido; I lack a libido because I am dead. Yes, yes, I know that

he also said, "A man sometimes needs a woman just as he sometimes needs a well-cooked meal." But that very statement indicates
his lack of a libido. Pussy cannot be confused with meat loaf! Even
when he meets the single so-called love of his life, Lou Andreas-
Salomé, his address to her is entirely devoid of libido. "What
stars," he asked, "have sent us orbiting toward each other?" No
wonder she refused to marry him. Nietzsche went crazy from
sperm backup, not from a dose of the pox picked up at a cathouse.
Without a libido, he took long walks during which he formulated
his philosophy. "Never believe ideas that come to you indoors,"
he wrote. On these walks he invented the Individual: a creature
who had not existed in Europe until Nietzsche came upon the
scene. Friends came to visit and Nietzsche would drag them up and
down country roads for twelve hours. So he could never have felt
sexual temptation. He could never have been a satyr.

I, Muldoon, have many temptations. I shut my eyes and they
crawl up and down the insides of my eyelids: undulating, nubile
bodies, money, fast cars, the privileges of power.

Isn't it greater to have temptations and resist them than to have
no temptations at all? Isn't the man who yearns for the hot flesh
of little boys and yet denies himself a better Boy Scout leader than
the one who is without temptation? "Verily," says Zarathustra, "I
laugh at those who are weak and think themselves good because
they have no strength in their claws."

Let us consider Michael Marmaduke, whom I love as my own
son. After all, I helped to create him. What seems pure about
Michael is the singularity of his nature, but this is in fact a decep-
tion, because his nature is childish. He is a twenty-five-year-old
man trapped in an eight-year-old's sensibility. He is an animal who
has never been let out of his cage. You think perhaps there is no
cage, that he is naturally simple with a vanilla-flavored soul: soul
of sweetness, soul of light? I grant the possibility. But what of his
other soul, the one that has not yet revealed itself, that is still
folded within his darkness like a tulip bulb beneath the ground, a
black flower which has yet to poke up its first green shoots? No,
you say: what you see is what you get.

Can one, like Faust, have two souls in a single breast?

I say there is another soul within Michael Marmaduke which lies dormant because it has never been summoned. Perhaps he has even repressed it. Perhaps he once caught sight of its twisted face and it frightened him. Perhaps its appetites disgusted him. What would it mean to release that soul? Let's look at him now, torn by the trauma of Rose White's kidnapping. Certainly I see changes within him: beginnings of anger and impatience, the glow of un-released violence. Is the Boy Scout leader who feels no temptation in fact a cripple? Is a saint without temptation truly a saint? Both Saint Francis and Augustine had to subdue the flesh. By calling it bad, they were able to reject it. They were cripples who could only walk with the crutch of morality. Isn't this rejection of the flesh a weakness? A living thing above all needs to vent its strength. And what happens if one represses that desire so that it seethes and burns within one unreleased? Does one then like Nietzsche go crazy at the age of forty-five? Sperm backup.

I am amused by the arguments of contemporary thinkers who say we must slap ourselves on the wrist for our nasty thoughts. The genitalia of each human being, they suggest, should be put in a genitalia bank, and a person—man or woman—should only retrieve it if he or she promises to use it with minuscule pleasure and then return it right away, carefully scrubbed. They want to create a world in which there is nothing to be afraid of. They confuse stability with morality. Let's make everyone the same size and have the same intelligence and wear the same clothes! Moral-ity is no more than timidity, which is the enemy of the will to power. My friends, there is no such thing as the common good. It is a contradiction in terms. What is common has no value.

It is Muldoon's belief that the emotions of hatred, envy, covet-ousness and lust for domination are life-giving emotions which need to be heightened if life itself is to be heightened. Without them, one might as well retire to a lawn chair and lick sherbet forever. Lust for domination is the little engine which powers each of my wrestlers. Even Michael must have it buried within him. But it frightens him. He is afraid that if he releases it, he won't be able to control it, that Rose White won't like him. Why does Dentata feel comfortable in the company of Michael Marmaduke? Because she feels he has no lust for domination: a lust which, we can surmise, once victimized her in her earlier life when she was merely Maud.

Nietzsche wrote, "We think severity, force, slavery, peril in the street and in the heart, concealment, stoicism, the art of experiment and devilry of every kind, that everything evil, dreadful, tyrannical, beast of prey and serpent in man serves to enhance the species 'man' just as much as does its opposite."

If I were struck blind, I would print that sentence on little cards and sell them on the street. No wonder Nietzsche felt that he had to wear a mask! "Everything profound loves the mask," he wrote. "Every profound spirit needs a mask." He of course was the profound spirit he had in mind. You can't be the champion of the art of experiment and devilry and not need a mask. Otherwise, they won't let you out of jail! Genghis Khan is as necessary as Mahatma Gandhi. As John Wesley said, "No devil, no God." We are the sworn enemies of vanilla!

It is the mask that lets us live among our fellow creatures and not have them turn against us. When I shake the hand of a beautiful woman, what is it that keeps her from thinking I want to rip the clothes from her succulent flesh? My mask: the kindly mask of avuncularity.

But do not think that the mask hides only what the timid and hesitant call evil. Nietzsche writes, "I could believe that a man who had something fragile and valuable to conceal might roll through life as thick and round as an old, green, thick-hooped wine barrel." The mask hides whatever the wearer wishes to hide. Yet often it may conceal its opposite: beauty conceals ugliness, ugliness conceals beauty. That beautiful woman whose clothes you want to yank away might conceal the soul of a snake. You would do better seducing, or being seduced by, a frog.

What is the difference between the Mask and the Gimmick? That, my friends, is the big question. Let's say they are cousins. The Mask exists to protect. It is primarily defensive. The Gimmick exists to assert. It is primarily aggressive. And sometimes we can look deeply into a person and mistake his Mask for his Gimmick or his Gimmick for his Mask. And sometimes a person can look deeply into himself and do the same. "I am a good person," says Michael Marmaduke. Is that Mask or Gimmick?

When I was young, women wore falsies on their chests. Now they wear them on their shoulders. Who knows where they will put them next? Is that Mask or Gimmick? And isn't it possible that what is a Mask for one person may be Gimmick for another, and yet the two are the same? Perhaps the Mask is the emasculated Gimmick and the Gimmick is the masterful Mask? But do you know what else? Within a single person there can be layers and layers of interspersing Gimmicks and Masks. And doesn't this return us to the Gimmick Onion? When Michael Marmaduke looks into himself to make a list of his virtues and his faults, what is he seeing? What is true and what is false? So do you see why Nietzsche called truth an illusion whose illusoriness has been over-looked? The timorous sweep up fragments of a thousand masks and call them truths, and out of those little truths they make themselves a morality. Personally, I prefer the peril in the streets. Dare you call me a cynic? Nietzsche wrote that cynics were people who recognize the animal in themselves and yet still possess enough spirituality and appetite to make them speak of themselves and their kind *before witnesses*. And what happens to the person who does not recognize the animal within himself? He gets eaten.

And this brings us to the Wrestling Association. Let me say that my commission to create a combat between Santa and Satan has poisoned my life. I call to complain and I speak to secretaries or the person I need to talk to is out of town. I travel down to the main office near City Hall and find that this is not the main office after all. Rather it is where the paperwork is done but not where decisions are made. Who makes the decisions? I ask. Someone will phone you, they say. At last I receive a call from Johnny Korzeniewski, that dwarf, that walking turd, and he tells me that I am one of many managers and that my manager's license is granted at the discretion of the Wrestling Association and can be easily revoked. "Johnny," I shout, "is that a threat?" But the little weasel has already hung up the phone.

And do you know who must win this match between Satan and Santa? Once more will Satan be vanquished. It is not that I mind a rigged match. After all, we are engaged in theater. Does one complain that *Hamlet* always ends with the death of Hamlet? What I object to is the intention that lurks behind the majority of the matches arranged by the Wrestling Association, as if the value of the match resided solely in the value of its intention. And what is this intention? It is didactic, moral, trivial, and it assumes an audience of sufferers. Hidden within it is the belief that all those who suffer from life as from an illness are in the right. Why privilege the sufferers? My friends, they are the ones who put the bread on the table. They buy the tickets.

Among any wrestling audience, as among any large group, there is a surplus of failures, of the sick, the degenerate, the fragile, of those who are bound to suffer. The intention of any wrestling match is to tell these people they are the opposite of what they are. Yet when the Wrestling Association gives comfort to the suffering, courage to the beaten and despairing, support to the irresolute, and lures those who were inwardly shattered into such places as Madison Square Garden, it works to preserve everything that is sick and in distress, which means in truth the corruption of the wrestling audience. With this intention, with such matches as Santa versus Satan, or even with Marduk against Rahab the Ragged Rascal or Tiamat or Pazuzu or the serpent Ur, the Wrestling Association smashes the strong, contaminates great hopes, casts suspicion on joy in beauty, breaks down everything autocratic, conquering, tyrannical, all the instincts proper to the best and most successful type of wrestling fan, into doubt, remorse of conscience, self-destruction; indeed the Wrestling Association reverses the whole love of the earth and the earthly into hatred of the earth and the earthly. And why does the Wrestling Association want an audience of the weak instead of the strong? The weak are easier to control. It is easier to make them buy the products of the wrestling advertisers. They always come back for more. They give up their money more freely.

I say let Marduk be beaten! Let Santa be cast down! Let's wrench wrestling away from this society of sufferers who now control it! Think of the damage done to Marduk that he has never been clobbered. No wonder Michael Marmaduke has a vanilla-flavored soul! One becomes human through adversity, and Michael has never experienced adversity. He needs to be slapped around!

My friends, the value of an action resides in precisely that which is not intentional in it. Free Marduk and Rahab from their chains! The morality of intentions must be overcome! Let this be the name for that secret labor which has been reserved for the subtlest, most honest and most malicious consciences as living touchstones of the soul. I, Primus Muldoon, will be a warrior, working to break the Association's stranglehold. The prospect of Satan versus Santa has made it impossible to go on as before. Muldoon is tired of following instructions. He was born not to direct but to create! But secretly. Within me a catastrophe is being prepared. I know its name but I will not pronounce it.

21

TRICKED

Do you know those October nights, when there is both drizzle and fog and each streetlight displays a nimbus like a golden coin, when the shiny black pavement reflects the taillights of cars and buses, making long red streaks down the avenues? On such nights the skyscrapers lose their upper stories to enigma. Who can tell what is up there? Of course we know that the top of the Pan Am Building is the same as ever, that the Union Carbide Building is flat and regular all the way up and the Chrysler Building still has its illuminated stainless-steel arches. But sometimes it seems that the upper stories of these buildings have not only disappeared visually, they have disappeared physically as well. Perhaps we can see the first twenty stories of RCA Rockefeller and perhaps after that in the golden gloom is the sculptured torso of a great bear. Perhaps the invisible top eighty stories of the World Trade Center have become twin dolphins. And the Empire State Building? The long neck of a giraffe. Of course we understand this is foolishness, but the fog and drizzle, the soft radiance of the disappearing stories, the hiss of tires on the black and shiny streets, the dancing reflections of the taillights—all this awakes a possibility beyond the quotidian, beyond taxes, the U.S. Mail and the reach of fax machines. The increased possibility of the improbable gives us more room to live. Mystery expands our options. How wonderful on these foggy nights to stroll up Lexington from the Chanin Building on 41st Street (fifty-six stories, 680 feet) to the Citicorp Center on 53rd (fifty-four stories, 914 feet) and see so many buildings disappear into the golden fog. The Mobil Building, American Brands, Chem-NY Trust, General Electric, the Waldorf Astoria. And what rises beyond our vision? The torsos of Gryphons, the head of a snake, a Centaur on its hind legs. And the day, which had been jammed with daily business controlled by the tyranny of appointment books, gives way to a night of unscheduled meetings and strange appearances.

For instance, take a look at this fellow coming up Lexington toward 42nd Street. He wears a ragged dark raincoat and a torn slouch hat from which sprouts wet black hair that looks more like the roots of some miasmic plant than anything naturally grown on the human skull. And is it possible that he actually grew such a beard, that accumulation of rat tails and the desiccated corpses of adolescent eels? Is that a mustache or a furry insect in the midst of preparing its cocoon? As the man limps along, he drags his right shoulder against the wall of the building and his head is bowed as if scanning the sidewalk for coins. Despite the murk and the fact that it is nine o'clock at night, the fellow wears dark glasses. Is he drunk or sober, panhandler or hobo?

But let's look more closely. Isn't he too well fed to be a hobo? His shoes—black leather Adidases—look almost new. His blue Levi Dockers still have a crease. Drawing his hand from his pocket to check the time, we see that his watch is a Rolex. And let's look more closely at that black straggly hair, because poking from underneath are a few golden strands. Need we say any more to establish that this is Michael Marmaduke in disguise? He turns the corner and looks up at the Chrysler Building, which stands across the street between Lexington and Third. At 1,046 feet, it is the third-tallest building in New York. Michael can see about fifteen stories of its seventy-seven stories, then there is that golden glow which we have been discussing. Chrysler, he thinks: Christ's Lair.

It has been a rough day for Michael: not just because of his grief for the missing Rose White, which is like a red-hot knife in his heart; nor because wherever he turns there is frustration and disappointment; nor because every member of the fourth estate within fifty miles is committed to tracking him down, but also because for a great many New Yorkers he has been transformed from the golden boy of the dropkick and headlock, the king of the wrestling mat, the brightest and most virtuous star in the Wrestling Association's vast firmament, to the dim-witted behemoth who has kidnapped and probably scragged his girlfriend. If Michael had a buck for every time some stranger has shouted, "Hey, big guy, did you kill her?" he'd be a rich man. It is not that Michael considers himself a saint, but on the other hand he normally thinks he's a pretty good Boy Scout, certainly not bad, certainly not a murderer.

Michael has tried to avoid these people, but he can't go back to his apartment, which is being watched, and he can't hang out on the street, where he is quickly recognized. In the early afternoon he went to a movie near Times Square, just to sit in the dark unbothered. He chose the theater without looking at the marquee and the movie dealt with murder and butchery and mayhem, which threw horrible images before his eyes. Even so he would have stayed had not an usher or popcorn salesman or ticket girl tipped off the press to his whereabouts, which he realized when about thirty people with small flashlights invaded the theater. Michael escaped out the back. Then, around three o'clock, he called Prime Rib, who, because he is short and fat, looks the least like a wrestler (do you remember that he is sometimes called the Death Buddha?). What Michael needed was a disguise, and his usual one was locked in his apartment. An hour later Prime Rib showed up at the dark bar on Tenth Avenue where Michael had gone to conceal himself and think: Thirty-three, Christ's Lair, the Aerie.

"You've become a real popular guy," said Prime Rib, wearing a raincoat and carrying an umbrella because of the drizzle. The raincoat was too big for him and made him seem perfectly round. Nobody would guess he was a wrestler—maybe a plumber or bookie. "A reporter from the *National Enquirer* called to ask me if you really drank blood before each match."

"Blood?"

"And if you'd once argued in favor of human sacrifices."

"I should have stayed in Paterson," said Michael unhappily. He opened the suitcase which Prime Rib had brought and which contained the raincoat, sloppy hat, wig, beard, mustache and even a black makeup pencil. "Thanks for this stuff."

"Just call me if you need anything," said Prime Rib. "I'm glad to help. And that goes for my brothers as well."

We skip over the hours between four o'clock and when we see Michael again on the corner of 42nd and Lex. He discussed his problems with Prime Rib. He ate a ham and cheese sandwich. He sifted his brain as California 49ers once panned for gold and came up with a few nuggets: Christ's Lair=Chrysler. The Chrysler Building is the third-tallest building in the city and is bounded on one side by Third Avenue, that is (thought Michael) it resides within the number thirty-three. The Aerie=top floor.

When the light turns green, Michael crosses the street to the building's Lexington entrance. The art-deco lobby is gray and full of haze. Even the representation of the building on the ceiling can barely be seen. The old guy running the elevator stares suspiciously at Michael's beard. "Where to?" he asks.

Michael tugs his hat down on his forehead. "The Aerie."

"You expected?"

"The Master of Ceremonies wants to see me."

"You're the boss," says the old guy. The door slides shut.

Even in the elevator the air feels thick, as if the fog had penetrated even here. The elevator shoots upward, and Michael swallows several times. He tries to look relaxed, but even a dummy could see that he is tied about as tight as the Gordian knot. Michael is not used to taking the initiative. The good things in his life have all dropped as gifts into his lap, and as a result, he's unsure how to deal with the bad things.

When the doors open, Michael takes a deep breath and steps out into a reception area. There are a desk and chairs but no people. Faded tapestries cover the walls. In one, a bunch of pilgrims in antique clothes ride on horseback through a forest. Another shows Galahad discovering the Grail. A third shows the burning of Giordano Bruno, although to Michael it is just some poor guy on the wrong end of a toasting fork. As Michael glances around, a door opens and a bearded man hurries out to meet him. He is a large man and wears a brown robe and sandals, which makes Michael think he must belong to a religious order.

"You're Michael Marmaduke," says the man cheerfully. "We've been expecting you. I'm Morgan the Pelagian."

"How did you know I was here?" asks Michael, surprised that his disguise has been penetrated so easily.

Morgan gestures toward a TV camera attached to the wall near the ceiling. "The Promethean said you might show up, although Brother Thomas and Sister Esclarmonde weren't so sure."

"I'm looking for the Master of Ceremonies," said Michael.

"He hasn't arrived yet. I've been designated to show you around because I'm generally thought to be the most reasonable, although of course that doesn't mean anyone agrees with me. They call me spiritually bourgeois." Morgan smiles, showing several gold teeth between his gray beard and mustache.

"And this is the Aerie?"

"Some call it that. Others have other names. Why don't you come in?"

"What sort of place is it?" asks Michael without moving. The elevator door has closed and he feels cut off.

"It's where the Disputants meet. There's a Theory Section and a Product Section, and both meet here."

Michael is impressed by how cheerful Morgan the Pelagian appears. "And who are the Disputants?"

"They're the ones who dispute. Each group seats one representative. There are Mandeans, Naassenes, Essenes, Ophites, Orphists, Magharians, Ebionites, Nicolaite Gnostics, Nazarenes, Simonians, Docetists, Apollos, Nicolaitans, Cerinthians, Judists, Cerdonists, Marcionites, the Peratae, Cainites, Montanists, Haematites, Encratites, Messalians, Patarenes, Mithraists, Archontics, Manichaeans, Prometheans, Clementines, Pseudo-Clementines, Valentinians, Sethians, Elkesaites, Barbelognostics, Paulicians, Bogomils (meaning 'lover of God'), Cathars (meaning 'the pure ones'), Borborites (meaning 'the dirty ones'), Coddians, Stratiotici, Phibionites, Athinganists, Montanists, Hemeticists, Sodomites (as opposed to sodomists), Neoplatonists, Carpocratians, Monarchians, Thonrakis, Cappadocians, Macedonists,

Apollinarians, Novationists, Quartodecimans, Subordinationists, Arians (Anomoians, Homoiousians and Homoians), Nestorians, Eutyches or Monophysites, Chalcedonians, Aphthartodocetists, Predestinationists (that's Augustine's party), Monoenergists, Monotheletists, Marcionites, Illuminists, Priscillianists and Pelagians (of which I am the chief). I'm sure I'm leaving out a few. There's a list someplace if you want me to look for it."

"So many?" Again Michael has a sense of threat but he can't explain to himself why he needs to be wary.

"We started with a couple, then the others began in reaction to the first. Of course they're not all seated together. We have twenty-four seats—one for every letter of the Greek alphabet. The groups rotate and try not to be too critical of each other. No ad hominum arguments are allowed."

"I've met some," says Michael. "They seem to hate each other." And he thinks: Maybe it's their hatred that bothers me.

"A few do. More than a few, actually. But you know those cartoons where steam puffs out of the ears of the angry person? Here's where the steam is made to work. Instead of bickering among each other, we discuss the conflict between evil and good. Where does evil come from and in what does it exist? Then our conclusions are synthesized. Actually we base our meetings on the First Ecumenical Council of the whole church which came together at Nicaea on May 20, 325."

"But this is a new organization?"

"Only the alliance that joins us. Most of the groups themselves date from the time of Jesus or shortly after. As the Roman Catholic Church grew in power, these groups disappeared, until with Augustine the church attained a unity of opinion which it held, more or less, until the Reformation, when it started to break apart again. Clearly, among the Protestants, there are hundreds of divergent voices. But despite their good intentions, have any done anything about the nature of evil? Isn't it more powerful? Consequently, many people have gone back to these pre-Augustine groups to see if the answer can be found there."

"The answer to what?"

"The answer as to the nature of evil. If we can define whence it came and why, this may give us control over it. By retelling the story of its birth, we may write the story of its death. That's why many differences between us—whether you accept this creed or that—are immaterial, because we're not discussing orthodoxy but evil. And so we work to channel our disagreements away from each other and toward evil itself."

"But where'd you come from? Why haven't I read about you in the papers?" Again Michael is aware of an unexplained anxiety.

"A few, like the Cathars and Bogomils, never disappeared. The Monophysites, for instance, remain active in Ethiopia. Mandeans are still found in Iraq. Others are recent reformings. As for the newspapers, they have no interest in a few crazy groups as long as they don't sell drugs or molest children."

"Do you belong to an old group or one of the new ones?"

"The Pelagians are a modern version of an older group. Pelagius was a British monk who showed up in Rome toward the end of the fourth century and was disgusted by what he found there. Too much sex, too much drunkenness and gluttony. He was an ascetic who believed that by living purely, you could get into Heaven. But where he made trouble was in his refusal to believe in original sin. Adam eating the apple, he thought, hurt nobody but Adam. Is a person born with a corrupt body and soul or does he become bad through evil deeds? Pelagius believed that each child is born clean, whereas the church believed that each is born damned and needs to be baptized in order to be saved. Of course there's more to it, and I'll tell you sometime if you wish. Pelagius was basically optimistic and infuriated Augustine, who wrote thirty-five books refuting him until Pelagius was driven into hiding. Saint Jerome was especially nasty. He called Pelagius a 'corpulent dog weighed down by Scottish porridge.' "

"And you decided to become Pelagius?"

"No, I decided to become a Pelagian and chose the name Morgan. I learned of the Disputants and was excited by their enterprise. Originally I was a Presbyterian, then I joined a variety of other groups. I mean, when something goes wrong, you want to know how to fix it, right?"

"And what does the Master of Ceremonies do?"

"He guides the dispute, makes sure everyone gets a chance to talk and helps formulate the conclusion. Then he's very involved with the product side of our work. But come in! You can't just hang around the elevator. We've all been expecting you."

Somewhat reluctantly Michael follows the Pelagian across the reception area to a large pair of double doors. Morgan opens the doors and waves Michael through.

Beyond is a dimly lit hall with a cathedral ceiling. A semicircle of twenty-four desks occupies the center, each with a little halogen lamp and a Greek letter carved from a block of wood. At the front is a raised dais with a podium and a large Toshiba projection monitor. At the back of the hall is another raised area with several levels of theater seats. About thirty people are in the room. Most are back by the theater seats, but perhaps half a dozen are scattered at the desks, reading or studying papers. People speak quietly, and there is occasional laughter. The room is windowless and on the walls are about forty framed posters. One depicts Achilles in his chariot, a second shows Saint George slaying the dragon, a third shows Horatio at the bridge. But there are more recent heroes as well: Cyrano de Bergerac and Admiral Nelson. Michael is startled to see posters of wrestlers: Gorgeous George, Hulk Hogan and, most surprisingly, himself.

Among those gathered near the theater seats, he notices not only Brother Thomas and Timaeus the Promethean but a few of the gang members from two days earlier. Clemency, the Valentinian Gnostic, is chatting affably with Rattler, the Ophite. Clemency sees Michael and waves. Others turn toward him as well: men and women wearing monk's robes or togas, some in peasant costume, some in business suits. The noise of conversation fades, and Michael feels everyone watching him. As if sensing his discomfort, people begin to turn away again, but Michael notices that many continue to sneak quick looks. Glancing back, Michael sees someone else who looks familiar: a large bald-headed man wearing a ragged fur jacket and fur pants.

"I know that guy, he's a wrestler." Michael snaps his fingers, trying to bring the name to mind. "He retired a couple of years ago."

"That's Sembak the Thonraki," says Morgan. "It's an Armenian heresy, dualist, of course. It's the old question: how could a good God create evil? But you're right about the wrestling. He used to wrestle under the name of . . .''

"Ahriman, Prince of Darkness, and sometimes Iblis. My manager was trying to set up a match before he quit the ring."

"Representing darkness grew difficult for him," said Morgan, "so he put away his Gimmick and came to us."

"Isn't becoming Sembak the Thonraki like putting on another Gimmick?"

"Not at all. We each had a name we left behind to become a Disputant. But in addition to our names, we set aside our entire lives. In a way, we became nobody at all. We're Disputants. We are idea. We exist to discuss and dispute certain questions."

And Michael wonders what it would be like not only to stop being Marduk the Magnificent but to stop being himself as well. To be no one, only a face with the name of an idea attached.

As Morgan has been talking, about a dozen men and women have sat down at their desks and turned on their lamps. A very thin man in a torn gray robe stands up and begins to speak.

"All human beings are born to the Spirits of Truth and the Spirits of Error and into these two divisions all human acts are divided. Between Truth and Error, God has set an eternal enmity. Deeds of error are an abomination to Truth, while deeds of Truth are an abomination to Error, and there is a constant rivalry between them, for they march in discord."

"That's one of the Essenes," says Morgan. "They quarrel with everybody."

Another man stands up. "We mostly agree that Satan was no more than an officer in the court of God whose function was to roam back and forth on earth and report on the doings of men. This is why he was called 'the Eye of the King.' He was sent to earth as the head of the Watcher angels and they mated with human women and bred giants. The question is, were they seduced by the women or did they rape them? Who was at fault?"

"That's one of the Nazarenes," whispers Morgan. "He wants to bring back the Book of Enoch as part of the Canon."

"The Watcher angels violated their very nature and office," says an elderly gentleman. "They fell into lusting after virgins and became slaves of the flesh. Among them was this prince of matter and its forms who became negligent and wicked in managing what was entrusted to him. They fell through their own free will. Even if the virgins tried to seduce them, the angels could have turned aside."

"Athenagoras," whispers Morgan.

"The real sin of the Watcher angels," says a woman wearing a dark blue robe, "was to renounce the beauty of God for a beauty that fades, and so they fell from Heaven."

"How do we know they were really angels?" asks someone else.

"True angels," says a bearded man, "weep freshwater tears. That is how they are recognized."

"Origen," whispers Morgan.

"Are they disputing?" asks Michael.

"No, no. The Master of Ceremonies hasn't arrived yet. They're just chatting. But he should be showing up at any minute. Let's go out to the lobby and wait."

Passing through the door, Michael glances at the poster of Marduk. It shows him in the ring with his hands victoriously over his head and his foot on the neck of somebody or other: perhaps Pazuzu, perhaps Rahab. Michael can't remember.

He is just turning back when he hears the elevator slide open. "Here he comes now," says Morgan the Pelagian.

Michael turns to see a white-haired man in an old overcoat and carrying a cane exit from the elevator. It is Jack Molay.

"That's the Master of Ceremonies?" asks Michael, surprised.

"Do you know him?"

"That's Jack Molay."

"Just one of many names," says Jack Molay in his slight French accent. He reaches out his hand to Michael, who begins to take it and then decides not to.

"So you were the person you told me to find?" Michael feels he has been tricked. "Why didn't you just bring me here yourself if it's so darned important?"

"It wouldn't have been important unless you had found it yourself. You needed to be activated, to engage yourself. There are two reasons for you to be here. First to learn about heresy. In the words of Augustine, 'The process of refuting heretics brings to light the content of sound teaching. There must be heresies so that those who are tested and proved genuine might be manifested amidst the weak.' Clearly he is echoing Paul."

"Can't you understand that I don't care?" says Michael. "My fiancée is in danger . . ."

"The second reason," says Jack Molay, as if he hasn't heard, "is to discard the Gimmick of Hero. You can't act heroically until you have put aside the illusion of heroism. The Gimmick of Heroism is to true heroism what heresy is to true faith. You won't find Rose White until you correct this error."

If we stand back a little, Michael's confusion grows more apparent. In his old raincoat he seems shabby and his brow is wrinkled with doubt. He turns from Morgan to Jack Molay with his hands slightly raised as if trying to lift something: the granite blocks of his own ignorance. Slowly, however, his confusion and anxiety begin to coalesce into indignation, which allows him to forget his lack of knowledge. It even becomes comforting.

"But you were the one who said I could find her myself!"

"True, but your sense of heroism is dualist. It derives from wrestling. Cartoon heroism: action without thought. It is the fog which keeps you from seeing clearly."

"I can see perfectly clearly."

"Then why haven't you found her? It's not muscle that matters. You need to use your brain. I believe we can help you, but you can help us as well. We'll help you in the retelling of your story and you can help us in the telling of ours."

These words make no sense to Michael, but he doesn't care. He feels he is being made fun of in some new and peculiar manner. Didn't he need muscle when he faced Troll, and hadn't that use of muscle resulted in knowledge? Surely he can take pride in that. He goes to the elevator and pushes the button. "I don't want to help you! I just want to find Rose White."

"Remember the proverb," says Jack Molay with a certain asperity: " 'For the turning away of the simple shall slay them, and the prosperity of fools shall destroy them.' "

At that moment the doors opens. "To heck with you," says Michael, entering the elevator, "and I don't like my poster on the wall either."

"That's the wrong guy to have mad at you," says the old elevator operator as the doors close again.

"I don't want to hear about it," says Michael. Actually, he is rather pleased with himself. He feels he has stood up for himself and spoken his mind. Although he has often assumed the Gimmick of anger in the ring as Marduk the Magnificent, he has rarely had it come to him naturally. Even in heavy traffic he doesn't get angry. He puts a finger to the pulse in his neck and feels the speed and strength of it. He feels curiously excited.

22

SWORD

We are again in a van which is moving quickly, although to compare this van to the one owned by the Vals is like comparing a Learjet to a roller skate. This is the van owned by the three brothers Prime Rib, Prime Rate and Prime Time and it has every modern convenience, including hot and cold running water. If we were outside the van, the inside would be a mystery because of its tinted windows. The van is silver and has the shape of an oversized doorstop. Five antennae bristle from the roof to indicate that even in the remotest locations, this van is in touch with the rest of the world. The vanity plate carries the simple boast: "Prime."

It is Monday night, nearly eleven o'clock, and still drizzling. Seconds ago the van exited on the Queens side of the Midtown Tunnel and soon it will turn south on the Brooklyn-Queens Expressway. Prime Rib is driving but his black leather seat is like the reclining lounge chair of a basement rec room and he treats the world beyond the windshield with all the attention he might give a bad TV show. Attached to the steering wheel is a small Lucite knob, of the sort once called a "suicide knob," and implanted within the knob is a small yellow rose. Prime Rib steers with his left index finger resting on the center of the rose: that is his only

contact with the wheel. The driver's seat swivels and Prime Rib is
turned half toward Michael Marmaduke in the other front seat,
who is wearing every seat belt he can find. It is not that Michael
is afraid, but he understands how a flight through the windshield
would cleave his face and by belting up he is only protecting his
equity. No face, no job.

Deep Rat leans forward between Prime Rib and Michael to give
directions. Prime Rib feels that Deep Rat smells oddly like axle
grease: it's not a bad smell, but neither is it a good smell. In the far
back, Prime Time and Prime Rate are sitting side by side, looking
rather like fat twins. Both wear black turtleneck sweaters, as does
Prime Rib, and whenever Michael glances back he sees their two
faces suspended at the rear of the van like twin moons. Muted
salsa music plays over the stereo system. The van has sixteen
speakers, and with the music turned up loud it is like riding inside
stereo headphones. The music is now low because Deep Rat hates
music and has asked that it be turned down. If he had his way, he
would break the stereo system.

Michael called Prime Rib from the lobby of the Chrysler Building. He was still angry and strangely invigorated by his anger.
Apart from several security guards, there was no one in the lobby
and Michael had a queer desire to roar. He imagined stamping
back and forth across the lobby, throwing back his head and
roaring like crazy. In his mind he kept seeing Rose White in the
cage swinging from the crane while far in the distance was the
New York skyline with the Metropolitan Life Building on 23rd
Street just to the right of the crane and the four smokestacks of the
power station on 14th Street to the left. Brooklyn, Michael had
thought. Why can't we find that place? Meaning not Brooklyn but
the building under construction. And so he had called Prime Rib,
firstly because he had transportation, and secondly because he had
two big brothers as well.

On the phone, Prime Rib said, "Do you know a guy named
Deep Rat? He's been calling me. He says he's got information for
you about some place in Brooklyn."

Michael had a sudden recollection of what it had been like to be
squeezed tightly by Troll.

"How'd he know you?" Michael asked.

"He says he recognized me yesterday at the Meat Market when he went to talk to you. He says he's been calling several people who were there. I got his number. What do you want me to do?"

Michael felt like saying, "Do nothing." Then he thought he should forget his indignation, go back upstairs and see why the Master of Ceremonies had arranged such an elaborate scheme to get him to discover the location of the Aerie. Instead he said, "Call Deep Rat and bring him along. And you'd better call your brothers as well."

But thirty minutes later when the van stopped in front of the Chrysler Building and the side door opened to reveal Deep Rat and his smile, which, because his teeth inclined inward, was both toothless and toothful at the same time, Michael felt a tinge of anxiety and a chill gripped the nape of his neck much in the way a pet shop owner grips a kitten.

"The only purpose of my life," whispered Deep Rat, "is to help you. There is a chance that your fiancée is in Brooklyn."

Michael climbed into the front seat and exchanged a brotherhood handshake with Prime Rib. Then waved to Prime Rate and Prime Time in the back.

"Hey, hey, hey," said Prime Time, "we're on our way!"

"There's a new building on Wythe," said Deep Rat, "although they stopped working on it last year. The company went bankrupt. The basement of the building has been taken over by strange people and now it's called the taurobolium."

As Deep Rat pronounced the word, the van entered the Midtown Tunnel. The wrestlers felt they should know what a taurobolium was and when no one asked the inevitable question, each decided he was the only one who didn't know, and each felt his duty was not toward knowledge but toward protecting himself from the accusation of ignorance. But that was not Michael's way, and after a minute of silence he asked, "What's a taurobolium?"

"The taurobolium," said Deep Rat, "is the place where Taurus hangs out."

"I know that name," said Michael Marmaduke, trying to remember more exactly.

"He had these horns implanted as part of his Gimmick," said Prime Rib. "Then he had this match with Ormuzd the Primal Man and gored him. Right in Madison Square Garden. There was lots of blood. It was bad enough to gore him, but he wasn't even supposed to win. I never could figure if the Wrestling Association thought the winning was worse than the goring or the goring worse than the winning. In any case, they canned him."

A quarter of an hour later Prime Rib is driving down Metropolitan Avenue near Bedford. He sits straight in his seat with both hands on the wheel and he tells himself that the neighborhood is full of people who would like to relieve him of the Flying Wedge, which is what he and his brothers call their vehicle. And although Prime Rib feels that he and his brothers are more than a match for any yoyo who wants a fight, he suspects the local car thieves do not play with their bare hands. Prime Rib has spent thousands of hours lifting heavy objects to make himself a monster of strength, and while lifting these objects he has often considered the great injustice by which a ninety-seven-pound weakling becomes a five-hundred-pound muscle man with the simple purchase of a .22 revolver.

But then, even if they get past the car thieves, they have to deal with Taurus and his craziness. Prime Rib once knew Taurus or at least they shared chitchat in a dozen different locker rooms. It wasn't enough for Taurus to be an ugly oversized wrestler with a big salary, he wanted to be Taurus all the way through. He wanted to be Taurus on the inside as well as on the outside. So he checked into a special clinic and got himself a bull's jaw and a snout. Then he got a pair of horns. Then he had work done on his spine so he would be comfortable on all fours. Then he got himself a tail. Prime Rib realized something was wrong when Taurus stopped engaging in locker-room chitchat and would only snort and paw the floor with his feet. "What's the harm?" people said. "If he wants to be a bull, let him be a bull. What're you, a taurophobe?" So Prime Rib tried to be forbearing even though his brothers kept asking, "Would you want your daughter to marry a bull?" And not long after that, Taurus gored Ormuzd the Primal Man and his wrestling career was over.

The unfinished building is off Wythe near 13th Street. Prime Rib pulls the Flying Wedge up to the fence and sets his various security systems, including the tape of the barking dog. Everyone climbs out of the van. It is still drizzling and they draw up their collars. No one is wearing a hat and each thinks this is not the sort of situation where you carry an umbrella. Michael and the Prime brothers huddle in a little group and consider what might lie ahead. Deep Rat stands a few feet away sucking his teeth. Next to them is a wooden fence covered with graffiti. Above them metal girders disappear into the fog.

Michael ponders the nature of fear. He doesn't quite feel it but he can see it in the distance. It has a shape like a giant spider and it wants to suck his heart. He wonders if it will make him a better wrestler to understand the nature of fear. Then he wonders if he's really a wrestler or only a weight lifter with a Gimmick, an actor in a lifetime role. Embodied in this thought is a touch of cynicism, and perhaps we should mark it with red pencil because it may be a first for Michael Marmaduke.

"Can't we just talk to this guy?" asks Michael.

"He doesn't know English anymore," says Prime Rib. "He only grunts."

"He's transformed himself into a monster," says Prime Rate.

"I say we go back to Manhattan," says Prime Time.

The others, except Deep Rat, look at him as if wondering whether they can really go back to Manhattan without making themselves appear bad. They have all been hurt in a variety of ways, but none has been gored. Deep Rat has found a loose board and pulls it aside. "Come on," he whispers.

The four wrestlers squeeze through the opening. Michael wonders how you talk to a person who only grunts. Could Taurus really have forgotten the English language?

"This way," says Deep Rat. He leads them through piles of construction material: metal bars, a stack of two-by-fours, piles of sand. There is a path of sorts and Deep Rat has a light.

"Over here."

They join Deep Rat at a low fence and he shines his light forward into the murk. Some kind of pit lies in front of them and the light doesn't reach the bottom.

Prime Rib considers articulating the sentence "I don't like this" but thinks better of it. He and his brothers are in their early forties. They have maybe another few years of wrestling, then they will retire, move to the Florida Keys and buy a charter boat: take wealthy Yankees out looking for game fish and do some fishing themselves. Their kids have grown up; their wives could open a gift shop in Marathon or Key Largo. Now these dreams appear very frail: tissue-paper dreams.

"Should we go around to the left?" suggests Prime Rib.

"Or maybe the right?" asks Prime Time.

"Or maybe go over the side right here?" says Prime Rate.

But before they can decide there is an electronic crash and one hundred lights blaze on. Even Deep Rat jumps.

Spread out beneath them is a brightly lit cellar hole with a drop of about twelve feet to the bottom. No ladders, no stairs, no dangling ropes. Instead of being square, like the building above, the hole is round. The floor is covered with sand, and resting in the center is a small rectangular object that resembles a videotape. Nobody else is visible, but, as all five men think simultaneously, somebody must have turned on the lights. On the other side of the hole is a large double door.

"I don't like the look of this," says Prime Rib.

"What is this place?" ask his brothers.

Deep Rat sniffs the air. "A taurobolium."

"A bull ring," says Michael.

No one asks what they should do next. They know, but they don't want to know. They want to take rubber erasers and scrub the knowledge from their minds. Is this also true of Deep Rat? Let it be said that even Deep Rat is impressed. The lights are very bright. The sand has recently been raked and is very white and smooth.

Michael begins to ask, "What do you think that thing is out there in the middle?" but he understands what it is and he sighs. He swings a leg over the wooden fence. "I guess I better go get it." Actually he doesn't feel too bad, because for the first time in several days his course seems absolutely clear.

Prime Rib raises his eyebrows in admiration. He has never

thought Michael a coward, but neither has he thought him brave. As wrestlers, bravery and cowardice were just part of the game. "I'll come too," he says.

"Why don't you wait till we see what we're up against." Michael swings his other leg over the side and lowers himself down the wall. At last he is hanging with his fingers gripping the edge. When he lets go, he still has a three-foot drop.

The sand is soft. Plodding toward the center is like plodding along a beach. It's not good for running or doing anything fancy. Looking back, he sees the others up by the fence: the three brothers close together, then Deep Rat off to the side. Michael plods forward. Yes, the rectangular object is definitely a videotape. He makes his way toward it while keeping an eye on the double door. He is not sure what will happen next, but he knows that the double door will be part of it.

When Michael is halfway to the videotape (about twenty feet), there is a blare of a trumpet. This is very easy to say: a blare of a trumpet. What is more difficult is to chart the progress of this sharp quasi-musical sound within the brain and body of Michael Marmaduke, as well as within those of the three wrestlers waiting above. First of all, their adrenaline takes an abrupt jump. If one were to imagine an old-fashioned thermometer with the temperature measured in red, then one could see the red part swiftly zoom to the top. That's the adrenaline. This is followed by a profound sinking feeling, as when a small plane hits an air pocket and drops several hundred feet. Then, to each, the sound of the trumpet also resembles a physical blow, like being jabbed with an icicle in the softest part of the belly. Finally, the blare of the trumpet is clearly not an end in itself. We are not going to have the trumpet and nothing else. The blare of the trumpet, in all its awfulness, exists to introduce something even more awful. The twin doors (did we say they were painted blood red?) slide open.

It is at moments such as this that phrases like "rooted to the spot" are most useful. Michael is unable to move. The others see him as continuing bravely to face the open doors, but, in truth, he is rooted to the spot. In the darkness beyond the doors, he sees something nasty: i.e., a pair of eyes that don't look quite human.

They are oversized and bloodshot. They are also at a peculiar height: high but not high enough. The eyes stare at Michael and Michael stares back. He has no doubt that the eyes belong to Taurus. It occurs to Michael that he was angry at the Master of Ceremonies because he felt the Master of Ceremonies wanted to change him in some way. But at least the Master of Ceremonies didn't want to hurt him. An unpleasant cow smell emerges from the opening, and Michael wrinkles his nose.

The second blare of the trumpet is not quite as startling as the first, but this is followed by hoofbeats and the shaking of the earth as Taurus gallops into the ring. In the brains of the three wrestlers waiting at the rail, the word "Big" flashes on their mental screen. This is followed by the word "Ugly." It is clear that Taurus, down deep, is still human, but he has gone so far to transform himself into a bull (look at those hooves) that the effect is startling. He is covered with brown fur and he gallops on all fours. His horns are curved and protrude about a foot from his head. Each horn is tipped with a steel point which looks very sharp. He easily weighs over four hundred pounds.

Taurus gallops once around the ring, thrusting his head at the wall and snorting. The double doors slide shut. When Taurus has made a complete circuit, he stops, turns toward Michael and begins pawing the earth with his front hooves, which are in fact hollow stainless-steel hooves with hands inside of them. He tosses his head and snorts.

"Mr. Taurus," says Michael, "I'd like to check out that videotape over there. You see, my fiancée has been kidnapped . . ."

Even as Taurus charges, Michael is saying, "Can't we discuss this like rational human beings?" As he speaks, Michael thinks how fast Taurus runs and he experiences a sensation which, if not fear, is at least something close.

Up along the rail, Prime Rib is glad that he is up above and Taurus is down below. Taurus lowers his head to gore Michael with his great horns and at the last moment Michael puts out his hands to stop him. As a result, Michael is thrown in the air, as if he were a wad of paper, thinks Prime Rib. Michael lands on his back in the sand at the same moment that Taurus turns and charges again. Michael rolls aside and again Taurus spins around and charges. Michael is wearing a brown leather jacket, and the next time Taurus passes, one of his horns catches the shoulder of the jacket, ripping it.

"Ah, shit," says Prime Rib, and he scrambles over the rail and into the taurobolium. "Hey, bull!" he shouts. "Hey, you furry asshole!" Then he runs along the wall, limping and dragging his foot, not because he is hurt, but because Prime Rib likes to hunt birds in the fall and this is what the birds often do in order to lure him away from their nests. Behind him he sees his two brothers climbing down the wall as well.

Taurus turns away from Michael and charges Prime Rib, who jumps aside. Then Taurus charges Prime Rate and Prime Time. Prime Rate leaps out of the way but Prime Time gets trampled and is slow getting to his feet. Fortunately, Prime Rate grabs Taurus's tail to keep him from goring his brother when he is down, but then Taurus spins around and slashes Prime Rate's jacket, so that, still standing at the rail, Deep Rat can see blood. This makes Deep Rat nervous and he has a mental image of all four wrestlers lying dead in the sand and what the personal consequences of this would be for Deep Rat.

Taurus again charges Michael and Michael again jumps out of the way, but he is slower. The other wrestlers shout at Taurus and he charges back at them and this time he throws Prime Rate high in the air and would gore him as he lies sprawled in the sand, but he is distracted by the shouts of Prime Rib and Prime Time. Deep Rat sees a suitcase off to his left and he runs to it. The suitcase is made of tan pigskin and on the side is a bumper sticker reading, "Yo ♥ Madrid." Deep Rat opens it and draws out a red cape. He hurries back to the rail. "Here!" he shouts to Michael Marmaduke. "Take this!"

Deep Rat throws the cape and Michael grabs it. Even as he unfolds it, he feels the earth shaking and hears the snorting of Taurus behind him. Michael spins around with the red cape held in front of him, then dodges aside as Taurus rushes through its empty folds.

Michael gets a better hold on the red cape and is ready when

Taurus charges again. Even so, when Taurus rushes by, there is perhaps an inch between Taurus's right horn and Michael's right hip. Michael is struck by the cheeriness of Taurus's expression, as if only now has he found true happiness. Taurus turns and charges again, flinging the cape in the air. For a breather, he chases Prime Rib, Prime Rate and Prime Time before returning to Michael. Taurus is snorting more violently and isn't as fast as earlier. Michael knows there are many fancy moves he can make with his cape, but, really, all he wants is to get the videotape and call it a night. At the moment, Taurus is standing directly over the tape considering his next charge. Michael lowers the cape and shakes it. Abruptly, Taurus lunges forward, veering to the left and nearly ripping the cape from Michael's hand.

"Hey, hey!" Michael hears Deep Rat calling. "Take this!"

Michael sees a sword flying toward him. It lands in the sand and he picks it up. It's a long thin sword and Michael knows he's supposed to use it to stick Taurus. Taurus charges and again Michael deflects him with the cape. Should he stick this guy? Michael lifts the sword. Taurus waits with his head down, trying to catch his breath. Michael takes a step toward him. He knows he's supposed to stick the sword in the back of the bull's neck. He lifts the sword higher. Taurus looks up at him and grins. "What am I doing?" Michael asks himself. He flings the sword away. Taurus almost appears disappointed.

Prime Time, Prime Rib and Prime Rate have moved up to within fifteen feet behind Taurus. At a secret signal they all begin to run at once. It should be said this is a maneuver they perfected in the wrestling ring but have never done in real life. When they nearly reach Taurus all three leap into the air with their feet sticking straight out in front of them. This is called the triple dropkick, and when they simultaneously hit Taurus, who has reared up on his hind legs and is apparently deep in thought, they drop him like Paul Bunyan drops a tree. One imagines stars forming in Taurus's brain.

Michael runs to retrieve the videotape, then all four wrestlers dash for the side of the ring. Prime Rib gets on Prime Time's shoulders and the other two scramble to the top, then Prime Rate reaches down to drag up his brothers while Michael Marmaduke holds his feet. How complicated it all is. Michael lifts up the videotape. "I got it," he says.

From the taurobolium there comes a disappointed roar. Taurus is standing up and pawing the sand with his hooves.

"Let's get outta here!" says Prime Rib.

At one a.m. Michael Marmaduke is in the precinct office of Brodsky and Gapski. They are not there and he has been told to wait. What Michael really wants is to go to bed. He has asked Prime Rib to book him a room at the Gramercy Park Hotel and he is getting ready to leave Brodsky and Gapski a note, along with the videotape, and then hit the hay. As an athlete in training, Michael isn't used to late nights. He also has sore places from where Taurus threw him. Still, Michael feels good about himself. He feels he had a problem and has solved it.

He wanders through the office, glancing at the doodles on each police officer's blotter. Some show aggressive tendencies, some show sexual yearnings, some show hidden anxieties. He tries the door to Sapperstein's office and finds it unlocked. He considers taking the cellophane off Sapperstein's Yasir Arafat dart board but he doesn't know where Sapperstein keeps his darts. At last Michael turns on Sapperstein's VCR and inserts the videotape. He has already seen it at Prime Rib's apartment, but he wants to watch it again. He finds it a comfort to glimpse Rose White's face, even though she is suffering.

After a moment we see a close-up of Rose White. Her face forms a perfect oval and seems to have been carved from white marble. When Rose White was fifteen years old she cut back on her smiling so she wouldn't develop wrinkles around her eyes that would deepen as she grew older. She learned to smile only with her lips and a friendly twinkle. Her wish was to be beautiful until she was eighty but maybe she won't live that long. Her face is suddenly transformed into a desperate cry. "Help me, Michael! You must save me! I'm being . . ." As Rose White cries out, the camera pulls back and we see that she is tied to a railway track which appears to be inside a building. She is wearing a white nightgown. Then the screen goes dark. Michael lowers his head and presses his hands to his eyes. He wonders what he would do if he caught the person who kidnapped Rose White, and he imagines the weight of the sword, which Deep Rat threw to him, balanced again in his hands. But then Michael's thoughts frighten even him and he looks around for a sheet of paper in order to write Gapski and Brodsky a note.

And where are the police detectives? At the moment they are visiting a garbage dump in Long Island. They have lights. They have shovels. They have twenty big guys to help them. Bones have been discovered much like the bones found on the floor by Troll's king-sized bed below the subway station at Union Square. Those bones have made a big impression on Brodsky and Gapski, and the word has gone around the department *sotto voce* (because Sapperstein wants to keep this out of the papers) that the bones are human bones. Right now many people are looking for Troll and absolutely nobody—other than Michael Marmaduke—is looking for Rose White. Brodsky and Gapski have forgotten all about Rose White. In fact, considering all these bones lying about, it's hard to think about anything else. Hard, but not impossible, because as Brodsky was digging, he threw (accidentally, he claims) a shovelful of trash at Gapski, and Gapski (also accidentally) threw a shovelful of trash at Brodsky. Both men are wearing fedoras and raincoats and black rubber boots because of the drizzle, and as the twenty big guys look on, and backhoe operators look on, and landfill personnel look on, Brodsky and Gapski continue to throw shovelfuls of trash at each other (still, they claim, accidentally), getting faster and faster so their raincoats are smeared with old potato peelings and ancient hamburger and archaic carrot scrapings, yet still they shovel faster and each thinks, in his heart of hearts, that if he can only shovel fast enough, then he can bury that short little sucker who has made his life such a misery.

23

Runrun Undone

Join me in the belfry of this church steeple: St. Ignatius Loyola at Park and 83rd. We are here to make use of a high place and perhaps it is appropriate that we are in a spot named after that great battler of heretics and enemy of Luther who saved Moravia, Bohemia, Poland and a good chunk of Germany for the Roman Catholic Church. No unnecessary abstractions for Señor Loyola, for whom the evil you see (heretics) was worse than the evil you don't see (Satan). Looking out we have a clear view of Park Avenue. It is nine-fifteen Tuesday morning and the sky is blue with a brisk breeze containing a hint of winter. Everything is clean after a night of drizzle and the only obvious discontent is shown by the honking cars far below. This is a working day and people are in a hurry. There's money to be made, commodities to be bought and sold.

On the sidewalk men and women are walking briskly with their attaché cases banging their legs. See that young fellow running? He's across the street down by 81st and he's coming our way. At first we might think he is late for a meeting, but then we see it is Seth, the kid who is searching for the bottle of aquavit for Marcello, his ailing father. He hasn't found it yet, nor has he located

his missing brothers. However, his jaw is squarely set and he has
no intention of giving up. Let us also say that within his jacket
pocket rests the lucky two-headed coin. Seth remains unaware of
its presence, but he feels he is running faster than ever. Maybe the
coin has some power after all.

If one followed him exclusively and forgot about Michael Marmaduke, one would be plunged into another series of stories.
Where did Seth spend the night? Where is he going now? As he
nears the corner of 82nd, we see a fellow with a shopping cart
approaching the same corner from the side street. Just as he pushes
past the corner, he meets Seth, who smacks right into the shopping
cart and knocks it over. Even looking from this height we can tell
that both men are distressed. And don't we know that old fellow?
That's Beetle and he's anxious that Seth might steal some of his
returnable bottles. Seth rights the cart and sticks one of the black
plastic bags back inside. Beetle says something and Seth shakes his
head. Perhaps Beetle has said, "Would you like to hear a sad
story?" Seth turns away and begins to run north again. Beetle pats
his bags to make sure they are all right and turns south. Either
could lead us to new narratives. But isn't this true of anyone on the
street? They all have stories which are the passionate concerns of
their lives.

In the church beneath us priests are hearing confession. Think
of the sad tales that prick their ears. And beyond some of these
nearby windows, psychiatrists, therapists and analysts are being
paid big money to hear even more stories. Some listen without
making a peep. Others might say, "Why don't you share your
feelings about that?" Some are more high-pressure and say, "That
was a pretty stupid thing to do." At which point the patient paying
one hundred smackers per hour feels he's getting his money's
worth. And maybe there's a shrink who says, "You dumb bozo,
what a feebleminded fuckin way to act!" And his patient thinks,
Hot damn! This is cheap at the price.

Have you ever wondered how often you might form part of one
of these narratives, even though you have never met the person?
Let's say you are coming up the stairs off the IRT at Astor Place.
The pebble which has been nestling beneath your sock slips forward under the ball of your foot and you come down on it hard.

Ow, that hurts! You make an awful face. Later that day a middle-aged gentleman in a three-piece suit tells his shrink, "Just this morning in Astor Place a handsome young person made a terrible face at me. I've felt dirty all my life!"

You see how easily it could happen? Even now, as we look from this steeple, we see dozens of people who know something of our narrative. Maybe they have read the story in the *Post* or in one of the other papers. Maybe they have seen something on TV. Maybe, like Beetle or Seth, they are small participants in our drama. For instance, we didn't get a close look at all of those Disputants, or those guys helping Brodsky or Gapski search the garbage dump on Long Island, and maybe some are strolling along down below or are riding by in a cab. They are thinking about something we too know about—the discovery of a human thighbone or that angels cry freshwater tears—and they are saying, "How strange! How peculiar it all is."

Let's look directly across the street through that sixth-story window. Do you see the woman lying on a couch and the man at his desk fiddling with a yellow pencil? She is talking and her eyes have the fixed attention of someone recalling something that happened long ago. Perhaps she is forty-five. She is well dressed, has thick blond hair and holds a white handkerchief, because even though her eyes are dry, she is prepared to weep. The psychiatrist is of the modern type: no beard or German accent. His name is McRoy Phillips and as he listens he tries to keep his mind off racquetball and he is failing. He has a lunchtime match with another shrink who consistently beats the pants off him and McRoy Phillips is trying to analyze the weaknesses in his game, while occasionally saying, "Tell me more about that," and "How did that make you feel?"

"I was very young and I met these women at a party and they invited me to this loft," the woman is saying. "I didn't know what I was doing. I only went for the dancing."

"How did the dancing make you feel?" asks McRoy Phillips. He leans back in his swivel chair and presses the yellow pencil to his lips. I need to work on my backhand, he thinks. That's my big problem. You can't win without a backhand.

"It was wild," says the woman. "This wasn't ballroom dancing or anything like that. There were flutes and drums and it kept getting faster and faster. Mostly there were women, but some men as well. The flutes got inside you somehow. And the drums, they never stopped."

"Tell me more about the flutes getting inside you." McRoy Phillips begins to nibble his pencil.

"It just felt that way—being filled with music and all of it getting louder. We had been drinking wine, lots of wine. The room was a blur. I didn't even know where I was. Then the god came among us and urged us onward, touching and caressing us."

"What sort of god? What are your thoughts about that?" If he went to a backhand clinic three times a week for an hour, how much improvement could he show in four weeks? McRoy Phillips considers the pleasure of whipping his fellow shrink.

"It was exciting, passionate. He wore a mask with horns. He weaved in and out of us, as if he were part of the music. We wore white robes with nothing beneath them. Sometimes he would touch me, touch my breast, and my feet would move even faster. I don't know why I never fell."

"Share your feelings about that."

"At last the music would end. The crescendo would build and then it would be over. I'd fall right where I'd been dancing, just collapse on the floor. Once he came to me. I felt him lie across me and open my legs. It wasn't rape. I let him take me. I could feel him inside me, feel him thrust against me even though I was hardly conscious. It was like the dancing, except now it was inside me."

"Don't hold anything back," says McRoy Phillips. And dietary supplements, he thinks. Perhaps I need vitamins. Maybe my back-hand is congenitally weak.

"When I had the baby, I had it there in the loft and the other women were with me. I knew it was his. I don't know why I felt no anger. It was a crazy period in my life. Years later I felt anger, felt cheated of something. They took the baby. They said the god took it. This wasn't uncommon. Other women had gotten preg-nant as well. And there was more than one man. The sex was just part of it, part of the whole crazy scene. After a while I quit to go to graduate school. When I went back months later to see them, to find what had happened to my baby, they weren't there anymore. I don't know what happened to them."

"And what did you feel about that?" Maybe I'm too old for racquetball, thinks McRoy Phillips. That's right, I'm getting old. It's not my backhand; it's decrepitude!

Down below the traffic is still honking. Up above the sky is still blue. To the south we see Beetle pushing his cart. The story in his brain is like a gerbil on a wheel and it spins round and round. To the north we see Seth still running. His father is sick. His brothers have disappeared. Actually, the oldest is neck deep in a poker game and can't get free. The other is hip deep in his neighbor's wife and feels as if he has ridden into a canyon on horseback and gotten stuck. Both brothers are squashed in a tight place by circumstance and have forgotten about their father and his need for aquavit. As for Seth, he keeps running. He came out of the darkness and he will return to the darkness, but at the moment he is like a string, tying our story together. See that cab waiting for the light at 95th? That's Morgan the Pelagian sitting in the backseat. He looks at Seth running across the street and thinks what a pleasant face he has and wonders why he is in such a hurry. Then he passes from view. And as Seth runs, the coin in his jacket pocket takes a little bounce each time his right foot hits the pavement. It keeps flipping over right inside the pocket. First the angel face points upward with its beatific smile, then the cynical demon face. There's no humor in the demon's grin: just malice.

Wally Wallski sits on the pier of the South Street Seaport Museum and looks over at Brooklyn. That's where I used to live, he thinks. That's where I was happiest. Maybe all his troubles started when he lost his job with the fishing boat. Hadn't Claudine liked him better when he was hauling in the flounder, nabbing a tuna now and then? Perhaps he has been emasculated by the money crunch. There are fish in the water right now. Wally Wallski can feel them. Although any fish hauled out of the East River would surely glow in the dark. Perhaps his loss of work is not the result of an economic crisis, but an ecological crisis. Nobody wants to eat fish that glow in the dark. But doesn't he also know people who refuse to eat their little four-legged brothers and sisters, as they call them, their little silver cousins covered with scales? Perhaps he's out of work not because of an economic or ecological crisis, but a spiritual crisis. Nobody wants to eat their little silver cousins anymore.

Wally Wallski sighs and gets to his feet. He needs a new profession. Here he is thirty-five years old—what can he do? Wash dishes? Sweep floors? Where's the romance in those jobs? Where's the glory? He begins to walk back toward Fulton Street. His ribs hurt and he has a limp. Yes, let's not conceal the news any longer. His wife Claudine has beaten him up. He returned to their condo on West End Avenue last night and said they were lucky to have what they had, and he refused to go begging to Mr. Lenguado again, and Ernest Hemingway never begged nothing from nobody, nor did Marduk the Magnificent, if truth be told, and Claudine punched him out. She hammered on his ribs and kicked his shins and when she had finished, Wally Wallski said he would see Mr. Lenguado first thing in the morning and that if Claudine wanted a house on Gramercy Park, with a key to the park to go with it, then he, Wally Wallski, would make sure she got it. But there was no happiness in his surrender, no sense that he was doing the right thing. Might makes right, thought Wally Wallski. It's a shame but it's true.

It was a bright blue morning when Wally Wallski sat down at the end of the pier, but as he waits for the light at South Street, he feels a drop of rain. The wind has picked up and it whistles through the girders of the overpass. Pigeons flutter off to protected places. Several cars turn on their lights. There's a rumble of thunder. As Wally Wallski crosses over to Fulton, he wonders if he loves his wife or if she is merely a powerful habit. Perhaps he stays with her only because she frees him from the painful decision-making process of having to run his own life. With Claudine, there is no question about what Wally Wallski will do next, because she tells him. Maybe I've let her make a baby outta me on purpose? Wally Wallski asks himself. Maybe I lost my job on purpose? And next I'll let her put a diaper on me and stick a bottle of warm milk in my mouth.

On the other hand, maybe everything will be okay after Claudine has this place on Gramercy Park. Maybe Gramercy Park will be her saturation point and she'll be happy. She'll bake Wally Wallski a chicken pot pie and let him have ice cream for dessert. The wind blows harder and Wally Wallski zips up his jacket. Bits of paper and plastic bags rush past him. From somewhere comes the crash of breaking glass. What would Marduk the Magnificent do with a wife like Claudine? And Wally Wallski imagines Marduk and Claudine in the ring together. Both are naked and they are wrestling like crazy but Marduk has the upper hand and Claudine clearly likes it. Wally Wallski shuts down his scary thoughts. Sometimes his brain is just a pest.

The wind makes it hard to walk. Wally Wallski squints to keep the dust out of his eyes. Mr. Lenguado's building is half a block away. Over the rush of wind, Wally Wallski hears rousing music, a march of some kind, and with it comes singing, but he is too far away to make out the words. No one else is on the street. Wally Wallski tries to imagine Claudine happily whistling in her new kitchen on Gramercy Park. Maybe they will have kids at last and in the spring Wally Wallski will take his little son or daughter over to the park and teach him or her the names of the flowers. "Crocus," he will say proudly. "Daffodil!"

"Können ihm Essig holen," sings a male voice as drums pound in the background. Can bring him vinegar . . .

"Können sein Gesicht abreiben . . ." Can wash his face . . .

Wally Wallski has seen a lot of World War II movies and he correctly identifies the language as German. The pounding drums and the martial music make him nervous. Maybe it's a Nazi opera.

"Können einem toten Mann nicht helfen!" You cannot help a dead man! This is followed by a blare of trumpets, and Wally Wallski scrunches his neck into his shoulders. He could bust his brain all day long and never guess this is the last scene of *The Rise and Fall of the City of Mahagonny,* by Kurt Weill and Bertolt Brecht. The characters are having a protest march and they carry the belongings of a man who has just been executed on the stage. Wally Wallski wonders how Mr. Lenguado will ever hear him. He stands beneath his window. Gusts of wind whip the geraniums in their green boxes and red petals flutter through the air.

"Mr. Lenguado! Are you in there? I got a favor I gotta ask! My wife Claudine finds the condo on West End too small! She wants a nice place on Gramercy Park! Mr. Lenguado! Do you hear me? It's Wally Wallski. I saved your life!"

"Können einem toten Mann nicht helfen!" sings the chorus of men, followed by the trumpets. You cannot help a dead man!

It rains harder and thunder bangs around the sky. Wally Wallski grips the collar of his coat. He wishes he had a hat. "Mr. Lenguado, you gotta help me out! I saved your life. My wife Claudine punched me in the snoot!"

A woman is singing. It is Widow Begbick. She says you can put money in the hand of a dead man, dig a hole for him, stick him in the hole and fill the hole with dirt, but when all is said and done: you cannot help a dead man. "Können einen toten Mann nicht helfen. . . ."

Wally Wallski puts his hands over his ears. "Mr. Lenguado!"

The trumpets sound. "Enough!" cries a loud voice. "Didn't I warn you about bothering me again?"

The voice is so angry that Wally Wallski hopes that it's the opera, but he knows it's Mr. Lenguado. "My wife told me I had to come back. The place on West End isn't right for her."

"What's wrong with it?"

"It doesn't have a little park. My wife Claudine needs a little park with a private key. Flowers mean everything to her. Please, Mr. Lenguado!"

"Do you know I could have you sunk ten feet in concrete?" shouts Mr. Lenguado. The sky is pitch-black.

"Können wohl von seinen grossen Zeiten reden . . ." sings a male voice. We can speak well of his great times and forget his great times.

"Please, Mr. Lenguado, I saved your life. This is the last time, I swear it!"

"I could have you turned into dog meat!"

"Please, Mr. Lenguado. We're planning to have kids. I want to teach them the names of the primary plants! I want them to know what's important among the flora and fauna!"

"Go!" shouts Mr. Lenguado. "The truck's already on its way. But if you ever come back, my dogs will eat you!"

"Never," shouts Wally Wallski, as lightning strikes. "You'll never see me again! Oh, thank you, thank you!"

"Können uns und euch und niemand helfen!" sings the chorus. We cannot help ourselves and you and nobody!

The trumpets fling their noises into the surrounding air, but Wally Wallski is running back toward South Street as fast as his legs will carry him. The music is already a dim memory and he can see a little blue sky over Brooklyn. Then Wally Wallski slams on the brakes at the corner as a young man dashes in front of him. "Sorry!" shouts the young man in a voice that is both friendly and exhausted. Then the young man slams on the brakes as well. "You know where I can find some aquavit?"

"Never heard of it," calls Wally Wallski. "Do you know how I can change my life?"

The young man gives Wally Wallski a friendly shrug, then turns away and starts running. Now there, thinks Wally Wallski, is someone working hard to solve his problems. Then he thinks: Just like me. Wally Wallski turns north. Am I really working hard to solve my own problems? he asks himself. No, I am just taking orders. I take orders from whoever frightens me most.

Sparrow Gonzalez leans across the table and stares into Bernard's dead fish eyes. "I may be talking through my hat," he says, "but I think the world's falling apart."

Bernard is gazing at something in the middle of the air of the hospital dayroom. Perhaps it is the ghost of a former patient. It is ten o'clock in the morning and the only other people in the room are half a dozen zombies in front of the TV, where a quiz show is in progress. They are pointed at the TV rather than looking at it. We must salute the efficacy of modern medicine, which has replaced the ball and chain with a tiny pill.

"I had this wonderful two-headed coin," says Sparrow, "and some guy came running along and knocked it right outta my pocket. In a well-ordered world things like that wouldn't happen."

There is no response from Bernard. His hands are posed in midair as if he were typing without a typewriter. Every so often Sparrow kicks him in the shins to make sure he is alive. Sparrow also keeps a sharp eye on the doors. He wants to avoid the Grabber, who he keeps brooding about. He wishes he could think of a big punishment, one that will take the place of a lot of little ones. Sparrow regrets that he quit the Golden Gloves, that he didn't push forward as a fighter. He feels that his skills of retribution are being wasted as a window washer.

"First this awful stuff happens to Marduk the Magnificent," says Sparrow, "then I lose my lucky coin. Who knows what'll happen next?"

As if in response to this question, the Grabber appears in a doorway on the other side of the room. His eyes focus on Sparrow and his eyebrows rise in anticipatory pleasure. The Grabber is very big and the doorway fits him as a tight skirt used to fit Marilyn Monroe. Not only is his Elvis Presley haircut perfectly coiffed, but he wears a net over it as well. The Grabber is one of those people who believes that the King still lives ("You can't tell me he died taking a dump, no way!") and right this moment he is belting his heart out in the Yucatán. A little light goes on in the Grabber's eyes and he surges forward.

"Hey, Bernard, I gotta hit the road," says Sparrow. "Maybe I'll catch you tomorrow."

"Ahhh," says Bernard and he slightly moves two fingers, as if hitting the "k" and the "f" on his invisible typewriter.

The dayroom is a large room, and for the next few minutes the Grabber and Sparrow Gonzalez run around it at high speed. The Grabber is faster on the straightaways. Sparrow is faster on the curves. The other seven people in the room, including Bernard, do not appear to take any interest as the Grabber and Sparrow rush past so close as to make their hair flutter. In fact, the Grabber even knocks over the TV, which shoots up a lot of sparks, but the six zombies go on staring at the spot where it had stood as if their interest in the quiz show continued undiminished.

One could try to work up a little sympathy for the Grabber. In high school he was a big flabby kid who could never get a date and who the other kids all picked on. Alcoholic parents, abusive older siblings, traitorous acquaintances—the Grabber's seen it all. He might have gone into therapy, he might have gone to jail—instead he changed himself into the Grabber, the nuthouse tough guy who gets to punch people who can't punch back. It is only in those quiet moments in his room when listening to "Heartbreak Hotel" that something vaguely human emerges. We will not see those moments, but we want to take the opportunity to say they exist. It would be nice if the Grabber were one hundred percent bad; then our delight in his sufferings could be absolute. But like anyone, the Grabber gets lonely in the night and sometimes he looks in the mirror and just shakes his head, confused. If the Grabber's high school had possessed one of the President's F-16 fighter-bombers to peddle to the Arabs, it could have used the money for better teachers and counselors and maybe the Grabber would have turned out differently. But the President needs those F-16s, so let's cut out the traitorous chitchat.

We now move quickly through the remainder of this section. As the Grabber hustles around a couch in pursuit of Sparrow, the frustrated window washer slings a straight chair into the bully's path and it connects with his left ankle. One can chart the course of the pain by watching the wrinkles blossom on the Grabber's round face. See how his mouth puckers and his eyes squinch up? See how he hops up and down on his right foot? These are the outward manifestations of an inward experience.

"Owww, that hurt!" says the Grabber.

"It didn't hurt enough," says Sparrow, making for the exit.

The Grabber limps after him. He thinks if he had a gun, he could shoot Sparrow, and he plans to drive over to the Bedford-Stuyvesant section of Brooklyn where he can buy one cheap.

When the Grabber gets outside, he sees Sparrow on the other side of the parking lot staring intently at the Grabber's car. This is a cream-colored '57 Chevy and the Grabber has put a lot of work into it. The chrome is without a blemish and the red leather tuck-and-roll upholstery is as soft as chamois cloth. For a foolish moment, the Grabber thinks he still has a chance to catch Sparrow, but then he notices just the smallest white whisper of smoke rising up from the back of his Chevy.

"Hey!" says the Grabber, fearing the worst.

This is followed by an explosion and a flash of fire which transforms the Chevy from an immaculate automobile into a fleeting orange flower. Rarely does one have such a perfect enactment of the words "totally engulfed." The force of the explosion is like a fist that smacks the Grabber's belly and knocks him down. He lies for a moment with his hands over his head. Looking up at last, he sees Sparrow standing on the other side of the burning automobile with his arms crossed.

"I'm poor, I'm poor!" says the Grabber.

"Not poor enough yet," says Sparrow.

We now move over to the Gateway Plaza and back in time about thirty minutes. It is seven minutes before ten o'clock and a hooligan wearing a double-breasted sport coat with a bulge over his heart which is neither tenderness nor compassion steps up to an intercom, pokes a few buttons and, through a red silk handkerchief, pronounces the words "Clean as a whistle."

If we pull back, we see six of these thugs and their master, a rectangular-looking bald guy. All have their right hands inside their jackets as if suffering from a simultaneous case of heartburn. They form a semicircle around an elevator door and the bald guy stands in the center because he wants the pleasure of being first. Remember? The Snowman is about to ride that elevator, which is attached to the side of the building, and these guys want to transform him from a living, breathing, feeling (occasionally) human being into dog meat.

If we look around, we find other oddities. For instance, poking up among the bushes by the wall are four shoes with their toes pointed toward Heaven. Their occupants are headed for the other place. They are two of the Snowman's bodyguards, and even though they were pretty good at their job (despite this ultimate lapse), they were pretty bad at everything else, so bad that Saint Peter needs only a glance at their vitas to send them packing.

On the other side of the elevator is something even stranger: a two-story construction made out of plywood resembling a cross between a skateboard ramp and a ski jump. It goes up and up and at the top is an orange tent of the sort that utility workers use to obscure their mysterious enterprises. Some kids with skateboards were hanging around it earlier, but the hoods chased them away. There is no sound from the tent, no evidence of occupation. There is only this anxious waiting. It is as if a great clock were hanging in the air above the elevator. For the seven hoods that clock is as real as Miami Beach and right now it says three minutes before ten o'clock.

A cough floats down from a high place and the seven hoods wrinkle their foreheads in thought. Maybe it was a pigeon, thinks one. Maybe it was an angel, thinks another. The bald rectangular hood goes by the name of Runrun Lowensohn, and we wish we had time to review all the bad things he has done. There is little to choose between when comparing the Snowman and Lion Boy, as Runrun likes to be called. Sleaze for these guys is like a hometown. Sadism is the middle C of their peculiar musicale. Hearing the cough, Runrun Lowensohn glances warily toward the orange tent at the top of the plywood structure, and if he had time, he might investigate. But the time for investigation is past. The lighted numbers above the elevator are dropping down from the thirty-fourth floor. It is almost exactly ten o'clock.

When the number above the elevator registers "10," there is a dull rumbling from the plywood structure and the whole contraption begins to shake. Several of the hoods glance at it nervously, but now the elevator is nearly at the bottom and the hoods cannot afford to be looking elsewhere when the doors open. The Snowman hasn't succeeded in the fast lane of criminal enterprise by being slow on the draw. The hoods begin to remove large revolvers from the holsters above their hearts.

What happens next happens fast, and we need to artificialize the scene by presenting it in three sections. First the elevator door slides open to reveal the Snowman and his daughter, Beacon Luz. The Snowman has his hand inside his sport coat and pressed to the revolver over his heart, because he was not quite happy with the voice that had called up, "Clean as a whistle," and he is vigilant. Next to the Snowman is Beacon Luz, and she wears her green Marduk the Magnificent sweatshirt and she holds a red beach ball. When the doors open and the Snowman and his daughter see what is to be seen, they open their mouths very wide.

Second we have the seven hoods with Runrun Lowensohn in the center. All seven stare not at the elevator but at the great plywood structure, and their expressions range from astonishment to exasperation. Their guns are in evidence but they are not pointed at anything. They are simply dangling from their fingers while their minds are busy elsewhere.

Third we have the skateboard ramp cum ski jump. Plummeting down it at fifty miles per hour is Zapo, the fifteen-year-old syringe salesman, wearing a New York Giants football helmet and his red Marduk the Magnificent sweatshirt. He is strapped to his stumpboard and holds an iron bar about ten feet long. He moves so fast that if we had not slowed him down, we wouldn't see him. Let us also say that his chin has a resolute jut to it. He doesn't know what will come next, but he is ready for anything.

Now most of the guns in evidence begin firing. However, it is a wild and unfocused sort of firing, because Zapo, going more than sixty miles per hour, has reached the seven hoods with his iron pole, which he holds at knee level. Zapo tears through the hoods like a high-production cane cutter through a canebrake. Those crack-crack noises are not gunshots but the sound of the iron pole against kneecaps. Zapo manages to mutilate six of the seven hoods, missing only Runrun Lowensohn himself, who jumps craftily in the air. In a more exact world, he might be shot by the Snowman, but the Snowman is in the process of unpeeling his daughter from his legs. Beacon Luz has panicked and grabbed him. Her red beach ball bounces across the sidewalk toward the damaged hoods. Runrun Lowensohn comes down on his two feet and takes aim at the kid on the skateboard who has messed up his plans.

Indeed, this would be the end of Zapo, but at that moment who comes barreling around the corner in his quest for aquavit but Seth, still running hard and not watching where he is going. Before Runrun can fire, Seth smacks right into him.

"Sorry, sorry, I just didn't notice, sorry, sorry!" And Seth scrambles to his feet, accidentally kicks the red beach ball and disappears around the other corner.

Zapo has managed a pirouette and comes zooming back again. Runrun Lowensohn is depressed by how the morning has fallen out but he lifts his pistol for at least one shot at the Snowman.

Again there is a cracking sound and again it is kneecaps not gunshots. Runrun topples to the sidewalk. Zapo begins to collect the revolvers from the unhappy thugs.

The Snowman steps from the elevator. He has freed himself from his daughter's panicky grasp and he is all set to shoot somebody, but there is nobody left to shoot.

"I guess I owe you one, little guy," he says.

"I'm not so little," says Zapo. "It's just the fact that I don't have any legs that makes me short."

Zapo wants to stare at Beacon Luz but he feels too shy. And Beacon Luz would like to stare at Zapo, her daddy's rescuer, but she feels shy as well. But even though they don't look at each other, the picture of Marduk on Zapo's red sweatshirt and the picture of Marduk on Beacon Luz's green sweatshirt make eye contact and a long and intimate glance is exchanged.

24

KEEPING MUM

Who we become, who we are, who we have been in the past—are most people unchanging throughout their lives? They are born with a nature in the same way one is born with brown eyes and they keep that nature until they are lowered into their graves, at which point the worms get to share it between them? And if someone's nature seems to change, does that prove that one's nature is capable of change or is it simply one's true nature rising to the surface? Take Michael Marmaduke, who has always been a kind man—if he commits a cruel act, is this a change in his nature or the disclosure of a hidden nature?

If one's nature changes or one's hidden nature rises to the surface, this event needs a cause. Something happens to make one want to change. As Lactantius said (more or less), danger makes us smart. The stimulus of danger forces change. Perhaps this is not a change in one's nature, but utilizing a muscle or talent hitherto unused. Some will argue that one's intrinsic nature cannot change. One is born with a certain potential and at best one can explore that potential. If one finds something nasty in one's psychological stewpot (a desire to sock short people), one attempts to squelch it. If one finds something nice (the ability to play the conga drums like crazy), one heightens it. But for each person this potential is a poorly mapped territory. There must be many nasty occupations that could give lasting pleasure. There must be many gifts we never explore, such as playing the trombone or speaking Urdu or learning to wrestle. And it is mostly chance that sends a person in one direction or another.

This returns us to Michael Marmaduke. For twenty-five years his life was as simple as a ball rolling down a hill. He had brains he never used, emotions he never explored. If vanilla was his favorite flavor, it was because no one had offered him tutti-frutti. One should feel sorry for those even-tempered people for whom puberty is no more than a mild merry-go-round ride. Their lives are as smooth as Nebraska. Instead of burning with a hard and gemlike flame, they simmer like a bowl of Cream of Wheat. But even to them something can happen—a child can die, a loved one can be taken away—and they change. "He became a different person," we hear people say. But has he intrinsically changed or has he dredged up something from his own unexplored potential?

The disappearance of Rose White and the inadequacy of the police pose a terrible problem for Michael Marmaduke. His love for the missing woman and his sense of justice demand that he act, while the attention of the mass media and the prodding of one hundred nosy reporters make it impossible for him to sit still. *He must act.* What an elementary sentence and what a distance exists between it and the completed action. A great deal of head-scratching goes on between those two events.

For Michael much of the head-scratching occurred Tuesday morning as he sat in his room at the Gramercy Park Hotel, just a stone's throw from Wally Wallski's new red-brick townhouse. When he awoke, he called Brodsky and Gapski. They were not in their office. The man to whom Michael spoke said they had watched the video which Michael had dropped off for them, but they had left no message. Michael is in a quandary. He doesn't know what to do. But this is not quite accurate. He keeps remembering the previous night when he faced Taurus with the sword and the complicated feelings he experienced. He believes he came very close to sticking that crazy man turned animal, but probably he didn't. Probably the idea just zipped through his brain and disappeared. But to Michael it seems he came within an ace of killing Taurus, and this alarms him. It also makes him remember what Jack Molay said about the Gimmick of Heroism. Would killing Taurus have been a heroic act or would it have meant surrendering to the illusion of heroism? Would killing Taurus have helped find Rose White, or would it merely have bolstered Michael's own sense of himself as a hero? And what defined heroism? Bravery, prowess and muscle. Where did these values come from? Weren't they at odds with his own gentle nature?

But let's consider Michael's gentleness. As Primus Muldoon points out, what is it in Michael's nature that allows him to put on the Gimmick of Marduk the Magnificent so easily? Is violence antithetical to him or just part of his own unexplored potential? Perhaps violence frightens him and his apparent gentle nature is a reaction to that fear. Perhaps what scared him was not Taurus but that the sword, which Deep Rat flung to him, gave Michael a glimpse of his own capability for violence.

But for Michael the big problem is what to do next. And he asks himself what Marduk would do in this situation. The answer is not long in coming: Marduk is a problem solver, not a problem sufferer. Marduk would act. This realization leads Michael to don his wig, beard, mustache and slouch hat and take a cab uptown to the Chrysler Building. What does it mean to put aside the illusion of heroism, to discard one's Gimmick? Michael will eat crow if he has to, but if the Disputants can help him, then he must return and apologize. Surely, he thinks, they cannot lead me to any place so dangerous where I might be tempted to stick some poor demented creature with a sword.

When Michael gets off the elevator at the Aerie, he finds a receptionist seated behind a desk: a middle-aged woman with a beehive hairdo and a crossword puzzle.

"I'd like to see Jack Molay," says Michael.

"I'm sorry," says the woman without glancing up from her crossword puzzle, "he's not available."

"What about Morgan the Pelagian?"

"Mr. Morgan? I'll buzz him. Who shall I say is calling?"

Michael wishes he had some innocent and anonymous nom de plume. "Michael Marmaduke, I guess."

The woman appears unaffected by the power of his name. She says something into her mouthpiece, then tells Michael, "Please take a seat. He'll be with you shortly." As he waits, Michael removes his black wig and slouch hat, then he peels off his beard and mustache. He's tired of looking like a bum.

Five minutes later Morgan the Pelagian comes through a side door that Michael hasn't noticed. "Mr. Molay is very disappointed in you," he says. He has changed out of his brown robes and is wearing a business suit. He doesn't even offer to shake hands.

"I wanted to hear more about what it means to get rid of the Gimmick of Heroism."

"It may be too late for that."

"I'm worried sick about my fiancée and it seems I'm the only one who can help her. I know I behaved badly. I didn't mean to offend anybody."

Morgan gives Michael a thoughtful look. His beard is neatly combed and he is dapper enough to model a Brooks Brothers shirt. "You won't go storming off again?"

"I never lose my temper. I don't know what got into me."

"Whatever you see here, you don't talk about. Okay?"

Michael nods. He feels embarrassed about himself and wishes he had more of Marduk's self-assurance.

"Come with me." Morgan leads him through a door which puts them at the rear of the Hall of the Disputants. A few people are seated at the semicircle of desks and the lamps at those places provide the only light. Morgan climbs the steps onto the raised area, then leads Michael back to the last row of theater seats. "Let's sit here," he says, moving to the center of the row.

Morgan looks at Michael, then sighs. "I expect what the Master of Ceremonies means by putting aside the Gimmick of Heroism is to accept the God which appears in the Book of Job."

Again Michael's awareness of his own ignorance creates within him a sense of anxiety. He's never read the Book of Job, which he always thought rhymed with Bob. "What do you mean?"

"In the Book of Job, a good man is tormented by God for no clear reason. Satan appears as God's helper and his role is to see what human beings are doing and report back. There's nothing malevolent about him. Satan is not even his name; it's his job title. Satan's change to a specific angel with an evil agenda came out of the wish to free God from blame. Man couldn't permit God to have a different morality from his own. As a result, if bad things happened, they weren't done by God, but by Satan: a new Satan, an evil Satan, a fallen angel. But to accept the God in the Book of Job means to accept that man can suffer without having done wrong. It also means that God—the God in the Book of Job—finds human ideas of justice simplistic. To accept the God of the Book of Job means going beyond conventional ideas of good and evil to a place where nothing is clear. The trouble with the Gimmick of Heroism is that it is dualistic. The hero fights evil like Saint George fought the dragon. To give up your Gimmick means to give up this dualism and to seek more sophisticated definitions of justice."

"But I thought the Disputants were full of dualists."

"They are. But we work to transcend dualism and help others transcend it as well. Look again at Lactantius, for whom Jesus and Satan were brothers. Not only are they brothers, they form the right and left hand of God. These hands are in constant battle, but they also derive from God. Take away either and God is diminished. Or look at the goddess Kali, who is called 'the Ferry Across the Ocean of Existence.' She is both horrible and benign. She gives life and she takes it away. In her, all opposites are reconciled. Is an earthquake evil? Is a hurricane malevolent? Kali represents the wholeness, the sum of all there is. Or look at Dionysus, who is also the god of opposites: birth and death, destruction and creation, comedy and tragedy, joy and sorrow. There are many such gods. Symbols, really. The problem with dualism is that it either makes evil something outside, or makes it a flaw in oneself, like the dualists perceive matter to be flawed. They argue that you cannot help being bad because the matter out of which you are made is bad. Such a theory saves you of blame. It's not your fault you are bad; rather, something made you bad. This dichotomy leads one to view the world in the same terms. It also gives value to the Gimmick of Hero: he who combats evil. That's your position. You see the kidnapping of Rose White as an evil act and you try to find her by learning the nature of that evil. But perhaps it wasn't done out of evil. Perhaps she was kidnapped for another reason."

"But what could it be?"

"I don't know, but when the Master of Ceremonies said that you would discover her by putting aside the Gimmick of Heroism, he might have meant that you need to stop looking for evil motives for her kidnapping and look for others instead."

"Like what?"

"That's for you to discover. But it's like Job. Terrible things happened to him, but as long as we think those things are evil, then we can have no understanding of the God who appears in the Book of Job. You want one answer. Perhaps there isn't one answer. When Pelagius went to Rome, he had faith in a book of the Bible which has been expelled from the Canon called the Apocalypse of Baruch. It's main difference was that it didn't blame Adam for everything. It didn't make everyone suffer for Adam's sin. It said, 'Adam is not the cause, save only of his own soul, but each of us has been made the Adam of his own soul.'

"This made sense to Pelagius. It meant that human beings commit evil not out of their natures but their will. It made each person responsible for his own evil. But Pelagius wasn't much of a sinner and his idea was too commonsensical. He didn't see that a religion doesn't just need to teach, it needs to govern. And it governs by offering people something they want. First it convinces them they need to be saved, then it offers salvation. Augustine had a far clearer idea of evil. He had his sexual obsession and his body tormented him. Consequently, he also espoused the will, but he put the will in a corrupt body: a body in need of salvation. And Pelagius was driven away. But I'm sorry that the Apocalypse of Baruch fell into disfavor. That, too, was because of Augustine, no doubt. 'Each of us is the Adam of his own soul.' That's not a bad idea, do you think?

"In any case, the Hall of the Disputants is where we discuss these ideas. What is good, what is evil, what is responsibility and what is the basis of our interpretation? For instance, one thinks of theft as evil. But perhaps it's not theft that is evil, but property that is evil. That is very simplistic, but it indicates how these ideas must be reassessed."

"But why?" asks Michael. "What does it lead to?"

"Through disputantship we articulate priorities. Then, in the Product side of our enterprise, we communicate them."

"How? Do you distribute pamphlets?"

"No, no, our communication is nonverbal. Language is a diminishment, a reduction. At best, a written text is to its subject what a map is to the territory it represents. But how can a map of Manhattan give you any feeling for Manhattan? Therefore we move past the map, past language, to give the very essence of the dichotomy. We don't reduce it, we recreate it."

"Can you give me an example?"

"I can do better than that," says Morgan. "I can show you how it works. Look down at the Disputants."

Michael sees that as they have been talking, the Disputants have entered the hall and the twenty-four desks are now occupied. A spotlight blinks on and focuses on the stage in front. Someone mounts the steps and walks to the podium. He wears a dark robe with a hood, but then he pushes back the hood to reveal his face.

"It's Jack Molay!" says Michael.

"The Master of Ceremonies," says Morgan the Pelagian. "Now you'll get a sense of the product side of our work."

One of the Disputants stands up at his desk. "I have known my soul and the body that lies upon it, which have been enemies since the creation!"

"That's one of the Manichaeans," says Morgan. "Probably a Greek. This should give you a good sense of dualism."

Another Disputant gets to his feet. "We know what is said to have been before there was earth and darkness; we know why God and Satan fought, how Light and Darkness mingled, and who is said to have created Heaven and Earth; we know why Earth and Heaven shall pass away, and how Light and Darkness shall be separated from each other, and what shall happen thereafter."

"He's a Persian," says Morgan. "He and the Greek mostly differ in the names they give to the Darkness. Out on the street, they'd probably kill each other. Here they dispute. This actually is a synthesis of previous discussions, with the two sides compromising in order to dramatize the narrative."

Both the Greek and the Persian are middle-aged bearded men wearing monkish robes.

"The Dark was divided against itself," says the Greek, "the tree against its fruit and the fruit against the tree. Strife and bitterness belonged to the nature of its parts; gentleness was unknown to those filled with every malignity."

"Yet it was their very tumult that gave them the chance to rise up to the worlds of Light," says the Persian. "For truly, these members of the Tree of Death did not know one another. Each had only his own mind, each knew nothing but his own voice. Only when one of them screamed did they hear him and turn hungrily toward that sound."

The Greek Manichaean speaks again. "Thus aroused they fought one another, and did not cease to press each other until at last they caught sight of the Light. For in the course of the war they came, some pursued and some pursuing, to the boundaries of Light, and when they beheld it—a sight wondrous and glorious— they marveled at it; and all the Matter of Darkness assembled and conferred how they could mix themselves with it."

Then the Persian rises to his feet. "But because of the disorder of their minds they failed to perceive that a mighty God dwelt there. Thus without understanding, they cast a mad glance upon the Light from lust for the spectacle of these blessed worlds, and they thought it could become theirs."

Then the Greek spoke more loudly. "And carried away by their passion, they wished to fight against it and mingle their own Darkness with the Light. They united all the dark and ruinous Matter and with their forces they rose together, and they opened the attack without even knowing their adversary, for they had never heard of the Deity."

Michael notices that the Master of Ceremonies is lifting up two hand puppets. The one on his left hand is blue and twists back and forth with quick staccato movements. The one on his right hand is red and perfectly still.

A woman Disputant in a gray robe gets to her feet. "God had nothing evil with which to chastise Matter, for in the house of God there is no evil. He had neither consuming fire with which to hurl thunder and lightning, nor suffocating water with which to send a flood, nor cutting iron nor any other weapon; but all with him is

Light and noble substance, and he could not injure the Evil One."

A fourth Disputant stood up: a young man in a dark robe. "The Father of Greatness called forth the Mother of Life, and she called forth Ormuzd, the Primal Man, and Ormuzd called his five sons, like a man who puts on his armor for battle. The Father charged him with the fight against the Darkness. And Ormuzd armed himself with his five sons: the gentle breeze, the wind, the light, the water and fire. He made them his armor and plunged down from Paradise until he came to the border of the area adjoining the battlefield."

Now Michael sees the red hand puppet swooping down like a bird upon the blue one. The large screen behind the Master of Ceremonies lights up but remains blank.

The Greek Manichaean speaks again. "Ahriman, the Archdevil, also took his five sons—smoke, consuming fire, darkness, fog and the scorching wind—and he armed himself with them, then rushed to meet Ormuzd, the Primal Man. As the King of Darkness beheld the light of the Primal Man, he spoke: 'What I sought afar I found nearby.' After they had struggled long with one another, the Archdevil overcame the Primal Man."

Through this part the two hand puppets have been twisting together in a conflict resembling an elaborate dance. Two men have appeared on the screen behind the Master of Ceremonies. Both are wrestlers, and Michael, in his role of Marduk the Magnificent, has wrestled each of them. They are Ormuzd, the Primal Man, and Ahriman, Prince of Darkness.

The Persian Manichaean begins to speak. "Thereupon Ormuzd, the Primal Man, gave himself and his five sons as food to the five Sons of Darkness, as a man who has an enemy mixes a deadly poison in a cake and gives it to him. As the Sons of Darkness ate them, the five luminous gods were deprived of understanding, and through the poison of the Sons of Darkness they became like a man who has been bitten by a mad dog or serpent. And the five parts of Light became mixed with the five parts of Darkness."

During the Persian's speech the two hand puppets continue their dance, but very slowly, while behind them on the screen the two wrestlers, Ormuzd and Ahriman, meticulously duplicate the movements of the puppets. The Master of Ceremonies again has his black hood over his face so it seems that the puppets are alone behind the podium. They struggle together, rocking back and forth, while on the screen Ormuzd and Ahriman swirl around in an embrace and it is impossible to say who is winning and who is losing. Indeed, they no longer seem to be fighting but each appears entangled with the other.

"This is your product?" asks Michael, astonished.

"Yes, this is the translation of the dispute."

"Then you're the Wrestling Association," says Michael.

Morgan nods. In the dim light Michael sees only the glimmer of a gold tooth.

We now move forward to midafternoon. Michael is seated in Primus Muldoon's office separated by only a partition from the gymnasium called the Meat Market and which Muldoon calls Pforta. From nearby we hear the sounds of weights clanking together and human grunts indicative of strenuous effort. On the wall behind Muldoon is a photograph of Friedrich Nietzsche in profile. Primus Muldoon is also in profile and Michael is struck by the similarity of their mustaches: big, brazen and self-important. Michael reaches up and pulls off his own false mustache and throws it in the trash. He vows never to wear a disguise again. His mind is a jumble, and transposed across his thoughts he sees the hand puppets of the Master of Ceremonies weaving through their intricate dance.

"Prime Rib went back to Brooklyn this morning," Muldoon is saying. "There was no sign of Taurus and the taurobolium was just a basement again. He said if his brothers hadn't been with him, he'd have thought the whole thing a dream. I remember Taurus: one of those fragile egos, torn between his wish to do bad and his wish to do good. How clever to avoid the human dilemma by becoming an animal."

But Michael's mind is elsewhere. "You know, that morning you found me pumping iron at Bernie's Pump House, I'd never been there before. Some guy gave me his card. It was a lousy place, full of cockroaches, and I almost didn't stay. What if I'd left before you got there? I'd still be in Paterson keeping little kids from playing too rough on the slide."

"You were my great discovery," says Muldoon.

Michael isn't sure who discovered who, but clearly his whole present life stems from that encounter. Were it not for Muldoon, Michael would never have met Rose White. "What do you think of the Book of Job?" He is careful not to rhyme Job with Bob.

"Job is the victim of the Jewish God," says Muldoon, surprised by the question. "He teaches the slaves that you can do everything right and still get a kick in the pants. What's got you wondering about Job? Having trouble with pimples?"

Michael shakes his head, not understanding the reference. "Why do you think Rose White was kidnapped?"

"At first I thought someone was going to use her to get money out of you, but now I don't know. I don't understand those videotapes. They do nothing but make us mad. Who'd want to hurt anyone as gentle as Rose White?"

"I just don't see how I can find her," says Michael, putting his head in his hands. "It's been five days."

"Nietzsche said, 'Belief in truth begins with skepticism about everything held to be true.' Look at the obvious reasons for the kidnapping and dismiss them. Then look at all the implausible reasons and consider their validity."

"What do you know about the Wrestling Association?" asks Michael. This is a question that Michael has wanted to ask all along but he has felt hesitant.

"Those cretins!" shouts Muldoon. "Did I tell you that I have to rig up this ludicrous match between Santa and Satan by tomorrow afternoon? They are the tyrants that bind my hands and feet! The despots that provide me with my daily bread! I give them my genius and they treat me like a servant!"

"Did you ever hear of the Disputants?" asks Michael.

"No. Are they a tag team?"

"It's just a name someone mentioned." Michael dislikes lying. He feels that Muldoon has given him everything and now he is hiding something from him. What if Muldoon knew that the Disputants are the Wrestling Association? Michael considers Jack Molay's anger: "For the turning away of the simple shall slay them, and the prosperity of fools shall destroy them." If Muldoon knows nothing about the Disputants, then that's how they want it. Consequently, Michael should keep his mouth shut, not because he is afraid of Jack Molay, but because he doesn't want to lose the chance of his help. But even thinking this, Michael sees the widening crack in his own divided nature.

On the wall across from Muldoon is one of Nietzsche's slogans in Gothic letters: "A more complete human being is a human being who is more completely bestial." Michael looks at it. What does it mean to be more completely bestial? If he were more bestial what would he be like? And he imagines himself squatting in the mouth of a cave gnawing on a bone. Within the cave he sees a woman wearing what looks like a fur bathing suit. She is pushing away the brats who reach for her breasts. Is it Rose White? Michael isn't sure. Then a chill slides down his spine and he turns away from the vision.

25

MULDOON:
I INTEND TO EXPLODE

Do you admire my pinkie ring with a single red ruby or my hand-painted silk tie with miniature Grecian wrestling figures? Giving style to one's character is a great art. It is practiced by those who see all the strengths and weaknesses of their own natures and then comprehend them in an artistic plan until everything appears as art and reason, and even weakness delights the eye. Surely it is strong natures who are happiest with such activity. Only when a person has achieved this satisfaction deriving from a sense of style is he tolerable to behold. Whoever is dissatisfied with himself is always ready to revenge himself, and we others will be his victims, if only by always having to stand his ugly sight. For the sight of the ugly makes us bad and gloomy.

But now my own sense of well-being is being attacked by the Wrestling Association. For years I was able to suffer their foolishness. I dismissed their meddling. They are no better than cunning pleaders for their own prejudices, I told myself. Occasionally I would visit their offices to protest. There was no one to listen to me: secretaries and functionaries, there was no one with any power. It was like being surrounded by cows. Because I could find no one who was accountable, I learned to practice subterfuge. I chose a middle road between servile obedience and outright rebellion. I prided myself on the artistic merit of my own path. I saw myself as a secret soldier skirmishing with their intellectual inconsequence. But how bad every protracted war makes a person when it cannot be waged with open force. My very subterfuge diminished me. I wanted to spit on the city of narrow chests and constricted souls, beady eyes and sticky fingers, the city of the importunate, the shameless, scribblers, screamers, overheated fortune hunters. This too diminished me and at last I turned to the words of Zarathustra: "Where we can no longer love, we must pass on."

Couldn't these functionaries see that I wanted to turn wrestling into a high art? Conflict is the soul's chosen diet, and through wrestling it seemed possible to achieve an art form which would touch the human soul with no intruding medium, with no dividing barrier, just as the lips of lovers touch. Clearly Michael Marmaduke was part of this new aesthetic, as were Thrombosis, Dentata and the others if only I could free them from their assigned Gimmicks. But for the Wrestling Association what is new is invariably *evil*, wanting as it does to break through the old limits and subvert the old pieties. But I have my plans. If the Wrestling Association wants Santa versus Satan, then I will give them a Satan they will never forget. My Satan will knock their socks off. Unfortunately, they will not be daunted for long and this could mean the end of me as a manager within the Wrestling Association.

But of what is great one must either keep silent or speak with greatness. To speak with greatness means to speak cynically and with innocence. That is my duty, and after I have enunciated my words about Santa and Satan, silence will be my only recourse. You say, why not become a teacher? Why not speak to those whose ears are ready to hear? But I don't want believers; I think I am too sarcastic to believe in myself. Nietzsche said, "Only great artistic spirits can learn from history the one real lesson—how to live." This is what my humiliation by the Wrestling Association will teach me: how to live.

I have my wife, my mistress, my two daughters. I have my little house in Summit with my workshop above the garage. I have books. I have Wagner. I have the memory that I have taken the broken, the downtrodden, the desperate and turned them into, well, if not warriors, then at least creditable actors and grapplers with the chimaera, strugglers against desolation, contenders with the mystery. I have the knowledge that I have given Marduk the Magnificent to the world. But just as Michael Marmaduke has been laid low by the abduction of his fiancée, so I have been laid low by this final humiliation by the Wrestling Association: the need to set Satan against Santa. As something was taken from him, so has something been taken from me: my pride, my sense of well-being, my self-esteem as an artist. But you lied for them in the past, you say. You created foolish matches for their foolish pleasure. But what I find in this proposed match between Santa and Satan is an eruption of madness—an outbreak of arbitrariness in feeling, hearing, and seeing; pleasure in mental indiscipline; joy in human unreason. It is the collapse of everything and I am left to either retreat into my isolation or . . . what? That is the question. Am I courageous enough to face the alternative?

I have a secret that I have never told. Think of how my genius has been bludgeoned by the interference of the Wrestling Association. Only a few times have they accepted my ideas for wrestling matches, and even then they have tampered and intruded. Yet I have composed other matches, dream matches, brutal encounters of my reverie. What could I do without real wrestlers, without an audience, without the means of artistic production? I drew them. I drew hundreds of pictures: scene after scene of one great hero lifting some great villain into the air and throwing him as I felt he should be thrown. Yet sometimes the villain fought back and was triumphant and stamped goodness into the mat. I drew hundreds of these fictitious matches. I colored them and improved upon them. Then I hung them upon the walls of my workshop, so that when I am working, I am surrounded by the triumphs of my imagination. And as each match controlled by the Wrestling Association has its hidden intention, so do my sketches of wrestling matches have their hidden intention. But mine reflect the world! Evil triumphs more often than good! And what is this evil? Is it evil to be strong? Is it evil to be new? My paper heroes and heroines bear evil and good within themselves equally. They are made up of equal portions of saint and sinner. This is my lesson to my nonexistent audience. We must accept ourselves in our entirety. We must love our own dirt! We must not try and scrub from ourselves the human in order to become the superhuman. My heros fart and belch and lose and die. They hurl rocks at the clouds. They raise themselves above the petty by tunneling through the commonplace and coming out the other side!

Indeed, these drawings covering the walls of my workshop are the arrows I loose against the heavens. If you could only see their brilliant colors, the grace and humanity of my paper wrestlers. But in truth, how petty it is. How grim! How you must mock my little endeavor! At the moment, I am an artistic middleman, the servant of the Association. And soon I will be nothing at all!

This is the darkest moment of my soul. Even as I speak, I doubt myself. How can I believe my own words? You think I speak in order to describe myself? My words are the building blocks with which I construct my hiding place. Isn't this how books are written: not to reveal the writer but to hide what is within him? And isn't it equally true that a great wrestler like Marduk the Magnificent wrestles not to manifest the true nature of Michael Marmaduke but to disguise it? Nietzsche wrote, "Each philosophy *conceals* another philosophy; each opinion is also a hiding place; each word is a mask." And if each word is a mask, then each word can be Gimmick. Each word contains within it some element of how the speaker sees himself and wants to be seen. When I knit together sentences which are designed to play upon your sympathy, how can I even believe myself? In truth, when I use words to communicate to myself, how can I even know what is true?

Do you see why Nietzsche called language a "net" and a "prison house"? He said that language can never describe a thing. It can only show our relationship to the thing. How can it describe a thing? Can language have taste or smell? How can a word be the thing it represents? Words have only the vaguest of relationships with their subject matter, as a stick figure may represent Marduk the Magnificent. Nietzsche said that between language and the object of language, there can only be an aesthetic interaction: no causal connection, nothing precise or expressive. Language is the transmission of hints! Not only did he teach the truth that we have to live without truth, he taught that we have to live within a noisy and meaningless silence. What is language? Consider the hostility of the universe. That hostility is like the fierce sun burning down upon us. Language is the parasol we hold above our heads to protect ourselves. Oh, we say, we are safe here. Nothing can harm us because we have our parasol of little words!

My friends, my words are the hiccoughs I fling to the dark. They show pain, they show frustration, but they conceal more than they show. What is needed is not words but action. Instead of the word "love," we need a kiss. Instead of the word "hate," we need a kick in the pants. Oh, I have prepared an action which will stun my enemies and drive them back to their holes. Sad to say, it will also destroy me as a wrestling manager. But perhaps it was of me that Nietzsche was speaking when he said that some men are born posthumously. My life will begin after my life is over! Perhaps some other genuine artist will find his way into my workshop and see the watercolors attached to the wall. His genius will recognize my genius. Perhaps this is enough. But for too long have I bruised my understanding by bumping my head against the limits of language. Sometimes I think the life I am living is really dangerous. Sometimes I think I am one of those machines that could *explode*!

26

REGENERATION

Occasionally life's details can be so terrible that the mind retreats from their unpleasant glare and recasts them into a more pleasing aspect. The woman who has slipped from a yacht and is going under for the third time may think how she has always liked the sea. The man who is sucked from the emergency exit of a Boeing 737 at thirty thousand feet can look out at the green hills of Vermont and be transported by the view. So it is with Wally Wallski.

When he completes his walk from Fulton Street to Gramercy Park, he finds his wife Claudine already at home in a four-story red-brick building on the west side of the square with beautiful filigreed balconies. The house is spacious and furnished with expensive antiques and original paintings. Not modern stuff, more like Constable and Stubbs. Even Claudine has been improved. Her hair has been freed from the stainless-steel rollers and is genuinely attractive: a glossy mouse brown. She wears a pretty blue dress with large white polka dots that flatters her full figure. Lipstick, eye shadow, rouge on her cheeks—she appears healthy and full of life. When Claudine greets Wally Wallski at the door, she gives him a kiss on the cheek. True, it is a little rough and later raises a bruise, but it is inspired by affection. Even if this is not the sweet young thing that Wally Wallski once married, she seems a reasonable alternative. She gives him a pinch and invites him inside.

For the rest of the afternoon they explore the house, and each discovery is more exciting than the last. Within a drawer of a rolltop desk, they discover a stack of hundred-dollar bills. Within a drawer of the First Empire dressing table is a jewel box with emerald earrings and a diamond ring. The men's clothes in the closet fit Wally Wallski perfectly: silk shirts and cashmere sweaters. Maybe Claudine has been right. Maybe he was smart to keep nagging Mr. Lenguado after all. Although even as he enunciates Mr. Lenguado's name to himself, there is a rumble of thunder and a chill wind caresses the back of Wally Wallski's neck.

But then Claudine cooks him dinner and even though she burns the lobster and undercooks the cabbage, everything is really wonderful. Claudine tells Wally Wallski about the inadequacies of her childhood (a father who wouldn't let her play Little League baseball; a brother who wouldn't let her borrow his motorcycle) and for the first time Wally Wallski sees his wife as a woman who has been damaged. The term "male hegemony" doesn't quite leap to his mind, but if he knew it, then it would.

By midnight they go to bed and actually make love, although it has been so long that Wally Wallski at first cannot imagine what Claudine is doing. And he doesn't mind that she insists on being on top and hurts his back, he's only glad that she's happy.

So where is the wrinkle? you say. How is this like someone falling out of a plane?

It is while they are sleeping, or at least Claudine is sleeping. The bed is a king-sized bed with a canopy, something like the great Bed of Ware in the Victoria and Albert Museum, and for once Claudine has enough room so that Wally Wallski doesn't have to sleep on the floor. Wally Wallski lies on his back staring at the designs on the underside of the canopy, which are just visible in the glow from the street. He is trying to let himself be happy even though he feels he is trusting himself to thin ice. Not too far away his wife Claudine is purring softly.

What's wrong? Wally Wallski asks himself. Why can't I accept my good fortune?

It is then that Claudine mumbles something in her sleep. Wally Wallski is instantly alert. What has she said? Again something is mumbled. Is it a name?

"Pierre," says Claudine quite distinctly. "Oh, Pierre!"

Wally Wallski checks to see that Claudine's eyes are shut. They are.

"Oh, Pierre, Pierre, Pierre, Pierre, Pierre!" Then Claudine rolls over and becomes silent.

Wally Wallski is stunned. He assumes that Pierre is the doorman, even though he hasn't noticed a doorman. But perhaps he is a doorman over at the Gramercy Park Hotel. Wally Wallski has never thought that Claudine might be unfaithful. She never seems to notice another human being except when one gets in her way and needs shoving aside. Wally Wallski wonders what he should do, and after a while, he decides: Maybe it is not so bad after all. If she wants the doorman, then at least Wally Wallski won't have to go to Mr. Lenguado to get him. And who knows, it might make her more relaxed. Isn't it wrong of him to possess her as if she were his private property? Isn't this another example of how she has been mistreated by the male world? If she wants Pierre, then it is unfair for Wally Wallski to object. He'll stay home and raise the children, whosever they are. He'll take them for walks in the park and show them his Marduk the Magnificent videotapes. Maybe he could even name one of the kids Marduk, or Marduka if it's a girl. It would make up for a lot.

In the morning Claudine seems grumpy, but she is always grumpy in the morning. Wally Wallski brings her a breakfast tray: poached eggs on an English muffin, freshly squeezed orange juice, coffee with sugar and real cream.

When she is half finished eating and somewhat perked up, Wally Wallski begins to broach the delicate subject.

"You know, I've been thinking," he says. "If you want to have an affair with the doorman, I won't stand in your way."

Claudine looks up from her poached eggs as if someone had bitten her foot. "Doorman!" she barks. "What doorman?"

"Pierre. You mentioned him in your sleep. If you want Pierre, I'm sure the three of us can be happy."

"Not Pierre, you idiot!" says Claudine. *"The* Pierre. I want *the* Pierre."

It is a pity there are not eye sizes in the way there are hat sizes —size six representing a tiny head and size nine being a monster —because then we could say that Wally Wallski's eyes leapt from size six to size nine and one would know what is meant. "Do you mean the hotel?" he asks.

"You're darn right I mean the hotel. I want the Pierre. I want the ballroom. I want the banquet halls. I want the spas and gift shops. I want all one hundred and ninety-five rooms. You go back to that goddam Mr. Lenguado and tell him that I have to have it. He's got to give it to me. After all, you saved his lousy life, the creep!"

So it is that a half hour later Wally Wallski has been bustled out of his beautiful house on Gramercy Park with firm orders to go back to Fulton Street and tell Mr. Lenguado that his wife Claudine must have the Pierre.

But Wally Wallski has changed in the time we have known him. As we look at him sitting on his front steps, he appears older than his thirty-five years, and even though he is not exactly brainy, he has developed a kind of wisdom. He knows, for instance, that he cannot go back to Mr. Lenguado. It would mean being turned into dog meat. He also knows that he will never be Ernest Hemingway, no matter how much he drinks. He is Wally Wallski, an out-of-work fisherman, and he is in a fix.

Now watch carefully. Wally Wallski gets to his feet. He doesn't know where to go but he realizes if he keeps sitting on the front steps, his wife Claudine will come out and abuse him. He moves one foot, then another. All of a sudden a young man comes tearing around the corner and smacks into him so that both Wally Wallski and the young man fall down on their butts.

"Ommph!" says Wally Wallski.

The young man jumps to his feet. It is Seth, who is still looking for a bottle of aquavit. "Ah, I'm sorry, jeez, I'm sorry. You okay? Anything I can do for you? Jeez, I'm sorry."

"Go find a truck," says Wally Wallski, "and hit me again."

"It can't be that bad," says Seth, for whom any person who does not require aquavit must, by definition, have a happy life. "Nothing's that bad. Cheer up!"

"Easier said than done," says Wally Wallski, standing up.

"Hey," says Seth, "you know where I can buy some aquavit?"

"Not me," says Wally Wallski, "I'm a Canadian drinker." Meaning he sometimes sips a little Seagram's 7.

"Thanks anyway," says Seth, who is already running again. He turns left at the corner, lopes past the National Arts Club and the Evangeline Home for Women, then right at Irving Place and past Pete's Tavern, where that jailbird O'Henry used to hang out.

At eighteen years old Seth is more like an Irish setter than a human being. Running is what he does best. As he passes Pete's Tavern, the collision with Wally Wallski has already slid from his mind. It is nine o'clock on a Wednesday morning. The street is quiet; the sky is blue. Every so often Seth finds some helpful person who tells him, "Sure, I know where you can find some aquavit. Nothing easier. You know Whitehall?" Or maybe they say, "You know Morningside Heights or Yorkville or Fort George? Well, you go down this street, I forget its name, but you can't miss it because there's a Chinese restaurant on the corner or maybe it's Puerto Rican, anyway, about halfway down the block there used to be this little bodega, it's been years since I was over there, but places like that never change, right? They had aquavit, I know they did, or was it pisco?"

As for the lucky two-headed coin, it remains undiscovered in Seth's jacket pocket. Perhaps this is just as well. Perhaps Seth doesn't need further complications in his life. Every now and then he stops to call home. Marcello is still hanging on and the nuns are bringing him bowls of rice. There's been no word from the two older brothers. "Okay," shouts Seth, "okay, I'm on the right track, I can feel it. I should be home by lunchtime or maybe dinner."

Most people have hundreds of little problems. Seth has one big problem. Perhaps this is preferable. But perhaps it is also inaccurate. Seth also has a problem seeing where he is going. Days of running have so jiggled his eyes that everything is a blur. Watch him now as he makes the turn at 16th Street toward Union Square. Bam! He smacks right into a guy with a shopping cart. Of course it is Beetle. Between the two of them, Seth and Beetle cover more streets than a yellow cab.

"Sorry, sorry, sorry!" shouts Seth, and he begins to pick up the black plastic bags that he has knocked out of the cart.

"Leave it lay, leave it lay!" shouts Beetle.

Seth helps put everything back into the cart. "My fault, my fault entirely!" He has no memory of having seen Beetle before.

"I once found a baby in a trash barrel," says Beetle. "Its ankles were handcuffed together!"

Even though Seth is eighteen and innocent, he feels that Beetle's remark is a ploy to make him listen to what will turn out to be a very long story. He begins hopping up and down. "Can't stop, can't stop!" And he takes off down 16th Street toward Union Square, right past Eddie Condon's, from which a muted trumpet might be heard.

"I took a kid out of the trash basket!" shouts Beetle. "And I carried him to New Jersey! I carried him even further than New Jersey!"

But no one is listening. Beetle sighs and pats his black plastic bags to make sure nothing is broken. Then he starts pushing his cart north on Irving toward Gramercy Park. He thinks what it would be like to have a gigantic voice: a voice as loud as the atomic bomb. He would tell his story in this voice and the very noise of it would pin people to the wall and blow their hats and hairpieces down the street. The noise of his story would just wad everybody up like crumpled paper and when they were all wadded as tightly as they could be wadded, Beetle would flip them over his shoulder and stroll away.

By now Seth has crossed 14th Street and is running down Third Avenue. The coin continues to bounce in his pocket, sometimes landing angel side up, sometimes demon side up. Seth has a casual lope and his long brown hair bounces up and down with each step. He's had a tip about some aquavit in Chinatown and he's full of hope. He'll buy a quart and take it to his dad and his dad will get better and they'll go to the park and shag balls all afternoon. But with this nostalgic thought, Seth once more stops watching where he is going. He's down to Great Jones Street right by the Jean Cocteau Repertory theater, when, bam, he runs into not one person but two. Although to Seth's furry vision it looks like one person, as if he were staring at one person and that person suddenly split into twins. But it's not twins, it's the two policemen Brodsky and Gapski.

"Slap the cuffs on him, slap the cuffs on him!" shouts Gapski, rolling around on the sidewalk where he has been knocked.

Brodsky starts digging for his cuffs, then says, "You slap the cuffs on him, if you want to so much!"

"Sorry, sorry, sorry, sorry," says Seth, helping both men to their feet. "I'm looking for some aquavit."

"Never touch the stuff," say both men in unison. Then Gapski and Brodsky glare at each other.

"Your old lady sniffs glue," says Gapski.

"Your old lady sniffs dog poop," says Brodsky.

It should be said that Seth is now half a block away and the two small men are already fading from memory. But let's stay with Brodsky and Gapski. They have been working overtime ever since Rose White's disappearance, and double overtime since the discovery of Troll's lair. Never have they spent so much time together, and consequently each is seething with hatred for the other. At the moment they are walking over to some kind of hospital on First Avenue called El Instituto Estético. Brodsky and Gapski are already suspicious: meaning if the place is legit, then why does it have a fancy foreign name?

In their investigation of Troll's lair they found a business card with the name of El Instituto Estético to which they paid scant attention because of all the interesting bones. Then when they visited Brooklyn to check Michael Marmaduke's story about a bull ring, they discovered another El Instituto business card in a kind of smelly stable. Of course they didn't find Taurus, but neighbors were able to describe him in such a way as to tweak Brodsky and Gapski's interest so that they were able to curb their mutual hatred until Seth smacked into them and they began saying rude things about each other's old lady.

We, who know more about El Instituto, can surmise that both Troll and Taurus had major body work done at the clinic, for although these gentleman were born ugly and raised ugly, neither was truly as ugly as he wanted so they had paid big money at El Instituto for further heavy-duty uglification.

We skip over the rest of Brodsky and Gapski's quarrel and subsequent shaky truce, and when we next see them they are seated in the office of Dr. Florabunde, age fifty-five, the director of El Instituto. Dr. Florabunde's office resembles the library at the Harvard Club: lots of dark bookshelves and leather furniture. The doctor is seated at his desk with a brass lamp with a green shade and a green blotter with brass triangles at the corners. He has just hung up the phone where he has told someone to "Hold all calls" and now he tilts back his leather chair and folds his hands across the front of his gray tweed suit. Dr. Florabunde has tiny ears and his head is absolutely hairless and round. He doesn't even have eyebrows. Never, think Brodsky and Gapski, have I seen anyone who looks so much like a cue ball. Dr. Florabunde's eyes are pink and watery behind thick glasses, and it becomes clear to the detectives that he must be an albino. Since Dr. Florabunde could change himself in any of a million ways within his own clinic, his decision to look like a cue ball with pink eyes must be commented on, as if to look like a cue ball with pink eyes was Dr. Florabunde's chosen Gimmick.

"What we do here, gentlemen," he is saying, "is to perfect the imperfect. We are in the business of transformation. If you wish to look like Cary Grant, we can make you look like Cary Grant. If you wish to look like Lassie the Wonder Dog, we can make you look like Lassie the Wonder Dog. The choice is yours."

This is the moment when Brodsky and Gapski should be at their sharpest, because, if they thought about it, many of their clues bring them into the neighborhood of El Instituto Estético. But neither is thinking as clearly as he might. Instead each is thinking how either he or his partner might himself be altered at El Instituto, so instead of appearing as twins, they would look as much alike as Winston Churchill and Uncle Joe Stalin.

"Can you make people taller?" asks Gapski.

"We can add ten inches to any human being," says Dr. Florabunde, and his voice is so warm that it makes the detectives think of heating pads and fur blankets.

"Can you make people bigger all over?" asks Brodsky.

"We can add three cubic feet of mass to any man or woman."

"Is it expensive?" asks Gapski.

When Dr. Florabunde smiles, one notices that his tongue exactly matches the pink color of his eyes. "There are many forms of payment," he says.

It is here that certain authorial limitations are most apparent. How many times in a movie theater have we wanted to rush to the screen and shout, "Don't do that!" as the hero or heroine embark on an activity which we perceive to be life-threatening? Just as Brodsky and Gapski are closing in on their goal, which is the question of what happened to Rose White, they have been sidetracked by personal interests. That is the trouble with working with characters who are human beings. We can't just have two policemen with a clear case to investigate, we have to have living, breathing, feeling human creatures who, apart from any criminal investigation, have their own personal agendas.

"So for instance," asks Brodsky, "you could take this fellow right here and make him look like Groucho Marx?"

"Nothing would be easier." And again Dr. Florabunde smiles.

Brodsky and Gapski look pensively at the ceiling. Right now their minds are far from their professional obligations, and by following them into Dr. Florabunde's office, we have strayed into a narrative cul-de-sac. The door is shut behind us and ahead stretch many pages on the subject of full body reconstruction. But look, there is some movement outside the window. We see ropes. We see a platform. We see pails and brushes indicative of window cleaning. And just as the platform rises and goes past Dr. Florabunde's window, we observe the face of Sparrow Gonzalez glancing casually into the room. Let us join him.

If one is not afraid of heights, one can easily envy Sparrow his occupation. Plenty of fresh air and wonderful views. Of course Michael Marmaduke wouldn't like it, but he hates heights. We, however, have always appreciated high places and so we relax and enjoy the ride as the platform carries us aloft. Already we see the East River and there is the Williamsburg Bridge.

Sparrow has no mind for the view. Instead, his head is full of his own problems. Just this morning he went to visit Bernard at St.

Elmo's nuthatch and the nurse refused to let him in. Then she tried to keep him busy until the police arrived. It seems there had been a problem about several blown-up vehicles. But Sparrow hasn't been paranoid all his life without it paying off. He could tell that the nurse was up to some monkey business and so he slipped away. But how terrible to leave his friend Bernard in such a dreadful place. And he is so overswept by hatred for the Grabber that he nearly tumbles from his own platform, and he has no appreciation of the view whatsoever.

The Grabber's ugly kisser is projected so big on Sparrow's mental screen that when he glances through a window on El Instituto's tenth floor and actually sees the Grabber, he has the awful idea that he has brought him to life just by thinking about him so hard. Sparrow clutches his safety rope and looks again. Yes, there indeed is the Grabber. He has his pants off and he sits on a table and he wears the embarrassed expression that one wears when a doctor is inspecting one's genitalia and one is pretending that all this poking and prodding means absolutely nada, as if hardly a day goes by without this sort of suprapersonal intrusion so that now it is no more bothersome than brushing one's teeth. But even Sparrow can see through this charade and he kneels down on the platform so that his eyes just peek over the sill because his one desire is to find something which will facilitate his revenge. Inside this room is the man who has wrecked Sparrow's first friendship since high school (twenty years ago), and Sparrow's single purpose is to make him poor, in the way total destruction makes one poor.

The doctor steps away from the table and an intimate scene is revealed. It seems the Grabber has had some work done on his penis and today the bandages have come off. We won't describe this penis except to say that it is circumcised. Additionally, it has been reddened by its recent trauma and has little black stitches along both sides. More important than the penis is the rubber tube hanging from the Grabber's scrotum: a tube which ends in a rubber ball. Sparrow keeps his eyes peeled as the Grabber lifts the rubber ball and squeezes it, once, twice, three times; and as he squeezes it, the penis becomes engorged and points toward the ceiling like an admonishing finger, as in fact the Grabber's third-grade teacher, Mrs. Ernestello, used to admonish him for, oh, at least a dozen infractions ranging from pulling the wings off flies to keeping a toad in his desk to scare the girls. And now it seems that Mrs. Ernestello's admonishing finger is furiously waggling itself between the Grabber's legs.

As for Sparrow, he nearly falls off his platform. He has known something of the nature of El Instituto—after all, he has been cleaning windows here for some years and has seen many bandaged faces—but this is the first time he has seen an inflatable penis, although he has heard of such things. Peeking again over the sill, Sparrow sees the Grabber give the red ball another squeeze and the jumbo red member deflates. The doctor and the Grabber both nod and smile at each other and although Sparrow can't hear what is being said, he knows it is happy talk.

But let us not stay on this platform too long. As Sparrow quickly lowers himself past the eighth floor, he glances through a window and sees a beautiful black-haired nurse seated at a desk and pondering something on the wall beyond Sparrow's line of vision. This is Violet White and her face bears an expression of calm expectation that makes it appear almost gentle. At least that is what Sparrow thinks and he would look at it longer if he didn't have more important business to attend to, but we have a few minutes so let us see what Violet White is doing.

Violet is staring at a bulletin board. Thumbtacked to it are the faces of twenty women. We know these faces. They have occupied our adult hankerings. We have spent much time worrying about their celluloid comings and goings. They are famous movie actresses: Joan Crawford, Ginger Rogers, Jane Russell, Kim Novak, Piper Laurie, Lauren Bacall, Marilyn Monroe, Grace Kelly, Jane Fonda. These are publicity shots and the women look vibrant and full of life. Across the face of Lauren Bacall a red X has been drawn, and Violet seems to stare at that photograph in particular.

Then she sighs, opens the drawer of her desk and takes out still another photograph in a silver frame. It is a picture of Marduk the Magnificent in a Speedo bathing suit with his arms raised triumphantly above his head. This too is a publicity shot and Marduk looks fit as a fiddle. Violet touches an index finger to the scars on Marduk's ankles. Where did they come from? If Marduk desired, those scars could be removed at El Instituto. They constitute a blemish, the evidence of a wrinkle in Marduk's past. Even that past could be removed. One of the clinic's psychiatrists could erase its memory, since it has been Dr. Florabunde's discovery that not only does one's body need to be changed, one's memory often needs to be tinkered with as well, or at least brought into line with one's new appearance.

Violet has a mental image of Michael Marmaduke and Marduk the Magnificent as Siamese twins lying on an operating table. They are naked. A doctor enters. It is she, Violet White, wearing a white dress and black shoes with four-inch stiletto heels. She strokes the cheek of the sleeping Marduk. The two men are joined at the hip. A nurse gives her a surgical machete, and with one powerful sweep of her hand, Violet separates Michael Marmaduke from Marduk the Magnificent. For Michael the result is disastrous. Like a party balloon losing its air, he deflates until he resembles nothing more than an old condom. A nurse picks it up with the tips of her fingers and drops it in the trash. But Marduk the Magnificent seems bigger and stronger, even more handsome. Suddenly he is awake. He sits up rubbing his eyes and stares around him. Roughly, he reaches out for Violet White, tearing her uniform and exposing one of her breasts. He puts his mouth to the breast as he snaps off her buttons with his thumb and index finger. They fly around the room. Then Marduk lifts her onto the operating table. Her bright red fingernails carve sensuous messages on his back.

Violet White shakes herself out of her dream and stands up. She has work to do. Looking in a mirror, she pats her black hair and adjusts her cap. Staring into her eyes, she sees they still have a yellow tint but it's fainter. Perhaps it is going away. She imagines a time when her eyes will be completely clear.

Out in the hall, Violet turns left. Here there is more bustle. Doctors, nurses, an occasional patient in a wheelchair, orderlies pushing carts. As she walks she glances into different rooms. Some patients are talking to visitors, some are reading or watching TV, some are asleep. The vast majority have their faces bandaged. At times they remind Violet of that old movie *The Invisible Man*. When the bandages were unwrapped from his face, there was nothing to be seen. But these people have the opposite of nothing; soon they will have the fulfillment of their dreams. And for a week or so, they might be happy. Maybe even longer. Others will return for more work, further modifications.

Violet White opens the door of a room and enters. There is a single bed where someone is sleeping. The shape under the blanket is small: perhaps a woman or child. The figure's face is hidden by bandages. Maybe it is Deep Rat in disguise again. But believe us when we say that it is not Deep Rat. Almost crossly, Violet White takes the person's pulse and blood pressure. Then, opening a drawer of the night table, she removes a syringe and a vial of liquid. She fills the syringe, then pushes back the person's sleeve. Certainly it is a woman, look at that white skin. When Violet inserts the needle into the patient's arm, there is no response. For a moment Violet watches the person in the bed, then she puts away the syringe and leaves the room.

She walks briskly down the hall. Several people greet her and she nods. She checks her watch. It is just ten-thirty. At the end of the hall is a closed door. Violet White unlocks it, then passes through a small anteroom into a larger room where a dozen young women are seated on couches or chairs. They look up as if they have been expecting her, which of course they have.

Violet White walks to a couch and sits down. Taking off her white nurse's cap, she pushes her hands through her black hair. She leans back and begins to tell her story.

"But the wife of Semele's lover knew that the child Bromios still lived. She could feel the child's presence each time she took a breath. As a broken rib cuts into the lung, so the knowledge of the living Bromios cut into her body. When she could stand it no longer, she went to the Titans, who were the children of Heaven and Earth, and she said, 'Kill this child and I will reward you.' And the Titans traveled to where the baby Bromios was hidden and they found him sitting on the floor playing with knucklebones and they knew him by the horns on his head and by the crown of snakes nestled in his hair. The Titans rushed at the baby Bromios and Bromios changed himself into a serpent, and still the Titans pursued him, and Bromios changed himself into a bull, and still the Titans pursued him, and Bromios changed himself into a lion and the Titans leapt upon him and tore his head from his neck, and tore his arms and legs from his body, and some of these pieces they cooked in a caldron and some they ate raw, shoving the pieces into their mouths and chewing them and swallowing them, then they belched and spat out the bones and went away. And where the blood of the baby Bromios spilled upon the ground, a pomegranate tree grew up and the wind blew through its branches and made a mournful sound. Then, when night fell, Rhea, the mother of Semele's lover, came and gathered up the bones of her grandson and she carried them home in a bag. She joined the bones together in a caldron and said words over them and added the leaves of holy plants and reaching into the caldron she withdrew the baby Bromios and he was more beautiful and stronger than before, and his father gave the baby into the safekeeping of Persephone, the queen of regeneration and the bringer of destruction, and the baby Bromios grew powerful."

Leaning back against one of the other women, Violet White thinks of how the baby Bromios was ripped apart and then rejoined to be made more beautiful and powerful. And she thinks how Michael Marmaduke is being ripped apart, how all that was weak in him is being scraped away. Violet puts her fingers to her own cheeks and lets the nails press against her flesh. And isn't she also a bringer of both destruction and regeneration?

27

No Gimmick

Even though the air conditioning is on, the hall of the Disputants must be eighty degrees. From our spot near the double doors we can see a dozen men and women fanning themselves with paper fans. In the dim light the fans resemble fluttering birds. They nibble the sweat drops as pigeons gobble kernels of corn. The semicircle of twenty-four desks is occupied and the Master of Ceremonies stands at the podium directing his hand puppets—one blue and one red—in their intricate dance, even though the screen behind him is dark. About fifty men and women sit in the theater seats at the back and another twenty stand by the wall. All listen attentively, at times leaning forward or tilting their heads to hear better. The only empty seats are on either side of Michael Marmaduke, who sits in the last row. Possibly the seats are empty out of deference to his notoriety. Possibly they are empty because he is so big that he overlaps into these other spaces, so that sitting beside him one would be squeezed. Or possibly they are empty because this last row, being the highest part of the room, is also the hottest. Beads of sweat trickle down Michael's brow and he wipes them away on his sleeve. It is Wednesday evening and he has been in the hall about ten hours.

A Manichaean is speaking. He is a balding man in a black robe. "And the Spirit said, 'I am in the midst of my enemies. They are the beasts which surround me, the powers which burn in their wrath and rise up against me.'"

The Master of Ceremonies raises the blue puppet. "We see this as a single kick of the left leg. Full extension. Agreed?"

"Agreed," come a dozen voices.

The Manichaean stands at the Epsilon desk on the left side of the semicircle. "Matter and her sons divided me among them, they burnt me in their fire. They tasted my sweetness and wanted to keep me with them. I was life to them, but they were death to me; I bore up beneath them, they wore me as a garment upon them."

The blue puppet is raised again. "One leg kick followed by a shoulder lock."

"I think he threw him," comes a voice.

"No throw," says the Master of Ceremonies.

"Was that one leg kick or two?" comes another voice.

The Master of Ceremonies seems annoyed. "One kick of the left leg, followed by a shoulder lock on the right shoulder."

Another man gets to his feet. He is in his sixties, is bigger than the others and has a shaggy beard. It is Augustine, the Predestinationist, but to Michael he looks like an ex-wrestler. Augustine wears a gray robe and stands at the Sigma desk. "It is the mark of a weak mind to be displeased with any single thing in God's creation. There may be things which are thought evil because they do not harmonize with all elements; yet with further elements they are able to harmonize and so they are good. And these things which cannot fit with each other are still able to fit with that lower part of creation we call the earth and which has its own cloudy and windy sky which again is fitting to it."

The red-colored puppet grapples with the blue one. "I see that as a shoulder lock reversal and a throw," says the Master of Ceremonies. "Agreed?"

"Agreed," come a number of voices.

Fanning himself with a paper fan, the Manichaean gets to his feet. "Jesus came into the Garden in the guise of a serpent. He showed Adam how the Father on high and his own Nature had been cast into all things, into the teeth of panthers and elephants, devoured by them that devour, consumed by them that consume, eaten by dogs, mingled and bound in all that exists, imprisoned in the stench of darkness."

The blue puppet is raised. "One body block off the ropes."

"Agreed."

The Manichaean continues. "Jesus raised Adam up and made him eat of the Tree of Life. Then Adam cried out: terribly he raised his voice like a roaring lion, tore his clothes, smote his breast, and spoke, 'Woe, unto the shaper of my body, unto those who fettered my soul, and unto the rebels who enslaved me!' "

"Second full body block and a fall." The red puppet collapses. "Agreed!"

Augustine mops his brow with a handkerchief. "What the serpent signifies is the poison of the heretics, and especially of the Manichaeans. For no one more brazenly promises the knowledge of good and evil. Take even those words 'Ye shall be as gods.' Isn't this the claim of the heretics, when through their proud vanity they try to persuade others to the same pride and affirm that the soul can be that which only God is?"

"Double foot lift. Blue on top. Do I see a fall?"

"No fall," comes the reply.

"Foot lift and a full body suspension. Do I see a twirl?"

There is disagreement as to the twirl. The red puppet is on its back with its legs in the air suspending the blue puppet.

"Incipient twirl," says the Master of Ceremonies.

Throughout Wednesday Michael's thinking about the Disputants has increased to the point of bewilderment. Certainly before each match, he received directions which he could memorize within ten minutes, although earlier in his career it had taken longer. Sometimes the directions were more complicated and required practice matches with his adversary. He rarely thought about this process. He understood that what he did was closer to theater than sport, and he understood that heroes were more popular than villains. He knew that Muldoon received these directions from another source and this often irritated the wrestling manager. But as long as Michael got paid and did his job in a way that gave him satisfaction, he never bothered about the rest. He saw himself as working for Primus Muldoon, although he knew that wasn't really accurate. And even though he had ambivalent feelings, he took pleasure from raising his hands above his head and hearing everybody cheer.

But to understand the nature of the Disputants was to have certain definitions overthrown, like seeing rocks rise against the force of gravity, and Wednesday morning Michael returned to the Aerie to see more. He went without his false beard and mustache and when people pointed at him on the street and nudged each other, he tried to not let it bother him.

Michael sat in the last row of the theater seats, although most of the seats were empty and he could have sat anywhere. He told himself that the view was better from the top, but perhaps he also didn't want to completely commit himself. Way at the top of the room he was almost outside of the room.

The first dispute took place between Valentinians and Barbelo-Gnostics: a battle between Jave the Bear-Faced and his brother Eloim the Cat-Faced. Eloim was also called the Just and he ruled the upper elements of Fire and Wind. Jave the Bear-Faced was the Unjust and ruled the nether elements of Water and Earth. Together Jave and Eloim ruled over the Tomb: their name for the human body. Jave and Eloim were the two sons that Ialdabaoth begat upon the Virgin Eve. In their battle, Jave the Bear-Faced slaughtered his brother.

As the two sides conducted their dispute, the Master of Ceremonies manipulated his hand puppets so that physical movements corresponded to narrative or intellectual movements. Sometimes the movements of the hand puppets were translated to actual movements of wrestlers upon the screen.

"The puppets are called the Combatants," said Morgan the Pelagian, who kept checking on Michael throughout the day, "in order to differentiate their rhetoric from the Disputants. The wrestlers of course are just wrestlers, but the Combatants are the means by which the dispute is translated to the wrestlers."

The second match was between two Sumerian sister goddesses, Inanna, goddess of light, and Ereshkigal, goddess of darkness. Together they represented two aspects of a single goddess, and at the conclusion of their match one goddess devoured the other. In the next match, according to Morgan, the one who had been last devoured would be the devourer, and so they would alternate between devourer and devouree.

"The dispute concerns the assimilation of opposites," said Morgan, "the devouring of one's own unsuspected self. To keep from being devoured one must put aside pride, vanity, virtue, anger, even life itself, and submit to what is most intolerable. Once the side of light has submitted to the intolerable, it discovers that it is no different from its opposite and that the two are of the same flesh."

The two hand puppets rocked back and forth in an embrace while on the screen two women wrestlers were equally caught up and neither seemed capable of victory.

Afterward came a battle between the Egyptian god Osiris and Typhon, the child of Mother Earth and Tartarus. In place of hands Typhon had the heads of hundreds of snakes. His arms reached six hundred miles and coiled snakes formed his legs. His head was like the head of a donkey and bumped against the stars.

The Disputant spoke in the voice of Plutarch. "Even though Osiris is stronger yet it is impossible for the evil of Typhon to be destroyed, since it is innate and exists in both the body and soul of the universe. So in the soul, Intelligence and Reason, the Ruler of all that is good, is Osiris, but Typhon is that part of the soul which is impressionable, impulsive and irrational, and that part of the body which is destructive, diseased and disorderly. Consequently there is no end to their combat and the two are locked as if one."

And again the hand puppets pushed back and forth in an embrace, while on the screen two male wrestlers appeared to hug each other and neither seemed capable of decisive victory.

For most of the day Michael watched from the last row. And whenever Morgan the Pelagian joined him, Michael had questions.

"There are several kinds of matches," explained Morgan. "The most common are between two dualist characters within the same religion. For instance, David and Goliath, Cain and Abel, Jesus and Judas, although we've also matches where the villain becomes the true hero. Then we have battles between concepts of good and evil. Tomorrow night we'll have a totally new match between Santa Claus and Satan. We have great expectations from that one. Then there are matches between different sects or religions, such as between Prometheans and Bogamils or between Licentious Gnostics and Non-Licentious Gnostics. The best are between the Manichaeans and the Predestinationists directed by Augustine. We'll have one of those this evening."

Let us return to the conclusion of the dispute between Augustine and the Manichaean. Augustine is speaking: "But envy follows pride, it does not precede it: for envy is not the cause of pride, but pride is the cause of envy. The exact time when pride threw Satan down scripture does not say. But it's obvious it must have happened before man's fall, and it was because of pride that Satan envied man. The first sin therefore is pride."

The Master of Ceremonies raises the red puppet and brings it down upon the blue one. "We see this as a tackle and a fall. The red Combatant presses blue to the canvas."

"Agreed," answer the Disputants.

"Yet," continues Augustine, "we should not vainly imagine that Satan fell from the very beginning of time through pride, nor was there any previous time in which he lived with the holy angels peaceful and blessed. Rather, from the very beginning of *his existence* he turned away from his creator."

"The blue Combatant's shoulders are pressed to the mat. The referee begins his count."

"Agreed."

The Manichaean gets to his feet. "Since the ruin of Matter is decreed by God, one should abstain from all ensouled things and eat only vegetables and whatever else is nonsentient, and abstain from marriage, the delights of love and the begetting of children, so that the divine Power may not through the succession of generations remain longer in Matter."

The hand puppets separate. "Blue executes elbow strike to the ribs and crawls to the ropes. He is weakened and in pain."

"Agreed."

The Manichaean is not happy with this call. "The liberation of the parts of Light is helped by the pure word and pious works. Thereby the parts of Light which are the souls of the dead mount up by the pillar of dawn to the sphere of the moon, and the moon receives them from the first to the middle of the month, so that it waxes and gets full, and then it guides them to the sun until the end of the month, and thus effects its waning so that it is lightened of its burden. And in this manner the ferry is loaded and unloaded, and the sun transmits the Light to the Light above it and does not cease its labor until no part of Light is left in this world."

The two hand puppets grapple. "Blue Combatant leaps on the back of the red and attempts a neck choke. Are we convinced?"

There are yeas and nays, but the nays are louder.

"We feel the blue Combatant is no longer in his first strength and weakens quickly," says the Master of Ceremonies.

Augustine stands up and lifts his voice. "Let them perish as empty talkers and seducers of the soul, who, having observed there are two wills in the act of deliberating, conclude from this that we have within us two minds of two different natures, one good and one evil."

"Red Combatant flings blue over his shoulder onto the mat!"

"Agreed."

"They themselves are evil when they hold these opinions," continues Augustine, "but they are just as capable of becoming good if they will realize the truth, so that the Apostle may say to them, 'Ye were sometime darkness, but now light in the Lord.' "

"Red Combatant falls onto blue with a full body press."

"Agreed."

"But these people," concludes Augustine, "by imagining the nature of the soul is the same as the nature of God, want to be light, not light in the Lord, but in themselves, and the result is that they have reached an even deeper darkness, since in their shocking arrogance they have forsaken the truth!"

The Master of Ceremonies raises the hand puppets with red on top. "Blue is unable to throw off red. Referee slaps the mat three times. Red Combatant is the winner!"

People call out "Agreed!" and "Winner, winner!" There is applause from the Disputants as Augustine goes over to shake the Manichaean's hand.

"Actually," says Morgan, who has joined Michael again, "the difference between their systems is about one millisecond. Mani believes the creation of the world and the creation of evil are simultaneous events. Augustine believes that the creation itself was good but soon corrupted. How soon, is what I'd like to know."

"And now a match will be made from that dispute?"

"That's right. I don't know who will be assigned. Perhaps you'll get it, who knows? But come meet Augustine. He irritates me at times, but he's one of the founders of the Disputants. His ideas (the original Augustine of course) in *De Doctrina Christiana* were what first led us into the wrestling business."

"It was Origen," Augustine is saying an hour later, "who first used the word 'Fall' to describe what happened to Adam and Eve. Even in its Christian cloak, his thinking is Gnostic." Augustine sips a glass of ice water. He and Michael and Morgan the Pelagian as well as the Master of Ceremonies sit in a small library off the Hall of the Disputants. "He uses the word *descensus,* saying that the material world came into being from a *descensus* of spirit into matter, a 'Fall' from essence to existence. Later Origen's heresy became obvious and he was condemned. One wonders if he was yanked out of Heaven three hundred years after his death. But surely he should be praised as one of the first to argue that man fell—experienced a *descensus*—not by his nature but by his will. So perhaps he too is a soldier in the final battle."

Michael's brain feels like a beehive knocked on its side. "And you believe in that battle?"

"Some of us do," say Augustine. "Personally, I've never been convinced by the validity of the Book of Revelation. It's convenient because it rounds out the story—it points the finger of blame at the Serpent—but even that, to my mind, makes it suspect. But those who believe in the final battle also believe that through the Wrestling Association, we can effect its course. This is the passion that motivates some of our best Disputants."

"And what is yours?" asks Michael.

"I believe that by debating the nature of our lives, we can influence the times in which we live. This means exercising our will and gaining insight into the nature of pride. One cannot eradicate evil until one eradicates sin; one cannot eradicate sin until one eradicates pride, not that it can ever be erased completely. Through the Disputants we create combats that articulate the struggle of human beings for their own souls, their struggles against pride. To my mind pride becomes the villain, whether he be called Rahab or Cain."

"But why wrestling?" asks Michael. He thinks of the various kicks and blocks and throws he has accomplished in the ring and tries to imagine them as points of logic within an argument.

"Because physical reenactments of verbal disputes are the best way of communicating certain truths. In *De Doctrina Christiana* the original Augustine set down his ideas on a language of signs which he saw as coming into being after the Fall. Before the Fall, Adam and Eve were united with themselves and with each other. They had no need for language. They had no self-consciousness. They were one with God and with themselves.

"But afterward how did God know they had eaten the fruit? He saw them trying to cover themselves. They were aware of their nakedness in a way that would have been impossible earlier. They had lost this sense of oneness. What Adam and Eve experienced was a dislocation of consciousness, and as the word 'apple' is separated from the true Apple, so were Adam and Eve separated from the mind of God. How did language come into being? It was invented by Adam and Eve desperately striving to reattain this unity with God, to repair this dislocation of consciousness. Language was the attempt to recreate oneness. Before the Fall, they could see into each other's mind and the wish of one was immediately known to the other. After the Fall, there was only barking and gesticulation.

"The Word of God became veiled for them and so they created their own words, which in their clumsiness were also part of the veil but which were the only possible way of reaching God once again. But don't you see, they bargained without Satan, who is the Prince of Confusion. Language is inexact. It aims, it never achieves. And what stands between the word 'apple' and the true Apple? That's where Satan lives, where he weaves his confusion.

With the Wrestling Association the Disputants bypass language. Through their disputes they create an argument which is then translated into a nonverbal form that communicates the relationship between evil and good. At worst the wrestling is metaphor; at best it is a new language. And what we do with a proscribed series of Gimmicks and scenarios is establish a canon, which is the attempt to create a perfect teaching, that will recreate the 'oneness' experienced by Adam and Eve in the Garden. The Bible itself attempts to be such a canon."

"But doesn't the Bible contain contradictory stories?" asks Michael. "For instance, how will it help me find Rose White to accept the God in the Book of Job?"

The Master of Ceremonies taps the floor with his cane. "Heraclitus said, 'To God all things are fair and good and right, but men hold some things wrong and some right.' To accept this means to question your ideas of wrong and right. Perhaps your fiancée was not kidnapped out of evil. That is what you need to learn. But you wouldn't need to do this alone. We'd help you."

"How?" asks Michael.

"We want you to join the Disputants," says Morgan.

It is difficult to give a sense of Michael's surprise. It wasn't like being hit with anything. It was more like driving along on a clear afternoon and suddenly entering thick fog.

"But I don't know anything," says Michael. "I mean, I'm not even a Christian or believe in God or anything."

"That's not important," says Augustine. "What we desire is a wrestling manager who is also a Disputant. So far we have only used managers who know nothing about us. That has made problems. Some managers wish to pursue their own scenarios, and this defeats our purpose. But if you joined us, you would see why certain combats must be performed in a certain way. Our communication to the ring would become more exact."

"But why me?" asks Michael.

"Because you are the best wrestler within the Association," says Morgan the Pelagian.

"Because you are young and can be taught," says Augustine.

"Because you are gentle," says the Master of Ceremonies. "Working with the Disputants and the Wrestling Association, you will confront hundreds of contradictory opinions and ideas. Only through gentleness and endurance can you find a path among them."

"But what if I think I can find Rose White without you?"

"That's up to you," says the Master of Ceremonies, "but we feel we can help you see through the illusions which surround you, thus enabling you to understand what has happened to Rose White. We can help you to think."

"What would I have to do?" asks Michael. And he wonders: What sort of illusions surround me, and can't I think already?

"To become a Disputant," says the Master of Ceremonies, "you'd have to give up your Gimmick. You'd have to discover who you really are. It would also mean you could no longer wrestle. You could no longer be the partisan of Marduk, you'd have to become the partisan of all, of the Association itself."

28

Pre-Weenie

Not many flowers are left in Gramercy Park in late October—marigolds mostly—and at midnight not many of these can be seen, just a few drowsy orange blooms bordering the orderly paths. Wednesday is over, Thursday has just begun. Streetlights create a ghostly glow within the park, and between the marigolds poke the delicate snouts of several rats, because rats dearly love the shelter of foliage and how the twigs scratch their long spines. Not many questions in a rat's life, not much philosophy. For a rat, either you do it or you don't. And if you do it and don't succeed, then you don't complain. You eat that morsel of bad cheese and end up puking your guts out, well, that's the breaks. This philosophy explains why we have so many rats. They do what they must do and don't fuss. We should be glad that humans are more finicky, because if humans were tough as rats are tough we'd be up to our necks in humans. And of course rats look out for each other, take care of their young, lead upstanding lives. Philosophically, one could do worse than to study the rat.

See how these rats with their inquisitive snouts don't even duck when the slap slap of human feet come running along the sidewalk on the other side of the fence. The rats realize there is no danger.

It's only Michael Marmaduke getting his exercise, doing laps around the park before he retires for the night. He's had a busy day and his mind is in a whirl. No, the creature who makes the rats uneasy is that dark figure under the awning of the National Arts Club: black suit, black fedora hat, narrow face, delicate little hands. Being nonverbal (could rats be preverbal?) they are unable to articulate just what about this fellow makes them unhappy. But this of course is Deep Rat and what makes the rats uncomfortable about Deep Rat is just what bothered Neanderthal man about the Cro-Magnon. They see in him their evolutionary replacement. And the rats sniff the air once or twice, then return to the safety of their sewers.

As for Deep Rat, he is waiting for the right moment to make himself known. Personally he sees no point in exercise: all his actions are purely product-oriented. Exercise seems decorative, and he has no use for decoration. But he also knows that Michael Marmaduke is running to relax himself, to soften his brain for sleep. And Deep Rat wants Michael's brain as soft as possible before he interrupts him. As he waits, he hopes that Michael might fall and scrape a knee or twist an ankle—something to bring a little additional tribulation into Michael's life—but Deep Rat knows he will most likely be disappointed in this.

As for Michael, his brain is like a bag of question marks: What?, Why?, When?, Where?, Who? and How?—just like a high school journalism class. He is thinking what it would entail to give up his Gimmick, to become Idea, to be a conduit between the discussions of the Disputants and the battles within the ring, to stop being Marduk the Magnificent. Transcending his Gimmick would mean moving to a higher plane, saying goodbye to the ego, embracing the totality of the group; it would mean becoming stronger, worthier, more noble etc. But to give up being Marduk would result in losing a big chunk of himself, and although Michael would gladly do this if it meant finding Rose White, he is not one hundred percent positive it is necessary. And if Deep Rat had the gift of telepathy (as perhaps Adam and Eve did before the Fall) he would rub his paws together, for he would understand that Michael's brain is ripe for picking.

Michael likes running at night. It means fewer distractions, greater privacy. But each time he rounds the west side of the park he hears shouting from the windows of one of the houses. It sounds like a woman's voice, but in its anger and indignation it is almost sexless. "You little shrimp . . ." he hears. And next time he comes around, "If you don't get your ass back there . . ." And again, "You tell that sleazeball . . ." And once more, "Of course you're sleeping on the floor!"

This is Wally Wallski being addressed by his beloved, and we mention it because it comes at a time when Michael should be thinking as clearly as possible, and the anger in Claudine's voice creates an unpleasant buzz in Michael's brain, leading him into the embrace of non sequiturs and confusion. You know how when you are trying to count and someone else shouts numbers at you and so you lose count? It is like that. And through his faulty cogitation—made faultier by Claudine's foul temper—Michael thinks: But if I become a hero, then I can find Rose White all by myself and still be Marduk the Magnificent.

And this is the point when Deep Rat steps from the shadows and calls, "My friend, is that you?"

"Who's there?" calls Michael, startled.

"It is Deep Rat and I am here to serve you."

But now let us move forward two hours to another fast-moving vehicle: a black Porsche 941 driven by Michael's fellow wrestler Cashback, who wrestles under the name Hephaestus the Hunchback, Vulcan the Vicious, or Mulciber the Maniac. Mostly he engages in comedy matches because of his physical peculiarities. Cashback has a single black eyebrow like a bar code across his forehead and each of his big red ears resembles half of a broken heart. His legs are short and his hands hang to his knees. He wrestles as the powerful smith of mythology who can make the gods laugh and he is built like an anvil. Cashback also has a passion for small fast cars and small fast women. But there are no women with him tonight, only Michael and Deep Rat. Michael sits in front and Deep Rat sits in back. It is something to be said for Deep Rat that he can be comfortable in the back of a Porsche.

Deep Rat has come forward with new information. It seems that the railway track to which Rose White was tied in the video found at the taurabolium has been recognized. Ticket stubs were lying in the gravel around Rose White's feet, shadows of girders, architectural idiosyncrasies, and just how many railway tracks are indoors anyway? Deep Rat has been talking to people. When something odd happens, it is hard for anyone to stay quiet for long. The video was taken within Grand Central Station. At night the place is full of bums and they can't keep their mouths shut. They heard a woman screaming, was it just last week? Great Father Snake knew something about it. He's crazy about amateur videos and sometimes he shows them to his pals.

"Great Father Snake," Michael said. "Didn't he wrestle?"

"Once upon a time," said Deep Rat.

"I think Cashback wrestled him. Then he quit or retired. Something like that."

This is when we should bring in Primus Muldoon for a brief speaking engagement, just like those times when the President is pounding the bejesus out of Baghdad, and TV stations get some bearded fellow who has been to Baghdad and they say, "Tell me, what do you think those people in Baghdad are doing right now?" What we need to ask Primus Muldoon concerns the danger a wrestler faces in being consumed by his Gimmick. Let's say you put on a mask: does an uncrossable millimeter of space remain between your face and the mask, or do the two start nibbling at each other? Just how stable is the human personality, anyway? For how many years can we take our Gimmicks off each night before we reach a point when we forget or it gets stuck or we just don't care anymore? I've been a tough guy all my life, says the shrimp. I've stuck more chicks than a shishkabob stick has stuck tomatoes, says the shyest guy on the West Side. When we look in a mirror, do we see ourselves or a committee? All this talk about poor clunks with multiple personalities and how they need shrinks to have their personalities fused because they get up in the morning as cheerleaders and go to bed at night as organic chemists—give me a break! A multiple is a someone who drags around a bag full of Gimmicks at the same time, while we healthy people move more slowly between one Gimmick and the next.

And now we have Great Father Snake. Sure he used to wrestle, and he was pretty hot. Like others we know he had some uglifying done at El Instituto Estético and he looked the part. But one day he was staring into his dressing-room mirror after a match and just as he was about to splop a great blob of cold cream on his puss, he asked himself, "Why bother?"

And isn't that the big question? Why shouldn't I become my Gimmick? Who's going to care? Maybe it'll change my life. Maybe I'll have more friends. Girls and money and fast cars, maybe I'll have more respect. I'll quit smoking. I'll start smoking. I'll lose weight. Gain weight. I'll buy a flashy tie. I'm sick of being a chump. From now on, it's all Fast Lane.

So Great Father Snake walked out of Madison Square Garden and some fans ran up to him and said, "Aren't you Great Father Snake?" and Great Father Snake, who used to be called Benny McGuire in what the Premodernists referred to as Real Life (you remember back when we had Real Life and how comforting it was?), Great Father Snake said, "Fuckin A!"

Now days when we hear the question "Why bother?" we pay little attention. I want to be a snake, why not be a snake? It used to be the church would say, you'd better not. You'll jeopardize your soul. But who goes to church these days? Kooks and old people. It used to be we could say, it's against the spirit of this country and the ideals expressed in the Bill of Rights. You'll jeopardize your position as a citizen. But here's the President pounding the bejesus out of Baghdad to show the world he's got a big weenie. Hey, if he can do it, I can do it! Then it used to be the question of Why bother was affected by cultural considerations, history of ideas, great books, extension of moral experience through art. You'll jeopardize your intellectual standing. But you remember our pals DeMaus, Vogel and Sosage? You know the expression "to throw a moon"? They're all dropping their drawers and throwing a moon at that one. You're valorizing and privileging and claiming that apples are better than dog poop. How crude of you, how old-fashioned! It used to be that if your Gimmick got too flashy, too socially aggressive, you'd get bounced from your job. But now the Gimmick itself is a full-time occupation. If you get fired, there's always another job. Anyway, if you paint your nose red and the telephone company tries to fire you, then you can haul them into court. "Why bother?" That's the big question. You want to have yourself turned into a cocker spaniel? Who's going to stop you?

Now days Great Father Snake has got himself a job at Grand Central Station between one A.M. and five A.M. That's when the homeless, the half-mad, the unemployed, drunks, weirdos, creeps, crooks and old-fashioned bums all want some shut-eye and there needs to be a bruiser in charge to make sure no one tries to snitch their plastic bags or swipe their shopping carts. The cops don't care; they just stay out of it. The train people don't care; they're home in bed. So all these disenfranchised pool a few returnable bottles and they hire a guy. He's like a bouncer and he likes his work. Short hours, adequate pay and nobody minds his kinky habits. This is Great Father Snake. One day he looked in his mirror and said, "Why bother?" And now he's going to be Great Father Snake forever.

"When I used to wrassle him," says Cashback, "he was a shy kinda guy. Sad eyes, I remember he had the saddest eyes."

"And you used to lift him over your head?" asks Michael.

"Sure, that was the big joke. We'd do a Heracles and Antaeus number. I'm five foot two and he's six-eight. I'd pick him up and twirl him around and everybody'd laugh. The longer he was up in the air, the weaker he'd get. Then he had some body work done and gave up the Antaeus bit. He wanted to be a snake."

It was this memory of a link between Cashback and Great Father Snake that led Michael to telephone his friend around one A.M. and to ask for his help. Cashback has already talked to Liquidity and the Prime brothers about their nocturnal travels with Michael Marmaduke and was not eager. Still, Michael is his pal and if he can do anything to find Rose White, then he wants to be counted in, even if it means a few bruises. Now they are on their way up Park Avenue to Grand Central Station and Cashback tells himself he feels perfectly relaxed, except that his hands are sweating and his pulse rate is up.

As for Michael, he is thinking it is six days since Rose White disappeared and seven since he saw her last. He finds he can no longer remember her face with any exactness, meaning he has to take her picture out of his wallet to refresh his memory. He tries to think of her voice, her smell, the touch of her skin. He saw her just a week ago and now she is moving into what the world calls history. These thoughts lead Michael's eyes to mist over, although whether he is more upset at Rose White's absence or the nature of the world it is hard to say. A lesser person would complain that it's not fair, whatever fairness is, but Michael won't do that. He just doesn't like the whole setup: life changing and things being forgotten. Maybe he should stick with the Disputants after all. At least they have a positive attitude. And he wonders how the Disputants worked out those matches between Heracles and Antaeus, and how Great Father Snake had fit into their schemes.

As for Deep Rat, as the Porsche speeds north, he thinks how he hates having his hatreds inhibited. He thinks how handsome Michael is and how pure his feelings seem to be. Will he ever have the chance to smack Michael with a brick? To scar him just a little? Then he thinks of Nurse White and he folds his little paws together. Even to recall her is to have his fingers ache.

Cashback parks his Porsche in a garage on East 41st Street, then they walk back a couple of blocks to Grand Central. It is breezy and cool and they pull up their collars. Cashback is even shorter than Deep Rat but three times as wide. It is amazing what stubbornness can do in the field of body sculpting. Cashback spends five hours a day in the gym and even though he looks like a little guy, he's basically a monster, if that word can be used nonpejoratively. Right now Cashback wonders if he could still throw Great Father Snake, but he doubts it. In the ring the big guys let you throw them. In real life they don't.

They pass through a side door to Grand Central Station. The Oyster Bar is closed, everything is closed, and the lights have been turned down low. It's three a.m. and very quiet. This is why Michael walks on tiptoe. It seems important to be quiet. Cashback and Deep Rat also tread softly. Cashback casts his mind back to his private money matters to make sure that his health insurance is paid up and his Keogh account is looking good. They descend the stairs to the waiting room, where four football fields could fit easily. It resembles one of those scenes after a Civil War battle: lots of chewed-up men looking as if they are sleeping but we know they are dead. Here lots of chewed-up men look dead but we know they are sleeping. Bundles of people line the walls. Snores can be heard, moans, nocturnal noises, the smells of several hundred people who haven't brushed their teeth.

"I hope we can surprise him," says Cashback.

"I just want to ask a couple of questions," says Michael.

Deep Rat sucks his teeth. He doesn't believe in talk. "Bop 'til you drop" is his motto, and when he bops, he uses a baseball bat.

"This shouldn't take long," says Michael, glancing over the sleeping bodies. "It looks like a pretty relaxed place."

At this moment we hear a loud electrical click like a public address system being flicked on. This is followed by a burst of feedback which plays havoc with Cashback's adrenaline. Some of the reclining figures stir in their sleep. Some sit up and rub their eyes.

"Maybe a train's coming," says Cashback, although he knows no train is coming.

Then a voice booms over the public address system. There is something so unpleasant about this voice that Cashback wants to vanish. If a snake could talk, this is the sort of voice it would use: lots of S's and breathy noises.

And what does the voice say?

"The Great Father Snake smells your foreskin; he is calling for it!"

Even Michael hopes the voice is talking to somebody else, that it isn't a response to his presence.

Although nobody has moved, the hundreds of reclining forms seem very alert. Michael is poised on the steps with his left foot in midair. He feels ambivalent about moving forward. Somehow it wouldn't be so bad to be threatened with death, but having already been circumcised he doesn't have much foreskin left and what remains he'd like to keep.

"Go on," says Deep Rat, nudging him. "It's only a snake."

Michael takes another step, then another. There is a sudden movement on the other side of the waiting room. Again his foot is poised in midair. Michael sees Great Father Snake slithering toward him across the marble floor, making a noise like sandpaper blocks rubbing together.

"It is more than just a snake," says Cashback in a high voice.

Let's take a moment to see what Great Father Snake looks like. First of all, he is long. It seems that Benny McGuire, as he was called, has had his legs lengthened and fused together. The feet are gone entirely. Then his shoulders and hips have been narrowed. Is he wearing any clothes? Maybe a loincloth. It's hard to tell. Are those greenish scales natural? But it is the head that bothers Cashback the most. No hair, no ears, no nose, no chin, oddly shaped hypnotic eyes, and all of it green. Those doctors at El Instituto must have gotten lots of pats on the back for Great Father Snake. They must have won a prize.

Cashback tries to imagine the mental process that would lead a person to believe that such radical changes might make him look nice. Not many girls in Benny McGuire's life these days, thinks Cashback. And does he ever go home to see the old folks? But maybe he's wrong. Maybe old Benny's got girls up the wazoo. Maybe his dad is proud that Benny has broken free from the herd.

Michael continues down the steps, but his pace has slowed. He thinks Great Father Snake moves pretty fast, considering he has no legs. The snake is about fifteen feet long. The word "slither" takes on vigorous proportions in Michael's brain.

"Excuse me," says Michael to the snake. "I wonder if I could have a word with you about a private matter."

The former Benny McGuire raises a cordless microphone to the place where his lips used to be. "The Great Father Snake smells your foreskin; he is calling for it!"

As a child Michael collected stamps in bound books with thousands of stamps held in place with little paper hinges. He imagines such books full of foreskins. Then he takes hold of himself. This is not how heroes behave. Being brave means never worrying about the consequences.

"I need to talk to you about a videotape showing a young woman tied to the railway tracks. That woman is my fiancée and I believe you know something about it."

Great Father Snake is coiled up about ten feet away. His head weaves back and forth and he hisses. A forked tongue pokes from his mouth. The loincloth around his middle (one can't call it a waist) appears to have pockets.

"Well," says Michael, stepping forward, "I want an answer."

Great Father Snake rushes forward and a period of violence ensues, during which Michael learns that the snake feels slick and unpleasant to the touch. We must imagine a cartoon circle of activity: a pink-and-green ball with hands and feet protruding. Very soon Michael finds himself lying on his back with the wind knocked out of him. He jumps to his feet to see Great Father Snake swing Cashback over his head and bowl him across the floor. A dozen homeless people stand together watching the action. The marble floor is slippery and Cashback tucks his head and rolls. He hits the homeless people dead center and they scatter.

Michael wonders what the snake has in the pockets of his loin-cloth. Trying to rid his mind of ugly consequences, he rushes at Great Father Snake and we have another period of violence: a circle of activity like a Ferris wheel gone amok, which ends with the snake lifting Michael off the floor in a tight embrace. "Fore-skin!" whispers the snake. He opens his jaws to bite Michael, then he is hit from the side by Cashback. Great Father Snake drops Michael, grabs Cashback and once more bowls him into a group of homeless people.

Slowly Michael gets to his feet and runs at the snake for a third encounter, in which he tries to keep his mind totally blank: no fear, no scruples, no doubt. Michael attempts a flying kick, but Great Father Snake bats him away with his tail and Michael goes sliding across the floor on his stomach. He realizes he is getting bruises on top of the bruises he got from Taurus, which were already on top of the bruises he got from Troll. Michael comes to a stop by a bench where a homeless fellow is sitting.

"Ain't you Marduk the Magnificent?" the man asks.

Michael feels it would be pointless to deny it under these circumstances. He nods.

"Try singing," says the homeless fellow. "Great Father Snake loves music. You know, it was great what you did to Rehab last week. He really had it coming."

"Thanks," says Michael, getting to his feet. "What's that snake got in his pockets?"

"That's where he keeps his movies," says the homeless fellow. "Great Father Snake's crazy about the tube."

Two thoughts occur to Michael. First, he doesn't see how his present activity requires anything but brute force, meaning that the Master of Ceremonies would seem wrong about the need for Brain. Second, he is fighting far more easily—meaning he is being more heroic—than he had fought with Troll, even though he is still being beaten. Both of these thoughts please him. In fact, they strike Michael as examples of how well he can think.

Great Father Snake has curled himself up and his head is weaving back and forth about six feet off the floor. He wears a complacent, smug expression.

Michael thinks of the songs he knows. To tell the truth, he's never cared for modern music and little comes to mind. He thinks back to high school chorus. Great Father Snake raises himself up for a strike.

"Beautiful dreamer," sings Michael, "awake unto me." He forgets the next line. "Open your eyes and see what you'll see."

A sleepy expression suffuses Great Father Snake's features. He sways back and forth to the music.

"Beautiful dreamer," sings Michael, "I like you a lot. My heart's beating quickly and my blood's getting hot."

Great Father Snake's eyes drift shut. Immediately, Deep Rat appears at Michael's side. He holds a baseball bat. "Hit him with this," he says.

Michael pushes him away. "That wouldn't be fair." He approaches the snake. "Beautiful dreamer, you're okay in my book. So what does it matter if you cannot cook?"

Michael leaps forward to snatch the loincloth. Unluckily, Great Father Snake is not quite comatose. Another period of violence ensues, which ends with Michael being lifted over the snake's head and bowled across the floor. Michael slides about thirty feet and smacks against a bench. A homeless person is sitting on the bench. We know this person. It is Beetle.

"You want to hear a sad story?" asks Beetle.

It occurs to Michael that he himself is a sad story but he doesn't want to complain. "I'm busy right now," says Michael.

"I found a baby in a trash can. A living baby."

"Maybe later," says Michael and he limps back toward Great Father Snake.

In the meantime, Cashback is trying to lift the snake above his head. He used to lift Benny McGuire with no trouble but now he's heavier. "Benny!" says Cashback. "It's me, Cashback."

Effortlessly, Great Father Snake wraps his tail around Cashback and sends him skimming across the floor into another group of homeless people.

Michael approaches again. "I dream of Jeannie with the light brown hair," he sings. Again he forgets the next line. "Her cheeks were chubby and her skin was fair."

Great Father Snake appears to be getting drowsy again.

"I dream of Jeannie with the light brown hair. For a great big girl, she seemed lighter than air."

The snake closes his eyes.

Again Deep Rat appears at Michael's side with the baseball bat. "Hit him with this! Don't be stupid."

Great Father Snake seems asleep. Michael approaches him, intent on grabbing the loincloth. The bulky shapes in his pockets are just the size of video tapes.

"Way down upon the Swannee River, far, far away . . ."

Michael leaps forward, snatches the loincloth and yanks. The belt comes free in his hands. Unfortunately, Great Father Snake opens his eyes and grabs him. Worse, he opens his mouth, exposing big teeth. Michael tries to twist away but can't get free. The fangs approach his throat. Suddenly there is a loud crack and the snake goes limp. Michael slides to the floor.

Cashback stands on one side of the comatose snake with the baseball bat, while Michael and Deep Rat stand on the other. Further away is a ring of homeless people. "If you can't do it," says Cashback, "then I can. I'm sick of bowling strikes. Let's get outta here."

Now it's time to introduce a new character. His name is Smitty. Let's first look at his face. Pink, right? This young man appears eighteen but he's actually twenty-four. Blond hair, blue eyes, ruddy cheeks, glasses in flesh-colored frames. He's trying to grow a mustache to make himself look older, but it's just fuzz. His whole round face is fuzzy and undeveloped. But look at his eyes.

See how they express shock and dismay? Let's pull back to see what he is staring at.

He's sitting at a desk piled high with papers. More papers are piled on the floor around him. And don't we recognize this crowded office with awful green walls? This is where Brodsky and Gapski used to work, but at five o'clock yesterday afternoon they went on indefinite medical leave. This pink-faced young man is their replacement. It is four in the morning and he is trying to catch up. Isn't it touching that he thinks he can succeed? He's got fat files marked Rose White, fat files marked Troll and fat files marked Taurus. Last week he was a traffic cop, and since he was a good traffic cop he was promoted up into this bureaucratic hell: like winning in a quiz show and for a prize they shoot you. Before the budget cuts, five people used to do this much work. Now there's only one. Hey, not only should every high school get one of the President's F-16s, some other places need them too.

Smitty is trying not to be depressed. His father was a cop. His grandfather and great-grandfather were cops. Smitty always wanted to be a cop as well. Now he thinks he could do better as a dogcatcher. For the past ten hours he has been reading as fast as he can, but it's like trying to climb out of quicksand by swallowing the muck. He's going under. Still, he feels he has a tiny chance of success, just as long as nothing new happens.

Unhappily, at this moment Michael Marmaduke enters the office carrying a videotape. He has already seen it at Cashback's apartment and he is deeply upset. He hopes Brodsky and Gapski will help him. He knows nothing about Smitty, and when Smitty bursts into sobs right in front of him in a few minutes' time, Michael will want to join him.

And what does the videotape show?

It begins with Rose White lying in what appears to be a glass coffin. She wears a white nightgown. Her hands are folded across her breast. Suddenly she begins hammering at the glass lid. We hear a slight thumping noise. Then, as if from very far away, we hear, "Michael! Michael! you must help me, I'm . . . !"

Smitty is going to see this video in Sapperstein's office with its plastic-wrapped Yasir Arafat dartboard and green venetian blinds.

He is going to hear about Great Father Snake and all the rest. Right now Smitty feels so awful that he can't imagine feeling worse. Soon he will feel worse.

And Brodsky and Gapski? Where are they?

At the moment Brodsky is in a hospital room studying his face in a mirror. In a few hours he will go under the knife, and not only will his face be changed, changed utterly, but he is going to be made taller as well. Fuck you, Gapski! he thinks to himself. Fuck you, Sapperstein!

The doctors have asked him, Who do you want to look like? Clark Gable?

But deep down Brodsky has a sentimental streak, so he wants to look like someone named Brodsky. There are no actors by that name, no rock stars, fashion models nor rich gangsters. However, there is a Russian Nobel Prize–winning American poet named Brodsky, so the doctors dig up his picture and Detective Brodsky likes what he sees. "That'll do just fine," he says. "Make me look like this guy. As long as I'm taller, what's it matter?"

And Gapski? Gapski is in a similar room just down the hall and he too is staring in a mirror. He doesn't care what he looks like as long as he doesn't look like an animal or a broad. He wants to look like a man, a taller man. "Surprise me," he says. "Make me different, but surprise me."

29

POST-WEENIE

Before describing Wally Wallski's suicide attempt we need to take a moment to discuss the reasons for the growing popularity of biographies, memoirs and autobiographies at the expense of what is disparagingly referred to as fiction. "Movie star tells all!" "President's spouse spills the beans!" "Auto exec reveals how he racked up big bucks with little brains!"

"We read them because they're true," says the man on the street.

So we open a book at random. "I was there and this's how it happened," says the movie star. "I am an unimpeachable source!"

Then why do one hundred other people say it happened one hundred other ways?

What we see in biographies etc. is just a cagier form of fiction. Sure the guy was born on such and such a date and made his first million exactly twenty-one years later (inherited), but all this let-me-tell-you-how-it-really-was and to-the-best-of-my-recollection: my friends, it wouldn't stand up in a court of law.

What biographies, memoirs and autobiographies do is make life seem manageable. They allow us to say to ourselves: If he can do it, then I could have done it, if I'd had the right breaks, right connections, right looks, right checking account.

Biographies etc. remove the improbability factor and make life look causal: first we have this rational activity, then that rational activity. Nobody likes a Monday-morning quarterback, yet we increasingly privilege a form of writing which is one hundred percent Monday-morning quarterbacking. "I went into my first screen test for the following excellent reasons," says the movie bimbo who was actually so hopped up on coke that she believed she was trying on a miniskirt at Saks Fifth Avenue.

Biographies etc. remove the peaks and valleys from human existence. The random, ridiculous, zany and hysterical—all get evened out in *My Life* as told to Jerry McGillicuddy. But look at the second section of the *New York Times* any day of the week—that's where life hides. The first section is full of big-time manageability with the Big Weenie saying this and Big Weenie saying that. The second section has Man Turns Himself into Dog and Baby Eaten with Mustard. But we don't mean to give free advertising to the *Times*. The same is true of the *Post* and the *News*. Back pages, that's where life hides out. You think Troll, Taurus and Great Father Snake stretch the limit of credulity? Check the back pages and see their footprints.

But even better, maybe we should ask why we need to find such actions improbable: why do we prefer to read Auto Exec Tells All? In reading about auto execs and development kingpins what we are really doing is valuing falsehood over truth. Maybe we are afraid to discover that life isn't manageable in the least. "Count no man happy until he is dead," our pal Solon used to say. Biographies try to disprove that claim, and we read them because we want to disprove it as well. "Sure I was unhappy last week, but tomorrow I'll be happiest man alive because I'm going to hit the lottery and I believe that life zaps along as straight as a line drive, didn't these kingpins and Hollywood bimbos do it? Well, I can do it too."

But let's get chummy for a moment. Is this what you think? I worry about you, pal. You keep acting like that and life will squash you. You know when you see a cockroach creeping along the dark places on your kitchen counter and you keep quiet hoping

the cockroach will feel safe and wander into the open? Then,
BAM! You squash him. Reading that biography stuff, that causality fiction, those manageability fantasies, you watch it, you're
going to stray into the center of life's big counter. BAM!

All of which returns us to Wally Wallski. One could say his
good fortune began when he caught the lucky coin. Or one could
say that his bad fortune began when he caught the lucky coin.
Then he drops it and it rolls into an alley and he bumps into a
couple of bozos with guns so that he saves the life of Mr. Lenguado, the real estate tycoon. These things happen all the time.
What we demand, however, is causality: a clear line of cause and
effect. It was caused by Wally Wallski sneaking into the Marduk
vs. Rahab Wrestling Extravaganza against the wishes of his wife
Claudine. By betraying her wishes, Wally Wallski brought this
trouble down upon himself. As for getting a new apartment, then
going back and complaining and getting a bigger place, then complaining, etc.—all this has been in the papers. Or we have heard
about it happening to our second cousin's best friend. It has already taken place.

Rock falls out of the sky and hits a guy walking to work—it has
happened. Man walks down the street and a building falls on top
of him. It has happened. Consider the death of Aeschylus. He was
strolling along minding his own business and an eagle dropped a
turtle on his head. People read about it in the back pages of the
Athens Tribune and said he must have deserved it. He must have
insulted the wrong person. But rocks and turtles falling out of the
sky don't need explanation—they just happen. And that's also true
of the rest. A lucky golden coin falls into your life—it just happens.
You fall in love—it just happens.

Now for Wally Wallski. This Thursday morning he is sitting on
his front steps. He is both mentally and physically unhappy and
where he doesn't have bruises it would take a specialist two weeks
to discover. Wally Wallski holds his ten fingers in front of his face
and he is saying, "First this happened, then that happened, or did
this happen because that other thing happened, but then this third
happened because this second thing happened and . . ." Poor
Wally Wallski! He has read too many biographies, memoirs and
autobiographies. He is caught up in a causal cul-de-sac. He feels

that if he can discover the original thread then he can untangle the whole mess. Hey, Wally Wallski, it was just chance, like a big turtle falling out of the sky. Look at the back pages of your favorite paper and see how it works. "Baby Born with Face of Bear!" "Woman's Head Falls Off During Nap!" "Man Eaten by Car Radio Waves!"

But when Wally Wallski stops banging his head with his fists it is not because he agrees, it is because he feels he is not smart enough to figure out the system of cause and effect and he thinks he should visit the New York Public Library and read more biographies just to see how life works. But actually he is too depressed to read and he has been banging his head for so long that his eyes are all wobbly. What he understands is that if he goes back into the house on Gramercy Park, a house more beautiful than any in his entire life, his wife will kill him because for his wife this place is a dump and she wants the Pierre, meaning the hotel. And if he goes to Mr. Lenguado and tells him that his wife wants the Pierre, then Mr. Lenguado will kill him, because Mr. Lenguado is sick to death of him. And so Wally Wallski is being forced to choose between two disagreeable forms of death, and he is wondering if there isn't a third form more suitable to his particular tastes— because he feels that with all his burdens death is all he's good for —and what he wants is a Wally Wallski–type death, not a Claudine death or a Mr. Lenguado death, and at that moment Wally Wallski sees Marduk the Magnificent.

Michael Marmaduke has just left the Gramercy Park Hotel through the side door in the company of Primus Muldoon. He is groggy from lack of sleep but he is also optimistic. Not many places make Plexiglas coffins, and he feels he can trace the coffin featured in the videotape which he gave to Smitty only several hours earlier. It should be said, however, that this idea was not originally Michael's. Deep Rat suggested it as a possibility. But when they heard it, both Michael and Cashback thought it made sense. And Muldoon thinks it makes sense too, but he is distracted by his own concerns, about which he is strangely silent. And when Michael asks what's bothering him, Muldoon only says, "The Devil, he's got a plan." Which is a remark that makes no sense to Michael except to remind him of the dualist world of the Disputants and make him feel guilty that he has kept quiet about them to this man to whom he owes his entire career and everything good in his life (although at the moment like Wally Wallski he could also say everything bad in his life).

But it is a warm morning at the end of October and a few robins remain in the park and although the air carries a touch of winter, we feel it will be a mild winter. Michael exits from the side door of the hotel because he doesn't want to be recognized and he and Muldoon are heading for Muldoon's big black Volvo when suddenly the sidewalk is blocked by a insane-looking bozo who is crouched over and stretching out his hands and wriggling his fingers and stamping his feet and clamping his jaw so tight that it makes his face look like a squashed pillowcase and he says, "Come on, big guy! Let's go, big guy! Kill me if you can!"

It is Wally Wallski and he has decided how he wants to die.

"Pardon me?" says Michael.

"Hey, fella," says Primus Muldoon, "cut the jokes, we're in a hurry."

"I can't stand it anymore!" says Wally Wallski. "I'm going crazy!"

Both Michael and Primus Muldoon feel that Wally Wallski has gotten his verbs mixed up because he doesn't seem to be "going" crazy. He seems to have "arrived." But before they can tackle Wally Wallski's grammar, he rushes at Michael Marmaduke.

Wally Wallski hopes that Marduk will lift him up and impale him on the spikes of the fence surrounding the park, or maybe he will throw him in front of a bus, or maybe lob him through the fourth-floor window of Wally Wallski's own house so that he can land in a broken and bloody heap at the feet of his beloved Claudine and she can see what a mistake she has made.

Michael indeed catches Wally Wallski and lifts him over his head. Wally Wallski weighs about 150 pounds, which is absolute peanuts for a muscle man like Michael Marmaduke. Then Michael begins to spin him around and around. Let us look closely at Michael's handsome features, because we are surprised by his action, just as Muldoon is surprised.

Michael bears the expression of a man pushed too far. He is tired of people bothering him and wanting to wrestle and not

letting him have his own life and here comes this maniac who
wants to go ten rounds and Michael is tempted to throw him
through the fourth-story window of that big handsome house just
across the street. All Michael wants is to find Rose White, get
married and settled down. He is sick of people confusing him with
his Gimmick. And the look in his eyes, which should surprise us
and which surprises Primus Muldoon, is that Michael wants to
hurt Wally Wallski. He wants to do him harm. And any second he
will throw Wally Wallski just as far as he can throw him and
without a doubt this will be the end of Wally Wallski.

But then Michael realizes what he is doing and a look of embar-
rassment suffuses his face. Quickly he drops Wally Wallski, catching him again before he hits the pavement. Then Michael embraces
Wally Wallski, squeezing so hard that Wally Wallski goes
"Oooph," and tears come to Michael's eyes because he feels confused and tears come to Wally Wallski's eyes because he is being
squeezed so hard. Abruptly Michael lets him go and marches off
down the street. Wally Wallski spins around in a dazed sort of way
and says "Oooph" several more times, but then Muldoon takes his
arm and when Wally Wallski is looking fairly normal, Muldoon
gives him his card and says, "Here, young fellow. Call me this
afternoon. I think I've got work for you."

Before hurrying on to other business let's take a moment to visit El
Instituto Estético. This is a busy place on a Thursday morning, any
morning for that matter. Stretchers are being rushed up and down
the halls. The operating rooms are a flurry of activity with scalpels
flashing and more stitches than Madam Lafarge could manage in
a lifetime. You say life dealt you a bum hand? Here's where you
get new cards. A lot of dreams hang out at El Instituto. If one could
inject pink dye into the dreaming capability of El Instituto's patients in the same way doctors can feed you radioactive gunk to
make a map of your innards, then the sky around El Instituto
would be one vast pink fog bank. At El Instituto all futures are
rosy. Clouds with silver linings, pots of gold at the end of rainbows
—this is where it happens.

But that's not to say mistakes can't occur, which brings us to Brodsky and Gapski. Rush, rush, rush, anybody can goof up in these situations. Probably it comes from the high value placed on money in places like El Instituto. Carving up twenty patients an hour means twice the bucks of carving up ten. And Brodsky and Gapski—if you glance quickly at their charts, the data look the same. Same age, same height, same weight, same occupation— even their names are almost the same. So what happened? you ask. Perhaps it is too soon to tell. After all, the detectives are bandaged and each looks like a mummy. But two points can be made. One is that both Brodsky and Gapski are now exactly six feet tall. And two is that Gapski is in Brodsky's bed and Brodsky is in Gapski's bed. Maybe this means nothing, but, on the other hand, we are the only ones to know about it.

As for Brodsky and Gapski themselves, both men are awake, groggy but awake, and in their separate rooms both are looking through their peep holes at the ceiling. Brodsky can't wait until his bandages are peeled away and he stands revealed as the Russian Nobel Prize–winning American poet Joseph Brodsky. And Gapski can't wait until his bandages are peeled away and he learns the nature of his surprise.

But now we have some good news, and this too is of a medical nature. We are downtown in the neighborhood of the Gateway Plaza and we see a young couple walking toward us. The woman is quite young, no more than thirteen, and she stares adoringly at the young man at her side. You may say that a woman so young cannot afford to be in love. She needs to finish school and get a good job, but this is Beacon Luz and her daddy is worth millions and if she wants to fall in love and get married at the age of thirteen, then her daddy will buy the church and make it happen.

The young man at her side walks unsteadily as if recovering from a long illness. He has a cane which is doing a lot of work and maybe he should have two. Staring into his face, we find it familiar. It is clean, happy and vibrant; the blue eyes have a bright look; the skull has a nice haircut; the body is clothed in a blue pin-striped suit. Looking more closely we realize that the young man is Zapo, the fifteen-year-old syringe salesman, now ex–syringe salesman. We have never seen him so clean before.

But I thought Zapo was a little guy on a stumpboard, you say. That was the old Zapo, the unimproved Zapo. But now the Snow-man has bought him the best phony legs that money can buy and Zapo is getting used to them. He has his own physical therapist, his own gym, his own masseur, and in two more weeks he'll be able to tap dance.

But it is not only in the areas of physical and emotional improve-ments that life is looking up. Zapo also has a chance at a new job. Aha, you say, the Snowman will give him half his crooked king-dom. But you are wrong. Zapo has no desire to be beholden to Beacon Luz's daddy for his dinero. He wants to make it on his own. Just this morning as Zapo was tottering along on his new pins, a black car pulled up and a man shouted, "Hey, kid, are those fake legs?"

Zapo admitted that they were.

The man gave Zapo his card and said, "You like show biz? I got a job for you, kid. Give me a call this afternoon."

Zapo has the card in his vest pocket and every now and then he pats it to make sure it's still there. Let's take a peek at it. Name: Primus Muldoon. Job title: Trainer of Champions. Location: The Meat Market, followed by an address in New Jersey. And a big reason Zapo is happy is that he reads the wrestling magazines and recognizes the name. Primus Muldoon is the trainer of Marduk the Magnificent. Let it be said right away that Zapo and Beacon Luz are deeply in love, but they are also in love with the fact that Primus Muldoon is somewhere in their future. Love grows best on fertile soil, and Muldoon is the Rapid-Gro sprinkled across Zapo's particular half acre.

But now look what's going to happen. Zapo and Beacon Luz are approaching a corner. From our high vantage point we can see someone else approaching the corner from the other direction, and he is running as fast as he can run. Of course it is Seth and he is not paying attention and he crashes smack into Zapo, who finds walking a hard proposition on his phony legs and now some guy is trying to whack him thirty feet. But Zapo doesn't fall. He spins

around and comes to a stop still standing up, and he feels good
about this and he looks at Beacon Luz proudly and she looks at
him proudly. Just a few days ago a scene like this would have had
Beacon Luz blowing her whistle and calling her tough guys, but
now she has tossed away her whistle and turned over a new leaf.
Love is like that.

"Sorry, sorry, sorry!" says Seth, and he's grinning all over because he has managed to find a bottle of aquavit and he is heading
home. Sometimes bad things happen to good people and sometimes good things happen to bad people, but also sometimes—
more rarely—good things happen to good people and right now
good things have not only happened to Zapo and Beacon Luz, they
have also happened to Seth, and so all three are grinning and Seth
is saying, "Sorry, sorry," and Zapo and Beacon Luz are saying,
"No harm done" and "It doesn't matter in the least." So what that
all three are mortal and will someday be dragged from this vale of
tears in a nasty manner. On this particular morning it is warm and
sunny and love is in the air and after Seth says sorry several more
times, he runs off again and he's got the bottle of aquavit under his
coat and nobody is going to take it from him.

Seth had a problem and he solved it. His father Marcello was
sick and now he'll get well. Tomorrow his two older brothers will
come home, sheepish but okay. Even better, Seth was a boy without a future and now possibility has knocked, because he too is
carrying a little card just like Zapo's and Wally Wallski's. Primus
Muldoon, that busy man, has given it to him. As for the lucky
two-headed coin, it continues to bounce up and down in the
pocket of Seth's denim jacket and Seth still has no idea it is there.
Perhaps Seth is our happiest character. He has run through danger
and ill fortune without being aware of their existence. He has had
a problem and solved it all by himself.

As for where he got the aquavit, he was running through Battery
Park twenty minutes ago, in his own blind fashion, and he crashed
into a holdup in progress, almost like Wally Wallski several days
earlier. By chance, he saved the life and fortune of some old
codger, and the codger said what can I do for you, and Seth said
I need a bottle of aquavit lickety-split and the codger gave it to him
just like that. If we were writing Seth's biography we would need

to invent a complicated system of cause and effect just to show how it was destined to happen. But since we are dealing with real life we can say it happened otherwise. Sometimes turtles fall out of the sky and sometimes bottles of aquavit. Maybe Seth found the bottle because of the lucky coin. Maybe he found it because he has been searching for it for five days without interruption. Maybe he found it because he deserved to find it. In any case, he has it and now he is going home.

But not quite yet.

He has one more person to bump into.

Let us look at this person as he strolls down Water Street smoking a pipe. He is in his late thirties and although he is handsome and well dressed, we feel there is something wrong with him. For one thing, his clothes are old-fashioned: that double-breasted overcoat and out-of-date gray suit and gray fedora and those old-timey wing tips. He looks like someone on a late-night movie, although we can't say exactly who. Even his mustache is old-fashioned. Even his pipe. And what is this fellow doing that keeps him from seeing where he is going? He is reading a book. He is walking along and reading a book. In fact he is reading the book out loud.

"They had the calm weathered faces of healthy men in hard condition. They had the eyes they always have, cloudy and gray like freezing water. The firm-set mouth, the hard little wrinkles at the corners of the eyes, the hard hollow meaningless stare, not quite cruel and a thousand miles from kind. The dull ready-made clothes, worn without style, with a sort of contempt; the look of men who are poor and yet proud of their power, watching always for ways to make it felt, to shove it into you and twist it and grin and watch you squirm, ruthless with malice, cruel and yet not always unkind. What would you expect them to be? Civilization had no meaning for them. All they see of it is the failures, the dirt, the dregs, the aberrations and the disgust."

This fellow is reading about policemen in Los Angeles and he is eating it up. His name is Philip Kyd and he is a private detective. And just as he pauses to turn the page, Seth runs smack into him.

"Sorry, sorry, sorry!" says Seth, bending over to pick up the man's book from the pavement. Seth hands Philip Kyd the book, bobs his head apologetically and trots off down the street. Kyd feels stunned and jolted but what interests him most is the gold coin which he suddenly finds in his hand. On one side is an angel face with a pretty smile. On the other side is a demon's face with an unpleasant leer. Philip Kyd flips the coin and watches it spin into the sunlight. Then he sticks it in his pocket. Even though he is an honest man, it doesn't occur to him to call after Seth and say, "Hey, buster, you dropped something!"

Instead he thinks, He was a game little rooster. Then he hurries on to his appointment.

Ten minutes later Philip Kyd is leaning across the desk of an attractive secretary on the fiftieth floor of the Chase Manhattan Building. "Anybody ever tell you you're a cute little trick?" he is saying.

"There are magazines on the table, Mr. Kyd, if you need to entertain yourself while you wait."

"You wouldn't mind calling me a goddam cheap double-crossing keyhole peeper, would you, baby?"

"I don't care to call you anything," says the secretary, surprised. A red light flashes on her telephone. "Mr. Roskommen can see you now."

Philip Kyd smiles, showing his healthy white teeth. He's not a bad guy. He's just got too much borrowed dialogue buzzing between his ears. He's been victimized by midcentury nostalgia, whacked by detective sentimentality. He reads a little more from his book as he strolls into Mr. Roskommen's office: " 'In Bay City,' Maglashan said, 'we could murder you for that.' 'In Bay City you could murder me for wearing a blue tie,' I said."

Mr. Roskommen looks up from his desk. He is a man with a problem and he hopes this private detective can solve it. He went to college in the sixties as part of the love generation, kept his nose to the grindstone in the seventies and got rich in the presidential giveaway in the eighties. He quit smoking ten years ago and every day he rides a stationary bike for thirty minutes. He has a wife who successfully manages her half of their marital partnership, a mistress who does what she's paid for and three unmarried daughters who worry him silly. Mr. Roskommen is a responsible citizen and he is in a pickle.

Philip Kyd thinks, He had a long narrow head packed with shabby cunning, a long nose that would be into things. The whole face was a trained face, a face that would know how to keep a secret, a face that held the effortless composure of a corpse in the morgue.

The two men shake hands.

"I'm glad the agency could send a man over so quickly," says Roskommen. "This is hard for me. I don't want to be unfair."

"Sure," says Kyd, "you want to hire a nice clean private detective who won't drop cigar ashes on the floor and never carries more than one gun."

Roskommen doesn't say anything.

Kyd thinks, He nodded and let that one drift with the tide.

"I have three daughters that I love very much," says Roskommen. "For the past four weeks they've been going out every night, not returning till five or six in the morning. I don't know where they go and they refuse to tell me, even though we've always been on the best of terms. But what's odd is their shoes. They keep wearing out in just a couple of days. You're the fourth detective I've hired. The other three quit."

"Maybe you should buy them higher-quality shoes," says Kyd.

Roskommen gives him a puzzled look.

Kyd says, "You're supposed to say, 'It's a waste of time talking to you. All you do is crack wise.'"

An expression crosses Roskommen's face which is like the expression of a man forced to carry a heavy load up a mountain. "You want the job or not?"

Philip Kyd removes the gold coin from his pocket, glances at it, flips it and looks at it again. The angel's face smiles up at him. "Count me in," he says.

Now we come to the difficult part of the chapter, the part we have been avoiding. As already indicated, sometimes bad things happen to good people, sometimes good things happen to bad people and so on. But is any person completely good or bad? Take the Grabber. He is as mean as any human being can be. But he wasn't born mean. Meanness wasn't scrawled across his genetic makeup. In other circumstances, he might have grown up to be Pope. Rather his meanness is linked to his upbringing and maybe he is a little dyslexic so he didn't do well in school and the smarter kids laughed at him and the girls wanted no part of him and he got made the butt of a lot of jokes until he learned that if he whacked the smaller kids, they'd shut up; and when he grew bigger all the kids became smaller kids and first he whacked them to make them shut up and then he whacked them just for the fun of it, because whacking them made him feel good, so he'd whack them and listen to Elvis singing "Don't be cruel to a heart that's true" and he'd feel that life wasn't so bad after all.

But there remained a problem. Girls. Whacking them didn't help. What they liked was sweet talk. No kisses for the Grabber, no holding hands, no nuzzle nuzzle. But it was worse than that. Anyone can find someone, and if that someone doesn't offer him- or herself willingly, then a place can be found where money can be exchanged and he or she can be bought.

The Grabber visits his first prostitute when he's in the military police in Germany. What a terrifying experience! As he later told the doctor at El Instituto, "My weenie lay there like a sick dog!" This experience was repeated a number of times and always, "My weenie lay there like a sick dog!"

So all the meanness that developed in the Grabber's life cranked up a little. He hit people a little harder, he shouted a little louder and he got the job at St. Elmo's, where he was a big success. The doctors found that with the Grabber around they could cut down on the patients' knockout drops and what they saved on knockout drops was twice what they paid the Grabber for doing the job manually. But there remained this problem with impotence. Several times at St. Elmo's female patients responded to his advances (or at least they didn't reject him but perhaps they were too doped up to notice), but, as he told El Instituto's specialist, "My weenie lay there" etc.

But we have nearly reached the year 2000. Any problem can be solved, and one night a guy in a bar tells the Grabber about El Instituto, and when the Grabber talks to Dr. Florabunde he hears about implants, corrective surgery and easy payment plans, and now, on this Thursday, the Grabber has been home from the hospital for several days and he is sitting on his bed at St. Elmo's with his pants down to his ankles and his shorts at his knees and he is saying, "Cock-a-doodle-do," and when he says "Cock-a-doodle-do" he squeezes the little ball in his hand three times and his weenie stands up as straight as a Fascist salute. Then the Grabber says, "Awwwww," and his weenie deflates and then he says, "Hey, diddle, diddle," and his weenie pops up again, then he says, "Bye-bye," and his weenie falls down again. The Grabber has been doing this for the entire morning and he is one happy *Homo sapiens.* He wishes he could go down to the Yucatán, or wherever Elvis is hiding out, and show Elvis his new trick. "Hickory, dickory, dock!" he'd say, and his weenie would leap to attention like a singer doing "The Star-Spangled Banner."

But sometimes success arrives too late in a man's life. The required serum reaches the hospital after the poor child is dead. Even without this potency problem the Grabber would be a bully. It was already too late when he hit puberty, although with a better home environment and so on, sexual potency might not have been a heartache. Maybe he would have been a little nicer, who knows? But now, as soon as his stitches are removed, he plans to check out eight or ten of the semicomatose female patients right here at St. Elmo's, because the Grabber has got himself a powerful hunger. He feels like a farmer with a sharp scythe looking at a ripe field of wheat which he is all ready to cut.

But sad to say, the Grabber has forgotten about Sparrow. All of us have a line we should never cross, and usually this is a line we don't even realize is a line until we have crossed it. So it is with the Grabber. Here was this little shrimp trying to keep him from doing his job, making threats and trying to stop him from tossing Bernard into the back of his truck. Clearly it was an insult to the power granted him by the trustees of St. Elmo's Hospital and the State of New York. Whack him! Knock him down! Who is he, anyway? Ah, Sparrow Gonzalez is the Grabber's Waterloo. Too late to make amends. Too late to say sorry. There comes a moment in every Grabber's life when the tables get turned around, even if it's only death that does it. That's the nice thing about death—it rejects no one.

So now it is after lunch and the Grabber wants his nap and,

because he is so excited and has been up half the night playing with his new toy and because he's afraid he won't be able to fall asleep and the doctors have said that he needs to get plenty of rest, the Grabber takes a little sedative. And as he lies on his couch trying to get comfortable with his pants still at his ankles and occasionally giving the little rubber ball a few squeezes ("Jack be nimble, Jack be quick") and letting his mind drift off to rosy scenarios with semicomatose female patients, what should be occurring outside St. Elmo's at this moment but that a taxi putt-putts up to the gate and Sparrow Gonzalez climbs out. Then the driver opens the trunk and Sparrow removes a gray metal tank. Sparrow tips the driver and they exchange a few cheerful words about the weather and the taxi drives away. Then, turning up his collar, Sparrow starts sneaking from tree to tree toward the building where the Grabber is just falling asleep.

Sparrow is leaving nothing to chance. He carries a blackjack, a rope, a hypodermic full of horse tranquilizers and a variety of keys. He has already done his preliminary work, knows where Grabber hangs his hat, has learned his habits and knows he takes a snooze after lunch. What he doesn't guess is how the Grabber has made his job easier by popping a bunch of sedatives. When our time has come, it is amazing how we often give destiny a helping hand without knowing what we are doing. As for Sparrow, he is like a locomotive rushing toward its destination. He sneaks into the building and up to the third floor. He finds the door of the Grabber's apartment. He enters on tiptoe and suddenly freezes at the sound of a peculiar noise. Muted chain saw? Faulty plumbing? No, it is the Grabber snoring.

Sparrow enters the living room and there on the couch is the Grabber fast asleep with his pants at his ankles. Sparrow tosses off a little sigh to whatever fierce god of retribution keeps his motor ticking. Quickly he wraps the rope around the Grabber, tying him to the couch, then he sits quietly for a moment as he contemplates the spicy cinnamon flavor of revenge. At last he bestirs himself. Time to get to work, Sparrow thinks. We don't want to shoot the whole afternoon on this bag of bad business.

Sparrow carries the gray metal tank over to the bed and removes a rubber tube from his pocket. And just what is this tank? Painted on its side in red letters are the words "Danger Hydrogen Gas." Sparrow attaches the rubber tube to the nozzle of the tank and connects the other end to the rubber ball dangling from the Grabber's scrotum. Then Sparrow opens the valve.

At a hundred carnivals we have seen helium balloons being filled by happy roustabouts. There is a distinctive hissing, an obvious swelling and a growing eagerness on the part of the lucky youngster who has chosen this particular balloon as his own. So it was for Sparrow. In no time the Grabber's penis is three feet long and getting bigger. Even Sparrow, who often feels there is nothing left in life to surprise him, experiences surprise. The weenie is huge and pink and shiny and smooth.

We won't describe what the Grabber was dreaming in the moments before he wakes up, but it concerned sexual relations with a grizzly bear and the bear was doing the major part of the relating. Then the Grabber opens his eyes to see that he is being attacked by a gigantic pink dirigible. He swats at it and yelps. The dirigible is pulling at him something terrible. Then the Grabber realizes he is roped to the bed. Turning, he sees Sparrow Gonzalez tying off the rubber tube hanging from his scrotum. The expression "The scales fell from his eyes" is useful here, because it seems to the Grabber that everything has been made clear and he understands how big a mistake it was to throw Bernard into the back of his Ford van.

"I'm poor, I'm poor!" shouts the Grabber.

"Not poor enough yet," says Sparrow. He takes out a knife and cuts through the ropes binding the Grabber to the couch.

Immediately the Grabber begins rising toward the ceiling. His penis looks like a pink torpedo. The ceilings in these old buildings are pretty high, at least twelve feet, but the Grabber gets there anyway. The tip of his penis bumps the ceiling. "Ow!" says the Grabber. He bounces slowly across the cracked plaster. "Ow, ow, ow!" His penis is taller and fatter than the Grabber. It looks like the boss of the family. It looks like it should be wearing the pants. The Grabber tries to kick his feet but his own pants are still down around his ankles. He bats at his gigantic pink penis, trying to locate the rubber tube, but Sparrow has tied it off close and the Grabber can't find it.

"I'm poor, I'm poor!" shouts the Grabber.

"Not poor enough yet," says Sparrow. He walks to the door and opens it. Then he flicks on the overhead light. It is a 250-watt bulb hanging from the ceiling. The Grabber is slowly bouncing toward it. Each time his penis pokes the ceiling in one of its slow-motion bounces a little bit of plaster falls. "Ow, ow!" The Grabber flaps his arms.

"I'll be seeing you," says Sparrow, "in all the old familiar places." He walks out of the room and shuts the door. Then he hurries down the hall.

When the explosion comes, it knocks out all the windows in the building and sends Sparrow sliding down the hall on his belly. Doors are blown open or shut. Leaves are ripped from trees. It would not be an exaggeration to say that each of the five thousand men nearest to the explosion, without knowing he is doing it, touches a protective hand to his own genitals. This is what Carl Jung called the Collective Unconscious.

Sparrow gets to his feet and dusts off his clothes with his hands. "Poor enough now," he says. Then he checks his pockets to make sure he hasn't lost an important card just like he lost his lucky coin. No, here it is: Primus Muldoon, Trainer of Champions. Sparrow sucks his teeth and thinks of the future.

30

FREE TASTE

The time has come to watch a little TV. Indeed, for many of us the world only exists as phenomena that reach us through TV: life is not seen till it pops up on the screen. And the big reason we are so attached to TV is that we too have wonderful tales to tell. Just as the TV is a box full of stories, so is a human being a bag full of stories. And just as the TV needs to be unloaded by flicking on a switch, so the human being needs to be unloaded, and he or she waits eagerly for the opportunity. "You want to hear a sad story?" says Beetle.

We are up to our earlobes in stories. It is as if we were standing at the base of the Grand Coulee Dam and we found a spigot and all we needed to do was turn it on. You might say, "These are not stories, these are complaints." But to the complainer, every complaint is a story. Every dream is a story, every worry is a story, every ingrown toenail is a story. This is why TV shows with audience participation and call-in talk shows are so popular—they allow human beings to unload their bag of stories into the big boss of stories itself. It's hard to drag these stories around all day long. They get heavy and shopworn. "If I could tell my story, I'd make a million," says a guy. "I'm full of best-sellers," says another. This is what is so sad about DeMaus, Sosage and Vogel. "Stories are no longer important!" they say. "Words can't communicate!" Poor fellows! And they wonder why nobody listens. A human being is composed of stories in the way that a balloon is composed of air or an egg roll is composed of God knows what. And the ambition of each person is to broadcast his story in a pleasing and entertaining manner. The ambition of each person is to become a TV. And that's why we watch so much of it: to learn the tricks and see how it's done. Like Beetle, we want to find a way to tell a story that is so compelling that our listeners are pinned to their seats like a butterfly to a collector's cushion.

On this rainy Thursday evening we find a lot of TV being watched in New York City. A lot of ghostly blue lights can be seen through the darkened windows of a lot of apartments. In hospital rooms, restaurants, bars, offices the televisions are shining. Boob tubes, jerk boxes, flickering witchery—how can we speak so disparagingly? In ancient Greece an idiot was someone who refused to take part in the life of the community. These days an idiot is someone who refuses to watch TV. This machine connects us all. It makes us part of the same great animal.

Let us hurry across this wet sidewalk to look through the rain-streaked window of this First Avenue bar. Thursday night is wrestling night and along the line of bar stools a lot of necks are cultivating incipient cricks as they crane upward to watch the cruel commotion on the screen.

Consider the strategy of the Disputants. Here we have a horde of heretical groups each holding fierce opinions about the nature of evil: groups resurrected from the past because of pessimism about the future. And indeed, their opinions are so fierce that the members of one group would gladly bust the noses of another group even when their opinions differ by no more than a jot or tittle. The Disputants take this energy and translate it into verbal disputes on the nature of evil, which are then retranslated back into nose bops—but not amateur, disorderly, illegal nose bops, but professional, instructive, ennobling nose bops: the nose bops of the Wrestling Association. Isn't it by a similar process that mediocre grapes are turned into good brandy?

The arguments of Mani and Augustine, of Valentinus and Tertullian, of Brother Thomas, Timaeus the Promethean and Sister Esclarmonde—all are being closely followed at the bar. Each hammerlock, leg kick, elbow jab, body block and whizbang off the ropes corresponds to a fine point of logic. Within the grammar of muscle and syntax of sweat a dispute is being conducted. And watching from the bar, the men and women think to themselves: How true, and I never thought of it like that. What does it mean to be convinced? Language arranges marks on a page and barkings in the ear to make them correspond to the matter of life itself. Apple, we say. Big, green, ripe, juicy, flavorful apple. Then we move to simile and metaphor. Apple like a dream. Apple like a spring day. Apple like a home reached after months of weary travel. Apple of truth, apple of first love. But can we ever taste it? Are we ever convinced? On the screen Killer Coyote (Liquidity) lifts Wolfboy (Jimmy Holblock) over his head and bounces him onto the mat. What words can possibly correspond to the grimace of pain suffusing Wolfboy's features? His face contorts like a crumpled paper bag as Killer Coyote stamps on his hand. This is a logic the audience comprehends. Indubitably correct, think the men and women at the bar.

But the big match of the night is between Santa and Satan. Never, in the minds of many viewers, have Hegelian Thesis and Antithesis been so neatly posed. Both are red. Both have tails (Santa has a sort of cottontail). Satan has his pitchfork. Santa has his bag of tricks. Satan has his horns. Santa has his wreath of holly. And their names are nearly the same. Indeed, the three thousand dyslexics watching the match are thoroughly perplexed. There are a number of baffling features to this match tonight. For instance look at the participants. Wally Wallski, sitting at the bar of Pete's Tavern, grows suddenly alert. That guy dressed up as Satan is none other than Primus Muldoon. Wally Wallski recognizes him by his mustache even though it has been dyed bright red for tonight's event. He is short, stout and middle-aged and by all rights should be playing Santa if he must play somebody. Wally Wallski has watched a lot of wrestling and he has never seen Muldoon wrestle before. Nor, if the truth be known, has anyone else.

But look at Santa. He's quite a young fellow despite the white hair and whiskers. And why does he walk in that funny limping way? That oversized tummy is clearly somebody's pillow. And look at that girl with the blond braids in his corner. She can't be more than thirteen. How happy and innocent they both appear. They're even holding hands! Then Slick the referee raises his arms, a bell is rung and the match begins.

Nearly everyone we know is watching television this evening. Brodsky and Gapski are peeping through their bandages as Satan hurls Santa into the ropes. Smitty, their replacement, is taking a break from the Himalaya of paper on his desk and sneaks a look at Sapperstein's dusty set in time to see Satan whack Santa on the head with his pitchfork. Somewhere Troll is watching. Somewhere Taurus is glued to the tube. Great Father Snake is coiled around a portable Sony. All watch Satan stick his pitchfork between Santa's legs, making him trip and slide across the mat on his chin. Seth and his father Marcello are sitting side by side on the sofa as Satan smacks Santa in the snoot. Wally Wallski scratches his head as Satan pulls Santa's big rubber nose two feet from his face, then lets it snap back. Ouch! That hurt. There's something weird with this match, Wally Wallski thinks.

In a West Side bar called the Library the detective Philip Kyd sits in a booth with Mr. Roskommen's three daughters, who are sipping Singapore slings. Philip Kyd is drinking a gin gimlet. He has decided that the best way to see where the daughters go each night is to join them. All four stare at the TV, where Satan has turned Santa upside down and is using him as a pogo stick. Bounce, bounce, bounce across the ring. Philip Kyd thinks that Santa is having so much trouble that a little more will seem like frosting. He is struck by how much Satan appears to be enjoying himself. Odd match, he thinks. Santa hasn't had the chance to strike a single blow. Even though he is focused on the TV set, Philip Kyd is alert enough to see one of Roskommen's daughters slip something into his drink. Ah-ha, thinks Kyd, the old sleepytime trick. No wonder those other shamuses quit.

Somewhere Claudine is watching, somewhere Mr. Lenguado is watching. Prime Rib, Prime Time and Prime Rate all feel bewildered. Primus Muldoon never wrestles; Satan never wins. How is this professional, instructive and ennobling?

In a Brooklyn bar not far from St. Elmo's nuthatch, Sparrow

Gonzalez watches Satan give Santa a karate chop. Santa is expressing pain in the same way that Pavarotti sings. Satan stamps on Santa's foot, then laughs and laughs. Sparrow has been trying to figure out a way of freeing his pal Bernard from St. Elmo's (guns or dynamite, that's the question), but at the moment all his attention is on the TV. That guy playing Satan, he thinks, he's the guy who offered me a job!

Michael Marmaduke and Morgan the Pelagian are sitting toward the back of the Hall of the Disputants. It is clear to Michael that nothing in the match is going according to plan, and he worries that Primus Muldoon might get in trouble. Beside him, Morgan keeps saying, "For Pete's sake, will you look at that?"

Satan has Santa on his back and yanks at one of his legs. Santa's face is contorted with pain. Satan laughs gleefully.

On the floor of the Disputants, Augustine stands at his desk, proceeding through the dispute planned for this evening. "Even now when someone sins nothing different happens from what happened to those three: the serpent, the woman and the man. For first comes the suggestion, whether through thought or the bodily senses. If our desire doesn't lead us into sin, then the cunning of the serpent will have been overthrown. If we sin, however, then we will have been persuaded just as the first woman was."

The Master of Ceremonies pounds the blue puppet—meant to be Santa—on top of the red puppet—meant to be Satan. But no one notices. Everyone is looking at the screen. Several people cry out. Satan has just pulled off Santa's leg.

"Good grief!" says Wally Wallski, sitting at the bar of Pete's Tavern. Satan has yanked off Santa's leg and is waving it over his head. The bar has grown silent and the only noise is the sound of Satan's happy laughter.

In their separate rooms Brodsky and Gapski push themselves up on their elbows in bed at exactly the same instant. Balanced on his single remaining leg, Santa is hopping around the ring. "For cryin out loud," say Brodsky and Gapski in unison.

"For cryin out loud," says Smitty, glued to Sapperstein's lousy set. Satan has just knocked Santa down with his own leg.

"How mean!"

"How cruel!"

"How vicious!" say Roskommen's three daughters. Their names are Betty, Loulou and Phoebe, and they are all set for a night of dancing, just as soon as they can get rid of the creep with the funny hat. But what is happening to Santa Claus? He's being smacked with his own leg. While the three daughters stare at the TV, Philip Kyd pours his drink with the Mickey Finn under the booth. He tells himself that Satan beating Santa with his own leg is about as subtle as a tarantula on a piece of angel food cake. Then he touches the gold coin in his pocket. This is going to be his lucky night, he thinks.

Troll in his new lair, Taurus in his smelly stall, Great Father Snake wrapped around his Sony—all think that wrestling is beginning to look like fun again. Maybe they retired too soon. Santa Claus is hopping around the ring and Satan is chasing him while taking swings at him with his leg.

Michael Marmaduke feels strongly ambivalent, torn between his love of Muldoon and his love of Christmas as an institution. Muldoon's actions make no sense to him. Where's the educational value? He knows that Muldoon has been worried of late and he feels bad that he is so busy with his own troubles that he has been unable to help him. And even as he thinks of his troubles, Michael pulls out his wallet and checks Rose White's picture, just to remind himself what she looks like.

"He's going to get himself in a real jam," says Morgan.

Satan is smacking Santa with his own leg in the way that Babe Ruth used to smack baseballs.

Augustine is on his feet again. "The heretics ask, 'Why did God make man, if he knew he'd sin?' Because even from a sinner God could make good things. If man hadn't sinned, there'd be no death; but because he sinned, others are taught by his sin. For nothing so recalls man from sin as the thought of his own death.

" 'Then,' say the heretics, 'who made Satan?' God made Satan, but Satan was not made evil. He became evil by his sin. 'Well then,' say the heretics, 'God shouldn't have made him if he knew he would sin.' But why shouldn't God have made him, when through his justice and providence he is able to teach so many men and women with the malice of Satan?

" 'Then,' ask the heretics, 'is Satan good because he is useful?'

No. Satan is evil, but God is good and omnipotent. Even from the malice of Satan, God can create many good things. Only to Satan's evil will should we impute the attempt to do evil, not to the providence of God, who from evil makes good."

This is the end of the dispute and the Master of Ceremonies shows the hand puppet representing Santa Claus to be victorious. But no one is paying attention. On the screen Satan has ripped off Santa Claus's other leg and stands on Santa's chest holding both legs above his head. Satan is grinning as if he were the happiest troublemaker in God's great kingdom. Slick the referee reluctantly begins the count. It should be noted that the audience at Madison Square Garden is completely silent. And in their hospital rooms Brodsky and Gapski are silent. Seth and his father Marcello are silent. Mr. Roskommen's three daughters are silent. Troll, Taurus and Great Father Snake are silent. Wally Wallski is silent. Sparrow Gonzalez is silent.

Michael says to Morgan the Pelagian, "If Satan didn't exist, there would be no danger, and thus no basis for wisdom."

"You're quoting, I hope," says Morgan.

Are there any other responses? Yes. In her office at El Instituto Estético, Violet White holds her belly and she is laughing. Her ribs hurt, her chest hurts, and she is laughing. She sees Satan lifting Santa's legs above his head and she howls. She rocks back and forth and her hair is a black cloud around her beautiful face. She guffaws, chortles, chuckles, she roars with laughter. And up and down the hall the patients staring at their TVs hear her laughter, and anxiously they touch their bandaged faces and the future's rosy pinkness turns a little gray.

Michael and the Master of Ceremonies are in the small library which is attached to the Hall of the Disputants. A fire burns in the fireplace and the two men sit in leather wing chairs on either side of it. Each has a brandy snifter containing an amber fluid and each occasionally takes a little sip. It is ten o'clock in the evening and many of the Disputants have gone home.

"No man, not even Muldoon, can be esteemed more than we esteem the truth," says the Master of Ceremonies. "Consequently

I want to say that all imitations of wrestling are ruinous to the understanding of the audience. Is that not correct, Michael?"

"What do you mean?" asks Michael. The Master of Ceremonies has asked for a private talk and the prospect makes Michael nervous, even though he cannot explain his nervousness. But he feels that Muldoon will come under attack and he reminds himself that Muldoon is his friend. He also feels that his own Gimmick of the heroic Marduk may be made to seem silly. Even though he has wrestled as Marduk for several years, Michael is only now learning what it means to have a Gimmick and what it is to be a hero. For instance, wasn't it heroic to face Great Father Snake?

"Here in the Hall of the Disputants we have our disputes and, through the Wrestling Association, we have the imitation of our disputes. And then we have what Primus Muldoon performed this evening. What would you call that?"

"Maybe an imitation of an imitation?" suggests Michael.

"Precisely. So we have three disputes. We have the one made by the Disputants, who we may call the natural authors of the dispute. We have the one made by the Wrestling Association, which imitates our dispute. And we have the one that Muldoon did tonight, which we may say is third in descent from nature."

"Sure," says Michael, sipping his brandy.

"Now let me ask you another question: what was Muldoon's performance designed to be—an imitation of things as they are, or as they appear? Of appearance or of reality?"

"Of appearance," said Michael.

"Then Muldoon is a long way from the truth, and perhaps we can say that he can do many things because he lightly touches on a small part of them, and that part is actually an illusion. For example, he'll imitate a dispute between Mani and Augustine even when he knows nothing of their arguments, and if he does it well, he may deceive children and simple persons, is that not correct?"

"Certainly."

"And whenever someone informs us that he has found a man who appears to know more about wrestling than anyone else— whoever tells us this, I think we can only imagine him a simple creature who is likely to have been deceived by some wizard or actor, whom he thought all-knowing, because he himself was unable to analyze the nature of knowledge and ignorance and imitation."

"I guess so," says Michael. He finishes the brandy in his glass and looks around for the bottle.

"So when we hear people say about Muldoon that he knows everything about wrestling, knows all the arts and all things human, virtue as well as vice, we should think here we have a similar illusion. They may have been deceived by Muldoon's match tonight and didn't know it was an imitation thrice removed from truth, and made without any knowledge of the truth, because Satan's defeat of Santa was an appearance only and not reality."

"That sounds likely." Michael pours himself more brandy, then offers some to the Master of Ceremonies, who shakes his head. Michael thinks it is quite hot in the library and he tugs at his shirt to get some air under his arms.

"Then the real wrestling manager," continues the Master of Ceremonies, "the one who knew of the Disputants and knew what he was imitating, would be interested in realities, not imitations, meaning he would be interested in the disputes themselves; and would desire to leave as memorials of himself many true wrestling matches; and, instead of being the author of encomiums, he would prefer to be the theme of them."

"The author of what?" asks Michael.

"Encomiums: distinction, high praise."

"Ahh," says Michael.

"Thus far we are pretty well agreed that an imitator like Muldoon has no knowledge worth mentioning of what he imitates. The imitation he engaged in tonight was only a kind of play or sport. But tell me, what is the faculty in man to which that imitation was addressed?"

"What do you mean?" asks Michael.

"Well, we may say that the soul contains both superior and inferior principles. The higher principles are always ready to follow the suggestion of reason, but the lower principles lead us to remember our troubles and thus to lamentation and complaint, and they never get enough of this activity; so we may call these principles irrational, useless and cowardly, isn't that true?"

"Sure."

"But these rebellious principles furnish a great variety of materials for imitation, whereas the wise and calm discussions of the Disputants are not easy to imitate because they require a keen knowledge of the nature of the dispute. By showing Santa defeated and legless, Muldoon was able to prey upon the fears of the audience, fears which arise from these rebellious and nonrational principles. Indeed, in order to be popular he will have to appeal to the passionate and fitful temper of the audience."

"I guess so."

"In his pride and ignorance of the Disputants, Muldoon's wrestling match displayed an inferior degree of truth. It also appealed to an inferior part of the soul. Therefore we shall be right in refusing to admit him to the Disputants because he nourishes the emotions and impairs the reason. The wrestling manager who knows nothing about the Disputants implants an evil constitution into the soul of the audience, for he indulges the audience's irrational nature. He is a manufacturer of images and is very far removed from the truth."

"That sounds right," says Michael. He sips some brandy, then wonders if he should really be drinking if he wants to keep a clear head concerning what the Master of Ceremonies is saying.

"But we have not yet brought forward the heaviest charge in our accusation, which is the power that Muldoon's wrestling match had in harming the good. Is this not an awful thing?"

"Sure, I mean if that's what he did."

"Hear and judge: the best of us, when we see Santa weeping and smiting his breast because Satan is beating him with his own leg, delight in giving way to sympathy. But when any sorrow of our own happens to us, then you may see how we pride ourselves on the opposite quality—we try to be quiet and patient, to bear our troubles without complaint. So how can we be right in praising and admiring another who is doing that which any one of us would be ashamed of in his own person?"

"I don't know." Michael looks at his glass. He thinks it is too late to stop drinking. He is already confused. He squints at the head of the Master of Ceremony's cane and can't be sure which face is looking at him: angel or devil.

"So in misfortune we feel a natural desire to relieve our sorrow by lamentation, and this feeling which we try to keep under control in our own troubles is aroused by ignorant wrestling managers like Primus Muldoon. An innocent occurrence, you might think. But few people reflect that from the evil of other men something evil is communicated. And so the feeling of sorrow which has been increased at the sight of the misfortunes of others is with difficulty repressed in our own souls."

"That seems to make sense," says Michael.

"And the same may be said of lust and anger and all the other emotions, of desire and pain and pleasure, which are held to be inseparable from every action—in all of them deeds like Muldoon's feed and water the passions instead of drying them up. Muldoon's match between Satan and Santa lets these emotions rule, although they ought to be controlled, if mankind is ever able to increase in happiness and virtue."

"Sure, that seems to follow."

"The labor of the Disputants is the study of good and evil, and this must be conducted logically and dispassionately if our ideas are to be conveyed through the Wrestling Association to our fellow creatures. Primus Muldoon may be a great artist, but we must remain firm in our conviction that only those who understand the work of the Disputants should become wrestling managers. For if you go beyond this and allow types like Muldoon to enter, then not logic and reason, which by common consent are deemed best, but pleasure and pain will be the rulers of our enterprise."

"Just what are you saying?" asks Michael, putting his glass on the floor.

"I am saying that Muldoon is out of a job and we want you to take his place."

"I owe a lot to Muldoon."

"I know that, but turning us down won't affect what happens to him. He's finished. Muldoon wants to be an artist, but we have no place for artists. Our duty is to defeat evil by the propagation of knowledge. You can help us to do that."

An hour later Michael Marmaduke is walking down Park Avenue with Morgan the Pelagian, who has changed out of his robes. Both men wear raincoats. It is midnight and the rain has stopped. The temperature has plummeted and a sharp wind cuts through from the side streets. Michael is on his way to the Gramercy Park Hotel and Morgan is keeping him company. Prostitutes huddle in doorways, hoping to pick up some trade from the Midtown Tunnel. They brighten up when they see Michael and Morgan, then stick out their lower lips when the two men continue on by.

"What I don't understand," says Michael, "is why they want me as a manager in the first place. I mean, what do I know?"

"It's the gentleness," says Morgan. "You're the only person in the whole business who doesn't want to hurt anyone else. They feel your gentleness would have great pedagogical value."

"But what's this stuff about being changed?" It now seems to Michael that his gentleness just gets in the way.

"You wouldn't really be changed, but certain things wouldn't interest you as much. To transcend your Gimmick means that all those things that made your Gimmick important to you will become unimportant."

"Like what?" Michael has his hands buried in his pockets. He wishes he had some more of the Master of Ceremony's brandy.

"Heroism, for instance."

"What's wrong with heroism?"

"First, it's at odds with your gentleness. Second, it sets the individual over the group. A person often behaves as a hero because he wants others to think he's heroic, meaning he wants to stand out from everybody else. To join the Disputants means you take on the concerns of the Disputants. You become a series of ideas in their vast dispute. Your own ambitions will no longer matter. Look at Buddha—he made a journey to achieve transcendence, and when he attained the profound repose of complete enlightenment, his original reasons for making the journey were no longer important. The world was different to him: what he once wanted, he wanted no longer. Or look at how Augustine described his conversion in the garden. 'I fought with myself and was torn apart by myself.' And afterward the things of this world no longer exercised their hold on him.

"Or look at me. I have a strong need of belief and I've belonged to many groups. Once I belonged to a pagan group with bacchanals and dancing and sex. You never knew who you had sex with. Some women got pregnant and had babies and one never knew what happened to the babies. I wanted to believe it but I didn't believe it, so I left and tried something else. When I joined the Disputants, I understood that these other groups had been my long pilgrimage and by becoming a Disputant I finally became idea. I became an argument about sin and Adam's Fall—that each person is the Adam of his own soul—which needs to be uttered, needs to be placed against those arguments which say we were born damned or that the body is bad. I am a moderating influence. When one wrestler begins to kick another in the balls or stick a thumb in his opponent's eye, it is my voice that stops him, my voice that preaches tolerance. I have moved beyond my human weakness and become what I admire most in civilization: a voice of restraint and reason."

"How would becoming a Disputant help me find Rose White?"

"If you abandoned your Gimmick and your aspirations to heroism, you would see a new series of motives for her kidnapping. This would lead you to identify the kidnapper and ultimately to find Rose White. But there would be a catch."

"What's that?"

"If you transcended your Gimmick you might no longer want her. You might still love her, but she would no longer be a romantic obsession for you. If you transcended your Gimmick you would leave behind many of the things that made her important. That's the catch: you might save her and lose her at the same time. You might become strangers to each other."

"How could that happen?"

"Your will would be different. You would be like a vehicle which has changed directions."

And it occurs to Michael that if he became a Disputant, he would not only stop being Marduk the Magnificent, he would stop being Michael Marmaduke as well. He thinks of Rose White's face and how far away it seems. How could he let it go away even farther? Reaching for his wallet, he steps into the lighted doorway in order to look at her picture. He slips the snapshot from its clear plastic sleeve. It shows Rose White sitting on the beach at Cape Cod with her body protected from the sun by a white robe. She stares up at the camera, holding up one hand to shade her eyes. She wears no makeup and her face is very white. To Michael her face seems unused, as if her life had not yet begun. It appears both sweet and empty, and this frightens him.

Then Michael becomes aware of people next to him. A hefty-looking prostitute stands on either side of him and they are also staring at the picture. If Rose White seems all potential, then these woman are all actuality.

"That girl won't wear well," says one. "It'd be like putting cheap Jap tires on a Mack truck."

And the other says, "Aren't you Marduk the whatever? I'll give you a free taste of my sweet flesh anytime day or night!"

31

MULDOON:
POWER AND SCORN

Am I the author of this tragedy? Are great artists a different breed from great thinkers? It seems to me that true wrestling managers, being necessarily men of tomorrow, have always found themselves in contradiction with the present times: their enemy is the tawdry ideal of today. And consequently they find their occupation in being the bad conscience of their age. They reveal how much hypocrisy, indolence and falsehood is hidden under contemporary morality. True wrestling managers reach for the future with a creative hand, and everything that is or has existed becomes for them a means, an instrument, a hammer.

For every elevated world one has to be *bred* for it: one has a right to wrestling—taking the word in the grand sense—only by virtue of one's origins, one's ancestors, one's blood. Many generations are needed to prepare for the true wrestling manager; each of his virtues must have been individually acquired, tended, incorporated, not only the bold and easy cadence of his thoughts but also his readiness for great responsibilities, his lofty glance that rules and looks down, his genial protection and defense of that which is misunderstood and calumniated, be it god or devil, his pleasure in and exercise of grand justice, the art of commanding, the breadth of will, his slow eye which seldom admires, seldom looks upward, seldom loves.

The true wrestling manager is a human being of incomparable worth, a priceless gem among the gravel of humanity. That is why it is incredible that the crazy incompetent clowns of the Wrestling Association cast me out! For the first time they had a wrestling match that showed the world as it exists and they fired me! Do those cretins believe that Santa defeats Satan in real life? The foul lucre that pays for the cheap baubles in Santa's bag is the blood coursing through Satan's veins! Hardly had I returned to the dressing room when the phone was ringing. "You're washed up!" shouted a voice who refused to identify himself. They stripped me of my wrestlers and threatened to take the Meat Market as well. Unluckily, they hold the mortgage. For the first time wrestling held up a mirror to life and the world was given a chance to see its true reflection, and the meddling hand of the Wrestling Association flicked out the light.

"What excuse can you possibly make for yourself?" shouted my mysterious caller.

I answered in the words of Zarathustra: "I find man in ruins and scattered, as after a battle or slaughter. And when my eyes fly from the present to the past, they see the same—fragments and limbs and gruesome accidents, but not men."

He slammed down the phone.

Was I broken? Did I weep? Strange to say, I felt liberated. I felt like a prisoner freed of his ball and chain. At last I could run! What I had for years imagined to be my means of expression—the access the Association had given me to the ring—was in fact the muzzle that kept me dumb. By providing me with wrestlers the Association had not given me freedom to speak; rather, it had forced me into silence. All my great endeavors—my creation of Thrombosis and Dentata, Prime Rib and Liquidity and Cashback, Michael Marmaduke my treasure—these great spirits were my shackles! They condemned me to dualist duplicity. They forced me into the simplistic conflicts which the Association claimed their audiences desired. My wrestlers were the stick figures in the moral lessons which the Wrestling Association felt compelled to present. Now they were gone!

Dazed with my sense of freedom, I looked around the dressing room. And there were my new heros: small, frail, adolescent, crippled—and yet they were tigers! Couldn't Zapo and Beacon Luz be the first warriors of my new army? And there were others as well. Not handsome, not strong, not mythic—no, they were as we all are: feeble, mortal and dull. I realized what was wrong with my former wrestlers: by being superhuman they denied the human. I realized I needed men and women who could understand how to be silent, lonely, resolute, steadfast and eager to be involved in turbulent activity: men and women with a talent to see in all things what needs *to be conquered*. These men and women would be the beginning of a new Association, but no, not an association, a federation, a partnership of like-minded souls to whom I would teach a series of great enactments, who would be my vehicle, the medium through which I would pass my ideas to the world. My new wrestling matches would present the emotions of hatred, envy, covetousness, and lust for domination as life-building emotions. They would go beyond good and evil; they would luxuriate in the will to power.

Even as my mind burned with these ambitions, I felt the drawings of my incredible dream combats flutter wildly on my workshop walls. These censored fictions, these epic novels of the flesh could now be brought to life! My private fantasies could become a public nightmare. The wrestling matches I had secretly committed to paper would be at last enacted in the ring!

And I saw that I hadn't been fired by the Wrestling Association; rather, I had fired them! I hadn't had my beloved wrestlers taken away from me; rather, I had cast them out. Again the words of Zarathustra came to me: "Whatever I create and however much I love it, I must soon be an adversary to it and to my love: my will wills it to be thus." Superficially it seemed I had been beaten, but truly I was the one who had done the beating. And for the first time I understood one of Nietzsche's greatest paradoxes: "I have never felt happier with myself than in the sickest periods of my life, periods of the greatest pain." Because wasn't I in pain? Wasn't I being expelled from Madison Square Garden for having forced the audience to eat of the Tree of Knowledge? But how could I be punished? With Zapo and Beacon Luz I would be like a phoenix rising from the ashes!

Policemen had to escort the three of us to my car—so great was the rage at Santa's defeat. This had been planned as a jape, a feeble rebellion against the Association. Instead, it was a mighty teaching. Santa had got his ass kicked and the audience got smacked in its complacent puss! We barely escaped with our lives. People threw bottles. My Volvo was chased. When we crossed into New Jersey, it was like reaching the promised land. I saw that for the first time a wrestling match had presented the audience with meat, with the flesh of the beast, and that for years the Association had been feeding its audience grass and assorted nuts. The audience had lost its teeth; people couldn't eat what I had given them. And another of Nietzsche's truths became clear to me: "The rule yielded by experience is that intellectually productive and emotionally intense natures *must* have meat. The other way of life is for pastry cooks and peasants, who are nothing but digesting machines."

Still, I'll have regrets. Despite their failings, my former wrestlers are dear to me. Now someone else will coach Thrombosis in the articulations of pain, assist Dentata in the elocutions of ecstasy. Take them with you, you say. They can be revitalized and sent forth into the battle. No, they are already the victims of dualist conspiracy. Isn't it deeply pessimistic to see our own bestial heart as being corrupt? To whimper in the face of our divided nature? To seek happiness in poverty, filth and wretched contentment? Where's the lightning to lick them with its tongue? Where's the frenzy with which they should be inoculated? In my future work the animal will be glorified. Meat, meat, meat! We will explore the labyrinths of savagery, the bloody caves of the unconscious. For this we cannot have heroes, we must have tools. Zapo and Beacon Luz are such tools. Others will come as well. Companions the creator seeks, those who will know how to wield their sickles. Destroyers they will be called, and despisers of good and evil.

Michael Marmaduke will continue on his personal quest. And somewhere Rose White waits patiently to be rescued. She is not meat but grass. Michael will feed upon her and his teeth will rot in his mouth and he will be left to gum her thin leathery breasts. The Gimmick he holds from the Wrestling Association will grow larger while he wastes away becoming no more than a shadow: a child lost in the clothes of a giant. Not long ago I had dinner with Michael, Rose White and Michael's parents at the Rainbow Room. Michael's parents—stepparents actually—are very sweet. The father, I believe, is a grocer. The mother teaches grade school. Gentle people who never lift their voices. And there was Rose White whispering as well. Please pass the celery. Please pass the parsley. I thought I was going deaf! Even Michael was whispering. The father plays badminton and kept trying to engage me in badminton talk. I felt like a clogged drain! When the waitress tiptoed by I wanted to bite her! All four ordered the vegetarian plate. Rose White and Michael's stepmother talked about casseroles and what wonderful things can be done with Jerusalem artichokes. Their chatter made one of Nietzsche's most virulent remarks clear to me: "It is through bad female cooks—through the complete absence of reason in the kitchen—that the evolution of man has been longest retarded and most harmed." Michael sat sucking a wedge of lemon. I wanted to lift him in my arms and escape into the street. I wanted to liberate him from his own temptation to do good!

But perhaps I am wrong about Michael's fate. I remember how yesterday he lifted Wally Wallski above his head, raising him nine feet above the street. For a moment I saw something strange in Michael's eyes. It was as if the curtain of his pupils had suddenly parted. In the canyons of his corneas hid an animal that wished to do Wally Wallski harm. For a moment I thought Wally Wallski might come crashing to the pavement or be pierced by the spikes of the fence around the park. Then the curtain closed and Michael set Wally Wallski gently down on the pavement and hugged him. But even that hug was illuminating: hug of Apollo, hug of Dionysus. That was not the hug of a grass-eater!

And I have been listening to the other wrestlers. I have learned about these dangerous visits to Troll and Taurus and Great Father Snake—poor benighted creatures enchained to the authority of their own Gimmicks. And are not these videotapes like will-o'-the-wisps leading Michael ever farther into the perilous swamp? Who is this Deep Rat and what is his purpose? More important, who does he work for? But can he be entirely bad if accustoms Michael Marmaduke to the taste of meat? At this rate, when he finds Rose White, he will no longer want her. She will offer him a cucumber sandwich and he will bite her leg. He will sink his teeth into the white softness of her belly!

Down with Gimmicks and all their lies! One must not run from one's opposite; one must embrace it. Does that mean I must shave my mustache? That I should hurl Nietzsche out the window? What a tangle is created by the tortuous road of truth! The Wrestling Association was my Gimmick and I have defeated it. I have taken the bellicosity that I needed and have discarded the rest as one discards the skin of a banana. Perhaps I was timid and my Gimmick taught me how to dance. Perhaps I was fearful and my Gimmick taught me how to fight.

Ah, but I have forgotten the Gimmick onion. By rejecting the Gimmick I received from the Wrestling Association, I have come to terms with a single layer of the onion. The new voice with which I speak is just another layer. It is unknown to me and I must study it. Eventually I will discard it and come to still another layer. There is always Gimmick; there is always mask. By embracing my opposite, I will make my way deeper into the onion. I will bring to the surface all that lies hidden.

Likewise in my new role of free-lance wrestling impresario I will present matches which will confront the spectator with his opposite nature and force him to embrace it. I will transfer my great scenarios from the walls of my workshop to the brain of the audience. The danger of dualism is that it divides the world into heroes and villains. It claims that evil lies outside us. Evil is not outside of us but part of us, part of our totality. To destroy that evil means one must become another person and perhaps lose the "I" that makes us "I." And isn't that a form of escape, of running away from the evil, of once more creating the illusion that the evil exists outside of us? Isn't it better to embrace the evil and come to terms with it? To hell with Galahad and his dainty ways! You found it horrible to see Santa bludgeoned to the mat by Satan? Isn't it possible that you found it horrible because you also found it exciting? What disgusts you, what frightens you, what do you hide from? My new wrestling matches will illustrate the darkness of your soul! The Wrestling Association teaches you how to be a responsible citizen, how to do your duty within the society. My wrestling matches will teach you how to be true to yourself, how to draw the beast from your hidden cage and set it free!

And so you are done with the Wrestling Association? you ask. Not quite. To sneak away would make me guilty of puffing up their vanity and pride. I must help to save the Association from itself. With Satan versus Santa Claus I showed them my genius and rebellion. I still must show them my power and my scorn!

32

SLASH

In late October there can be days so warm and clear that they appear as nostalgia dramatized. Not only do they echo the warmth of summer, but they bring to mind other autumns which the memory has scrubbed clean of discontents so that they seem part of a golden age from which we have separated ourselves. Somehow we got lost; somehow we took a wrong turn. This is when one finds oneself humming "September Song" or "Blue Moon" or something from the Beatles: "Yesterday" or "Eleanor Rigby." Our missed chances seem more obvious, but they don't bother us anymore. Regret mellows, heartache softens. Ex-girlfriends and -boyfriends, old high school chums, friends of one's youth—their faces pass before us like drifting leaves. I wonder what happened to old what's-his-name? we say. We remember football games from long ago and autumn dances. We think of the smell of the car heater and wool sweaters taken from the cedar chest. Beneath the warmth lie hints of a colder future. Soon we will wake up to winter's cruel inclemencies. But not yet, not yet. We wonder if we put away our good scarf in a drawer or if it is just wadded up at the back of the closet. Our minds move more slowly and we look from the window and sigh. We take longer lunch hours and enjoy the walk down the avenues to more distant restaurants recently recommended to us. We consider joining a health club and wonder how much effort it would take to get in shape by spring. We look at members of the opposite sex with a mixture of hope and melancholy: hope that our options are still open, melancholy from the knowledge that they are not.

Even the bitter and disappointed experience tender feelings on these warm fall days. The cynic modifies his jokes. The bully softens his blow. The paranoid and disillusioned—all remember better times and may even perform a small kindness for somebody else: open a door for an old lady or help a blind person cross the street. Sitting on a window ledge near City Hall Park this Friday morning, Sparrow Gonzalez remembers what a lion he used to be, even though he is only five feet tall. He recalls the Golden Gloves flyweight competitions of his teenage years and the pleasure of watching his opponent crumple to the mat. Not much fun of a similar nature these days. Even blowing the Grabber's prick to smithereens lacked the unself-conscious joy of youth. And isn't Bernard still locked up in St. Elmo's? How can Sparrow get him out?

Sparrow wishes he were driving through the country with Bernard at his side. They would look at the autumn leaves and Sparrow would describe his past failures. Bernard would nod sympathetically but without obvious emotion: a pale pastel sort of nod, a nod with the flavor of lime sherbet and half as cold. Dried leaves would swirl in a vortex of confusion behind the car as forest animals peeked from around saplings. Ahh, I'm sick of washing windows, thinks Sparrow, I wish I had something else. It is then he hears the boom-boom of a bass drum. A group of men and women are walking along the street carrying signs, and the man in front has a huge mustache. Some of the men are dressed in bathing suits. A woman in a fur bikini is beating the drum.

Sparrow packs his brushes and prepares to be entertained. He has always liked protest marches and has never been particular as to their philosophy. Pro-Vietnam, anti-Vietnam, pro-abortion, anti-abortion—Sparrow has marched in them all. And just what do those signs say? Their big black letters look righteously indignant. Sparrow squints down at them.

The nearest sign is being carried by a girl with braids. "Live dangerously!" it says in big letters. And on the other side: "Live at war with your equals and yourself!" Sparrow grins. He likes the tone of that: common sense for common people. Next to her is a young man who walks as if he were drunk. "Good and evil are the prejudices of God!" says one side of his sign. "Always live in disguise!" says the other. Not bad, thinks Sparrow. Am I a window washer or only disguised as a window washer? Then Sparrow nearly tumbles off his platform. There's the fellow who bumped into him and swiped his lucky coin! His sign says, "Contemporary New York stinks of sickly men!" And on the other side, "Never believe ideas that come to you indoors!" It occurs to Sparrow that some of his best thinking is done on window ledges. And another sign: "Morality is vampirism!" And on the reverse side: "I am not a man; I am dynamite."

That's me, thinks Sparrow, I'm as dangerous as dynamite! He begins lowering his platform. Whatever these people are selling, Sparrow is prepared to buy.

The protesters come to a halt before a squat brick building. Next to the front door is a brass plate with the words "Wrestling Association" and the Association's logo showing a male and female wrestler contorted into the shape of a pretzel beneath a plump apple. We of course know this is not really the headquarters of the Wrestling Association. It's where the secretaries hang out. It's where contracts are signed and health benefits are haggled over. Even Primus Muldoon knows this brick building is just a front. On the other hand, it's the only building he has. To his left is his secretary from the Meat Market, Speedy Babs, who has always wanted to wrestle but is too skinny: Flaquita, the latino wrestlers call her. She wears the fur bikini and beats the drum. With each loud blow her frustrations decrease: drum with the face of her father, drum with the face of every man who ever said no. All her life she has been waiting to beat such a drum.

To Muldoon's right is Wally Wallski. He wears only a black bathing suit and silver elf boots but he is not cold. He feels fierce. He feels he could push his wife Claudine downstairs (although he is smart enough not to try). He feels he has been waiting all his life for a pair of silver elf boots. He holds a sign which reads, "Within

Me a Catastrophe Is Being Prepared!" And on the other side, "A More Complete Human Being Is a Human Being Who Is More Completely Bestial!" It is a big sign, but Wally Wallski feels he could carry it forever. He knows if he went down to Fulton Street to see Mr. Lenguado he would hurl a brick through his window. Wally Wallski's consciousness has been raised. He is deeply in touch with the lost father hidden within himself. He never wants to be a fisherman again.

Nearby stands our friend Seth. He too wears a bathing suit but he is a trifle chilly so he is jogging in place. All this is new to Seth. He is surrounded by mystery. He had thought he would bag groceries at Gristedes and attend night classes at a community college but now he's going to be a free-lance wrestler instead. His father is proud of him. His brothers are proud of him. He'll start pumping iron. He'll bulk up. Even though he feels surrounded by a fog of unknowing, it feels like a rosy fog. He feels he could run down the street with his eyes squeezed shut and not hurt himself. He holds a sign that says, "Some Men Are Born POSTHUMOUSLY!" and "Dionysian Madness for Everyone!"

Behind him are Zapo and Beacon Luz. They are holding hands. Zapo feels more confident about his phony legs, more confident about everything. He has said goodbye to his stumpboard forever. He has said goodbye to syringes and street corners and cold rainy nights. The cheers he received as Santa Claus still echo in his ears. He feels all avenues are open to him, but he will stay with Muldoon because he was the first to show Zapo his own power. But nothing could have been achieved without Beacon Luz; and as Zapo says her name to himself, he grows weak in his phony knees. His love is like a torrent. His love is like a grizzly bear. True, they are young, but all their lives stretch before them. Think of their grandchildren, think of their great-grandchildren!

As for Beacon Luz, she's glad for the chance to be tough in the service of a terrific cause. She likes how Satan beat the shit out of Santa, and her daddy the Snowman liked it too. She intends to be a wrestler once she attains her full growth and she hopes she'll be seven feet tall. Already she has started taking hormone shots. She wants to start busting the bad guys. She wants to make the U.S. of A. a nicer place for people like Zapo and Primus Muldoon to live.

Just that morning she had her daddy the Snowman pay off the mortgage on the Meat Market. Now it is Muldoon's forever with her daddy as part owner. Her mind is full of expansion plans. Today the Meat Market, tomorrow the world!

The other dozen protesters are not people we know. Muldoon found them in various depressing locations. They were unhappy, unhealthy and broke and Muldoon picked them up. He has a plan, a great purpose, and his energy is infectious. You might think they came along because of the promise of a free meal, but that is not the case. "To abstain from violence is a denial of life!" he told them. "Life means overpowering the foreign and feeble!"

Some looked up and muttered, "Aw, go soak your head." But others felt hope. In rags and tatters they followed him to the Meat Market. He dressed them in wrestling finery and fed them slabs of red meat. He instructed them to make themselves strong, to turn their power outward. Now he has twenty men and women standing in front of the squat brick building, along with signs and a bass drum. "The future is everything!" shouts Muldoon. "To pause is to putrefy, to stop is to rot!"

Curiosity seekers gather across the street. "Sort of a pathetic little protest," says one man.

"Only twenty people," says another.

"They'll never make the nightly news," says a third.

Muldoon sees men and women staring from the windows. Their mouths form little zeros of alarm as he picks up a stone. "Our philosophy must begin not with astonishment but terror!" he shouts. He throws the stone. It hits a first-story window, breaking it. Wally Wallski throws a stone as well. Then Zapo throws a stone and Beacon Luz throws a stone. People passing on the sidewalk give these nutcases a lot of room. Cars slow down as their drivers take a better look. What's going on? It's just those crazy wrestlers again.

Across the street, a bystander says, "Someone will have to pay for that window."

"Nah," says another, "businesses are insured up the wazoo for stuff like this."

We have arrived at a tense moment. Some of our pals have slipped their moorings. They start to spin faster as the moral underpinnings that held them in check are torn away. They are belligerent conviction unmodified. They are Hegelian thesis suddenly inflated.

But wait. Next to the Wrestling Association's building is a garage with tall double doors. These doors begin to open.

"There is too much beer in the American intellect!" Muldoon is shouting, then he grows silent.

A great bulky thing standing twenty feet high, covered with canvas and crisscrossed with ropes, trundles out of the garage. It makes a rattling, clanking noise and dribbles a trail of slime. The doors close behind it.

"To live is to exploit!" shouts Wally Wallski, but the others shush him.

Appearing from behind the mysterious structure is the ex–midget wrestler Johnny Korzeniewski, whom we met before. He is dressed in a black suit and resembles a pygmy undertaker. Jumping up against the mysterious structure, he grabs the ropes, then pulls. Slowly, the canvas slides off.

"The Association has had just about enough of you!" shouts Korzeniewski. "We're sick of trying to be nice!"

Muldoon picks up another rock, then stops when he sees what is under the canvas.

If Muldoon and his protesters are Thesis out of control, then what faces them is Antithesis. Do you remember those iron Victorian banks which looked like clown heads? Press a lever and a red tongue snapped up a coin like a fat frog eating a fly. Green cap, white cheeks, big red nose—the giant object facing Muldoon is one of these clown heads: a blend of the cheerful and sinister, the kindly and demonic. Doesn't Antithesis always seem to arrive? The Bronx cheer that follows our finest speech. The decrepitude of age in response to our wonderful youth. But perhaps we can see Antithesis as balance. The gravity that curbs our energy. The fall that goeth after pride. Here is Muldoon ready to conquer the world. Here is a giant clown head ready to stop him.

It is not by accident that we have been discussing Thesis and Antithesis. In his spare time Johnny Korzeniewski has been reading Hegel. Placing his hands on his hips, he shouts: "Once a man's social instincts are dislocated, and he is obliged to throw himself into interests peculiarly his own, his nature becomes so deeply perverted that his energy is concentrated on refusing to conform!"

"Is that me you're talking about, you half-baked shrimp?" shouts Primus Muldoon, who hates Hegel. "I am all the fuckin names in history!" Muldoon flings his rock and it bounces off the clown's forehead with a clang.

Johnny Korzeniewski runs back behind the clown head and peeks around the side "The authentic truth," he shouts, still quoting Hegel, "is the transference of the inner into the outer, the building of reason into reality—this has been the world's task throughout history!"

"I know my fate!" shouts Muldoon, throwing another rock. "I am a bringer of glad tidings like no one before me. I am also a man of calamity! For when truth enters into a fight with the lies of millennia, we shall have upheavals the like of which the world has never dreamed!"

While Muldoon is shouting, the clown head moves forward. "Transcend your negative quality!" warns Johnny Korzeniewski. Now the clown's great mouth begins to open. People gasp. The crowd of curiosity seekers perks up. This little ruckus might make the evening news after all. The clown has a forked tongue that flicks between its red lips. Suddenly the two parts grow erect, transformed into twin hoses which shoot blasts of water from the mouth of the clown. "A water cannon!" say the curiosity seekers happily. Wally Wallski rolls across the street, soaked as he hits the pavement. Good thing he's wearing a bathing suit. Muldoon falls backward, waving his arms in the air. Zapo's phony legs are knocked from under him. Beacon Luz is bowled over in the act of throwing a stone. Seth and Speedy Babs run for cover. Speedy Babs drops her drum and a blast of water sends it bouncing down the street. Although the day is warm, no one wants to get wet. Besides, the water hurts. Even the curiosity seekers scramble. And look, there's Beetle pushing his shopping cart away as fast as he can. The protest posters are torn to shreds.

Muldoon gets to his feet. "Muldoon cut to pieces is a promise of life! He will return from destruction!"

The water cannon knocks him down again and he tries to crawl away. His hair lies plastered to his forehead and his thick mustache is bedraggled. His clothes hold more water than a wading pool. Again he tries to stand, only to be knocked to the pavement. The protesters fall back. Wally Wallski helps Zapo. Beacon Luz and Seth help Primus Muldoon. They retreat.

"I am the one," shouts Muldoon from half a block away, "who is constantly obliged to conquer himself!"

"I guess that's that," says a curiosity seeker.

"TV crews never had a chance to get here," says a second.

"Pure ephemera," says a third.

Muldoon's wrestlers shove the remnants of their signs into the trash cans and depart. Nothing proud now, nothing defiant. Hands in their pockets, dragging their feet—they are cold and hungry. Nobody's back is straight. Nobody walks with anybody else. But there is Muldoon in front. He has been humbled, but the best thing about humility is that it doesn't last for long. He puts an arm around Wally Wallski's shoulders. Beacon Luz takes Zapo's hand. Seth and Speedy Babs begin to talk, sharing their traumatic experiences. And here comes Sparrow hurrying down the street. He likes what he has seen and has dumped his window-washing equipment. Sparrow and Primus Muldoon shake hands. They continue down the sidewalk, Sparrow on one side, Wally Wallski on the other. Someone chuckles, someone whistles a tune. Their legs take on a certain elasticity, a little bounce. Their pride begins to return. The nuevo wrestlers are walking in step, side by side, lifting their heads. And then the police arrive.

Let's take a moment to check in with Philip Kyd, who sits in the waiting room of Mr. Roskommen's office on the fiftieth floor of the Chase Manhattan Building. Kyd is puffing on his pipe and reading: "I risk my whole future, the hatred of the cops and of Eddie Mars and his pals, I dodge bullets and eat saps, and say thank you very much, if you have any more trouble, I hope you'll think of me, I'll just leave one of my cards in case anything comes up. I do all this for twenty-five bucks a day—and maybe just a little to protect what little pride a broken and sick old man has left in his blood, in the thought that his blood is not poison, and that although his girls are a trifle wild, as many nice girls are these days, they are not perverts or killers. And that makes me a son of a bitch."

The secretary looks up from her desk. "Mr. Roskommen will see you now," she says.

Getting to his feet, Kyd reaches into his pocket for the lucky coin. With only the pressure of his thumb he thinks he knows which is the angel's face and which is the demon's face. He pulls out the coin to see if he is right. Nope, he's wrong. Today he is wearing a powder-blue suit, with a dark blue shirt, tie and display handkerchief. Looking at the secretary, he thinks: She had a lot of face and chin. She had pewter-colored hair set in a ruthless permanent, a hard beak and large moist eyes with the sympathetic expression of wet stones. There was lace at her throat, but it was the kind of throat that would have looked better in a football sweater.

Kyd approaches the desk. "Do you loathe masterful men?"

"I've never thought about it," says the secretary. She is twenty-five, blond and pretty in an ascetic sort of way: no love handles but lots of class. Her name is Ms. Cathcart.

Kyd proceeds into the office. He has a casual way of walking and lifts his feet no higher than he thinks necessary. Consequently he trips a lot. Stumbling on the corner of Mr. Roskommen's rug, he nearly falls flat on his face but is able to catch himself on the visitor's chair. He sits down and tries to look as if nothing unusual has happened. Glancing at Roskommen, he thinks, He was about six feet two and not much of it soft. His eyes were stone gray with flecks of cold light in them. He filled a large size in smooth gray flannel with a narrow chalk stripe, and filled it elegantly. His manner said he was very tough to get along with.

"So what did you learn?" asks Roskommen. He studies Philip Kyd with the expression of an investor who has just discovered that his favorite stock has dipped thirty points.

Kyd pops a kitchen match on his thumb and lights his pipe. "Your daughters belong to a peculiar dance club," he says. "I couldn't crash the place. They had a loogan outside the door."

"What do you mean, a loogan?" asks Roskommen.

" 'A guy with a gun.' "

" 'Aren't you a loogan?' "

Philip Kyd feels elated. Mr. Roskommen is responding with the dialogue from the book. " 'Sure,' " he says, laughing. " 'But strictly speaking a loogan is on the wrong side of the fence.' "

"I see," says Mr. Roskommen.

"No, no," says Philip Kyd, remembering the dialogue more precisely. "You are supposed to say, 'I often wonder if there is a wrong side.' "

"Of course there's a right and wrong side," says Roskommen. The stock that dropped thirty points drops another fifteen. "If there weren't a right and wrong side, I wouldn't be hiring you. Why am I supposed to say anything?"

"It's in a book I'm reading."

" 'We're losing the subject,' " says Roskommen, inadvertently quoting from the book. "What about my daughters?"

Kyd is glad to return to the context of detective fiction. He wonders how it is for people who don't have books to hang on to, who have to invent their own dialogue as they go along, poor suckers for whom all language is virginal. Think of the mistakes they must make. Don't they realize that the world is full of accidents just waiting to happen?

"I waited outside," says Kyd. "It's a place off Bowery. 'I found the fire door and pulled it open. The fire stairs hadn't been swept in a month. Bums had slept on them, eaten on them, left crusts and fragments of greasy newspaper, matches, a gutted imitation-leather pocketbook. In a shadowy angle against the scribbled wall a pouched ring of pale rubber had fallen and not been disturbed. A very nice building.' "

Mr. Roskommen has a swollen, reddish look. "Mr. Kyd, I am interested in my three daughters, not in seedy buildings off Bowery. What can you tell me about my girls?"

"Not much. Like I say, I couldn't get in," says Kyd. Then, though it makes him nervous, he plunges into unborrowed speech. "I stayed in my car and when they left this morning around six, I followed them home. But look, those people wear these white robes under their coats. If I'd been dressed like that, I could have slipped in with no trouble. So I'll get some of those robes and follow them again tonight. And if they go to the same place, we'll be sitting pretty."

Michael Marmaduke accompanies Muldoon's lawyer, Truman Butterfield, to the police station right after lunch. Muldoon and his pals have been charged with disturbing the peace and holding a march without a license. Bail is taken care of soon after Beacon Luz makes a phone call. In our pessimistic moments we feel that people like the Snowman should be appointed mayor. Got a problem? Shoot 'em! Got a complaint? Bop 'em on the head! Got a friend in jail? Let's make a call and spring 'em!

Michael waits on the steps of the precinct house soaking up the sun as papers are signed and declarations sworn. It is early afternoon and the sky has grown hazy. As he sits with his eyes closed he hears people say, "Isn't that Marduk the Magnificent?" He is struck by how it no longer bothers him to be confused with his Gimmick. Indeed, he can't imagine being bothered.

Along with making sure that Muldoon is okay, Michael wants to ask his advice. Late that morning Morgan the Pelagian called with the news of the attack on the Wrestling Association's offices. "The Master of Ceremonies is livid. He'd press charges if it weren't for the publicity. Have you thought any more about his offer? We need someone to replace Muldoon right away."

"I'm still considering it," Michael said.

It is this chance to become a manager that Michael wants to discuss with Muldoon. Michael sees no betrayal in this. Even though Muldoon is upset with the Association, Michael feels that Muldoon will talk to him frankly, if only because Muldoon has always talked frankly. Michael has doubts about tying himself to the Disputants and he is uncertain what it means to be changed. Of course, if he must do this to find Rose White, then he will do it. Rose White safe and unloved is better than Rose White loved and dead. But doesn't he stand a chance of finding her without the Wrestling Association? That morning he talked to Deep Rat, who had learned about someone purchasing a Plexiglas coffin. "We're getting closer," came Deep Rat's whispery voice over the phone. "You have to be ready for anything."

"Sure," Michael said, "I guess I'm ready. But don't you think we should take the information to the police?"

"What have the police done for you so far?"

"Not too much."

"My only wish is to see you and Rose White together again."

Sure," said Michael, "I appreciate that." And he wondered what it was about Deep Rat that he distrusted.

On the other hand, Michael remains impressed by the goals of the Wrestling Association. He likes Morgan and doesn't want Morgan to think badly of him. He has deep regard, tempered with nervousness, for the Master of Ceremonies. Also, there are many aspects to being a manager that Michael would enjoy. But Michael doesn't want to give up wrestling himself. He is young. He could be Marduk the Magnificent for many years to come. This is a new thought for Michael Marmaduke, but it feels as if he has always thought it.

What do I like about being Marduk the Magnificent? Michael asks himself. The money? The fame? He thinks how he has denied being Marduk when people ask for autographs, how it embarrassed him. What is it about Marduk that bothers him? Michael doesn't know. In Madison Square Garden there are air-conditioning vents blowing down on the ring. What Michael likes about being Marduk is that when he triumphantly raises his arms after putting some ugly bruiser to sleep in the Bosom of Abraham, the breeze from the vents tickles his flesh and gives him a little shiver. At the end of each match he experiences this shiver. He holds his hands over his head and his skin shivers like the skin of a horse and people in the first few rows see it and shout even louder. Sometimes Michael thinks he does the whole business only for that shiver. You are alive, it tells him. You are full of the world.

He has never mentioned this to anybody, not even Rose White. He has always told himself it was too small to bother about, but now he realizes it also embarrasses him, as if he had been caught doing something he shouldn't. Taking out his wallet, he studies the photo of Rose White at Cape Cod. He is struck by how young she looks. The white robe hides her figure, making her seem about twelve years old. Michael tells himself he is exaggerating. Rose White lives in New York and teaches third grade at P.S. 97. She is a mature and sexually desirable woman. The world is not a confusion to her. But Michael is not completely convinced, and he thinks about the difference between Rose White and her sister.

We should mark him here sitting on the steps of the precinct house on this sunny Friday afternoon. Hopeful pigeons have approached on the sidewalk (not too close!). Passersby glance at him with varying interest. Cars slow. Michael is a huge man. His blondness and youth and obvious health make him immediately noticeable, even to people who know nothing about wrestling. And his perplexity as he stares at the snapshot is also eye-catching. That smooth brow is unused to wrinkles. Seeing it, several matronly ladies want to console him. Michael feels as confused as a polar bear cub on a small iceberg: rough seas ahead of him, rough seas behind.

We hear voices and laughter from inside the precinct house, and moments later Muldoon and Truman Butterfield appear in the doorway, followed by the other protesters. Seth and Speedy Babs have blankets draped over their bare shoulders. Some generous soul has given Wally Wallski an old sweatshirt. Michael gets to his feet and returns Rose White's photograph to his wallet. Everybody is very cheerful. Seeing Michael on the steps, Muldoon claps him on the back.

"We have defeated the wasted dogs of the mob and all the ill-constituted brood of gloom," says Muldoon. "The laughing storm that blows dust in the eyes of the dim-sighted and ulcerated has been triumphant!"

"What are you talking about?" Michael's brow is still furrowed and his load seems heavy.

"I have canonized laughter and we have learned to dance!"

Muldoon comes up to Michael's shoulder. Butterfield is not much taller. Even so the group surrounds Michael and seems to pick him up as they proceed down the sidewalk. He is like a gloomy wood chip in their cheerful torrent. The pigeons flap away to the other side of the street.

"I was wondering if I could talk to you," says Michael.

Truman Butterfield gestures toward the curb. "My car's over here." His blue silk suit fits him like another layer of skin. His car is a chauffeur-driven Mercedes: not quite stretch, but definitely oversized.

Muldoon climbs into the back, lowers the window and addresses Wally Wallski, Sparrow Gonzalez and the others. "My friends, I will meet you at Pforta this afternoon. Lift up your hearts, you fine dancers, and do not forget to laugh well!"

The Mercedes pulls away from the curb. Looking through the side window, we see Michael Marmaduke leaning back against the gray leather seat. His brow is still furrowed. How sad it is: we learn to furrow our brows in reaction to the world and as we age the furrows remain as evidence of the world's visitation.

The Mercedes merges with traffic, then turns north on Church Street. Butterfield sits in front with the chauffeur, whose name is Lance. Butterfield is talking on the phone. He cups it with both hands, smirking into the mouthpiece in such a way as to suggest a pretty woman on the other end of the line. Muldoon is also grinning and slaps his chest. His big mustache bristles with cheerful aggressiveness. We don't know what he is saying, but we assume he is describing the victories of the morning. Michael nods and tries to smile but furrows still mark his brow.

The Mercedes stops for a light at Thomas Street and through the open rear window we can hear Michael's voice. "I know they fired you. They offered me your job."

"Ahhh," says Muldoon, frowning. "The world is deep."

The light changes and the Mercedes continues north. Lance is a practiced driver: fast and fluid. The gray Mercedes weaves between the yellow cabs. Sunlight bounces off the windshield. We see Muldoon and Michael talking more intensely. Muldoon doesn't seem so cheerful now. He keeps smacking his left hand with the fist of his right. Butterfield continues to chat on the phone. The Mercedes stops for another light at Worth.

"I haven't given them any answer yet," Michael is saying.

"But you're tempted?"

"It's flattering to be offered the job, and there are some interesting managerial angles. On the other hand, I'd have to quit wrestling. That whole part of my life would be gone."

Lance guns the Mercedes into the left lane to pick up Sixth Avenue. A yellow cab honks at him. Lance brakes quickly as a white panel truck covered with graffiti pulls out in front. We hear Michael saying, "I like wrestling. I like it more than I ever thought I did."

"If you become a manager," says Muldoon, "you'll be their animal. Of course as a wrestler you're also their animal but at least you have the illusion of freedom. . . ."

The Mercedes veers left onto Sixth. People are getting off work early this Friday afternoon. We can see several hundred people and all have weekend plans. For some the weekend means romance, for others it means raking leaves. Football, dog races, taking the kids on a bike ride. The desired future presses so close that the present becomes a trifle insubstantial.

The Mercedes stops at Canal Street. "Your duty is to yourself," says Muldoon. "If you're tempted to become manager but you still don't like the idea, then don't do it. Don't be their creature unless you want to wear their collar."

Michael has his chin in his hands "It's a much more complicated organization than you imagine."

"But you'd still be wearing their collar, wouldn't you?"

The light changes and Lance resumes his combat with the traffic: cabs attacking from the left, trucks from the right. It's hard to keep a Mercedes pristine in the city. As for us, we've heard enough. Michael has gone to Muldoon with a problem and the problem remains. He leans against the soft leather and presses his knuckles against his temples. This is meant to help him think. And what sort of activity is going on between those temples right now? Peering into Michael's brain we see Deep Rat in the middle of a stage. To his left is a sword representing the Path of the Hero. Sure it has childish qualities, but hasn't it produced results? Haven't they found those videotapes? To right is a candle representing the Path of the Disputants: not action but reason, not muscle but meditation. The path of the hero promises obliteration (death) as a result of failure. The other path promises obliteration (destruction of ego) as a result of success. Deep Rat gestures to both choices. "You pick," he seems to say. "After all, it's your life." Over Deep Rat himself there dangles a large red question mark.

And where is the real Deep Rat right now? Let's take a look at that as well.

Deep Rat has a couple of rooms in the Bronx, but he is so secretive that even we don't know where they are. Suffice it to say that he lives in a neighborhood with few buildings left standing and the only white faces tend to be on cops or people who have made a wrong turn and are getting out quick. Deep Rat doesn't think of himself as any color. Once some big black guys hassled him on the sidewalk, a little pushing, shoving and racial name-calling. Deep Rat bit them. He bit them with his teeth and bit them with his knife. Since then he has had no trouble.

Deep Rat's rooms have various oddnesses. For instance the windows are painted over and the walls are dark brown. The furniture tends to be Salvation Army modern and unworthy of our attention. But look at these posters. Hanging from wires strung from wall to wall in the small bedroom, living room and kitchen are dozens of posters showing Marduk the Magnificent. Here is Marduk stamping Rahab the Reckless into the mat. Here is Marduk putting Pazuzu to sleep in the Bosom of Abraham. How golden Marduk looks, how full of meat. Here is Marduk wearing only a male bikini and beating his chest. Do you see those scars around his ankles? Deep Rat wonders what could have caused them. Here is Marduk with a golden cape billowing around his shoulders and a golden crown on his head standing on the back of a white horse. Maybe more than one hundred of these posters clutter the air of Deep Rat's three small rooms. And where is Deep Rat?

We are getting to that. He is in the bathroom, preparing himself. We hear water running, a toilet flushing. Then the door opens and Deep Rat jumps into the hall. His eyes are black buttons. He wears a black turtleneck and tight black pants. In each hand he holds a knife with a thin blade. We have briefly frozen him here, but in truth he doesn't pause. He leaps out of the bathroom and begins slashing at the posters with his two knives. He stabs them. He slices them. He himself makes no sound, but the noise of ripping paper gets louder: crinkling, falling and being trampled on. Deep Rat runs hunched over between his three rooms slashing and cutting. There goes a knife across Marduk's handsome face. There goes a knife into his pink belly. Deep Rat breathes hard, a quick little panting noise. Beads of sweat run down his brow. He cuts and slashes, cuts and slashes. Within several minutes the posters have been ripped to shreds and the wires vibrate emptily in the still air. Deep Rat wades through the paper as if wading through deep snow. He lifts his head and sniffs. He smiles a little. Look at his teeth, how pointed they are. Then Deep Rat drops to all fours because in the privacy of his home this is how he is most comfortable.

33

DANCE—TWO

The police detective named Smitty is not someone we will ever know well. True, his hardships are nearly as great as any we have encountered but he is only twenty-four and young enough to be strengthened by failure. Pumping moral iron—that's what failures are about—but only to a certain age, then they create such moral hernias as creeping indifference and throbbing apathy. We bring in Smitty only long enough to take a look at his desk—an old gray metal affair but the papers on top occupy exactly the same volume as the desk itself. All these papers connect, if only tangentially, with Rose White. The police do their work by collecting bits of information and chewing on them. The papers on Smitty's desk represent this process: interviews with everyone connected with Troll, Taurus and Great Father Snake, interviews with everyone around Rose White's apartment house, interviews with habitués of the Blood Factory, fingerprint reports, dental reports, blood types, bone types, hair and skin reports. Again we are grateful to TV cop shows for teaching us about this relatively arcane aspect of life.

Smitty looks at this mountain of paper with all the gusto of an anorexic signed up for a pie-eating contest. He believes he could shut his eyes and pull out a paper and this could begin his task as well as any other. Looking at this mass of ex–wood pulp and cotton fiber, we feel it is wrong of Michael Marmaduke to accuse the police of not doing their job. Certainly they are working hard, and sometime around Christmas Smitty will be ready to act. He'll call up a few brave men and they'll have a raid, knock down some doors, shoot a few bullets and discover Rose White's desiccated corpse. Smitty sighs and looks forward to that time. Perhaps by then Brodsky and Gapski will have returned from sick leave. And as he thinks of Brodsky and Gapski, Smitty grinds his teeth and wonders if he could find reason to go on sick leave himself. Maybe he could raid a crack house and get shot. Given the choice between getting shot and climbing that mountain of paper, Smitty would pick a bullet in the leg any day of the week.

As for Brodsky and Gapski, they are resting comfortably. Beneath their bandages they detect their new faces (they burn a little) and they put the same amount of concentration into them as a hen puts into her eggs: soon they will hatch. Now and then a nurse wheels one of them down the hall for tests or some exercise, and each man knows he has laid eyes on his former partner but he has been unable to recognize him. This is how Brodsky and Gapski want it, although neither has grasped that they still—because of the bandages—look exactly alike.

If they think of Rose White at all, it is only to consider the oddnesses of the case—Troll, Taurus and Great Father Snake— but they don't miss it. Cases getting lots of attention always means trouble and trouble means getting yelled at. Better leave it to Smitty. Better just concentrate on getting better.

To prepare himself for his new face, Brodsky has been reading some of the poems of the Russian Nobel Prize–winning American poet Joseph Brodsky. They confuse him but he feels he sees within these poems a family resemblance. Isn't he confused by himself as well? As for Gapski, he is getting ready for the answer to the great mystery: who will he look like? Maybe he will look like a young Jimmy Stewart or Ronald Reagan. And to prepare himself he listens to music: Stockhausen and Schoenberg—all the music that has ever bewildered him. And when he finds a thread that seems to make sense, he says, "Aha," and he believes he is on the narrow and vaguely perceived path to self-knowledge.

As for this mix-up about Brodsky being in Gapski's bed and Gapski being in Brodsky's, a night nurse realized the mistake after Brodsky yelled at her for calling him Gapski and Gapski yelled at her for calling him Brodsky. She quickly switched their charts and removed from her mind the possibility of error. Mistakes are what other people make, right? "Everything will be fine soon," says the nurse. "Try to think forward thoughts."

El Instituto Estético is packed with people crammed full of forward thoughts: what they will look like when the bandages are removed, how people will treat them with more respect, more love, more awe. Its patients are in the process of becoming "other," which means, along with thinking forward thoughts, not thinking backward thoughts. Their pasts are over and done with. No use crying over spilt milk. But in a few cases this is not true and the past still looms large. Let us look at one instance of this.

We descend to the second floor, where several rooms have been knocked together to form the staff cafeteria. In a corner we see Violet White, or Nurse White as she is known at El Instituto. She is deep in conversation with a man who has his back to us. As we approach, something about him strikes us as familiar. He wears a ragged overcoat that is none too clean. His gray hair is unkempt; his dark pants are shiny with a mixture of dirt and grease and age; his shoes are on their last five miles. Then we catch the smell. This is a man for whom bathing is as distant as childhood. It is Beetle, and he is sipping hot chocolate and nibbling toast. He is also unburdening himself of his story.

"Tell me again what happened when you found the baby in the trash can," says Nurse White, and she smiles kindly.

Beetle has already told the story ten times but he has been so bottled up that he will have to tell it ten more times before he feels better. Volcanoes and carbuncles are like this when they pop. He has to drain himself of all the poison.

"I just found him. I mean, sometimes you take a look into trash cans just to see what's going on, and I found this baby with his feet handcuffed together. His ankles were all bloody."

"But why did you carry him out of the city?" Violet White leans toward Beetle across the table. Her face is composed and very white. A black strand of hair tumbles from her nurse's cap and she carefully tucks it back.

"Because once I'd found him, then I was gonna get yelled at for finding him. The cops don't like you finding things. So I carried him over to New Jersey. He wasn't heavy. I walked and walked. I could've walked for years. I swiped some milk for him and he slept. I liked him. He had real pretty blond hair."

"Was there anything else about the baby that struck you?"

Beetle scratches his scalp. No telling what sort of insect population he is disturbing. "Yeah, somebody had drawn a picture on his chest with lipstick. A picture of a leaf. I had the darnedest time washing it off."

"What kind of leaf?"

"Just a leaf. Pointy, like leaves are."

Violet unbuttons the top of her dress, exposing the tattoo of an ivy leaf on her left breast. "Did it look like this?"

"Yeah, sort of, except it was red."

"You know," says Rose White, putting one hand on top of Beetle's, "if these memories bother you, we can have them removed right here at the hospital. They need never bother you again."

We pity those people of past epochs and how they dealt with their primitive psychologies. When something bothered them they ran away to sea or joined the French Foreign Legion or stayed home and got drunk. Transformation: that's what the late twentieth century is about. Got a bad memory—we'll cut it out. Don't like your face—we'll make you look like a Nobel Prize–winning poet. Afraid to commit yourself to the pitfalls of language—use somebody else's. As for who we really are, well, that depends on the day of the week. On Monday we're Tarzan, on Tuesday we're Jane. Poor Christopher Columbus had to sail across the ocean blue to start a new life; we only have to call up El Instituto or our local street-corner therapist. I'm not really a cab driver, says the cabbie, I'm an actor. I'm not really a waiter, I'm a poet. I'm not really a lawyer, I'm a songwriter. I'm not really a banker, I'm a strip-tease artist. I'm not really a human being, says Taurus, I'm a bull.

This is what is so complicated about Michael Marmaduke's

dilemma. He is being asked to bid himself farewell just as he is learning—he thinks—who he really is. For at the very moment that Violet White is listening to Beetle's story for the tenth time (oh, is he glad to get it off his chest), Michael is talking to Morgan the Pelagian, Augustine and the Master of Ceremonies in the small library adjoining the Hall of the Disputants. It is early Friday evening and all four men hold cups of tea.

"But I'm not sure if I want to be liberated from myself," Michael is saying. He thinks how he faced Great Father Snake, Taurus and Troll, how he felt fear and how it wasn't so terrible, or at least not as terrible as he had feared. "If I were liberated from myself, I wouldn't be Michael Marmaduke anymore."

"But who is Michael Marmaduke?" asks the Master of Ceremonies. The three Disputants wear suits and could easily pass for stockbrokers.

Michael pokes a thumb at his chest. "Me! I'm Michael Marmaduke." The question makes no sense to him. He wears a brown leather jacket, blue T-shirt and blue baggy pants. He knows just what he looks like. He knows how his blond hair lies in studied disorder across his head. He knows how many push-ups he can do and how many chin-ups and how many pounds he can lift into the night sky. He knows all about himself.

"You've been invented by Primus Muldoon," says Augustine.

"He helped me, he didn't invent me. I've been Michael Marmaduke for a long time."

"But as a manager working for the Disputants," says Morgan the Pelagian, "you'll be helping your fellow human beings along the road to moral perfection."

Michael shrugs apologetically. "I'd rather wrestle. I mean, I'm flattered and I appreciate the offer, and as a wrestler I'll do everything I'm supposed to, but I don't want to give up being Marduk just yet. I'm too young to help anybody along the road to moral perfection. I'm nobody special. For years I've denied being a wrestler. I've felt guilty about it. But what I've felt most guilty about is that I like it. I like the action, I like the attention. Even if you signed me up as a bad guy I wouldn't care. Hero or villain—it's the muscle I like, not the meaning."

"What about Rose White?" asks the Master of Ceremonies.

"I'll find her without you," says Michael. "I mean, I'm on the right track and I've got people helping me." He feels uncomfortable about this claim, for he doesn't wish to explain about Deep Rat. Michael has no clear reason for this: it's just a guilty feeling. "Anyway, freedom from myself would also mean losing Rose White. I've given this a lot of thought, all this stuff about transcending the self. I don't want to be free from myself or escape myself. I don't want to become just idea. I want Rose White, I want to marry her. I'll find her by myself."

"And just who is helping you?" asks the Master of Ceremonies as he sets his teacup on a small table. They are drinking herb tea and there is a smell of peppermint in the air.

"Some people, that's all. We've been getting closer and closer." Again Michael experiences the guilty feeling.

"And why was she kidnapped?" asks Augustine.

"I don't have that clear yet. Probably somebody is trying to get even with me. Envy, isn't that what causes sin? Or is it pride? Anyway, she was kidnapped for one of those reasons."

"What if she was kidnapped out of love?" asks the Master of Ceremonies.

"That doesn't make sense to me. Bad's bad and good's good. All this talk about the God in the Book of Job. I've never even read it! All I want is to find Rose White, settle down and wrestle. Is that so complicated? I just want to be Michael Marmaduke."

Michael sits in a leather chair and he holds out his hands to the three men. He thinks he is asking a simple question with an obvious answer. In the country of Philosophy, he feels that Tautology is a nice town in which to live. Common sense will tell them that Michael Marmaduke is Michael Marmaduke. But is Michael on Tuesday the same as Michael on Friday? Look at how he has changed in the week we have known him. If we described to Michael what he had been like standing outside F.A.O. Schwarz holding a big talking bear, he wouldn't believe us. Already he has rewritten his past. For instance, ask about that night on Cape Cod when he proposed marriage to Rose White with Morse-code signals tapped on the motel wall. Already he has a different story. Not completely different, of course, but it's a story in which he plays a bigger part. "Marry me!" is what his new memory tells him he said, not "Will you marry me?" or "Please, please, will you marry me?" In all his memories of himself Michael has become more aggressive. Isn't it great how we go through life thinking we are on a straight and unchanging path? If there is a psychological wrinkle or some unhappiness, it is from too much coffee or too little sleep or perhaps we are getting a cold or a toothache or our period, but soon we will once again resume our undeviating course. We are like people lost in a snowstorm who feel we are traveling in a straight line but we keep coming upon blurry tracks that look a little like our own, but they can't be, right? They must belong to that person just up ahead and we must hurry to reach him, soon we will be safe, and oh look, he has been joined by someone else. Hurry faster, hurry faster!

"Traditionally," says Augustine, "there's no one as credible as Satan. If language for the rest of us is a bewitchment of our intelligence, then for Satan it is elementary. After all, he invented it. Language is the net in which we find ourselves caught. Satan is the fisherman. We use language thinking we are approaching the truth—after all, this makes sense and that is perfectly logical—but we wander deeper into perplexity. That's why the study of grammar was once thought to be Satanic, why the word 'grammar' is so close to 'grimoire,' which is a book of spells. At one point in history, the most plausible argument, the most plausible figure, the most plausible path was also the most distrusted. Plausibility was simply another of Satan's tricks."

"I still think I can find Rose White," says Michael.

"How will you recognize her?" asks the Master of Ceremonies. "She might be different. Even you might be different."

"Look, I appreciate your offer, but I'm just not ready to become a manager. Once I've found Rose White, then maybe we can talk again. I mean, I'm young, I've got plenty of time."

"Pride," says Augustine. "It wasn't envy that caused Satan to fall, but pride."

Augustine, the Master of Ceremonies and Morgan all look at Michael a little sadly. Although each has a slightly different interpretation of the problem, they understand that Michael's assessment is too naive. He sees himself as solid and as unchanging as stone. They see him as mutable as smoke. But perhaps they are

oversensitized to mutability. After all, despite the excellent philosophical reasons which led them to become Disputants, there were
also psychological reasons which influenced them in thinking that
transcendence and jettisoning the human personality was a smart
course of action.

And Morgan the Pelagian asks himself whether they weren't
mistaken about Michael's gentleness, or perhaps Michael is growing away from it. In any case, the attribute which they had sought
in a wrestling manager seems to be Michael's no longer.

The detective Philip Kyd sits in his car, an old Chrysler, on a street
off Bowery. It is about ten o'clock Friday night. The weather has
turned cold and he wishes he could start the car and turn on the
heater, but he doesn't want to attract attention. He is staking out
a doorway and trying to read by the light of the streetlight at the
same time. This is what he is reading:

"French said: 'It's like this with us, baby. We're coppers and
everybody hates our guts. And if we didn't have enough trouble,
we have to have you. As if we didn't get pushed around enough by
guys in the corner offices, the City Hall gang, the day chief, the
night chief, the Chamber of Commerce, His Honor the Mayor in
his paneled office four times as big as the three lousy rooms the
whole homicide staff has to work out of. As if we didn't have to
handle one hundred and fourteen homicides last year out of three
rooms that don't have enough chairs for the whole duty squad to
sit down at once. We spend our lives turning over dirty underwear
and sniffing rotten teeth. We go up dark stairways to get a gun
punk with a skinful of hop and sometimes we don't get all the way
up, and our wives wait dinner that night and all the other nights.
We don't come home anymore. And nights we do come home, we
come home so goddamn tired we can't eat or sleep or even read the
lies the papers print about us. So we lie awake in the dark in a
cheap house on a cheap street and listen to the drunks down the
block having fun. And just about the time we drop off the phone
rings and we get up and start all over again. Nothing we do is
right, not ever. Not once. If we get a confession, we beat it out of
a guy, they say, and some shyster calls us Gestapo in court and

sneers at us when we muddle our grammar. If we make a mistake they put us back in uniform on Skid Row and we spend the nice cool summer evenings picking drunks out of the gutter and being yelled at by whores and taking knives away from greaseballs in zoot suits. But all that ain't enough to make us entirely happy. We got to have you.'"

Philip Kyd wishes he could climb into his book and close the covers behind him. What's the point of real life? What's the point of all this uncertainty and insecurity and mystery? Philip Kyd likes that Ray Bradbury novel where people become books and he'd like to become one too. So what if a book isn't reality; what's so hot about reality? People become murderers and poets and assholes and crazy. Why not be a book? Why not enter a life where everything is settled already? So what if there are no surprises; at least there is plenty of style, lots of class. It would be like being a Gothic cathedral: everything known but everything nice to look at. Philip Kyd is aware of places like El Instituto Estético where you can be turned into anything from a goat to a gorilla. But their big problem is they can't turn you into a book: a book is the kernel without the chaff, it's the ultimate Gimmick. And if his lucky two-headed coin could grant him a wish, then he'd become a book in no time.

At that moment Philip Kyd sees Mr. Roskommen's daughters— Betty, Loulou and Phoebe—hurry into the building he is watching. All three have bright red hair and it peeks from beneath their white scarves. Under their coats, they are wearing long white gowns. Other people have also gone in and they too have been wearing white gowns, even the men. Philip Kyd is wearing a white gown as well and doesn't like it. He feels that the hero of his favorite books would not wear such a gown. He feels if he were a book, he would not have to put up with such foolishness.

Philip Kyd climbs out of his Chrysler, leaving his book, pipe and fedora on the front seat. Locking the car, he draws a white scarf over his head. He wears his pants under the white gown and the cuffs are rolled up. His lucky two-headed coin is in his coat pocket and he keeps turning it over with his thumb and forefinger. He wonders if it was a smart idea to leave his gun at home.

Kyd takes the freight elevator to the fifth floor, which is the top. He tries to think of parts of his favorite books, but anxiety keeps his mind a blank. Only one phrase comes to mind: "Dead men are heavier than broken hearts." This doesn't make him feel better. The elevator door slides open. He sees the loogan up the hall to the left. Actually, Philip Kyd isn't sure if the loogan has a gun or if he's really a loogan. The guy is about six feet six, four hundred pounds, wears a tiger skin, holds a club with a couple of spikes poking through it and probably doesn't need a gun. The books that Philip Kyd reads don't have such monsters, and again he considers the deficiencies of reality. In reality there is no control, no rules, and nothing has to be probable. If reality wants to be a mishmash, it can be a mishmash. What's the point of it? Philip Kyd walks toward the door taking shallow little breaths and trying to look relaxed.

"Better hurry," says the giant in a friendly voice. "They're about to begin."

"Thanks," says Kyd, opening the door. Before him is a large candle-lit space. Figures in white sway back and forth, some together, some separate. He hears the sound of a single drum—tum, tum, tum. Removing his raincoat, Philip Kyd leaves it on a pile of coats by the door. He holds the lucky coin in his hand, then plucks at the fabric of his white gown and sighs. It's hard to be a tough guy in a dress. Somewhere a goat is bleating.

We have observed this scene before but for Philip Kyd it is new and none of it is pleasant. As the door closes behind him a tambourine gives a sinister metallic rattle. The room seems without walls. About thirty women and a few men are spread across it, swaying to the rhythm of the drum. The faces of the women are powdered and look ghostly. Now a second, higher drum begins: tem, tem, tem. The candles flicker in their brass candlesticks. Philip Kyd moves forward. He feels his left pant leg slipping down and he bends over to roll it up. A streamer of ivy brushes across his face, making him shiver. As he moves along the side of the room he too begins to sway to the music, but the music is nothing he likes. Sometimes Philip Kyd dances the fox-trot, sometimes he dances the waltz, but he never does anything crazy like this. A third drum begins, a higher one—tim, tim, tim—and the speed increases. Philip Kyd wishes he could see the far wall but there are just distant shadows. He wonders if there is another way out. Ahead of him is a white goat with a golden collar tied to a white column. The goat looks nervous. Philip Kyd pauses to pat its head. "Brother, it's even worse than I expected." The goat shies away. At the top of the column is the mask of a bearded man with great black circles for eyes. Philip Kyd feels it staring at him but he knows that is not possible. It's just a creepy mask. He keeps turning the golden coin over between his fingers. His pant leg begins unrolling again. Bowls of wine and baskets of fruit stand on the floor by the column.

The squeal of a flute rising to a scream sends the hairs on the back of Philip Kyd's neck into a little dance of panic. Now a second flute joins the first. Kyd can see several women with tambourines—one of them is Mr. Roskommen's daughter Phoebe—but he can't see the drums or flutes. A tall black-haired woman circles near him and Kyd feels she is eyeing him suspiciously. He closes his eyes and tries to appear caught up by the music. He spins round and round, getting dizzy. He feels his pant leg sliding down his calf. He has only been a detective for six months and if it is going to lead him into jams like this, then he's going to recheck his options. Maybe he should have moved to L.A. and tried to get an office in the old Cahuenga Building like his hero. But maybe there wasn't any Cahuenga Building. Maybe there had been no Cahuenga Building in the first place.

The flutes slide up and down the register with no attempt to play any real songs. More people have begun dancing. They dance with arms outstretched, spinning and spinning, or they dip and turn, or they hold their hands high above their heads and whirl. In fact, they dance in all sorts of ways but none of it looks like the fox-trot. Their feet make a whispering noise on the wooden floor. Philip Kyd stays near the side, turning and trying not to get dizzy. He also tries to avoid the tall dark-haired woman who weaves between the others. While most of the dancers stay more or less in one place, the tall woman covers the whole floor. Sometimes she reaches out to touch someone, letting her hand trail across a shoulder or touch a cheek. She looks like trouble to Philip Kyd. The whole place looks like trouble. What he is afraid of would be hard to articulate, but it has to do with things out of control. No speed limits anymore, is how Philip Kyd puts it to himself. All he wants to do is keep an eye on Roskommen's three crazy daughters and stay cool. No wonder they wear out their shoes if they hang out in such crazy places.

More people are coming from someplace, so Philip Kyd knows there must be another door. Shortly, he finds a dressing room heaped with jackets and raincoats. There are briefcases, hats, blouses, neckties, bras, jewelry, scarves, pin-striped suits—all the usual clothing and accessories of daily life. At the far end of the dressing room is a flight of stairs. Satisfied at having found a second exit, Kyd returns to the dance floor.

The dancing has gotten faster and the dancers are swirling so quickly that they almost become one dancer or that all the dancers have come to look like each other. Still, the tall black-haired woman links them together. Philip Kyd tries to avoid her but it's hard because she moves quickly. The music is so loud and the scraping of the black slippers is so noisy that Philip Kyd feels he could shout and no one would hear him.

But suddenly he hears a woman's scream and after a moment he sees a new dancer wearing a red gown which is open at the top, exposing her breasts. She is not dancing but staggering and whenever she seems about to fall to the floor one of the other dancers lifts her up for a few steps. The new dancer wears the mask of a golden bull with a snout and two horns. She is tall and frail-looking and her hands are long and delicate. She keeps trying to remove the mask from her face but she can't and again she cries out. Philip Kyd moves toward her for a closer look. The tall, black-haired woman has disappeared. The new dancer falls again and two other dancers pull her roughly to her feet.

The music gets faster. Philip Kyd is several yards from the new dancer. Again she falls and is hauled to her feet. A deep drum begins to beat—thrumm, thrumm—and another masked figure appears among the dancers. At first Kyd finds her familiar, but then he realizes it is someone wearing the mask of the bearded man that had hung on the pillar. The dancer with the mask of the bearded man swirls past Philip Kyd, reaching out a white hand and scratching Kyd's cheek. Philip Kyd pulls back and touches his cheek. When he looks at his fingers, he sees blood.

The dancer with the mask of a bearded man spins toward the

masked dancer in the red gown and bangs into her, knocking her aside. Several dancers lift her up again. A second time the dancer with the mask of a bearded man knocks into her, knocking her down. This time Philip Kyd helps her to her feet, drawing her away, but still dancing, still spinning around. Other dancers bump into them, not brushing against them, but hitting them. The dancer with the mask of the bearded man appears before them and again bangs against the dancer with the red gown.

But look, the mask of the golden bull has been knocked off and slides across the floor. The woman in the red gown is bald, or perhaps there is a light fuzz on her scalp. Her white face is very delicate. There is something both familiar and strange about it. Philip Kyd stares at her. On both sides of her face and along the jaw are rows of black stitches. Philip Kyd knows the face, he has seen it hundreds of times. He has stopped dancing and hardly feels the other dancers who bump against him.

The dancer with the mask of the bearded man again knocks into the woman in the red gown, knocking her down. But this time Philip Kyd runs forward and picks her up, not to set her on her feet but to put her over his shoulder. He heaves her up and starts for the dressing-room door, not dancing, but running.

For the briefest moment the other dancers come to a stop, amazed. Philip Kyd runs across the floor with the woman over his shoulder. He knows who she is and he knows he will save her. Now the other dancers recover themselves and try to stop him, but being tough is what tough guy detectives do best. He straight-arms someone and slugs someone else. Reaching the dressing room, he slams the door behind him. The woman over his shoulder is sobbing and panting. Just as Philip Kyd reaches the stairway, the dressing-room door is yanked open and he sees the dancer with the mask of the bearded man. Philip Kyd hurries down the stairs, holding tight to the woman over his shoulder to keep her from bouncing. Footsteps echo in the stairway. Kyd passes the fourth-floor landing. The woman keeps slipping and he has to shift her weight. The dancer with the mask of the bearded man is getting closer. Kyd passes the third-floor landing. His hand holding the gold coin slides along the railing. The bearded man is only a few steps behind him. Philip Kyd hears his breath.

At the second-floor landing, Kyd turns slightly, holds up the gold coin, then flicks it backward just as he leaps down the stairs. There is a pause. The bearded man has stopped to pick up the coin. Philip Kyd reaches the door and throws it open. An emergency horn begins to blow. Kyd finds himself in an alley next to the building. He runs to the street and turns left to where his car is parked. Unlocking the door, he throws the woman in back, then jumps in front and starts the engine. He pulls into traffic just as the other dancers appear at the mouth of the alley. Philip Kyd heads across town toward the Holland Tunnel. He intends to get out of New York altogether. Maybe he can find a quiet place in New Jersey. He'll call Mr. Roskommen and warn him about that nutsy dance place.

The woman in the backseat has passed out. Kyd flips on the heater in case she's cold. He makes a few turns, to see if he is being followed, then drives to Canal Street. Traffic is piled up at the tunnel. Kyd decides to get gas on the other side and head for Atlantic City. The woman needs rest. She must have recently been operated on, something was done to her face, although it doesn't look too bad now. As he waits in traffic, Philip Kyd turns in his seat to get another look. Even bald, he recognizes her. It's General Sternwood's daughter, the older one, Vivian Regan, although in the movie of *The Big Sleep* she is called Vivian Sternwood. Philip Kyd feels he has been searching for her all his life. He feels he has gone into a book and found the world on the other side. He will live there now and everything will be okay. He won't even have to be a detective anymore.

The woman opens her eyes and looks at him. "Who are you?" she asks. "What happened?"

"We got away. Don't worry, I'll take care of you."

"I don't even know who I am," she says.

"You're Vivian Regan. I've known you since I was a child," says Philip Kyd as he drives into the tunnel. "I've seen the movie a hundred times. You don't have to worry ever again."

34

RAZOR WIRE

Somewhere between Friday night and Saturday morning it begins to sleet and the wind picks up. Men and women leaving the bars noisily scrape the ice from their windshields. Cars fishtail as they turn the corners and sidewalks grow treacherous. The branches in Central Park collect a thin layer of ice. They glitter and rattle in the glare of the streetlights; sometimes a branch breaks from the weight. It is very late or very early, depending on one's point of view. The wind careens down the avenues and in a few blustery locations the sleet flies sideways. The muggers feel sorry for themselves. Whores regret their miniskirts. Cops nap fitfully in overheated squad cars.

The sleet attaches itself to the sides of buildings, making them shimmer. The patina of ice covering the great apartment houses along Central Park West—the Century, the Majestic, the Dakota, the San Remo, the Kenilworth—transforms their turrets and towers from stone to glistening crystal. Let's look at one of them. See up there near the roof, say around the thirtieth floor? See that thing swaying up there? What could it be? Let's get a little closer. See that rope coming out of one of the windows in the turret? And there's another. Who is that man climbing down the first rope?

Not a gorilla this time. Look, it's Michael Marmaduke. We know he doesn't like heights. He must be scared to death. Above him on another rope is Thrombosis and next to him on a third is Dentata. And who is that just climbing out of the turret? It's Deep Rat.

If we focus on Michael's face, we can see he doesn't look happy. But this might be true of anybody hanging from a rope at the twenty-eighth floor of a building in a sleet storm at two o'clock in the morning. When Michael looks down he sees only a shiny blur. Bits of sleet sting his face. He wears gloves and running shoes and dark sweatpants and a dark sweatshirt with a hood. He tries to walk down the side of the building, holding the rope, but his feet keep slipping on the ice, which means that he bumps into the building with his shoulder, which makes him slide down a couple of feet until he can get his shoes wrapped around the rope. None of this is nice. But look more deeply into his face. Beneath the unhappiness resides a kind of pleasure. He hates heights, has always hated heights, and here he is sliding down a rope toward a balcony two stories below him. Along with his terror, Michael feels pretty good about himself. Even if he falls, he will feel satisfaction that he took the chance, faced his fear and climbed down the rope anyway. He'll be happy for most of his long tumble through the air, and when he starts to worry, it will be too late. Bam! He'll be just a memory in other people's heads. Climbing down this rope, Michael no longer feels like an actor with a Gimmick. He feels he's taken charge of his life and has no fear, or at least not an inordinate amount.

The one who is afraid is Deep Rat. He knows that if Michael falls, then he, Deep Rat, will have his hands turned to mush. Maybe Thrombosis and Dentata also have anxiety. When they agreed to help Michael they hadn't known it would mean climbing down the outside of a building in bad weather. However, they had already talked to Liquidity, Cashback and the Prime brothers; they knew about Troll, Taurus and Great Father Snake; and they understood that whatever they ended up doing with Michael would play havoc with their adrenaline. Really, Michael, Thrombosis and Dentata are in no danger unless they panic or a rope breaks or the ice gets worse. They spend hours every day working on their muscles and a climb like this is a piece of cake. The little survival creature that hides in their brains and makes their knees tremble is terrified, but the rest of them is doing all right.

Around nine o'clock that night Michael got home from the Hall of the Disputants to find a message to call Deep Rat. That day was the first since Monday that he had returned to his condo at Number One University Place. He saw no point in hiding from reporters anymore. If he didn't want to talk to them, he'd tell them to beat it. Several were hanging around, and that's what he did: "Beat it," he said. "I don't have anything to say." Later when he came home again he found more reporters. "I don't have time to talk to you," he said. "Get lost!" He was surprised how simple it was.

Then he called Deep Rat.

"You ever hear of the Pseudo-Marduk?" Deep Rat asked.

"Who?"

"Pseudo-Marduk—he's not a wrestler but he lives like a wrestler, twenty-four hours a day he lives like a wrestler. He lives like Marduk the Magnificent. He's got Rose White. He ordered the Plexiglas coffin. He's the one who had her snatched in the first place. And if he thinks she's going to be rescued, he'll throw her out the window."

"The Pseudo-Marduk?"

"We'll need some help. Is there anyone you can call?"

There was more. Equipment was discussed. Meeting places were arranged. Risks, inconceivable on Monday, were coolly evaluated. Fears, which would have been paralyzing on Tuesday, were examined and set aside. All that came and went like water down a river. How quickly does the impossible become possible. How fast does the monstrous become commonplace. The intervening hours slid by, and now, at two o'clock Saturday morning, Michael is hanging from a rope about twenty-seven stories above Central Park West, and beneath his trepidation, he feels a little smug.

Ten feet above him on another rope Thrombosis considers his weight of three hundred pounds and calculates the chances of the rope breaking. Sometimes in the summer he goes climbing in the Catskills, but it has never occurred to him to climb down a building in a sleet storm in the dead of night. "Dumb fuck, dumb fuck," is what he keeps saying to himself. And he thinks how his girlfriend would ask, "Sheee-it, man, whatchu doin?" And he might say, "Helpin a white brother," but even that seems like a weak response. They are sneaking down to rescue Rose White from the Pseudo-Marduk, and if the Pseudo-Marduk knew they were coming, he would toss Rose White out the window. Thrombosis has heard of the Pseudo-Marduk. He used to hang out at the Blood Factory but he wasn't happy just chatting with folks, he wanted to smack people. He wanted to be Marduk the Magnificent in action. So he was asked not to come back. And what does the Pseudo-Marduk look like? He looks exactly like Marduk the Magnificent except he wears contact lenses (El Instituto Estético couldn't fix his eyes) and so he squints a lot.

Not far from Thrombosis, Dentata isn't thinking much of anything. The rope is no problem and she doesn't mind heights. Fear as an activity is something Dentata gave up after becoming Dentata. What she has is curiosity. She too has heard of the Pseudo-Marduk and she finds it plausible that he might have snatched Rose White, but she thinks the police should have been called. It is not that Dentata minds rescuing Rose White to do Michael a favor, but it's not part of her normal job description. She believes the police could have rescued Rose White equally well and what interests her most is Michael's decision to be a hero. This is not a Michael she knows and she is not sure how she feels about it. She hasn't seen him for a week and she feels she hardly recognizes him, but that seems impossible. Yet when she met him outside the China Club thirty minutes ago, she felt he was different. He signed some autographs, said no to a few people and they hurried off through the sleet toward Central Park West as he described Deep Rat's plan. If Dentata has a big question, it concerns Deep Rat. Who is he and why is he helping Michael? Why doesn't he stand up straight? Why doesn't he look her in the eye? Why does she have a compelling desire to hurt him? She sees Deep Rat sliding down a rope ten feet above her and she is impressed by how easily he does it, as if he had been running up and down ropes his entire life.

Twenty feet below, Michael wonders if what he feels so intensely is life or the illusion of life. In the way that drugs or alcohol can create the illusion of wisdom, maybe danger can create the illusion of living. On the other hand, maybe this is really life and maybe Michael is living it to the fullest, or at least this is what he hopes. Ten feet beneath him a balcony juts from the side of the building. This belongs to the Pseudo-Marduk, who has a large condominium.

No telling who the Pseudo-Marduk used to be, other than a wrestling fan. He had a lot of money, he didn't have to work and so he made himself into the Pseudo-Marduk, just like there are a lot of Pseudo-Elvises and Pseudo–Richard Nixons and Pseudo–Hulk Hogans. For every famous personality there exists his duplicate who takes great pride in the duplicity. The big difference with the Pseudo-Marduk is that he takes it more seriously. It's his life's work. He is huge, he is strong and he likes to wrestle. And now he's got Michael Marmaduke's fiancée in a glass box.

Michael's feet touch the balcony's ice-covered balustrade. Lowering himself onto the floor of the balcony, he almost regrets that his descent is over. He wishes he could call up old friends, who know of his fear of heights, and tell them about it. He has half a desire to climb back up and do it again.

Thrombosis slides down beside him. "You okay, man?"

"I feel great," says Michael. "Not even cold."

Dentata comes down next. She doesn't even seem out of breath. She looks into Michael's face, studying it until he becomes uncomfortable. Deep Rat slides onto the balcony, then crouches down and shakes himself. He turns to the double doors and tries the handle. The doors are locked. Through the glass he sees a darkened room. The wind gusts around them and Thrombosis moves into the shelter of the balcony. Michael is sweating. He pushes back the hood of his sweatshirt. His blond hair lies in damp ringlets across his head.

Deep Rat has his head pressed to the glass.

"What do you see?" whispers Dentata.

"Candlelight," he says. "And a glass coffin."

Michael ducks down to look as well. He sees a large room, perhaps twenty-five feet across, and in the center on a trestle is a glass coffin. Maybe it's Plexiglas. Surrounding the coffin are circles of razor wire. Two burning candles in tall candelabra send their light skittering across the wire, making it sparkle. Someone is lying in the coffin. The light from the candles shines on the person's skin and blond hair. "It's Rose White!" says Michael. He realizes he hasn't thought they would find her. Maybe they would find another videotape, but Rose White herself seemed an impossible expectation.

Thrombosis ducks down to look through the window. "Sure is somebody in there," he says. "How we gonna get this open?"

"Break it," says Deep Rat.

"No problem," says Thrombosis and he begins to lean against the double glass doors.

"Do it fast," says Deep Rat, "so we can get inside before the Pseudo-Marduk knows we're here."

"What if he has a gun?" asks Dentata.

Deep Rat makes a snuffling noise which Dentata understands to be laughter. "People like the Pseudo-Marduk don't need guns."

"Here we go," says Thrombosis. He pushes hard. There is the noise of wood splintering, glass breaking. The four of them tumble into the room. Michael runs to the razor wire. At first he thought he could jump over it but the coils are too high and thick. The wire will have to be cut or pulled aside, and they have already made a lot of noise.

Thrombosis glances around. The room is nearly empty except for the coffin. But there are statues and pictures, some wooden benches and wall hangings. All of it looks like the Middle Eastern stuff that Michael uses for his Gimmick: Babylonian stuff, Hittite stuff. Odd, thinks Thrombosis. But before he can think anymore, the lights go on and the music begins.

It is always difficult to be on top of the description when the action starts. Everything happens at once, and of course it cannot be told that way. First this event, then that event—it's a real nuisance. The lights are spotlights set in the ceiling. They make no noise when they go on, but they are so bright that their very brightness seems like a noise. The music is Aaron Copland's "Fanfare for the Common Man." This is Marduk the Magnificent's theme music and it is played whenever he enters the ring. Michael, Thrombosis and Dentata register this fact at the same instant and each finds the music ominous and disturbing. These three stand near the razor wire. Deep Rat is back by the balcony near some heavy drapes decorated with Egyptian figures.

Although the light and music are astonishing, they are absorbed in the greater astonishment surrounding what happens next. Three people suddenly spring into an archway on the other side of the room: two men and a woman.

One of the men is Marduk the Magnificent; worse, he is Marduk in the full regalia of his Gimmick: white linen over which is a white robe that seems to have been dipped in blood. Written across the robe are the words "King of Kings." The man's face is powdered white and around his eyes are many shades of red, silver and gold so that his eyes seem to burn like flame. In his blond hair is a diamond-studded crown with strange writing. Marduk holds a short sword between his teeth. He wears ruby rings and gold bracelets. Tattooed on one bare leg are the words "King of Kings" in red letters. The other leg says "Faithful and True" in black letters. In his hands he holds the key to the abyss and an enormous gold chain.

Thrombosis, who helps dress Marduk before each match, is impressed. The bone structure, straight nose, square chin—this could be Michael's twin brother. The only difference is this guy squints a lot, but his eyes are the same shade of light blue.

Behind the Pseudo-Marduk is a huge black man dressed as Nasamon the Nubian Giant wearing golden robes with a golden turban containing a single star in the center of his forehead. He carries Marduk's weapons: a silver bow and a quiver of silver arrows, a silver club, several lightning bolts and the silver net which is held by the four winds.

Thrombosis is relieved that while this big fellow is dressed exactly like his Gimmick, his face is not Thrombosis's face. Maybe the guy could be a cousin: big round face, big splat of a nose. Nor does the woman, dressed as Nemesis the Goddess of Retribution with golden robes and a silver crown of stars, really look like Dentata, although she has a similar brooding quality.

Still, Thrombosis feels he would rather not have encountered this threesome. They are big and ready to wrestle. Thrombosis considers this paradox: that the three true wrestlers are not wrestlers at all, they are only actors, while the three fake wrestlers look pretty tough.

Dentata moves up beside Michael. She feels the evening has

been raised to a level of seriousness that she did not foresee. She wouldn't mind kicking that black guy in the balls, but she guesses she'll have to tackle the woman and she doesn't like wrestling women. She doesn't have anything against them: they're just women.

Michael stares at the Pseudo-Marduk. Does he really look like this? Of course he has seen videos of himself but nothing so realistic. The Pseudo-Marduk wears silver elf boots and Michael wonders if he has scars on his ankles. He thinks how handsome the other man is, how godlike, just like the Gimmick says he is supposed to look. Instead of anxiety, Michael feels anticipation. He takes another step toward the razor wire. Rose White wears a white gown and lies on her back with her hands folded over her breast. She is so pale that Michael would think she was dead except that there are air holes in the side of the coffin and he can see the rise and fall of her breasts.

"That's my fiancée," says Michael. "I want her back."

The Pseudo-Marduk takes a microphone and speaks into it: "Come, let us gather for a great banquet! Let us feast on the flesh of kings, of commanders, of mighty men, of horses and their riders, on the flesh of every one, free and slave, great and small!" Again Copland's fanfare bursts from a hundred speakers. The Pseudo-Marduk throws off his cape and his crown; he removes his rings and bracelets and championship belt. The Pseudo-Nasamon and Pseudo-Nemesis also remove their robes. The Pseudo-Marduk takes the sword from between his teeth and drops it onto his robes. He will wrestle without it.

For the first time Michael wonders if he should have called the police. Now it is too late. Thrombosis pushes past Michael. "I can take care of this," he says. "You stay put."

Thrombosis jogs around the razor wire toward the Pseudo-Marduk. When Thrombosis jogs, the floor shakes. He breaks into a run. Now watch closely. The Pseudo-Marduk runs forward four or five steps, flings himself up and kicks Thrombosis soundly in the chest and chin. No loud drumbeat accompanies this blow to suggest physical contact, the actual physical contact is loud enough. Thrombosis falls like big trees fall. He falls like the fall of night.

Dentata hurtles past Michael like a thrown spear. She leaps through the air at the Pseudo-Marduk with her kung-fu hands and karate feet ready to dismember and liquefy. The Pseudo-Marduk snatches her out of the air as if she were no more than a beach ball. He squeezes her and drops her. Dentata lies on the rug and does not move.

"Well," says Michael Marmaduke, hoping to lighten the mood with a little talk. But again he feels divided, torn between trepidation and exhilaration. He tries to think of what he knows about wrestling, but his knowledge consists of showmanship and illusion. He strips off his sweatshirt and the T-shirt beneath it. He kicks off his shoes and removes his sweatpants so that he is down to his navy-blue JC Penney jockey shorts. He puts his hands on his hips and walks back and forth before the Pseudo-Marduk. "Well!" he says again.

"Cast off the works of darkness and put on the armor of light!" roars the Pseudo-Marduk. "Sit at my right hand until I make of your enemies your footstool!"

Michael walks slowly forward. Not even in grade school was he a fighter, not even in kindergarten. He thinks that he has never bopped anybody for real in his entire life. Abruptly the Pseudo-Marduk rushes toward him. The men grab each other around the waist and squeeze. The Pseudo-Marduk's face is only inches from Michael's and he is grinning benignly. Michael is lifted off the floor and thrown. He hits the wall and slides down it. There is something sobering about physical pain. In its presence illusions retreat. Is it too late to become a Disputant? But no, we won't think like this.

Michael gets up and limps back toward the Pseudo-Marduk, who swings at him. Michael blocks his arm, then kicks the Pseudo-Marduk in the leg. Before Michael can jump away, the Pseudo-Marduk grabs his foot and throws him onto his back. Michael rolls aside as the other man leaps at him. The Pseudo-Marduk grins happily and grabs Michael again, squeezing him. Michael chops down on his neck but he is again lifted off his feet and thrown. Again he hits the wall and slides down it. The earlier pain, which seemed intense, has been surpassed.

Across the room both of his friends are being beaten. He looks for Deep Rat but there is no sign of him. If he looked carefully, however, he might see the tips of Deep Rat's black shoes poking out from under the drapes. But Michael has no time to look carefully. The Pseudo-Marduk is loping toward him in a cheerful sort of way. He is immensely happy. To wrestle Michael Marmaduke has been his greatest wish. His arms are outstretched and his fingers wriggle like little tentacles. Michael flings a chair in his path. The Pseudo-Marduk trips on the chair and falls. Michael tries to kick him in the head, but the Pseudo-Marduk grabs his foot and yanks it from underneath him so he tumbles to the rug. He tries to roll away but the Pseudo-Marduk is on top of him. Michael chops at his windpipe and gets free.

Michael stands by the drapes breathing heavily. The Pseudo-Marduk gets to his feet, grinning. Michael realizes that the other man is just having fun. He's not even trying. He wants the whole nasty process to last as long as it can, simply because he enjoys it. As for Michael, his body hurts and he is exhausted. The exhilaration which he felt earlier has been replaced by dread. Then Michael feels someone poke him. It is Deep Rat, hiding behind the drapes.

"What is your greatest weakness as a wrestler?"

"My weakness as a wrestler," says Michael, "is that I'm not a wrestler."

"Not that weakness," says Deep Rat. "The other one."

Before Michael can ask any more, the Pseudo-Marduk comes toward him in his cheerful hungry manner. He is blond, handsome and if it weren't for his squint, he would have a lot of people fooled, including Michael himself. Michael ducks to the side and tries to kick out. The Pseudo-Marduk bats his leg away. Michael swings a fist at him. The Pseudo-Marduk bats his hand away. Michael rushes at him, hoping to knock the other man down. The Pseudo-Marduk grabs him and squeezes him.

"Oh, you're hurting me!" shouts Michael.

The Pseudo-Marduk immediately lets him go.

Michael jumps back. That's my weakness in the ring, he thinks. I can't stand to see the other guy get hurt.

Michael again leaps at the Pseudo-Marduk, who easily grabs him and lifts him up. "Ow! Ow! Ow!" shouts Michael.

The Pseudo-Marduk drops him like a hot coal. As Michael's feet hit the rug, he hauls off and punches the Pseudo-Marduk in the chin so he staggers back.

Look at Michael crouched down and cunning. He has lied, he has caused pain, he is aggressive. He wants to hurt the Pseudo-Marduk, but hurting the Pseudo-Marduk isn't like hurting another person; it's like hurting himself, which isn't so bad. Michael wants to beat him. He wants to win. He wants to grab Rose White and get out of here. Across the room, he sees Dentata staring at him with a mixture of wonder and hostility. She has not seen him like this before. But we're not done yet. Michael has still more surprises.

As for the Pseudo-Marduk, he rubs his jaw and looks not so cheerful. The paint on his legs saying "Faithful and True" and "King of Kings" has smeared. The flamelike eye makeup has smudged.

"You're not Marduk," says Michael. "How come you squint in that funny way? I bet you don't have any scars on your ankles either. You're just a joke!"

The Pseudo-Marduk makes a roaring noise and runs at Michael, who jumps out of the way and trips him with a leg kick so that he falls to the floor and rolls. The Pseudo-Marduk isn't quite so confident and begins making mistakes. He starts squinting and blinking more. He rubs his ankles, where he doesn't have any blemishes of any kind. Michael backs toward the wall next to a straight chair. More slowly the Pseudo-Marduk comes after him. Michael tries to push him away but he is not strong enough. The Pseudo-Marduk grabs him around the waist and squeezes, lifting Michael off the floor.

"Oh, you're hurting me!" cries Michael. "It hurts a lot!"

The Pseudo-Marduk pauses. This is a difficult philosophical moment for him. Marduk the Magnificent is notorious for his soft heart, and if the Pseudo-Marduk ignores this cry of pain, then he will have failed to meet a major criterion of Marduk's Gimmick. In the midst of being more Marduk than Marduk, the Pseudo-Marduk, by ignoring Michael's cry, will cease to be Marduk.

"Ow, ow!" cries Michael.

The Pseudo-Marduk drops him and jumps back. In that instant

Michael grabs the straight chair and smashes it down on the Pseudo-Marduk's head so that he falls to his knees.

"Michael!" calls Dentata.

"Hit 'em again!" says Deep Rat. "Hit 'em again!"

Michael hits the Pseudo-Marduk again so the chair breaks to pieces.

"Kill 'em, kill 'em!" says Deep Rat.

Michael smacks the Pseudo-Marduk with the broken leg of the chair. The Pseudo-Marduk rolls onto his belly. There is blood on his forehead. Michael jumps on the other man's back, hitting his knees against the man's shoulders, knocking the wind out of him. Immediately, Deep Rat runs to his side. He slaps the floor. "One!" He slaps it again. "Two!" He slaps it a third time. "The winner! Michael Marmaduke!" He raises Michael's arm. The Pseudo-Marduk continues to lie on the floor. He is barely conscious and very unhappy.

Michael runs over toward Thrombosis and Dentata, who are still struggling with the Pseudo-Nasamon and the Pseudo-Nemesis.

"Let's go," says Michael. "Let's finish them off!"

The Pseudo-Nasamon holds up his hands. "Not me, man. I'm just getting an hourly wage. I'm done." He backs to the door. The Pseudo-Nemesis looks nervously at Michael and runs after the Pseudo-Nasamon. Up close she doesn't look a thing like Dentata.

Michael helps Thrombosis to his feet. "You okay?"

"When I get black-and-blue marks, they don't show," says Thrombosis. "You kill that guy?"

"Not that I noticed." Michael turns toward Dentata, who is sitting on the floor. He reaches out a hand and she ignores it, getting to her feet without his help.

"You hurt him," she says. "You took advantage of him and hurt him."

"He was hurting me," says Michael. He feels strange, as if just waking up after an operation. He likes how he feels.

"But he's not Michael Marmaduke."

"Then we should have gotten ourselves beaten?" asks Michael.

"We should have called the cops," says Dentata. She walks to the archway, limping slightly. "I can find my own way home."

Michael watches her go. He starts to say half a dozen things but says nothing. He doesn't feel bad about clubbing the Pseudo-Marduk with a chair. He doesn't think he had any choice.

"Women," says Thrombosis. But he feels surprised as well. He wants to get out of this funny place. He wants a few days to pass and then he'll see Michael again and he'll be the same guy as ever, a little absentminded, a little shy.

"Let's get that wire out of the way," says Michael.

They start pulling it aside. It's sharp and both men get scratched. Deep Rat watches but doesn't help. The Pseudo-Marduk lies on the floor and sometimes he moans. At last Michael makes a little path to the glass coffin. He lifts the lid. Rose White looks as if she has suffered a lot in the past week. Michael touches her cheek. Her hair is damp and he doesn't understand why. But then she opens her eyes and smiles. Michael feels as if something were squeezing his heart. He lifts her out of the glass coffin and she puts her arms around his neck. She stares at him uncertainly, then buries her face in his neck. Michael thinks of her blue eyes. They seem darker than before. He makes his way back through the razor wire with Rose White in his arms. He can feel her heart beating against his skin.

35

MULDOON: ZIGZAG DOODLE

Friedrich Nietzsche used to imagine a bird fluttering around his head twittering, "What do you matter? What do you matter?" Primus Muldoon has also had such thoughts, although in my case it is not a sparrow but a hawk. Only in this trifling difference of birds do I surpass my teacher.

Sitting in my workshop surrounded by the drawings of my unfulfilled dreams, I feel I might have thrown away my career for nothing more than hubris. I wanted to create, but I have over-reached myself and the Wrestling Association has expelled me. No more Madison Square Garden. No more television appearances. No more big Volvos. And who was chosen to take my place? Michael Marmaduke, my prize pupil. And didn't Nietzsche say: "It cannot be helped—each master has only *one* pupil—who will betray him—for he too is marked out for mastery."

But these fears don't last long. Mine is not a nature that is morbidly humble. And after a few gloomy moments my usual self-assurance reasserts itself. After all, Michael has turned them down. He has told the Wrestling Association to take a walk. Obviously, he feels that his first loyalty is to his teacher.

This confused story of Dentata's about how Michael half-murdered some schlepp by beating him over the head with a chair cannot be true. It must have been Thrombosis. Michael has trouble killing mosquitoes. But even Thrombosis has bragged how Michael climbed down a building with a rope in a sleet storm in the middle of the night. Pure childish storytelling! Michael is terrified of heights. Even stepladders give him nightmares. They are all in it together. They are conspiring to blur the boundaries between Michael and his Gimmick. Why? Because every time some wrestler bops a lout in a bar the ratings go up. The wrestling fans love to think of their heroes and villains as heroes and villains outside of the ring, as if Michael wore his silver elf boots twenty-four hours a day. So Dentata and Thrombosis have been told by the Wrestling Association to publicly confuse Michael with Marduk. And why have they done this? Because the Association has been thrown into a panic by the destruction I caused with Santa versus Satan. I confronted the Association's audience with the truth and so the Association has increased the magnitude of its lies. I Primus Muldoon have forced them to do this. In such petty ways do they think they can defeat me.

Of course these fabrications about Michael's heroism may be an attempt to make him look respectable in the eyes of the police. They have complained that they weren't called. They have spoken of vigilante tactics. A police detective named Smitty said he could make trouble if he wanted. Even though Rose White has been rescued there remain some questions about bones. What bones? All this is not clear to me. It has been difficult to get information. I offered the services of Truman Butterfield but was told he is not needed. I have become persona non grata. The Association has instructed all my old wrestlers to avoid me. This is the true antithesis: the degenerate instinct which turns against life with subterranean revengefulness.

Even so, you can imagine how hurt I was when I realized I was not to be invited to Michael's wedding on Tuesday. Of course my pain decreased once I realized it would be a tiny affair at the marriage bureau, but don't there need to be witnesses? Muldoon could have been a witness. Muldoon has always been a witness. Although Rose White is not exactly my kind of girl, I am still fond of her, and Michael Marmaduke has been like a son to me. But no, they wanted it private. She, I am told, has invited no one, and Michael has invited only his stepparents. But doesn't he at least owe me what he owes to his stepparents? After all, I gave him character. I gave him celebrity.

The Wrestling Association supposes that I have been beaten because they cast me out of their cheesy paradise. They say I am not sympathetic to their mission. They see themselves as being in the business of trying to abolish suffering, while I see myself as trying to increase it and make it worse than it has ever been. The Wrestling Association sees well-being as the final goal, while I see well-being as a state which renders man ludicrous and contemptible, which makes it desirable that he should perish. The discipline of suffering, of great suffering, is the discipline which has created every elevation in the history of humankind. That tension of the soul in misfortune which builds its strength, its terror at the sight of great destruction, its genius and courage in enduring misfortune, and whatever of depth, mystery, mask, spirit, cunning and greatness has been bestowed upon the soul—all this has been bestowed through the discipline of great suffering. In human beings, *creature* and *creator* are united: in human beings there is matter, fragment, clay, mud, madness, chaos; but there is also creator, sculptor, the hardness of the hammer and the divine spectator—do you understand this antithesis? The Wrestling Association pities the "creature in man" which has to *suffer* and *should* suffer. But my pity is for the Wrestling Association itself and for its pity, which is no more than pampering and weakening. There are higher problems than the problems of pleasure, pain and pity, and these are the problems which will be addressed by the newly established Muldoon Incorporated!

Yes, my friends, I have begun a new wrestling association. We are small but full of hope. And thanks to the Snowman's generous assistance the sketches on my workshop wall will be brought to life. The Snowman has a special interest in pain, and he will be the first to benefit from our discoveries. Once he had passions and they were called evil. Now he has virtues and they grew from his passions. Once he had fierce dogs in his cellar. Now they have been changed into birds and sweet singers. The Snowman understands that man is a rope fastened between animal and superman, a rope over the abyss. He has crossed that abyss. He has pushed people into that abyss. He is one of the great despisers and he has bankrolled Muldoon Inc.

And who are my wrestlers? Let's look at them. Once more we imagine a police lineup, but instead of sitting at the back, we sit in the front row because we are proud and full of joy. We sit on the edge of our seats and our expectation is a mighty churning within us. Before us is a brightly lit stage. A door slams open. A voice cries out, "Move all the way to the end!" A dozen men and women tramp onto the stage. They look happy and self-confident. They savor each moment of their present lives and eagerly look forward to the future. They blink their eyes against the light and squint into the dark room where we are sitting. Ah, they see us now. Look how their smiles increase.

Some of these people you have met. Wally Wallski now likes to be called Papa Deconstructor. Sparrow Gonzalez has chosen the name Sparrowhawk, but sometimes he is Condor and sometimes Dark Eagle. Zapo and Beacon Luz are variously Romeo and Juliet or Bonnie and Clyde. Seth is the one who runs through your dreams at night and soothes your troubled sleep. Water of Life, he calls himself, or Oil of Mercy. These other half-dozen men and women who joined me in my small protest against the Wrestling Association—they were empty, now they are overflowing; they were lost, now they are found. Men and women of all ages, all races, all backgrounds. And others will come as well.

But they don't look like wrestlers, you say. Beacon Luz is still a child and some of the others are pushing sixty. They are weak and small and ugly. They have serious blemishes and Zapo has no legs. My friends, you are still in the thrall of dualism. The problem I raise with the foundation of Muldoon Inc. is not what ought to supplant the Wrestling Association's heroes and villains in the sequence of species, but what type of wrestler one ought to *breed*, ought to *will*, as more worthy of life, more certain of the future. This type which I present to you has existed before: but only as a lucky accident, as an exception, never as *willed*. He and she have been the most feared, have hitherto been virtually *the* thing to be feared—and out of this fear the reverse type of wrestler has been created: the oversized, steroid-stuffed, galumphing, dualist monster who has no equivalent in that fantasy which we happily call Life. My new wrestlers are true representatives of the human species. They go beyond good and evil; they will wrestle in matches whose success and failure are not predetermined by dualist naiveté; they will accept a beating as easily as a victory.

My new wrestlers combine our faults and virtues. They are petty, puny and mortal. They mimic us in our dirty virtue and pristine sin. They kiss the child and kick the dog and sometimes they kiss the dog and kick the child. They are my gift to you. You know that face you show yourself first thing in the morning—face of weakness, face of exhaustion? That is the face my wrestlers will present to the world. And in seeing them, you will see yourself. In seeing them suffer, you will suffer. In seeing their elevation through suffering, you too will be elevated. You will be renewed! You will be forgiven! You will return to the struggle full of eagerness! You will embrace your ugliness, your inconsequential failings, your limitations. My wrestlers will teach you to kiss the dirt and love its taste!

Already I have rented an abandoned movie theater in downtown Newark. We will start slowly. Perhaps we will have access to one of the local cable stations. Yesterday we began practicing our first series of matches. These, which are also the oldest sketches on my workshop wall, will detail the didactic depredations of the wolf. Come to Newark and see Little Red Riding Hood (Beacon Luz) get eaten once and for all! Come to Newark and see that smarmy Russian Peter and his confounded whistling be devoured, along with the cat and bird and all that tuneful tribe. Come to Newark and see the three little pigs unable to find shelter, unable to find safety. See them hunted down one by one. See them dragged from their holes and eaten for the betterment of humankind! Through suffering we will be elevated! Our miseries will carry us aloft!

In conclusion, I would like to remind you that Nietzsche believed that his ailments and physical sufferings were caused by his capacity to attract electrical charges from the clouds. His blood was full of thunder and lightning. He wrote that he felt "like a zigzag doodle drawn on paper by a superior power wanting to try out a new pen."

And don't I feel the same way? Nietzsche could have been describing Primus Muldoon! That zigzag doodle—that's me! That's me! One day my name will be associated with the memory of something tremendous!

36

WRESTLE

First of all let us say that it was one of the luckiest mistakes imaginable that resulted in both Brodsky and Gapski being carved up to look like the Russian Nobel Prize–winning American poet Joseph Brodsky. And if they did not look exactly like the poet Brodsky, they did look exactly like each other: even more like each other than they looked as Brodsky and Gapski. Indeed, when they chanced to meet face to face in their wheelchairs in the hall of El Instituto Estético Tuesday afternoon they both tentatively reached out their hands expecting to touch the mirror which some joker had placed in their path. Their little exploratory fingers went out and out and instead of touching cool glass, they touched warm finger. And at that touch, from which each recoiled as if from the bite of an adder, they screamed such a scream of desolation that one hundred other patients frantically began patting their own bandages to make sure nothing was amiss. Naturally the nurses and doctors came running. A mistake had been made. Charts had been confused. Couldn't anybody make a mistake? And after all Mr. Gapski had said that he didn't care who he looked like. So why should he care that he looked like the Russian Nobel Prize–winning American poet Joseph Brodsky. "What," says Gapski, "do you mean there's a third person who looks like me as well?" Dr. Florabunde is sent for and he takes it upon himself to apologize for the employees, the stockholders, all the other successfully treated patients.

But it isn't good enough.

Brodsky and Gapski are now six feet tall, deeply in debt and both look like the Russian Nobel Prize–winning American poet Joseph Brodsky and all Dr. Florabunde can do is apologize? Can't the mistake be fixed? No. They could be changed into monsters, but they can't get new faces for at least a year. The tissue must heal, the bone has to fuse and harden. The other possibility is amnesia: their memories can be erased. Brodsky and Gapski consider the prospect of monsterhood and blissful forgetting. Even a face like a raw scab might be better than looking like each other, even a mind like a *tabula rasa*.

All this discussion takes place in Dr. Florabunde's office as Brodsky and Gapski keep looking at each other and sighing. Each sees the other as being made from the sediment scraped from a cesspool. Cheap, stupid, petty, ugly, depraved, unlovable—you name it. Yet, when each looks at this most hated of all human beings, what he sees is his own individual face.

There is a point, which happens most often in the novels of Zola, where fate deals such a succession of heavy blows upon men and women who are intrinsically innocent that it makes a (short) life spent at Ground Zero in Yucca Flats seem absolutely balmy. Terms like "mordant laughter" and "rictus grin" come to mind. Brodsky and Gapski have reached a place where it seems that nothing can get any worse. Of the options left open to them both suicide and murder loom very large, but after these have been rejected as counterproductive all that remains is to look their peculiar woes in the face, which means looking themselves in the face, along with looking the Russian Nobel Prize–winning American poet Joseph Brodsky in the face.

The hatred which Brodsky and Gapski bear for one another stems from the fact that each sees the other as a parody of his own Gimmick. And if the Gimmick is how we see ourselves and want to be seen, then the parody makes this desire seem cheap and foolish, so that each, basically, is left without a Gimmick to which to aspire: all Brodsky and Gapski have is anti-Gimmicks and a great frustration. The sum of their outward ambitions is nipped in the bud. At every gesture they see the other making a similar gesture and they see how ridiculous it is. They are condemned to being Gimmickless, which is as bad as being nobody at all. Worse, if the Gimmick is how we protect ourselves from fragmentation by concealing the natural drift of all life, then, because they are Gimmickless, both Brodsky and Gapski are constantly confronted with their own entropy and eventual dissolution. And with no Gimmick to put between themselves and this dismal fact, they have become melancholy, despondent and cranky. Their boss, Sapperstein, has foreseen this and it tickles him immensely. He laughs and laughs. Because Brodsky and Gapski are each the anti-Gimmick of the other, neither can ever become anything at all: they remain stuck in an eternal present. All roads are closed to them because at the start of every road is the mockery of the anti-Gimmick, which is an impassable obstacle.

It had seemed that El Instituto might be a solution. One of the police detectives could look like a Nobel Prize–winning poet, the other could look like Knute Rockne. But this would have meant not solving but avoiding the problem. Instead of facing their anti-Gimmicks, they would have fled them. It is hard to build a Gimmick based on lie. Did Brodsky imagine that he would write great Russian/American poetry? And Gapski, what were his dim plans?

Now their plans are kaput and they sit in Dr. Florabunde's office as if at the bottom of a deep well. All the doctors and nurses say they know just how terrible Brodsky and Gapski feel. But they don't, they can't. And then Brodsky and Gapski each realize (they come upon this mental discovery simultaneously) that the only person in the entire world who completely understands his present anguish and despair is the other. Brodsky knows what Gapski is going through. Gapski knows what Brodsky is going through. And at this sudden realization both men—who seconds before had thought each other no better than cow caca—fall into each other's arms and begin to weep. Dr. Florabunde is stunned. The doctors and nurses are stunned. Brodsky and Gapski both realize that each understands the other better than they have ever been understood in their entire lives. Not even their mothers knew them like this!

In this nanosecond of understanding Brodsky and Gapski are each transformed from being the other's anti-Gimmick to being his Gimmick, to being what the other truly aspires to: complete understanding, complete sympathy and the opening up of limitless possibility. For by becoming one another's Gimmick, each now has the prospect of going beyond his Gimmick, of transcending his Gimmick. In this moment when each is closer to the other than any other two human beings can possibly be, in this precise moment, each is freed of the other. It is astonishing to Dr. Florabunde to see these two men—who hated each other as human beings can rarely hate—fall into each others' arms and weep. But what is his astonishment when each falls back in his chair and begins to laugh. Howls of laughter. Whoops of laughter. "Shhh, shhh!" says Dr. Florabunde. "You'll upset the other patients." Brodsky and Gapski fall to the floor and roll around. They beat their fists against their knees. They make strange croaking noises as they gasp for breath. But let us bring this scene to a close.

In a purely classical melodrama Brodsky and Gapski would now become homosexual lovers. But they don't. They no longer need each other. They no longer even need to be policemen when they used to obtain what pleasure life afforded from pushing people around and seeing them cringe. They no longer need to live in New York City, where the scenes of so much daily suffering brought them a little cheer. In the next few days both quit the NYPD. Brodsky moves to Washington and obtains a job as a guard at the National Gallery. He learns to love El Greco and watch over his paintings with care. Gapski moves to Los Angeles and gets a job at the zoo. The way Brodsky feels about El Greco is the way Gapski feels about antelope. By unspoken agreement they split the United States between them and neither will ever cross the Mississippi. This is not to say that they never suffer from unhappiness and confusion. After all, no life is perfect. But when either feels unhappy and confused, he writes a letter to the other (maybe he sends a fax) and asks what is wrong. And the other, having complete understanding and complete sympathy, immediately responds. And each feels better.

Now let us relate a short scene that occurred on Sunday. It is family day at St. Elmo's nuthatch and Bernard's mother has come to visit. But it is not really Bernard's mother. It is Sparrow Gonzalez dressed up as a woman. Sparrow is being sought in connection with a mysterious explosion at St. Elmo's which liquefied that institution's beloved Grabber: the fellow who kept everything on an even keel. Many people have their eyes peeled for Sparrow and they want to put him behind bars.

As for Bernard, he is so medicated that if they introduced him to King Kong and said it was his mother, he would just nod and smile. He doesn't know if he has a mother. He doesn't know what a mother is.

It should be said that many changes must have occurred in Sparrow's delicate psyche for him to disguise himself as a short ugly woman. He has Muldoon to thank for these changes. Muldoon will make him a wrestler. Muldoon will make him a star. Already Sparrow has been tagged to play the wolf in a series of upcoming matches. Sparrow may be small for a human being, but he's just the right size for a wolf. A big wolf. The several days that Sparrow has been at the Meat Market have been the best of his life, and the only wrinkle was the absence of Bernard, who would love (Sparrow is positive about this) to learn to wrestle.

So here we are at St. Elmo's. It is a cool autumn day with racing clouds. Every so often we hear the honking of geese and looking up we see ragged V's streaming south. We can never observe these geese without wanting to travel ourselves, they are so evocative for us. The grounds at St. Elmo's are mostly covered with fallen leaves. Along the paths a few patients are walking slowly with members of their families and their feet in the leaves make a scritch-scritch noise.

And there is Bernard being led along by a short ugly woman in a plaid skirt, a bulky gray sweater and a blue handkerchief over her head. She is also wearing dark glasses and walks looking down at the ground.

"I have been very happy," says Sparrow Gonzalez.

"Ahh," says Bernard, looking at nothing in particular.

"I have met wonderful people," says Sparrow.

"Ahh," says Bernard and his beautiful blue eyes are as unchanging as blue saucers.

"I'm going to help you bust outta this joint," says Sparrow.

"Ahh," says Bernard. It is what he says to everything. It is what he says when brushing his teeth.

Sparrow and Bernard walk slowly toward the main gate. In former times the Grabber worked on Sundays and was ever vigilant to the possibility of nutcases escaping, but now the Grabber is no more. He has experienced the ultimate transformation: death. Of course there is a guard: an alert young man named Sammy who is eager for promotion. At the moment Sammy is deep in conversation with somebody we know. It is Zapo and he is showing Sammy how his legs snap off. Given the choice between watching nutcases or watching somebody snap off his phony legs, Sammy thinks there is no contest. Sparrow and Bernard walk right past him.

Now we have a moment with Sparrow and Bernard standing at the curb. Traffic is light. Dried leaves skitter across the pavement. A black 740 Volvo pulls up to the curb. Sparrow opens the back door and Bernard climbs in. *Tannhäuser* is playing on the tape deck: those brooding musical phrases, as if all the notes were brown. Sparrow also gets in back and shuts the door.

"Good afternoon," says Muldoon, turning down the volume. "I hear you like to wrestle."

"Ahh," says Bernard.

The black Volvo drives away.

Sammy and Zapo continue to stand at the gate. Sammy is hoisting up one of Zapo's legs in both his hands. How light it is. How lifelike. "Think of that," he says. "Think of that!"

In any long journey one reaches a point when the destination is finally in sight. The car bumps over the bridge and ascends the hill and there, twinkling through the trees, are the lights of the house which has been the object of one's thoughts for all these many miles. It is dark. A half-moon rides in the cool autumn sky. As the car turns into the driveway one hears the screen door slam. A dog begins to bark.

We too have reached such a place. It is Tuesday night, the last Tuesday in October. Early that day Michael Marmaduke and Rose White were married at the registry office. He wore a blue suit. She wore a white dress. Afterward they had lunch with Michael's stepparents at the Tavern on the Green. Then Michael and Rose White took a Circle Line boat around Manhattan and visited the top of the Empire State Building. All the usual tourist-type things. Wherever they went, Michael was recognized as Marduk the Magnificent, but it didn't bother him. He signed autograph books. Dozens of people told him they were glad he had his fiancée back again. Michael thanked them and Rose White smiled. She didn't say much and Michael felt she was tired from her long ordeal. She had been doped the whole time and told the police she remembered nothing. Her mind was a blank.

For their wedding night Michael and Rose White went to the Carlyle Hotel on East 76th. Bobby Short was playing piano downstairs in the café. People sent gifts to their room. There was champagne and flowers and fresh strawberries from Chile.

Now at last Michael is in the king-sized bed. Rose White is in the bathroom and Michael hears the water running. He wears a white pajama shirt but nothing else. A white sheet is pulled up to his chest and he leans back against several pillows. He has drunk half a bottle of champagne and feels blurry. He keeps receiving mental images of his fight with the Pseudo-Marduk, of confronting Taurus and all the rest. He wonders what happened to Deep Rat and if he will see him again. Michael hopes not. He remembers Deep Rat saying "Kill 'em, kill 'em!" about the Pseudo-Marduk and Michael's own complex feelings at the time. Maybe it would be better if Deep Rat just stayed away. Deep Rat on one side and Muldoon on the other—those parts of his life are over. In any case, now he's a married man with new responsibilities.

Michael glances at the side of the bed which will be his wife's. Even that word—"wife"—gives him a chill of expectation. Although they have kissed, they haven't made love. The sheet is folded back and soon he will hear her footsteps. On Rose White's night table, Michael sees something shiny. He reaches for it and finds it is a golden coin with a smiling angel face. He turns the coin over and sees a demon's face leering at him. Something about the coin strikes him as familiar but he can't think what it is. Perhaps he is thinking of the Master of Ceremonies' two-headed cane, but it is not that. Did he ever have a coin like this one? Michael can't remember.

He sets the coin on Rose White's pillow, then reaches into the drawer of his night table. The coin reminds him of a joke wedding gift that he was given by somebody—maybe Thrombosis or Liquidity or Cashback. The gift is a stick about six inches long. From one end dangles the head of an angel on a short thread. From the other end dangles the head of a devil. One is white, one is red. One is smiling, one is leering. In the center of the stick is a little cap which can be placed over the tip of a finger or over the head of an erect penis. Michael puts the cap over his left index finger and gives the stick a tap. The angel head and devil head spin round and round. They spin so fast that they blur into a single pinkness. Sometimes the devil ends up facing him and sometimes the angel: about half and half. Michael very much wants to put the little toy on his erect penis when his new wife comes out of the bathroom but he isn't sure if he has the nerve. It will depend on how she looks at him and if she seems ready to be amused. It will depend on her eyes.

Meanwhile, in the bathroom, Rose White is looking into the mirror. Her face is pale and very beautiful. She stares at her eyes and sees within them a faint yellow cast. Her eyes narrow slightly with displeasure. She turns away and puts on a red silk bikini halter. The fabric crosses her left breast just beneath a tattoo of a green leaf. She puts on red silk bikini panties. Over both she puts a white nightgown which buttons up the front. Rose White buttons it right to the top, then looks in the mirror, again inspecting her face. She touches a finger to her blond hair, pushing it aside and looking at the roots. She looks again at her eyes and the beauty of her face. Is she satisfied? Almost, but the yellow bothers her. She leans over the sink to look more closely. Then perhaps her forehead bumps the glass or perhaps, as in these old hotels, the mirror is just fragile and badly held in place. In any case, a crack develops and slowly wanders diagonally across the glass. Rose White steps back. The mirror splits from one end to the other. One piece falls into the sink, then another.

Lying in bed, Michael Marmaduke is still fooling with the joke wedding gift, spinning it around his finger. He hears the sound of breaking glass and he looks toward the hall leading to the bathroom. There is no further sound. Michael calls out to his new wife: "What was that?" There is no answer. He waits a moment, then calls: "Are you okay?" There is still no answer. Then he calls: "Are you coming to bed soon?"

And then Michael hears the bathroom door open and Rose White's footsteps approaching down the hall.

Let us pull back out the window. Do you remember that man —it now seems long ago—on the balcony of his East Side penthouse? He had to appear in court the next day? His ex-wife was trying to take the penthouse from him? Well, his ex-wife got the place and this Tuesday evening the man has been packing. Tomorrow the movers arrive. Now it is late and he paces back and forth on the balcony with a glass of whiskey—Jim Beam green for its smoky taste. Thirty stories below a car honks. Clouds scud across the face of the half-moon. The man thinks how he will miss this view and he grits his teeth at the thought of his ex-wife enjoying it with her lover. And where will the man be? In a hotel for a few days and then maybe over in New Jersey.

As he thinks of staying in a hotel, the man glances toward the Carlyle. When he had the money, he sometimes stayed there, but tomorrow he will stay at the Gramercy Park or the Excelsior. The man sees a lighted window around the thirtieth floor. The curtains are pulled aside. Curious, he fetches his binoculars and trains them on the window. Very small and far away, as if on a miniature television, he sees a man and woman. Both are naked; both are blond. They are wrestling on a large white bed. The man throws the woman onto her back. The woman twists and throws down the man. Now they kneel, grappling with their arms around each other, swaying to the left and right. Are they kissing or striking at each other with their mouths? Are they caressing or clobbering each other? Their bodies are golden and glistening with sweat. The bed is being ripped to shreds. The man on the balcony is surprised by how violent it all is. Again the blond man lifts the woman and throws her down on the bed. The woman reaches out her hand. The lights go out.

The man on the balcony continues to stare at the darkened room but all he sees is the white curtains blowing into the night sky. They flap and flap, as if a little echo of the violence. Then the man sees a glitter of something—just a flash and it's gone. He has no idea what it can be.

But if we look more closely, we can see it is a golden coin. It is falling through the air, turning over and over. Each side has a face but we can't quite make it out, although of course we know what it is. The coin spins down through the darkness, glittering in the light of the half-moon. It takes a long time to reach the bottom. Then it hits the sidewalk and bounces with a clinking noise.

One would think this is an event without a witness but that is not the case. A few feet from the coin is an old homeless fellow pushing a shopping cart. It is Beetle. He reaches down for the coin, which has come to rest on the sidewalk. Which face is on top? Neither is on top. The coin is wedged in a crack and is standing on edge. Beetle extracts the coin and looks at it: first the angel face, then the demon face. He feels himself lucky. He feels better than he has all day. For a long time Beetle has searched for something but he is not sure for what. Maybe this coin is what he was searching for. He has had something important on his mind but he can't remember what it was. It was a piece of amazing information, but the pretty nurse at the hospital took it away from him.

Narrative Bibliography

A number of books were useful in the writing of *The Wrestler's Cruel Study* and from some I appropriated various bits and pieces. Most helpful was Neil Forsyth's *The Old Enemy: Satan and the Combat Myth* (Princeton, 1987). From this I took several Middle Eastern prayers, although mostly I altered the language to suit my purposes. Forsyth also was the source for the quotes from Lactantius, the Apocalypse of Baruch, Plutarch, Athenagorus, Augustine and some of the Gnostic texts. Also useful was Hans Jonas's *The Gnostic Religion* (Boston, 1963), which supplied Gnostic and Manichaean texts (all changed slightly), and, to a lesser degree, Kurt Rudolf's *Gnosis: The Nature and History of Gnosticism*, translated by Robert Wilson (New York, 1987), and Elaine Pagels's *The Gnostic Gospels* (New York, 1989). Several other of the Marduk and Middle Eastern texts derived from S. H. Hooke's *Middle Eastern Mythology* (New York, 1963).

The book which originally aroused my interest in Manichaeism was Steven Runciman's wonderfully written *The Medieval Manichee* (New York, 1961). Other books which I drew on were David Christie-Murray's *A History of Heresy* (New York, 1989), Henry Chadwick's *The Early Church* (New York, 1967), Walter Burkert's *Ancient Mystery Cults* (Cambridge, 1987), W. F. Otto's *Dionysos: Myth and Cult* (Bloomington, 1965), St. Augustine's *Confessions* (New York, 1961), *the Bible,* especially *the Book of Revelation,* and Joseph Campbell's *The Hero with a Thousand Faces* (Princeton, 1968), where one reads: "When a little boy of the Murngin tribe is about to be circumcised, he is told by his fathers and by the old men, 'The Great Father Snake smells your foreskin; he is calling for it.' " The Master of Ceremonies' borrowing from Book X of *The Republic* is based on Benjamin Jowett's translation.

As may have been gathered, Primus Muldoon has an intimate relationship with the writings of Friedrich Nietzsche. Sometimes he quotes Nietzsche with an attribution, sometimes he doesn't. And mostly he distorts Nietzsche, changing words and generally making free. Most helpful was Ronald Hayman's *Nietzsche: A Critical Life* (New York, 1982). But I also drew heavily on Nietzsche's *Beyond Good and Evil,* translated by R. J. Hollingdale (New York, 1990). I also used Hollingdale's *A Nietzsche Reader* (New York, 1977), as well as Walter Kaufmann's translations of *Thus Spoke Zarathustra* (New York, 1978) and *On the Genealogy of Morals* and *Ecce Homo* (New York, 1989). Muldoon also swipes a few sentences from Roland Barthes's essay "The World of Wrestling."

As Muldoon made free with Nietzsche, so did the detective Philip Kyd make free with the works of Raymond Chandler, mainly *The Big Sleep, The High Window, The Little Sister* and *The Lady in the Lake.* To Chandler and Nietzsche and St. Augustine and others I make my apologies for wrenching them into new contexts. And that apology extends to the Brothers Grimm as well.

I would also like to thank Carl Rubino of Hamilton College for his translation of a paragraph from Tertullian's "On Prescription Against the Heretics"; my wife, Isabel Bize, for reading these pages and making excellent suggestions; and my editor, Carol Houck Smith, for her invaluable help in editing the manuscript.